# Sammy Rambles
# and the
# Fires of Karmandor

To Henry,
Validus Aureus Draco

J T SCOTT

Praise for the Sammy Rambles series:

*"The JK Rowling of the South West"* - Brad Burton,
*The UK's #1 Motivational Business Speaker*

*"A tale of finding yourself and achieving great things, the Sammy Rambles series of books keep readers of any age hooked through the myriad of adventures. JT Scott is the modern-day fantasy author whose stories are being brought to life by youngsters in the sports hall and playgrounds around the world." - Caroline Bramwell, Author of 'Loo Rolls to Lycra' and Inspirational Speaker*

*"Two hours to do the school run tonight. Sammy Rambles to the rescue, I turned on my Sammy Rambles and the Floating Circus audio book and kept everyone happy." - Francis, Plymouth.*

*"I loved it, only problem was I couldn't put it down. It's the first time in ages I have spent the entire day ignoring work and reading it from cover to cover." - L. Watts*

*"Great to hear about these fantastic books!" - Councillor Terri Beer (Cabinet Member for Children and Young People).*

*"It's a fantastic read, Lily is totally engrossed in the story, as am I! It's a huge hit here! We're looking forward to reading the rest of the Sammy Rambles books." – Jayne W.*

# Sammy Rambles and the Fires of Karmandor

First published in 2017
This edition published in 2019

ISBN-13: 978-1545317662
ISBN-10: 1545317666

# J T SCOTT

J T Scott lives in Cornwall with Ari and Sam surrounded by open countryside, sandy beaches, lots of historical castles, pens, paper and a very vivid imagination.

Also available in the Sammy Rambles series:

Sammy Rambles and the Floating Circus
Sammy Rambles and the Land of the Pharaohs
Sammy Rambles and the Angel of 'El Horidore
Sammy Rambles and the Fires of Karmandor
Sammy Rambles and the Knights of the Stone Cross

Find out more about Sammy, Dixie and Darius and their adventures on the Sammy Rambles website.

www.sammyrambles.com

# Sammy Rambles and the Fires of Karmandor

Chapter List:

# Sammy Rambles and the Fires of Karmandor

For Ari & Sam

CHAPTER 1

# FLYING BACK TO DRAGAMAS

Thirty thousand feet high in an aeroplane on his way back to England from Switzerland, thirteen-year-old Samuel Richard Rambles peered out of the small oval window next to his seat and he worried again about what would happen when he got back to Dragamas.

He had tried to convince himself it was all a bad dream. Over the summer holiday, Sir Ragnarok had told Sammy many, many, times that he had done the right thing out of the two terrible choices. But Sammy kept running the scene through his head, wondering if he could have done anything differently.

What if Dixie hadn't come with them to the den? What if he, Sammy, hadn't found the Angel of 'El Horidore? What if they had managed to overpower Alfie Agrock? What if Sir Ragnarok and Commander Altair had arrived earlier? What if? What if?

It made his head hurt and Sammy shut his eyes. But all he could see was Alfie Agrock holding the knife to Dixie's face, her bright green eyes full of tears, telling him not to give Alfie Agrock the Angel of 'El Horidore. She was telling him to keep the special Angel whistle, the whistle that would call all dragons, safe from the evil Dwarf, the same Dwarf Sammy had found out was the "A" in the Shape, the people who wanted to kill all the dragons and steal their draconite.

In his mind's eye, Sammy could see the shimmering blue-green draconite gemstone, the precious stone stored inside a dragon's brain which enables the dragon to breathe fire, to fly and perform magic. Without its draconite, a dragon would die instantly.

Sammy remembered how Sir Ragnarok had told him the Shape wanted all the draconite in the world so they could rebuild the Stone Cross and how this would give the Shape power over earth, air, fire and water. It would give them immortality and invincibility. Something that could never be allowed to happen again. He scrunched his eyes up tightly, wishing he could go back and change things. Put wrongs to right.

When he opened his eyes a few minutes later, he could see tiny buildings out of the oval aeroplane window. An announcement from the Captain informed the passengers they were flying over Northern France and that there would be some turbulence in the next few minutes.

'Are you all right babe?'

Sammy looked away from the window and shook himself. Louise Manning, the blonde air stewardess his mother had asked to check up on him every fifteen minutes from take-off, was leaning over the back of his seat.

'Are you sure you're all right babe?' asked Louise, flashing a gleaming smile at him. 'You were miles away!'

Sammy looked out of the aeroplane window and shuddered. The Captain had just told them about some bumpy bits and they were still several thousand feet in the air. He looked nervously at the aeroplane wings but they seemed to be fine and still attached to the aeroplane.

Sammy nodded, even though he felt really sick inside. He was feeling a bit airsick from the long aeroplane flight and a bit homesick as he was already missing his parents and his one-year-old baby sister Eliza.

But most of all, he was feeling sick with worry about what he would face when he got back to school.

Would Dixie be there? Would Sir Ragnarok have caught Alfie Agrock? Would all the dragons in the world have been summoned to the school?

As the plane lurched in the sky, Sammy looked up at the air hostess Louise Manning and nodded again.

'I'll be ok,' said Sammy, more bravely than he felt.

'That's good babe.' Louise smiled with her perfect teeth gleaming in her dark tanned face. 'It won't be long now until we land. Is anyone meeting you from the airport, babe?'

Sammy shook his head. 'I'm supposed to get my stuff and find a taxi. Then the taxi will take me to my school.'

'What, by yourself babe?' asked Louise. 'Didn't your parents organise a taxi for you?'

Sammy shook his head again. 'Nope. I have to do it myself. My Dad wants me to learn how to do things like that. It can't be that difficult, can it?'

'We'll see about that,' said Louise matter of factly and she flounced off towards the stewards' cabin, her blonde ponytail swishing behind her.

Louise returned about five minutes later, flashing her dazzling white smile at Sammy.

'I've been given an extended break before my next flight,' Louise grinned at him. 'How about we get a bite to eat and I'll help you find your taxi? We can get a burger and chips or whatever you want.'

'That would be very kind,' said Sammy in his politest voice, and thought his father would have been proud. Charles Rambles frequently told Sammy that good manners would get him anything he wanted.

'Then it's settled babe,' beamed Louise. 'You know, you remind me of my son. He's a right tearaway. He's always on about some dragon nonsense!'

Sammy pricked up his ears. It was the first time anyone had mentioned "dragons" in nearly ten weeks since he had left Dragamas School for Dragon Charming.

His face fell as he remembered that because the summer term had ended abruptly early there would still be some exams he had to pass to guarantee his place in the fourth year, his penultimate year at the school. He crossed his fingers, hoping Dixie would be there to meet him.

'We will be landing in thirty minutes,' the Captain's voice boomed over the loudspeaker. 'Please return to your seats and fasten your seatbelts.'

'Your son talks about dragons?' asked Sammy in surprise.

Louise pressed a finger to her lips and helped Sammy fasten his seatbelt. As she pulled the belt tight, Sammy felt his wooden staff with his onyx, ruby and amber gemstones press against his chest.

Over the summer, Sammy had spent hours trying to perfect techniques with his staff, practicing various manoeuvres, creating fire and casting different coloured sparks using the gemstones he had been given in each year he had been at Dragamas.

'There you go babe,' said Louise, checking the seat belt was fastened securely. 'We'll be back on the ground before you know it,' she added and disappeared down the gangway to attend to the other passengers.

'We get sapphire gemstones this year,' Sammy muttered to no one in particular.

The elderly couple in the seats next to him shuddered in their sleep. They hadn't said anything other than "hello" at the start of the flight. After turning up their noses as Sammy sat down with his crisps, cola and Dragonball Weekly magazine, they had hidden themselves under their newspapers and started snoring, occasionally hurrumphing in their sleep.

Sammy finished reading the last pages of his Dragonball Weekly magazine and gripped the arms of his seat, bracing himself as the plane came into land. He needn't have bothered as the plane landed on the runway as lightly as a feather.

When Sammy opened his eyes, the elderly couple were already at the front of the plane, shaking the hands of the stewards and stewardesses.

Sammy stood up and stretched his arms and legs. He picked up his magazine and checked his coat pocket to make sure he still had his passport and travel papers. He made his way to the front of the plane where Louise was waiting for him.

'Are you ready babe?' grinned Louise. 'I asked the Captain to get them to take your luggage off first. Staff privileges,' she winked at him and tapped her badge that read "Louise Manning, Senior In-Flight Air Stewardess", with the orange plane logo in the background.

'Thank you,' said Sammy, secretly glad the flight was over. He hoped he could manage to eat a burger and chips without throwing up.

Sammy was impressed when Louise's staff privileges got them through the express passport controls and out into the staff café in record time.

Louise found two empty chairs in a quiet corner of the café and handed Sammy a menu full of tasty options to choose from. Almost as soon as they sat down, a waiter came to the table.

'Hi Jack,' said Louise, 'I'll have the pasta salad, a slice of chocolate cake and a lemonade please,' she announced to the waiter whilst reaching for her purse. 'What would you like Sammy babe?'

'Just cola, please,' said Sammy, not daring to call Louise "babe" in the same infuriating but flattering way she did it to him. She's got a son my age, he grinned to himself.

Jack wrote down the order and Louise got up to use the self-service drinks machine.

'One pound eighty each!' said Louise as she returned with an orange plastic tray carrying the two drinks.

Sammy took out his wallet and counted out the coins.

'Oh, you don't need to pay babe,' said Louise, brushing his hand with the coins away. 'It's just the last time I bought a drink in the staff café it was thirty-five pence. You wouldn't get it in a can from the express stall for that price any more. I usually bring my own sandwiches and eat them on the plane.'

Sammy nodded and sipped his cola. When Louise's pasta salad and slice of chocolate cake drizzled in chocolate sauce arrived, he wished he had ordered some food.

Louise snapped the plastic fork away from the lid and started eating her pasta. 'Now, we've got your bags, your drink, just need to find your taxi and I need to be back for my next flight,' she recounted the items like a shopping list hardly pausing for breath. 'Then I'm on the next flight to Egypt. We fly right over the pyramids. You'd love the pyramids babe, they're amazing, especially at night. Have you ever been to Egypt babe?'

Sammy shook his head, amazed at Louise's ability to talk and eat continuously. 'I've seen other pyramids.'

'In books babe?' asked Louise, pausing to drink her lemonade in one gulp.

'No, not in books,' said Sammy. 'I've been inside a pyramid too!' he added, hoping he sounded impressive.

'Ooh babe, was it scary? Just they're supposed to be cursed, aren't they babe? Can't say I fancy being cursed with bad things happening to you.'

Without pausing for breath, Louise wrapped up the chocolate cake in orange and purple serviettes and handed the parcel to Sammy.

'I thought you might like this to keep you going on the motorway babe. It's about two hundred miles isn't it, to get to this school of yours babe?'

Sammy nodded. 'I guess so,' he said, even though he wasn't really sure how far away Dragamas was from the airport.

Louise laughed. 'By the time you're back at school, I'll be in Egypt, funny world babe, anyway I'd best get you to the taxi rank. I'll see if my Steve's on. He'll get you there safely.'

'Thanks,' said Sammy, putting the cake in his coat pocket. 'Are you sure I can't pay for this?'

'No way babe,' Louise held up a wadge of crisp twenty pound notes that Sammy thought were probably from his mother. 'This more than covers it and you've been a pleasure to look after babe.' Louise flashed him another gleaming smile.

Sammy grinned and pointed to a piece of green pasta stuck between her front teeth.

'Thanks babe,' said Louise, removing the pasta. 'Let's get you and your luggage to my Steve.'

Sammy picked up his grey suitcase with his initials sewn in green letters in the top corner and wheeled it to the taxi rank. He had to walk at a quick pace to keep up with Louise, who, despite wearing incredibly high heels, was walking as fast as he could walk in his trainers.

They went through the revolving door leading out of the airport. Sammy shivered as the cool air hit him but there was no time to stop as Louise whisked him along the concrete path to the taxi rank.

There was a long line of cars parked next to a bright yellow sign with the word "Taxi" written in black letters. All of the cars had their engines running and the drivers were ready to set off as soon as new passengers arrived.

Louise marched to the third taxi in the row and tapped on the window. Instantly a man dressed in a black suit leaped out of the car and gave Louise a lingering embrace.

'Hello babe,' said the taxi driver.

'Hi babe,' said Louise, breaking away from the man. She turned to Sammy and flashed a gleaming smile. 'Sammy, this is my Steve,' she said proudly.

Sammy looked at Steve. He was a tall, good looking man with twinkling brown eyes, light brown hair, broad shoulders and a cheeky smile that didn't really go with his smart suit and polished shoes.

Steve held out his hand. 'Pleased to meet you Sammy. I'm Louise's husband and chauffeur. Let's get your suitcase loaded up.'

Sammy shook hands with Steve and grinned. He got into the back of the taxi, looking forward to the drive back to Dragamas.

Steve gave Louise another long romantic embrace that made her late for her next flight. She had to be prised away from him by two security guards who had been sent looking for her.

Louise was still blowing Steve kisses as she disappeared back up the path towards the airport. Her high heels clicked on the concrete and she waved violently at her husband, promising him she would be home soon.

'Never get married to an air stewardess,' advised Steve, accepting the twenty pound notes Sammy held out of the window and lugging Sammy's heavy grey suitcase into the boot of his green Vauxhall Vectra. 'One minute you're the best thing since sliced bread and the next minute she's going off to look after some Pharaoh, gallivanting halfway across the world. Now, where are we going Sammy?'

Sammy handed Steve the Dragamas business card, the same card his father had been given by Sir Lok Ragnarok four years ago. Even though the card was scuffed with age, it had all the directions on the back.

'South West it is then,' said Steve, grinning at Sammy. 'Buckle up, you're in for a long ride.'

CHAPTER 2

# FOUR HOURS LATER

Four hours later, Sammy woke up with his head banging against the car window. Gone were the city lights and streams of cars and lorries on the motorway. They had been replaced with high green hedges and narrow twisting lanes that were only wide enough for one car at a time.

It was getting dark and there were no street lights, only starlight and the faint light of the moon trying to shine through the clouds.

'You missed most of the ride Sammy,' said Steve, grinning in the rear view mirror as he saw Sammy was awake at last.

Sammy noticed Steve's teeth were as gleaming white as Louise's teeth and he wondered for a moment if they had the same dentist.

'My Satnav is telling me we should be just about at this school of yours,' continued Steve. 'Do you know which way we go from here?'

Sammy looked out of the window. He had never forgotten the first time he had seen the beautiful grey stone

Dragamas Castle with its nine coned turrets complete with black flags with the golden "D" motif flying from the towering rooftops.

The castle was entirely surrounded by a large bubble of shimmering gold pearlescent mist that protected it from being seen by anyone who wasn't connected to the Dragon World.

'It's just round this corner,' said Sammy, anticipating the moment the castle would come into view, knowing he wouldn't be surprised if Steve couldn't actually see the castle. His parents couldn't see the castle, despite them owning a fully grown dragon each. The adult dragons were the size of his mother's Range Rover, but neither Charles Rambles nor Julia Rambles knew their dragons existed at all.

As they rounded the corner, Sammy noticed something new about the gold misty bubble around the castle. It was tinged with red, like blood.

'The blood of dragons,' Sammy whispered to himself, a shiver creeping up his spine.

'What's that Sammy?' asked Steve. 'Are we nearly there yet?'

'This is it,' said Sammy. 'We're here!'

Steve twisted round in the driver's seat and gave Sammy a funny look.

'Right-oh,' said Steve, looking a little bemused. 'Shall I just drop you off here, out in the middle of nowhere? What's your parents going to say to that?'

'It's ok,' said Sammy. 'Really. We are here at my school. It's just that you can't see it. Please pull over into the layby and I'll walk from here.'

'What that run-down building? It can't be a school. It just looks like a ruined farmhouse,' said Steve frowning and peering at the building. 'What does it say on that sign? Old

Samagard something?' He slid the Vectra neatly up against the hedgerow and turned the engine off.

'Honestly, it's fine,' said Sammy, trying to reassure Steve they were in the right place, but he had the distinct feeling the taxi driver thought he was mad.

Sammy opened the car door, swung his legs out and jumped into the lane. He looked up at the imposing castle and smiled. It felt like he was back home.

Still frowning and muttering to himself, Steve got out of the car and went to collect Sammy's suitcase from the boot.

'Well, if you're sure this is the right place,' said Steve, hesitating slightly. 'Maybe it's best if I come in with you.'

As Sammy wondered how on earth he could explain about the shimmering pearlescent bubble protecting the school, not to mention explaining how he would be able to study in a place that looked no more than a ruined farm house. He could even see the sign that outsiders saw, the sign that said "Old Samagard Farm". It was at that moment Sammy realised "Samagard" was simply "Dragamas" spelt backwards and he smiled.

'What are you grinning at?' asked Steve, lugging Sammy's suitcase out of the boot and into the layby. 'I hope you haven't got me on some wild goose chase.'

Luckily, at that moment another car turned up, followed by a bright purple, orange and lime green minibus with the words "Murphy Family Dragon Healers – Looking After Your Dragons Since 1980" painted in large white letters on the side door.

'Darius,' said Sammy gratefully spotting his best friend waving out of the passenger window.

'People you know?' asked Steve, his eyes wide as he stared at the garishly decorated minibus.

Sammy nodded. He looked up as he heard the beating of wings. Darius's navy blue dragon, Nelson, was flying in circles above the minibus. As he watched, Nelson was joined by two other dragons that Sammy recognised were Syren and Puttee, who belonged to his friends Gavin and Toby Reed. He guessed the twins were on their way to Dragamas and wouldn't be far behind their dragons.

'It's Darius,' said Sammy. 'He's in my house at school. His parents are dropping him off. They're Dragon Healers.'

'Right-oh,' said Steve, shaking his head and laughing. 'I'll leave you with them, if that's ok. If I right-foot it, I'll be back in time for last orders at the Draconian Arms.'

'Thank you for bringing me here,' said Sammy, shaking Steve's hand.

'No problem,' grinned Steve, 'and don't think I can't see them dragons up in the air! I may not be able to see your school, but I can tell when there's a dragon around!' he roared with laughter and started the Vectra. 'Bye Sammy!' Steve called out of the window as he sped off into the darkness.

'Bye,' said Sammy, waving and wondering why he found it so unsettling that a taxi driver he'd never met before could see a dragon circling overhead and his parents hadn't even smelt a whiff of five dragons, three fully grown dragons and two young dragons, when they had been living in the attic rooms right above them only a few months ago.

Sammy jumped out of the way as Darius rammed open the passenger door. He took a mistimed flying leap out of the minibus and landed in a heap on the road.

No sooner had Darius picked himself up than a smart blue Land Rover pulled up in behind the multi-coloured minibus and two boys, identical in appearance, sprawled out of the vehicle.

'Hey Sammy!' said the boys in unison and Sammy slapped hands with the dark haired twin brothers Gavin and Toby Reed who were also in his year and house at Dragamas School for Dragon Charming.

'Hey Sammy!' said Darius, dusting off his trousers which had collected some debris from the road.

'Hey!' Sammy grinned at his friends and waved to Mrs Reed, who had brought her sons to Dragamas in the shiny blue Land Rover.

Sammy wasn't surprised that Anita Reed didn't wave back to him, or that she gave him a very stony look that said "stay away from my sons, you've brought trouble to my home". He knew she blamed him for leading the Shape to her farmhouse and for the Shape killing her black dragon.

Sammy shivered, wondering what had happened to the Shape over the summer. In his first year at Dragamas, he and his friends had identified their Gemology teacher, Dr Margarite Lithoman, whose real name was Eliza Elungwen as the "E" in the Shape.

In his second year, with Dixie and Darius's help, Sammy had identified his uncle on his mother's side, Peter Pickering as the "P" in the Shape and at the end of the summer in their third year, they had identified the evil Dwarf Alfie Agrock, who hid behind the alias Alfie Grock, as the "A" in the Shape.

By Sammy's reckoning, they were on track to find who was behind the final letters "H" and "S" to find out exactly who was behind the Shape, the people who wanted to kill all the dragons.

Sammy wondered how many people had accepted money from the Shape in exchange for giving the Shape their dragons to kill and extract the draconite from their dragon's brain. He wondered how many people were in fact now working for the Shape, perhaps believing that if the Stone Cross was rebuilt with draconite that they too would have power over earth, air, fire and water as well as invincibility and immortality.

'Do you like my hair,' asked Darius, breaking Sammy out of his thoughts.

Sammy surveyed Darius's new close cropped style with blond highlights that were gelled into short spikes.

'You look like a girl,' scoffed Gavin. 'Come on,' he added pointing to the pile of suitcases, 'let's get this junk inside.'

Gavin tapped his suitcase with his staff, a wooden stick about six feet tall with black, red and yellow crystals on the end.

The suitcase quivered and took off, elevating itself to nearly shoulder height and moving slowly towards the castle gates.

'Cool,' said Toby and he copied his twin, raising his own suitcase off the ground using the invisible power of his own wooden staff with the same coloured crystals on the end.

Sammy noticed Toby was carrying a silver briefcase. It was identical to the silver briefcase he had packed inside his own suitcase for safekeeping during the flight.

'Dragonball,' said Darius, pointing to the silver case. 'You'd better have brought your set Sammy. It's much better than Toby's as it's got the Invisiballs.'

Sammy nodded. 'It's in my suitcase,' he said, pointing at the suitcase with his own staff. 'Up,' commanded Sammy, glad when the suitcase dragged itself along the gravel and then launched into the air with a satisfying swish.

Darius took a small half-moon shaped whistle out of his pocket and blew into the device. Without making a sound, Sammy knew the whistle would be calling Nelson to come to Darius's side.

Sure enough, the navy dragon landed beside his owner and blew two small smoke rings into the night sky.

Darius rested his left hand on his dragon's back. 'Come on Nelson,' muttered Darius. He pointed his staff at his suitcase, which begrudgingly lifted itself up, scratching along the road as it flew slowly towards the school gates.

Sammy noticed that Darius still needed the extra magic within his dragon to perform the simple uplifting command to mobilise objects, but he didn't say anything as he knew it would both upset and offend his friend.

'Where's Kyrillan?' asked Darius. 'You didn't take him to Switzerland with you, did you?'

Sammy laughed. 'No, Commander Altair said he would look after Kyrillan, Paprika, Cyngard and Jovah for me over the summer.'

Darius stopped in his tracks and turned to face Sammy with a look that made Sammy's blood run cold.

'You do know that Dixie's still missing, don't you,' said Darius quietly.

# CHAPTER 3

# A FIGHT OVER A DRAGON

Sammy stared numbly at Darius. Over the long summer holiday, he had all but convinced himself that his green haired best friend would be there when he got back.

He could picture her so clearly in his head. Dixie Deane with her genetically coloured bright green hair that she wore tied back in a ponytail, her bright green eyes, her smile and the way she laughed. He knew every detail about her, right down to the freckles on her nose.

'I…uh…no, what, she's still missing?' stuttered Sammy.

'Yup,' Darius nodded. 'It's been on the news and everything.'

'Since when do you watch the news?' asked Sammy, surprised that Darius, in his mobile minibus home, would have access to a television.

'My parents got me a pocket television. It does videos and recording as well.' Darius grinned and held out a shiny rectangular case. 'They said it would keep me out of trouble while my parents go round healing dragons. My Mum will go mad when she finds out I've brought it with me!'

'So, what do they say about Dixie in the news?' asked Sammy, guiding his suitcase over the cattlegrid and up to the school gates.

Darius shrugged. 'Not much. The Snorgcadell, you know, the Guardians of the Dragon Cells, they know something, but…' Darius paused and bent down to pick up his suitcase, which had given up flying across the road. 'Come on! Up!' shouted Darius, kicking the suitcase hard with his right foot.

'But what?' demanded Sammy.

'It's all top secret,' said Darius, tapping his nose. 'They're not saying anything. It's all classified. Eyes only. Need to know basis and all that.'

'But we need to know!' exclaimed Sammy. 'The Snorgcadell must know something.'

'Well, if they do know something, they're not saying,' said Darius. He knocked his staff on the gates and after a few seconds there was a scurrying of activity and the gates swung open.

Captain Firebreath, one of the Dwarves who mined precious gemstones in the castle's foundations appeared out of the shadows. The Dwarf was dressed as usual in his crisp white shirt with a red and white spotted neckerchief, navy dungarees and black boots. He stroked his fiery orange beard and stared at them with his beetle black eyes.

'Ger evenin' to y'all,' growled Captain Firebreath, tucking his thumbs into the straps of his navy dungarees. 'Yer can leave yer dragons and suitcases with me and scoot down the Shute.'

'Race you!' shouted Gavin, flinging his suitcase towards Captain Firebreath.

'You're on!' yelled Toby. 'Come on Sammy! Let's beat him!'

'I'll catch you up,' said Sammy, just managing to stop Gavin's luggage from thumping into Captain Firebreath.

'Are you sure?' asked Darius. 'I'll wait if you want.'

Sammy shook his head. 'I just want to ask a question.'

'Yer want to speak ter me, or just be a doormat for your mates' luggage?' growled Captain Firebreath, his cheeks puffing and turning a little bit pink.

Sammy looked at the angry Dwarf, the three dragons and the collection of suitcases. It would be worth carrying all of them by himself, if only Captain Firebreath could give him good news about Dixie.

'I wanted to ask, er, to ask...' Sammy faltered.

'Is it about your green haired Troll friend?' Captain Firebreath softened. 'Meant a lot ter yer, din't she?'

Sammy nodded, not trusting his voice not to crack. He felt like he should have done more, done something, done anything to stop her from being taken by Alfie Agrock.

'We're keepin' our fingers crossed an' our heads down,' said Captain Firebreath gently. 'Tha's all we can do, eh? An' tha's comin' from a Dwarf!' he laughed. 'Us an' Trolls don't usually mix too good.'

'Alfie Agrock is a Dwarf,' said Sammy.

Captain Firebreath nodded. 'Aye, a bad Dwarf an' all. Dixie'll be puttin' up a good fight. Thinks a lot of you she does. She'll want to thank you for tryin' to save her.'

'But I didn't!' shouted Sammy, kicking his suitcase. 'She's gone and Alfie Agrock's blown the Angel of 'El Horidore whistle and called all the dragons to come here to die!'

Captain Firebreath coughed. 'Well, I'm sure it could be worse, eh?'

'No it couldn't,' snapped Sammy. 'I'm going to take these down the Shute,' he pointed at the pile of suitcases, 'and then I want to know what we can do to find Dixie and get her back here.'

'An' I'll take yer dragons to the Dragon Chambers. Yer want some free advice, yer'll keep hopin' for the best. Too many give up when the end comes in sight.'

Sammy watched Captain Firebreath plod up to the castle. The flame haired Dwarf was almost hidden amongst Darius's navy blue dragon, Nelson, Toby's grey-green dragon, Puttee, and Gavin's pink dragon, Syren.

Sammy pinched his wrist to check he really was back at Dragamas, about to start his fourth year at the school, and that he wasn't in some horrible nightmare.

He stood on his own in the darkness for several minutes, until the Dragamas gates swung open again and Astronomics teacher, Professor John Burlay, nearly ran him over in the white school minibus that had twin gold dragon tails wrapped together along the side.

'Good evening Sammy Rambles,' shouted Professor Burlay out of the window. 'Do you need a hand with those suitcases?'

Sammy accepted Professor Burlay's help gratefully. He loaded the suitcases into the school bus, stacking them on any empty seats he could find amongst the returning students. Sammy recognised the familiar faces of the fifth years, returning for their last year at Dragamas. There were also lots of new, nervous faces belonging to this year's first year students.

At the back of the bus were two raven haired people, Alchemistry teacher Professor Simone Sanchez and her son Simon Sanchez, who was in the fourth year with Sammy, but in the East house, not in Sammy's North house.

'The traitor returns,' growled Professor Sanchez and everyone on the bus turned to look at Sammy. 'Surely Professor Burlay isn't letting this filth onto his bus?'

'Don't mind her,' apologised Professor Burlay. 'You'll find a few people blame you Sammy for, well, you'll see for yourself in a moment.'

Once he had secured the suitcases, Sammy sat in the first row of seats next to two girls from the fifth year. He was sure they were whispering about him from behind a glossy copy of SuperWoman magazine.

Sammy was feeling a little numb with shock at Professor Sanchez's reaction to him arriving back at the school. The feeling wasn't helped by Professor Burlay's erratic driving as the Astronomics teacher tried to avoid the pot holes in the driveway up to the castle courtyard.

Professor Burlay stopped the bus on the cobblestone courtyard, directly in front of the towering grey castle.

'Right then,' said Professor Burlay. 'Everyone off the bus!'

Sammy stood up. He turned around to pick up the first of the suitcases and Professor Sanchez gave him a piercing stare.

'Filth,' Professor Sanchez projected silently into Sammy's mind before disappearing with Simon into a faint red mist that left the first years speechless and the fifth years yawning as they too disappeared into clouds of coloured mist.

'Teleporting,' grumbled Professor Burlay. 'I wish they'd let the little ones out first. It's always the same, eh Sammy? I guess you couldn't really teleport with all that baggage.'

'It's not all mine,' said Sammy, smiling weakly. Over Professor Burlay's shoulder, he had seen a chilling spire of smoke coming out of a bonfire that looked suspiciously like it had been built out of a mountain of dragon bones. 'Is that…is it…' stuttered Sammy.

Professor Burlay cleared his throat. 'Um, yes, Sammy, that's well, you know what it is, don't you?'

'It's all my fault,' said Sammy. He felt hot tears blind him and he stumbled forward, abandoning the suitcases.

Sammy fumbled his way down the steps of the bus and ran out of the courtyard, making his way over to a solitary figure wearing jeans and a black hoodie, who was stoking the giant bonfire with a poker as long as a lamp post.

'Hi Sammy,' said the figure, who turned out to be his fourth year housemate, Jock Hubar, the son of Gemology teacher Mrs Hubar and head miner, Fignus Hubar, who preferred to go by his Dwarven nickname of Captain Duke Stronghammer.

'Hi Jock,' muttered Sammy. 'Is that the dragons?'

'Only the dead ones. I've been stoking this heap of bones all summer. Pay's good,' Jock grinned and held out a fist full of gold coins. 'Hey and guess what, I've got a dragon this year. After Giselle was killed, they've given me a new dragon.'

'Cool,' said Sammy, unable to tear his eyes away from the mountain of crackling bones. The flames shot high into the night sky and every so often there would be a fizz and a shower of scales would come falling at their feet.

'It's Kiridor,' said Jock, his eyes glittering with excitement. 'They've given me Kiridor.'

'Kiridor?' spluttered Sammy. 'Since when?'

'Since Dixie's not coming back,' said Jock. 'Sir Ragnarok's given him to me. That dragon needs a man looking after him – hey!'

In spite of himself, Sammy pushed Jock hard in the collarbone. 'She is coming back!' yelled Sammy. 'And she'll have her dragon back too!'

Jock threw down the lamp post poker and swung his fist in a right hook punch that would have struck Sammy on the knee, if he had still been there.

Instead, Jock's hand clashed with Sammy's staff. There was a nasty crack of bones and splintering shards of wood went flying into the air.

Sammy reached for the crystals on the end of his staff, intending to send a wave of green sparks at Jock, when he caught sight of a shadow in the corner of his eye.

Before he could see who it was, Sammy suddenly collapsed. His entire body seemed to shut down. Everything felt heavy, like he was wearing lead boots, and he crumpled to the ground, eyes rolling, clutching his stomach, where he had a fleeting memory of the chocolate cake Louise had given him coming back up his throat and burning him.

'Are you done?' asked a cool voice above him. 'Carry on with the fire please Jock. I will see to Mr Samuel Rambles.'

Sammy felt his body return to normal. He put his free hand to his mouth, trying to fight being sick. But it was no good and he saw the mucky brown cake mixed with the cola eject from his mouth and stain the charred grass.

Above him, there was the sound of cruel laughter. Jock was standing next to the fire but Sammy couldn't see who was with him. He could only hear their voices.

'Yes, you keep an eye on him. This year will be important. We must see what he brings us.'

Sammy shut his eyes. His head was spinning round and around. His stomach was churning. He felt himself lift off the ground and he was vaguely aware of a gold mist surrounding him.

'Wake up Sammy. We haven't got all night, eh?'

Sammy blinked. Instead of lying on the grass outside in the darkness, he was lying on a purple velvet couch in a circular tower room with big television screens on the wall.

'Sir Ragnarok's office,' whispered Sammy, sitting up and taking in his surroundings.

He saw the headmaster sitting at his desk opposite the couch.

'Hello Sir Ragnarok,' whispered Sammy, noticing how pale he looked.

The Dragamas headmaster nodded and stroked his long grey beard.

'Hello again Sammy. As I was saying, there is no way to tell where she went.'

CHAPTER 4

# THE STONE CROSS

Sammy stared blankly. It had been a tense summer after the climatic events at the end of the summer term. He had known Sir Lok Ragnarok, Headmaster of Dragamas School for Dragon Charming for nearly four years and not once had he seen him this pale, this tired or this angry.

'There is no way to tell where she went,' repeated Sir Ragnarok. 'I am sorry. We have done all we can.'

Sammy felt his hands shake. 'The bonfire by the courtyard?' he whispered. 'Is that all the dragons that have come here?'

Sir Ragnarok nodded. 'Alfie Agrock blew the real Angel of 'El Horidore whistle and he summoned all the dragons in the world, living or dead, to come here to Dragamas. So far, only fourteen live dragons have arrived.'

Sir Ragnarok pointed to a sketch of a Celtic cross on the noticeboard behind his desk. It had been coloured in using blue and green chalk on a white background. The cross was nearly all coloured in with very few white spaces.

'We believe this is how far the Shape have got in their quest to collect all the pieces of draconite,' said Sir Ragnarok quietly.

'No,' whispered Sammy. 'There must be more dragons still alive in the world.'

He stared at Sir Ragnarok's diagram, knowing that each individual blue and green dot represented a single piece of draconite, the precious gemstone that gave a dragon its powers. The draconite was being stolen from all the dragons' brains by the evil members of the Shape.

Sir Ragnarok sighed and shook his head. 'Perhaps there are more dragons. The Stone Cross has always been the guide we have used. Now that the Angel of 'El Horidore has been used, all of the dragons are on their way here.'

Sammy nodded solemnly. On one of Sir Ragnarok's large television screens he could see the bonfire flames burning brightly in the darkness.

'In the meantime,' continued Sir Ragnarok, 'please take good care of your own dragon. Kyrillan will be safe in the Dragon Chambers but promise me that if he goes outside, then you will not let your dragon out of your sight.'

'I promise,' said Sammy.

'Good,' said Sir Ragnarok.

The Dragamas Headmaster waved his right arm towards the curved wall of television screens. The individual screens merged into one picture showing the Main Hall and the students arriving for the welcome banquet.

'This will be your hardest year Sammy, but keep your head above the tide,' said Sir Ragnarok. 'We can all swim in shallow waters.'

'Yes Sir,' said Sammy, wondering if this was true.

Sir Ragnarok scratched his head and reached into his desk drawer. He pulled out a brown leather pouch. 'I nearly forgot these,' he said, passing the pouch to Sammy. 'It's draconite Jock has salvaged from the injured dragons that have died in our company. Please give it to Mrs Hubar, his mother, please. I dare say you'll see her before I will. You can look at the draconite if you like. It will remind you what we are trying to protect.'

Sammy took a deep breath and opened the bag of precious stones. He expected them to be cold and slimy with pieces of dragons' brains still attached. But it seemed as though Jock had painstakingly washed and polished the blue-green stones until they were shimmering and shiny.

Sammy knew, without being told, how important it was to protect the draconite and how the stones must stay away from the Shape at all costs.

'Work hard this year Sammy,' said Sir Ragnarok.

Sammy looked up at his headmaster. 'It is hard,' he whispered.

'It's hard on all of us, especially Dixie's mother, don't forget. Perhaps you could send her a card from your house. She has searched tirelessly for her daughter and I know, first hand because I have spoken many times with her, that she would like to hear your side of the story.'

'But,' Sammy pointed at the television screens, 'you can rewind to that day. You can show her exactly what happened.'

Sir Ragnarok smiled. 'Not when things are protected with these,' Sir Ragnarok reached into another of his desk drawers and brought out a shoebox that had a blue glow surrounding it.

Sammy gasped as Sir Ragnarok opened the shoebox. Inside were dozens of golf ball sized sapphires, all glowing with a deep blue haze. Sammy eyed the sapphires eagerly.

'You'll get one all in good time,' Sir Ragnarok smiled. 'In the meantime, go to your tower room and unpack, enjoy the welcome banquet and then tomorrow your lessons will keep your thoughts busy. Trust me, I will tell you as soon as there is good news.'

'And bad news?' asked Sammy. He could already hear Lariston purring at his feet and feel the smooth grey cat nudging his shins, urging him to get up and escorting him to Sir Ragnarok's office door.

Sammy was so busy looking backwards at the box of sapphires on Sir Ragnarok's desk that he bumped into short, plump, Mrs Hubar, who, as always had her hair pinned back in a bun fastened only by an orange pencil that you could see both lead and eraser poking out behind her ears.

'Watch where you're going,' snapped Mrs Hubar.

'Sorry,' muttered Sammy. 'Here you go Mrs Hubar,' he said, thrusting the leather pouch into her rough hands.

Mrs Hubar took the bag excitedly, her hands jittering as she opened it to inspect the contents.

'Oooh!' Mrs Hubar squealed. 'More draconite! Thank you!'

'Sir Ragnarok said you'd keep it safe,' said Sammy.

Mrs Hubar nodded vigorously and the orange pencil in her hair lurched violently, threatening to come loose. 'Of course I will young Sammy. Now, what's this tiff of yours with my Jock over Dixie's dragon?' I say bury the argument, like they'll probably be burying her, along with her poor father. It's such a shame.'

Sammy nodded, the idea of teleporting himself back to the North common room, that seemed such a good idea a second ago had vanished.

'Dixie will come back and I'll make it up with Jock,' said Sammy, taking small steps to avoid his brand new shoes squeaking on the stone staircase.

Sammy paused at the bottom of the stairs. He took a deep breath and pushed the tapestry aside and walked into the Main Hall.

As Sammy expected, the room hushed when he went in. There was a mixture of forgotten gossip and stares of sympathy that was broken by Sir Ragnarok placing two hands on Sammy's shoulders.

'Welcome to Dragamas!' boomed Sir Ragnarok, deafening Sammy, who extracted himself and walked as unobtrusively as possible up to the fourth year North table.

For the first time since he had been at Dragamas, Sammy couldn't pick out a single strand of green hair on anyone's head on any of the North house tables.

Dixie should have been the only person there with bright green hair as her brothers, Serberon, Mikhael and Jason had finished their education at Dragamas at the end of their fifth year, just a few months ago.

Sammy found two empty seats at the fourth year North table. He sat between Darius and Milly who, Sammy noticed, was now sporting pink train track braces on both her upper and lower teeth. The empty seat was a harsh reminder that Dixie should have been there.

'Here's the traitor,' muttered Gavin under his breath. 'All the dragons are dead. It's all his fault.'

'Liar,' said Toby, nudging his brother. 'There's our dragons, plus twelve others. Dad's newspaper said so.'

'Fourteen,' corrected Sammy. 'Anyway, what would you have done? Would you have let Alfie Agrock kill Dixie?'

Gavin shrugged. 'Who cares?'

'Yeah Gavin, what would you have done?' asked Milly, lisping slightly with her new teethwear.

'I'd have given it to Sir Ragnarok,' retorted Gavin.

Milly laughed. 'While you were frozen solid under the effect of the ruby? Don't be silly!'

'Thilly, whath's thilly ith your voicth,' mocked Gavin. 'Who cares anyway? Sammy's as good as killed all of our dragons.'

'Except Kiridor,' grinned Jock 'He's the same colour as your dragon Sammy, isn't he? Draconite blue.'

'Draconite blue,' echoed Sammy, grateful when Sir Ragnarok picked up his crescent shaped knife and five pronged fork and the Main Hall exploded into the merry sounds of vast quantities of delicious food materialising from the underground kitchens.

On the North table, each student had thought of their favourite food and the requested dishes were fizzing and popping as they appeared on their plates.

Sammy looked up and down the North table. To his left, he could see plates stacked high with sandwiches in white, brown and wholemeal bread, stuffed with fillings of chicken paté, cucumber and cheese, bacon and tomato, ham and mushroom and many others.

To his right, his friends had chosen plates filled with delicious looking bite-size mini pepperoni pizzas, loaves of garlic bread, small bowls of tomato soup with croutons, plates piled high with slices of cold meat, boiled potatoes, roast potatoes, chips and potato faces.

Sammy checked his own plate. When he had picked up his crescent shaped knife and five pronged fork he thought it would be nice to have a roast dinner, his favourite meal in the whole world.

As a welcome back treat, Sir Ragnarok always let the Dragamas students choose their own first meal. Sammy loved the way it was magically prepared and transported directly onto their plates from the school kitchens.

'Are you having roast dinner again?' asked Darius, tucking into a plate of spaghetti. 'You should try something different sometimes.'

Sammy nodded, staring at the empty wooden seat in front of him. Absent mindedly he stared at the Dragamas motif carved into the back panel of the chair. The twin dragon tails were intertwined like the past and the present.

Sammy felt the twin tails were mocking him, accusing him of losing the chair's occupant.

'You missed Dr Shivers handing out the Dragon Minder pins,' said Darius, winding strands of spaghetti around his fork. 'Me and Naomi are doing it this year. No-one else wanted to do it this year. Nobody volunteered at all.'

'No-one wanted "you" to do it,' added Gavin, staring at Sammy. 'It's your fault all these dragons are dead.'

'They were dead when they arrived,' snapped Sammy. 'Fourteen live dragons are here, aren't they Jock?'

'We're going to be fourteen this year,' said Gavin.

Jock shrugged. 'It doesn't matter really. Everyone knows the Shape are coming after the last ones. That's the real reason why no-one wanted to be a Dragon Minder this year. It's just too much responsibility.'

'You'd just give the dragons up to the Shape,' said Gavin. 'I want to keep my dragon and I want there to be dragons in the world.'

'You've changed your mind about the Shape, haven't you?' accused Sammy.

'It's different now,' said Gavin, dipping one of his mini pepperoni pizzas into a bowl of tomato soup.

'How?' demanded Sammy. 'Last year you couldn't care less. What would you have done? Would you really have let Dixie die?'

Gavin blushed crimson and there was a nasty silence for a few moments.

'Dr Shivers gave me and Naomi the Dragon Minder pins,' explained Darius. 'We didn't volunteer.'

'Ok,' said Sammy. He felt a little more at ease and speared a giant roast potato with his fork. He dunked the potato into the pool of gravy at the side of his plate and put it all into his mouth in one go.

# CHAPTER 5

# NELSON'S ADVENTURE

After eating more roast dinner than was sensible, Sammy made his way slowly through the North common room and up the boys' staircase to the second floor of the North tower. This would be his new dormitory bedroom, where the fourth year boys would sleep.

Sammy carried on up the stairs, first out of habit, then up a few more stairs out of nostalgia. He wanted to see his original bedroom, the first years' tower room, with the coned turret ceiling. A voice broke him out of his trip down memory lane.

'Hey Sammy! Are you lost?'

Sammy grinned at Nigel Ashford, the boy he was supposed to be mentoring and looking out for. Nigel was now in his third year at Dragamas and didn't really need any help at all.

'I'm just looking at the old rooms,' said Sammy.

'This is where you had that party, isn't it?' asked Nigel.

Sammy nodded, remembering how he had seemingly flown on Kyrillan through a solid stone wall.

'Awesome!' Nigel grinned but Sammy found he wasn't listening, or rather he was listening, but all he could hear was the rush of air in his ears.

The sound of Nigel's footsteps on the stone stairs was eerily distant and when the stairs actually faded away they were replaced with green grass in a familiar valley with a black shadow on the horizon.

'The Valley of the Stone Cross,' whispered Sammy, relieved as the grass disappeared and he could see the stone stairs beneath his feet again.

'The what?' asked Nigel.

'Uh, nothing,' said Sammy, looking up.

Nigel was holding his wrist and his housemaster, Dr Shivers, was propping him up by his shoulder. Dr Shivers held him in an iron grip, his skeletally thin fingers pinching Sammy's neck.

'You've been like it for five minutes,' whispered Nigel. 'Are you ok?'

'You have avoided another nasty fall Sammy,' said Dr Shivers coolly. 'What exactly were you doing two floors above where you're meant to be?'

Sammy looked down over the railings and agreed with the Dragon Studies teacher. It would have been a long way down if he had fallen.'

'Lucky I was passing,' said Dr Shivers, a cold smile filling his pale lips.

Sammy nodded. 'Thank you,' he said, rubbing his forehead and wishing he had seen more of the valley. He knew the Stone Cross was there and he wished he could go there again.

'Be careful what you wish for,' said Dr Shivers, smiling and tapping the side of his head. 'Now Sammy, make sure you're up early tomorrow. You may only have two more years here at Dragamas, but there is much to learn. Have either of you seen Mrs Hubar? I was hoping to have one or two lumps of draconite to show you something in your next Dragon Studies lesson.'

'She's probably in the mines,' said Nigel helpfully.

'Thank you Nigel,' said Dr Shivers. 'I will award you one star for your helpfulness. Good night boys.'

Without saying another word, Dr Shivers evaporated into a silver mist and vanished.

'He's creepy,' whispered Nigel. 'He does that at the end of all our Dragon Studies lessons and you're never quite sure if he's really gone.'

'He's gone,' said Sammy. 'Anyway, I'll see you later.'

'Night Sammy.'

Sammy waited for Nigel to go into his third year dormitory before making his own way back down the remaining stairs to make himself at home in the fourth year quarters.

The fourth years' dormitory tower door was made from solid oak with a plaque that said "Fourth Years" in Gothic scrawl. There was an old fashioned gold bell above the door and Sammy remembered how the bell would ring to wake them up in the morning. He ran his hand over the plaque and pushed the door open.

Inside the circular tower room, Sammy found because the room was much lower than the third year dormitory, he had lost even more of his favourite view of the Dragonball pitch. A row of silver birch and oak trees that lined the pitch were just too high to see over from his new window.

He also found that while he and his housemates had been stuffing themselves with the enormous welcome back banquet that all of their suitcases and luggage had been brought upstairs to their room.

Sammy looked at his new room. There were five beds with the familiar green duvets spread evenly around the room. Next to each bed was a chest of drawers with a small green lamp on top and a new three legged wooden stool underneath.

Above the chest of drawers was a long thin window filled with clear glass. Each window offered a slightly different view of the school and the grounds.

There was the same curtain rail with the thick green velvet curtains flowing from the ceiling to the floor that could be drawn around each bed for privacy.

He noticed the room was much bigger than the room they had shared last year. The tower seemed to be a lot wider as it got lower down and gave the five fourth year North boys plenty of room to spread out.

Sammy was pleased to see his grey suitcase was tucked neatly under his bed and also that on the end of his bed was the familiar year plaque which still read:

North House

Samuel R. Rambles

5 Years

Gavin was lying on his stomach, stretching out at full length on his bed with his feet on his pillows. It looked as though he was reading a magazine about fighter jets.

Toby and Jock were sitting on the floor exchanging dozens of the collectible Dragonball stickers to fill their albums with pictures of the popular players. The only person missing was Darius.

'Hi Sammy,' said Gavin, looking up from his magazine. 'Did you get lost on your way here?'

'Nice room,' said Sammy, ignoring Gavin and going over to his bed. 'Where's Darius?'

'Dragon Minder duties,' said Toby.

'He'll be here soon,' added Jock. 'Do you want this one of Nitron Dark?' Jock held up a sticker for Toby to look at.

Toby flicked through his album and shook his head. 'Got it already.'

Sammy quickly unpacked his suitcase, shovelling his clothes into the chest of drawers. He liked the new three legged stool that could be pushed under the bottom drawer to make a private study desk, complete with a small green lamp that could be turned on and off by tapping the base.

Just as Sammy was about to turn out his new desk lamp and change into his pyjamas there was a loud CRACK and Darius and Nelson appeared at the end of his bed.

Nelson thumped his scaly tail down hard on the floor and the draught sent Toby and Jock's stickers flying around the room.

'Oi!' grumbled Jock, picking up some of the stickers that had landed near him. 'No dragons are allowed in the tower room.'

Darius put his hands on his hips. 'It was an accident,' he said huffily. 'Nelson was supposed to stay down there in the Dragon Chambers.'

Gavin threw down his magazine and erupted into hysterical laughter. 'You'll never be a Dragon Healer at this rate!'

'At least Darius has got ambition,' snorted Jock. 'All you want to do Gavin is be rude to everyone and throw your weight around!'

'Like this!' shouted Gavin, leaping up and lunging at Jock, his fists outstretched.

Jock merely threw his leg out and tripped Gavin head first into the prickly spikes at the end of Nelson's tail.

'Oi! Dwarf breath!' yelled Gavin. 'I'll get you for that!'

'Mind my dragon!' screeched Darius as Nelson let out a cloud of blue smoke from his angry flared nostrils.

'He tripped me up!' squawked Gavin.

'You should look where you're going,' retorted Jock.

'You should be more careful!' shouted Darius. 'What on earth are you doing jumping around the tower anyway?'

'Don't ask,' said Toby. 'It's just Gavin being stupid again.'

'I'm not stupid!' shouted Gavin. 'You're supposed to be on my side Toby! Some brother you are!'

'Well you are stupid!' retorted Toby. 'Always throwing your weight around. Not everyone cares what you say.'

'No one cares what you say,' shouted Gavin. 'You can't stop me saying what I like!'

'Um, we should probably stop,' said Sammy, looking up at a grey shadow at the tower doorway.

'Having fun are we boys?' scowled Dr Shivers. 'That will cost you five stars each, plus fifteen for you Darius for bringing your dragon into the tower room. Now, give the dratted thing some of these.' Dr Shivers threw a handful of green pellets at Darius.

The pellets bounced away from Darius's clumsy catch and fell into Nelson's large nostrils.

'These are a new form of green pellets with a very strong sleeping draught,' said Dr Shivers, a smile on his pale lips. 'Make sure that dragon is moved by sunrise.'

'That's so unfair!' stormed Darius. 'Look at him!'

Sammy looked at the large navy dragon. Nelson was completely unconscious, his large tummy lifting up and down as he breathed heavily in a deep sleep.

'By sunrise boys,' said Dr Shivers. He laughed cruelly and whisked his grey cloak around his shoulders, disappearing into a cool grey mist.

'He's mean,' agreed Gavin, whipping his curtain around his bed. 'Anyway, I'm off to sleep.'

'No way!' roared Darius. 'This is your fault! You have to help!'

Gavin stuck two fingers out of his closed curtain and switched off his light.

'Come on,' grumbled Jock. 'We'd better get dragging.'

'No, no, no, no, no,' said Darius. 'There is no way my dragon is going to be dragged down those stairs.'

'Why not? It's not like we're at the top of the tower any more. There's only two flights,' said Sammy helpfully. 'Or we could teleport,' he added, not liking to share with the others that he'd been itching to try teleporting since they had arrived back at Dragamas.

Toby laughed. 'You can't do that!'

'How do you think I got Nelson here?' demanded Darius.

'Fluke?' suggested Jock.

'Pah!' snorted Darius. 'Come on, we'll just open the window and fly outside. The fresh air should wake him up.'

'Or you'll go splat,' said Gavin, his voice muffled from behind his curtain.

'Can't you just heal Nelson and wake him up?' asked Sammy. 'You know, with the gemstones on your staff?'

'Probably,' muttered Darius. 'But I'd need to research it first. All kinds of things can go wrong.'

Jock yawned, stretching his short arms up towards the ceiling. 'If you lot don't hurry up, I'll be asleep too.'

'Shhh,' hissed Gavin. 'I'm trying to sleep.'

Sammy shook his head. Gavin could be so awkward at times. He formed a ring around Nelson with himself and Darius at the navy dragon's head and Toby and Jock at the tail.

'On three,' said Sammy, wondering if this would work. 'One...two...'

'Three!' yelled Gavin at the top of his voice and suddenly there was an almighty explosion that rocked the tower.

'We did it!' shrieked Jock as the castle courtyard appeared and they all fell sprawling on the cobbles.

Sammy ended up entangled with Toby and Darius underneath Nelson, who was snoring gently, blissfully unaware his huge tail was preventing anyone from getting up.

'Cool,' said Toby, shifting his feet from under the enormous dragon. 'It's dark, isn't it?'

Sammy extracted himself and lit a fire with his staff, holding the flames above his head.

'I reckon we should be able to move Nelson to the Dragon Chambers from here,' said Sammy. He pointed to the gaping hole where the entrance to the Dragon Chambers was normally carefully hidden.

At the sloping entrance, Dr Shivers was talking with Captain Stronghammer.

'Hi Dad!' shouted Jock. 'Help us with Darius's dragon!'

Captain Stronghammer scuttled over, his black boots clicking on the cobbles. He tucked a spade into the front pocket of his denim dungarees.

'Holy smoke,' muttered Captain Stronghammer. 'A live dragon for a change!'

'It's Darius's dragon,' laughed Jock. 'Nelson was in our tower room and Dr Shivers made him go to sleep.'

'I see,' said Captain Stronghammer, frowning in the direction of where Dr Shivers had been standing. Now there was only a swirling grey mist. 'It's times like these when a Troll or two comes in handy.'

'Dixie's not here,' said Sammy. 'Neither are Serberon, Mikhael or Jason.'

'Can't you magic Nelson awake?' asked Toby. 'You know, like they do on telly?'

'No,' said Captain Stronghammer flatly. 'I'll go get me ropes. We'll have ter do this the old fashioned way.'

Half an hour later, there was a long skid mark on the cobbles where Nelson had been unceremoniously dragged into the Dragon Chambers.

Sammy thought to himself they would have done things far quicker if Darius hadn't insisted on checking Nelson was ok at every footstep.

Sammy also thought to himself that despite Captain Stronghammer and Jock proclaiming how strong they were, and they were pretty strong, he was sure that Dixie and Mrs Deane would have been able to move Nelson in half the time and made lighter work of the task.

'Phew!' groaned Toby when Nelson was safely installed in the Dragon Chambers. 'That was worse than one of Mr Cross's workouts in our Sports lessons!'

'I reckon Dr Shivers did this on purpose,' grumbled Darius.

'Of course he did,' said Jock. 'All the teachers are the same and that includes my Mum.'

'Don't let her hear you say that young Jock,' chuckled Captain Stronghammer. 'Anyway, you boys best get back to yer tower. I need to check all the dragons are settled in fer the night, do me rounds an' all.'

'Night then,' said Jock, waving to his father. His black eyes sparkled as he looked at Sammy, Darius, Gavin and Toby. 'Shall we teleport back?'

'North Tower, Fourth Year Tower Room, Boys!' shouted Sammy, reaching out for Darius's hand and missing.

Sammy was the only boy awake when Darius finally stomped into the tower room.

'Well, thanks for waiting!' said Darius, throwing himself fully clothed onto his bed.

Sammy grinned and turned out his new bedside light. It had been an exciting first day back at Dragamas.

# CHAPTER 6

# SLEEPING DRAGONS

Having had a night full of dreams of moving hundreds sleeping dragons and visions of the Stone Cross, Sammy woke early to an annoying thumping of footsteps in the room above them. He sat up in bed and looked out of the window.

Rows of trees covered in large plumes of leaves in many varying colours, from deep emerald green, to leaves fading into autumnal colours of orange, yellow and brown.

No matter what colour the leaves were, Sammy found they were all blocking his precious view of the Dragonball pitch which, to his surprise, he was quite possessive of. He wondered if the first, second and third years in the rooms above him appreciated the view as much as he had.

The morning sun was shining down in patches, soaking up the darkness like a damp sponge. There were some girls playing catch with pink and purple Firesticks balls in the courtyard.

For a split second, Sammy thought it would be fun to try and hit the Firesticks balls by firing the green sparks he could make with his staff out of the tower room window.

Then he considered the number of stars North had already forfeited the night before whilst helping Darius with his dragon and thought better of it.

Instead, Sammy opened the top drawer of his chest of drawers and picked out a clean pair of black socks, his school tie, black trousers and a freshly ironed white shirt with the North house compass logo on the pocket. He threw the clothes on, struggling with creating a neat knot in his tie after weeks of wearing t-shirts, jeans and shorts.

Sammy checked his yellow parchment timetable and groaned.

'Dragon Studies is first,' said Sammy to no one in particular.

'Great,' grumbled Darius. 'I bet Dr Shivers says something about Nelson.'

'You should have been able to wake up your stupid dragon,' shouted Gavin from the other side of the curtain. 'Anyway, hurry up! It's breakfast time!'

Sammy felt as though everyone was still staring at him at breakfast. He could hear faint whispers about how he had enabled Alfie Agrock to take and blow the Angel of 'El Horidore whistle.

He was glad when the gold bell above the double doors chimed loudly to signal the first lesson and everyone departed from the Main Hall to go to their lessons in the different rooms spread around the castle.

The uncomfortable staring continued, particularly from the students in the West house, as the fourth years sat down at the charred wooden desks in the draughty Dragon Studies classroom in room fifty-five in the East wing.

Dr Shivers appeared in a swirl of grey mist and stood at the front of the classroom. He was dressed in a pale grey suit with a white shirt and silver tie. A long grey cloak was wrapped around his shoulders, fastened with a silver dragon shaped pin at his neck.

'This morning we will be learning how to raise your dragons from slumber,' said Dr Shivers, with a smirk cast in Darius's direction. 'With just a sprinkling of earth and just the right touch between the ears. Like Darius Murphy failed to do yesterday,' he added spitefully.

Sammy nudged Darius. 'We didn't know how to do it either,' he whispered.

Darius shrugged. 'At least I'll know for next time.'

'You'll also need these,' said Dr Shivers, holding out a cardboard box brimming with the green pellets he had used to sedate Nelson last night.

'Sleeping draught pellets,' whispered Milly. 'I've seen them before. They're really strong.'

'I know,' grumbled Darius.

'You will have one pellet each,' continued Dr Shivers, 'and please don't eat them yourselves. Peter Grayling, that includes you! Obviously your forty dragons won't all fit in here at once so we will conduct this lesson outside. Teleport to the courtyard if you wish.'

Dr Shivers whisked his cloak around his shoulders creating a mini tornado that sent an icy breeze through the class. When the silver mist cleared, the Dragon Studies teacher had gone.

'Let's tele…uh…let's walk down the stairs,' said Sammy, catching a beseeching glance from Darius.

As the classroom filled with different coloured mists from the different students vanishing and teleporting down to the courtyard, Sammy and Darius picked up their things and walked the long way down through the corridors and out to the castle courtyard.

As they pushed open the heavy castle door, Captain Stronghammer was leading the forty fourth year dragons out of the Dragon Chambers into the cobbled courtyard. They could hear him tutting as he skipped out of the way as student after student appeared out of their teleporting mist and threatened to squash him.

Sammy felt a lump in his throat as Jock went to stand proudly next to Kiridor.

'Dixie should be here,' Sammy whispered to Darius.

Darius nodded, stroking Nelson's scaly back. 'At least Kiridor is being well looked after. Jock's dragon was killed so it's good he's got a dragon and after all, Dixie isn't here anymore.'

'That's not the point,' whispered Sammy. 'It feels too soon.'

Dr Shivers walked briskly around the class handing out the green pellets from his cardboard box.

Jock took the first pellet and held it in his open palm in front of Kiridor's nose. Dixie's large blue-green dragon inhaled the shiny pellet and promptly collapsed. Jock jumped quickly aside as Kiridor landed in a slumbering heap by his feet.

Kyrillan on the other hand did not seem to want to take part in the Dragon Studies lesson at all. Sammy had to practically force the green pellet into his dragon's mouth.

Kyrillan promptly spat the pellet out, stomping his feet and blowing burning smoke rings that unsettled the other dragons, especially Milly's pastel pink dragon, Bubbles. Sammy noticed Milly had parked her dragon inches from Kyrillan.

'Your dragon's really wild, isn't he? Full of spirit!' giggled Milly, holding out her green pellet at arm's length.

'I don't expect you'd like to be force fed,' Sammy snapped back at her.

'Ooo touchy!' Milly carried on giggling. 'Isn't that Dixie's dragon Jock's with?'

'He's mine now!' shouted Jock. 'Look everyone! My dragon is out like a mining lantern in a tunnel without oxygen! I'm a natural!'

Hearing the noise, Dr Shivers stomped over to Sammy, Darius, Jock and Milly. He wore an angry frown on his pale face.

'Do you want to lose more stars Sammy?' asked Dr Shivers. 'I clearly remember saying to feed your dragon the green pellet, not to let him set fire to the place!'

'Sammy is trying,' protested Milly. 'Look, my dragon won't eat it, um…well,' Milly tailed off as Bubbles obediently licked the green pellet out of her outstretched hand and fell flat onto Dr Shivers feet, pulling his grey cloak to the ground.

'Dratted thing,' said Dr Shivers, recovering his cloak from the cobbles and wrapping it around his shoulders. 'Get a move on Sammy. Feed your dragon the sleeping draught so we can practise how to wake him up again.'

'Yes Sir,' said Sammy, copying Milly and holding out his hand with the green pellet in his palm.

Kyrillan refused to eat the pellet, but lay down obediently with his head between his front paws and his scaly tail curled around his belly. He even made realistic heavy breathing noises.

'Good Sammy,' said Dr Shivers, surveying the class and all the sleeping dragons. 'Is that everyone done?'

Sammy put the green pellet into his trouser pocket. He felt a little guilty as Dr Shivers started stroking Kyrillan's ears and sprinkling some of the earth he scratched from between the cobbles over Kyrillan's nose.

With an almighty "hurrumph" Kyrillan got to his feet, scales clinking and he blew a belch of fire. Sammy ducked just in time and the flames missed him by inches.

'That is very responsive,' mused Dr Shivers. 'You have trained your dragon well Sammy. Now, let me see if the rest of the class can perform as well.'

Sammy helped Milly to collect a handful of earth and sprinkle the dust and grit over her sleeping dragon's nose.

With a loud snort, Bubbles sprang to life, knocking Milly off her feet.

Sammy reached out and caught her and she giggled at him.

'Oooer,' giggled Darius, who wasn't having much luck raising Nelson from slumber. The navy dragon was clearly in a very deep sleep.

'Concentrate!' scolded Naomi, putting her arm around Darius's shoulders, which he promptly shrugged off, his cheeks glowing crimson.

'Please write up this experiment as an essay entitled "Sleeping Pellets of the Modern World" and hand your work in on Wednesday,' said Dr Shivers checking his watch. 'Also, please give any unused green pellets back to me.'

Reluctantly, Sammy took the unused sleeping pellet out of his trouser pocket. He had been hoping to keep it for emergencies. As he placed the green rectangle into Dr Shivers's hand, Sammy caught Simon Sanchez's eye.

'We both did not use them,' said Simon Sanchez as he handed Dr Shivers his own green pellet. 'We will be good Dragon Knights one day.'

'Just you two is it?' snapped Dr Shivers, eyeing Simon's huge black dragon suspiciously. 'I might have known.'

CHAPTER 7

# BLACK ZYON POWDER

From somewhere deep within the castle, a bell chimed six times at full volume to signify that the next lesson was about to start.

Captain Stronghammer returned to take all of the forty multi-coloured four-year-old dragons back into the Dragon Chambers. Assisted by the Dragon Minders, he led the procession of dragons down the slope and out of sight.

The dragons clomped and stomped their way back to their quarters. Some of the dragons looked half-asleep after taking the sleeping pellet. Others yawned loudly, baring rows and rows of sparkling white teeth.

'Armoury is next,' said Simon, consulting his yellow timetable parchment. 'My favourite…not!' he laughed.

'Armoury Room!' shouted Sammy and Simon, at exactly the same and they bumped heads trying to be the first to get to the classroom.

Sammy rubbed his head and sat down at his favourite desk by the window. Simon sat at the back of the class, next to Amos Leech, who had also teleported, but arrived a few seconds behind them. Jock was next to arrive and he sat on the row next to Sammy.

Although the lesson wasn't due to start yet, the classroom filled up with students teleporting themselves into empty space between the desks and at the front of the classroom next to Commander Altair's desk.

Gavin and Toby sat next to Sammy and Jock. They each took last year's Armoury textbooks, paper and pens out of their rucksacks.

'You might have waited,' Darius grumbled some fifteen minutes later as he walked into the Armoury classroom via the door. 'I had to put all the North dragons away with Naomi and…' Darius paused dramatically, 'she kissed me!'

'Cool,' said Gavin, looking at Darius with respect.

Sammy choked. 'What?'

'She kissed me!' repeated Darius. 'And it was hot!'

'Like really hot?' asked Gavin. 'You know, like on TV?'

'Hotter!' said Darius, grinning widely at Sammy, Toby and Gavin.

'Like boiling bath water?' asked Toby grinning at Darius.

'Bath water!' snorted Gavin.

Darius cocked his head quizzically at Toby. 'It was hotter, much hotter.'

'Like…' Toby scratched his head and Sammy wished he knew how hot it might be to kiss someone.

Darius waved his hand dismissively. 'If you've done it, you'll know what it's like.'

'I've done it,' said Gavin. 'Me and Milly. We've done it loads of times!'

Sammy looked at Gavin with respect. 'Seriously?'

'Loads of times,' said Gavin. 'Ask her if you don't believe me!'

'Fine,' scowled Darius, turning round to where the girls were sitting in the next row. 'Oi! Milly!'

'No! Not like that!' moaned Gavin. 'She made me promise not to say anything!'

'Too late,' snickered Jock.

'What do you want Darius?' asked Milly. 'It's rude to say "Oi" to get someone's attention. Mummy says…'

'Did you kiss Gavin?' interrupted Darius.

Milly went bright pink. 'Gavin! I told you not to say anything!' she shrieked. 'You promised! It wasn't that good anyway. Toby was better!'

'Toby!' spluttered Gavin, grabbing his brother by the scruff of his neck. 'You bin at it with my girl?'

'Hah!' squeaked Milly. 'Your girl? I don't think so!'

Sammy was actually grateful when Commander Altair slammed the classroom door shut with a bang to let them know he had arrived. His face looked like thunder.

'What on earth is going on! Professor Burlay was right! You lot belong up there at the Floating Circus!' stormed Commander Altair running a hand through his corn coloured hair.

Sammy leaned back in his seat, glad that Gavin and Toby had instantly forgotten their fight.

'There are very serious issues we need to discuss this year and there's no room for slackers,' continued Commander Altair, putting a cardboard box on his desk. 'Is there anyone here who wants to skip my Armoury classes? Is there anyone here whose parents have forbidden you to learn with me?'

Gavin raised his hand, along with several students from the West house.

'Fine,' snapped Commander Altair. 'Get out and use these lessons for extra study in your other subjects. You probably need it.'

'I'm going too,' said Toby, shuffling quickly out of the classroom behind Gavin.

Within seconds, the classroom was half empty. There was an uneasy silence that was broken when Commander Altair finished writing names on a class register.

'Good,' said Commander Altair, smiling for the first time since he had arrived in the classroom. 'All the trouble makers are out and we still have an even number of students. Push the desks aside and then stand on your chairs please. I want to make sure you're all still on form with your Armoury skills.'

When the desks were out of the way, Sammy stood on his chair opposite Milly, holding his staff outstretched.

'That's a bit of an unfair match Sammy,' said Commander Altair, beckoning for him to change chairs and stand opposite Simon Sanchez.

Simon grinned and, without waiting for Commander Altair's instructions, fired a friendly volley of red sparks that Sammy found he could block easily.

When he was satisfied the remaining students were paired evenly, Commander Altair returned to the front of the classroom and stood on his desk.

In his dark jeans with the black belt with the silver stars and his black shirt under his grey jumper, Commander Altair looked every inch the warlord Sammy knew he was.

Commander Altair held his staff in his right hand and the coloured crystal gemstones glowed at the end above his head.

'When we are at war, we show no weakness. There is no mercy and no surrender,' said Commander Altair loudly. 'Do you hear me? Do you understand?'

From their elevated positions, every student in the classroom nodded. Sammy found he was holding his breath, mesmerised by his Armoury teacher who was also a Dragon Commander of the Snorgcadell.

'Good!' shouted Commander Altair. 'Now, attack your partner's chair, just their chair, until it collapses! Left of the room versus the right of the room. GO!'

Commander Altair ducked out of the fray as Rachel Burns let a volley of red sparks fly towards Darius, who, with more luck than judgement, ricocheted the red sparks back at her chair, making it rock unsteadily at her feet.

Sammy blocked another volley of Simon's red sparks. They bounced off his staff, fizzling into tiny red shards that disintegrated into red dust and vanished altogether.

Without a moment's hesitation, Sammy retaliated, letting one of his tower-rocking green sparks loose from his staff. The green spark catapulted into the legs of Simon's chair, knocking him flying over backwards and jolting the entire row of students on the right hand side of the classroom off their feet. The students fell haphazardly into twisted bundles of arms and legs on the classroom floor.

Commander Altair smiled at the devastation. 'We have a winner! Well done Sammy. Fifty stars for North.' He flicked his staff and a stream of gold stars exploded out of thin air and chased each other out of the classroom on their way to the noticeboard in the Main Hall.

'You were lucky,' Simon Sanchez grinned and got back on his feet. 'I was about to do the same to you.'

'Back on your chairs,' roared Commander Altair when the last of the gold stars had flown away. 'Now, block this!' He fired his staff at the ceiling and thousands of tiny jet black sparks fell like bats swooping down among the students.

'Ow!' shrieked Milly, as one of the black sparks hit her arm and dissolved into a black powder.

'Ow!' Sammy flinched as a black spark landed on his cheek. He brushed his hand over where the spark had hit him and felt sticky blood on his fingertips.

All around him, Sammy's classmates were busy shielding themselves from the black sparks with their arms over their faces or trying to hide under the chairs.

There was a thick layer of black powder forming on the floor where the black sparks hit their target and splintered into thousands of tiny pieces of dust.

Sammy risked looking up at the ceiling and pointed his staff at the centre of the black sparks. He flinched again as the charred remains of the falling sparks tore into his clothes, stinging his skin.

'Try harder!' shouted Commander Altair. 'You need to work together!'

'Will these black sparks come up in our end of year exams?' asked Simon Sanchez.

Sammy looked over at Simon and was impressed to see his classmate was blocking several black sparks with an umbrella he had created out of red mist.

'It will come up in your exams,' said Commander Altair, nodding and sending another volley of black sparks up towards the ceiling. 'Don't forget some of you still have last year's exams to take. Some of you might get put down a year!'

'I'm not staying down a year,' muttered Sammy to himself. He wished he knew how to create the sapphire shield of protection, feeling sure this would help protect himself against the raining black sparks that hurt every inch of skin they landed on.

Commander Altair waved his staff again and the room turned black overhead. Sparks rained down like burning coal.

'Good!' shouted Commander Altair. 'Work together and you will be able to control this attack.'

'Good?' puffed Sammy, as he shielded Milly from a large lump of the black material. 'This can't be fair. We're getting more black sparks this end.'

As yet another wave of the vicious black powder sparks descended, Commander Altair clapped his hands and the black sparks evaporated into a fine mist that dissolved almost instantly.

'That will do for today,' said Commander Altair. 'Let's sit down and discuss this. I want all of you to think hard about the benefits of this type of weapon...yes Simon?'

'The black sparks and the black powder will help us fight the Shape, yes?' asked Simon, picking up one of the broken legs of his chair.

'How will it help?' challenged Commander Altair. 'Tell me how it will help us fight the Shape?'

Sammy finished pulling the last desk and the remains of the chairs back into their usual places and raised his hand, remembering something from the past.

'Does it help us track the Shape when they teleport?' asked Sammy.

'Bingo! But more than that, it prevents someone from teleporting again for roughly an hour,' said Commander Altair. 'It is called Zyon powder and Sir Ragnarok is planning to dust everyone who comes through the Dragamas gates as a precaution...yes Simon?'

'Will you show us how to make the black sparks and the black Zyon powder?' asked Simon Sanchez, his black eyes sparkling.

Commander Altair shook his head. 'No, but I will teach you everything you'll ever need to defend yourselves. This year we will cover advanced outdoor skills including target practice, and I want to see you all create the perfect fire, with and without your staffs.'

'With and without our staffs,' muttered Darius. 'That'll be the day!'

'You all know me by now,' said Commander Altair, smiling at the class of attentive students. 'I'm not a great believer in teaching unless you are really interested in learning, so I won't ask you to write pages and pages about this exercise.'

Sammy looked up at the Armoury teacher. It was very unusual not to write up something as interesting as black sparks falling from the ceiling and dissolving into a black powder that would prevent anyone from teleporting.

'I would prefer,' Commander Altair continued, 'you to write two or three lines about your reactions to the black Zyon powder. Tell me what it feels like to be hit by the black dust, how it stings, how it hurts. Tell me how scared it made you feel. Tell me how you reacted to it so I would know what it felt like if I had ever been hit.'

'I bet he has been hit,' muttered Sammy, examining his torn white shirt, cut sleeves and bleeding forearms. He knew his mother would not be impressed that one of his new white shirts had been destroyed on his first day back at school.

'I have been hit with the black dust many times,' said Commander Altair. 'In the Snorgcadell, it is a weapon favoured by my father, General Aldebaran Altair, it is simple, painful, and in the right quantities, human flesh will melt before your very eyes.'

Commander Altair opened the cardboard box on his desk and took out three small brown bottles and slices of turnip that Sammy recognised instantly.

'When she heard what I had planned for this lesson, Mrs Grock made me bring these for you,' Commander Altair held up one of the brown bottles. 'She says it will cure anything and everything.'

Sammy wrinkled up his nose as he accepted the slice of turnip. He poured drops of the gloopy brown gravy-like liquid out of the bottle and smeared it over his skin.

In seconds, the cuts and bruises vanished and Sammy found his skin was healed and as good as new. The potion didn't fix damaged clothes so his shirt was still ruined.

Darius had been hit the worst out of everyone and he and Naomi giggled as they found each other's wounds and stroked the turnip over the scratches to heal them.

'You need Dwarf skin,' grinned Jock. 'It's as tough as old boots, tougher than Troll skin any day.'

'There isn't much of you to hit,' snapped Sammy, unnerved as he heard the word "Troll" which made him think of Dixie again. 'You haven't grown since I first knew you!'

'I probably won't grow any taller. My parents aren't very tall,' said Jock amiably.

'Shortness has its virtues,' said Commander Altair. 'I won't tolerate any bullying because someone is the wrong shape, size or colour,' he added, separating Darius and Naomi who were about to practice another kiss.

Above the door, the end-of-lesson bell chimed loudly and Commander Altair flung a green spark at it angrily.

'There is so much you need to know!' he exploded. 'How am I supposed to train you all in so little time?'

Sammy compressed his staff into three folded pieces and packed his pencils and paper away. He tucked his chair under the desk and headed out of the classroom.

As Sammy walked past the teacher's desk, Commander Altair called him back.

'Sammy, would you and Darius wait a moment please,' said Commander Altair quietly.

Naomi frowned and folded her arms. 'Don't keep him long,' she grumbled. 'I'll save you a seat in Alchemistry.' She blew Darius two kisses and Darius blushed.

Commander Altair raised his eyebrows. 'You students start younger every year,' he shook his head. 'Anyway, I wanted to talk to you both about Dixie.'

Sammy jumped. 'Have you found her?' he asked anxiously, holding his breath, hoping for some good news.

'No, but there is something I would like to ask you to do,' said Commander Altair.

'What?' asked Darius, staring absent mindedly down the corridor watching Naomi walking to the next lesson.

Commander Altair clenched his fists. 'This is really difficult, Sylvia Deane, Dixie's mother, she wanted me to ask you, since Dixie can't be there herself, and as her best friends, she'll understand if you'd prefer not to, I don't really want to go.'

'Where?' demanded Darius. 'How can we decide if you don't tell us?'

Commander Altair nodded and sighed. 'Sylvia Deane has asked whether you will go to Jacob's funeral? Will you go to Dixie's father's funeral?'

Darius gulped. 'You're joking?'

'No, I don't joke Darius. I've never been more serious. I can assure you, this is no joke,' said Commander Altair.

Sammy nudged Darius's elbow. 'We'll go, we have to, for Dixie. When is it?'

'It's this Saturday,' said Commander Altair, his voice hollow and strained. 'From what Alfie Agrock told you Sammy, we pieced together their last assignment.'

Sammy nodded. He remembered Alfie Agrock boasting in the clearing. It was the moment before Sammy handed over the Angel of 'El Horidore, believing he was saving Dixie from being kidnapped.

'Jacob's body was found by the side of the road. From the injuries, we think his dragon was trying to protect him from Alfie,' said Commander Altair. 'When the Angel of 'El Horidore was blown, Jacob's dragon's body arrived here and we had some more clues.'

Sammy gasped. 'Dixie's Dad's dragon was protecting him.' He felt a lump in his throat. Maybe one day Kyrillan would do the same for him.

'I found Jacob myself, completely by chance. I was flying overhead with my father. We were looking for places Jacob might be based on the co-ordinates of their last mission. We found him and brought his body home last week.'

'Was his dragon's draconite gone?' whispered Sammy.

'Nearly all the draconite in the world is gone Sammy. Piecing things together, it looks like there was no struggle. Jacob trusted Alfie. There were several deep cuts, here,' Commander Altair pointed to his throat. 'The coward got him from behind, probably when Jacob was asleep.'

'That's terrible,' muttered Darius, his voice choking.

Sammy found tears were prickling behind his eyes. 'We'll come to the funeral,' he whispered.

Commander Altair nodded. 'Thank you. It will mean a lot to Sylvia and to Serberon, Mikhael and Jason. Like I said, it's going to be held this Saturday morning. We'll fly at six am. Meet me at the school gates.'

Commander Altair teleported out of the classroom leaving a shining silver mist in his wake.

'Maybe Dixie will be back and we won't have to go,' suggested Sammy, when he was sure Commander Altair had gone.

'I've been to three funerals,' said Darius, 'and they're not so bad. At my Grandparents funeral, there was this massive party they'd put on afterwards with free beer in the local pub.'

Sammy looked at Darius, who cracked in front of him, his eyes streaming.

'I'm not crying,' snapped Darius. 'It's just some hayfever or something.'

'We don't have to go,' started Sammy.

'We do have to go,' interrupted Darius. 'You said we'd go and we're going to go.'

'Come on,' Sammy pulled Darius's arm away from his puffed eyes. 'Professor Sanchez doesn't like it if we're late.'

Darius gave a wry smile and wiped his eyes. 'I don't expect she'd take any stars off you,' he grinned.

# CHAPTER 8

# EXAMS

Sammy settled back into Dragamas life really easily and the rest of the week passed in a blur of activity. The highlight was when Mrs Hubar handed out shining blue sapphires to the fourth years in a Gemology lesson.

By now, Sammy had no trouble at all attaching and detaching the coloured gemstones on his staff. He clicked his piece of sapphire into place next to the onyx, ruby and amber gemstones.

Sammy knew the sapphire would give him the power to generate the layer of protection around a person or an object. The protective layer was like an oilslick. Nothing could penetrate in or out, unless the person who cast the protection allowed it, or, as they had found out to their cost, unless the magic faded over time.

Sammy remembered how the protection around the den, created by Dixie's brother Serberon, had faded over the course of the year. When it had gone completely, Alfie Agrock had been able to enter their den, seize the Angel of

'El Horidore and cause all this untold devastation in the Dragon World.

At the end of the lesson, Mrs Hubar took all of the sapphires away from the fourth years, promising them they could have them soon, when she thought they were ready for them.

Everyone grumbled, but handed back their blue stones. Sammy was desperate to know when she would give them out permanently but Mrs Hubar gave no clues.

In Astronomics, Professor Burlay had taught the fourth years the names of many new star constellations and refreshed their memories of the significance of the Dragamas Constellation.

Professor Burlay advised the fourth years to study the new constellations in great detail. He insisted this would be useful should they need to navigate at sea. Sammy didn't think this was very likely, but refrained from saying this to Professor Burlay as he didn't want to lose any more stars.

One evening just before bedtime, the fourth year North Housemaster, Dr Shivers, visited the North common room and handed out the list of exams they would need to take to guarantee they could stay in the fourth year and not go back to re-take the whole of the third year studies.

When Sammy had seen the list, he had groaned loudly. The list of exams included Dragon Studies, Astronomics, Alchemistry and, his least favourite subject, Ancient and Modern Languages.

Dr Shivers wasted no time explaining that there were several spaces in the third year should anyone need to repeat the year.

The following day, Sammy was in the fourth year bathroom, getting ready with his housemates.

'At least we had time for extra revision,' said Jock, grinning at himself in a mirror. 'I think I know everything we need to know for the exams inside out and back to front.'

Gavin peered around one of the shower curtains. 'Who cares what you know, Dwarf-breath,' he said, reaching for his emerald green towel and emerging from the shower a moment later with it wrapped around his waist. He stepped over to the wooden benches to change into his uniform.

'Shut it Gavin,' snapped Sammy. He was already nervous about the exams and didn't need the extra pressure. 'Was Professor Burlay being serious when he said we have to plot three navigation courses?'

'I could do it blindfolded,' boasted Jock. 'I plot star charts in my sleep! I can...'

'Yeah right!' interrupted Sammy. 'Like anyone could do that!'

Gavin laughed. 'Guess what! Mum's given me and Toby notes to get us out of doing the exams. She says we're traumatised by, um,' Gavin rustled a piece of paper out of his trouser pocket, 'traumatised by the unforeseen events caused by one of the troublesome students. My absolute recommendation is that my sons have excelled in all of their subjects, blah, blah, blah, and should not need to take their exams.'

'And they fell for it? You don't have to take the exams?' asked Sammy, flabbergasted.

'Hook, line and sinker,' said Gavin, grinning widely. 'Me and Toby don't have to take a single exam. We are staying in the fourth year and don't have to do any stupid exams to stay here.'

'That's not fair!' stormed Jock. 'I'll get my Mum to let me off the exams too. Darius isn't doing them because he's a Dragon Minder.'

'Hey Sammy, that means it's just you and Milly taking them,' cackled Gavin. 'Hope she stays down, useless horse!'

'Just coz she said you couldn't kiss!' grinned Jock.

Gavin stood up, his hands on his hips. 'Like you can?'

Jock laughed. 'Everyone knows a kiss from a Dwarf is as precious as the gemstones we mine.'

Gavin snorted, throwing his towel over his shoulders like a Roman Emperor. 'You talk so much junk!'

'Are we supposed to, y'know,' asked Sammy, not daring to say the word "kiss" as it was all so strange.

'It's up to you,' grinned Jock. 'You don't have to, but, well, you'll look a bit odd if you don't. Have you?'

'No,' Sammy shook his head.

'Not even with Dixie?' asked Jock.

'No,' said Sammy, a picture of green haired Dixie Deane forming in his head.

'Thought about it?' asked Jock.

'No,' said Sammy, not quite truthfully. He had been secretly reading the odd copy of SuperWoman that was occasionally left in the North common room and his ideas about girls were changing.

'Liar!' shouted Jock. 'I have. If she comes back, I'm gonna ask her to come with me to the next Nitromen game. We're gonna throw popcorn over Nitron Dark as he comes out of the tunnel!'

'If she comes back,' reminded Sammy.

'She will, um, I mean, probably she will.' Jock had a decidedly distant look and wouldn't meet Sammy's eyes.

Sammy finished brushing his teeth, trying to memorise the constellations he had sellotaped to the mirror, hoping it would help him get ready for the exam.

From what Gavin had said about he and Toby skipping the exams and Jock going to chat with Mrs Hubar, it sounded as though it would just be himself and Milly going to Professor Burlay's small office under the Astronomics balcony to sit the hour and a half test.

Sammy tore his notes down from the mirror, took a deep breath and marched off towards the Astronomics classroom. He met Milly in the corridor and they walked the rest of the way in nervous silence.

In the Astronomics classroom, the small square door by the blackboard was already open.

'Come on through,' called Professor Burlay. 'I've got the exam papers ready for you.'

Sammy crouched by the knee high door and crawled into the low passage that led from the classroom to the hidden room where Professor Burlay had his study underneath the Astronomics stargazing balcony.

Milly followed Sammy into the passage, around the corner and then scrambled to her feet as the passage ended and opened into the small rectangular room.

Professor Burlay was sitting in one of his high-backed emerald green office chairs hunched over exercise books scattered across one of his overcrowded mahogany desks.

Although the room had four diamond shaped lattice windows, which let in plenty of light, Professor Burlay was marking answers in the exercise books by candlelight and he looked up as Sammy and Milly walked in.

'Sit down please,' said Professor Burlay, smiling and pointing to the empty chairs by the second mahogany desk on the other side of the room. 'You'll find your exam papers are on my other desk. Sit on opposite sides and no conferring.'

Sammy pulled out one of the chairs and a dozen rolled up star charts fell off. He picked them up and stacked them next to a precariously leaning tower of old exam papers.

He sat down and looked at the two sheets of crisp white paper on the desk. One said "Samuel Rambles - 3rd Year Astronomics Exam" and the other said "Melissa Brooks -

3rd Year Astronomics Exam". Next to the paper were two green pens and two green rulers.

Milly sat in the chair opposite him and together they turned over their Astronomics exam paper in perfect synchronisation.

Sammy read through the questions as thoroughly as he could, then picked up one of the pens and a ruler. He chewed the end of the ruler for a couple of minutes, then lay it on the paper and began to draw some stars.

Despite Professor Burlay tutting from time to time as he marked students' work and Milly's groans as she tackled a hard question, the exam went fairly well in Sammy's opinion.

Sammy spent most of the exam time plotting a course from Dragamas to Dixie's house in the nearby village and back again using the stars as his guide. As he added the last star constellation to his map, Professor Burlay coughed loudly.

'Time's up,' said Professor Burlay from his desk. 'What do you think Sammy, the blue tie or the green tie?'

Frowning, Sammy stood up to find out what on earth Professor Burlay was talking about.

When he got to his Astronomics teacher's desk, he could see Professor Burlay had laid out a mens clothing catalogue over the exercise books he was marking. There were some fairly expensive suits made by designer labels he didn't recognise.

'The green tie,' said Milly, appearing suddenly at Sammy's shoulder. 'It will go best with your eyes.'

'And you're North,' added Sammy, feeling he had to say something.

'Green it is,' said Professor Burlay beaming at them. 'Emerald green will be perfect. Now, what do you think about these shoes?'

Sammy squirmed. 'I promised I'd meet Darius after the exam.'

Professor Burlay coughed nervously and accepted their exam papers, putting them to one side while he leafed through the catalogue. 'Yes, well, perhaps I shouldn't be discussing this with you. Best of luck with your other exams.'

Sammy crouched to leave Professor Burlay's study and made his way back down the L shaped passage and out into the Astronomics classroom.

Once they were walking down the corridor, Milly broke into a huge grin splitting across her glitter dusted cheeks.

'This is so exciting!' said Milly, grabbing Sammy's arm.

'What? Professor Burlay is getting a new tie and new shoes?' asked Sammy.

'The wedding!' giggled Milly. 'Professor Burlay's getting married! Those were wedding clothes magazines he was looking at!'

Sammy shrugged. 'Who's he marrying?'

Milly looked at him with one of Dixie's "don't you know anything" looks. 'I expect he's marrying that Mrs Grock,' she said, exceptionally snootily.

'Oh,' said Sammy, feeling stupid. 'That makes sense.'

'Not really,' whispered Milly. 'She can't get married twice.'

'Ancient and Modern Languages is next,' said Sammy, choosing to ignore Milly's bizarre comment and kicking a crumpled piece of paper halfway down the corridor. 'Then Alchemistry.'

'Then Dragon Studies,' said Milly, letting go of Sammy's arm. 'Do you like Dr Shivers?'

'He's alright, just a bit...' started Sammy.

'Shivery!' finished Milly, erupting into a fit of the giggles.

CHAPTER 9

# THE DRAGON STUDIES EXAM

Miss Amoratti scowled as Sammy and Milly arrived in the Ancient and Modern Languages classroom.

'You're late,' accused Miss Amoratti. 'Sit down at the front please and make sure you're on time for your next lesson. In my experience it is usually Trolls who are late so neither of you have any excuse for tardiness.'

Sammy slumped into one of the wooden chairs in the front row. Miss Amoratti hadn't changed over the holiday and seemed, if possible, worse now that Dixie wasn't in her classes.

The Ancient and Modern Languages teacher was tall, thin and scorpion-like with ice white skin, scraped back, jet black hair with electric blue streaks. She had coal black, birdlike, piercing eyes and a vicious tongue that she exercised in the softest tones.

'Tell me children,' she began sugar sweetly, tapping her large wooden ruler on her desk next to a large pile of fourth year textbooks, 'how do we say "Good Morning" in Troll?'

Jock put his hand straight in the air and Miss Amoratti pointed her ruler in his direction.

'Arug shura,' said Jock, without any hesitation at all. He seemed to have taken up learning Troll as a new hobby.

Miss Amoratti smiled and nodded. 'Very good Mr Hubar, but I would have picked you to have answered a Dwarf related question. You might not be so confident answering a tricky question in your own language compared with answering an easy question in an unfamiliar language.'

Sammy rolled his eyes. Miss Amoratti was so unfair.

'Pair up please,' said Miss Amoratti, waving her ruler. 'It is a pity Miss Deane isn't here after all. Perhaps she would have been able to pronounce things properly. Arug shura, good morning, repeat after me...arug shura, good morning, arug shura, good morning, arug...oooh.'

Sammy looked up. Dr Shivers was at the door. He pointed a long grey finger at Sammy and Milly.

'I need these two students,' said Dr Shivers. 'If they don't pass their exams they won't be coming back to your class Angela.'

Miss Amoratti laughed. 'That would be a pity. Pick up your books please Mr Rambles and Miss Brooks. Your evening studies will be answering the questions from two to twenty-four and eighty-one to one hundred and three from this year's textbook. Please hand your answers to me personally at the start of tomorrow's lesson.'

'Yes Miss Amoratti,' chorused Sammy and Milly, each taking a copy of the new textbook from the pile of books on Miss Amoratti's desk.

'You'll also need to revise chapters eight, nine and ten from last year's textbook for the third year oral exam that you missed. Please be ready for me this evening and you will be able to take the exam tonight.'

'As well as the other work you've set?' exclaimed Milly looking horrified.

Miss Amoratti nodded enthusiastically. 'You'll thank me for this in years to come.'

Dr Shivers tapped his watch with a long grey finger. 'Are you quite finished?'

Sammy loaded the new Ancient and Modern Languages textbook into his rucksack. It was a heavy leather-bound book with the words "Volume IV" written on the spine. He followed Milly and Dr Shivers at a brisk pace, hearing a few students sniggering about him having to take the exam as they left.

'You'll need your dragons,' barked Dr Shivers. 'Shall we teleport?'

'I don't know how to teleport,' said Milly.

'Sammy, hold Milly's hand and repeat after me, "castle courtyard outside the North Tower" and that should work,' said Dr Shivers.

Sammy gripped Milly's left hand, finding it warm and fleshy. A strange ripple of air fluttered in his stomach.

'Castle courtyard, outside the North Tower,' shouted Sammy, clutching Milly's hand as tightly as he could.

Wind blew in Sammy's ears as the corridor faded. He had kept his eyes firmly open and he was amazed that he could see the gold dust particles surrounding him and Milly in a private cocoon. Milly's mouth was wide open and there was a look of fear in her bloodshot eyes.

Unconsciously Sammy squeezed her hand a little tighter. Then the courtyard appeared and the gold dust faded away.

'You can let her hand go now Sammy,' said Dr Shivers. He turned to knock on the Dragon Chambers entrance with his staff. 'If you hadn't made a fool of yourself earlier this week, you could have been a Dragon Minder and let us in.'

'There aren't many dragons left to mind,' said Sammy, scowling at Dr Shivers. He got even more annoyed when Milly giggled at him. She was sniffing the hand he had held during their teleport. Sammy rolled his eyes.

The Dragon Chambers door opened and Captain Duke Stronghammer stood in the entrance with both hands on his hips.

'You'm supposed to be bin an' gone by now. Makin' 'em restless you are. They're not sure if 'ems comin' or goin' nowadays,' growled the Dwarf.

'Two dragons going please Captain Stronghammer. I just need Kyrillan and Bubbles so that Sammy and Milly can complete their exam from last year,' said Dr Shivers.

Captain Stronghammer laughed. 'An there's me thinkin' the green hair's returned. If I haven't only gone and got the only two blue-green dragons we've got left ready for yer. Will they do?'

'No,' snapped Dr Shivers icily. 'Melissa has enough trouble with her own dragon. I dread to think what she'd be like with someone else's dragon.'

'She's not a natural with dragons like my son, eh?' cackled Captain Stronghammer. 'I'll be back in a minute.'

Dr Shivers tapped his foot impatiently while Captain Stronghammer dragged the two reluctant dragons out of the Dragon Chambers.

Kyrillan broke away as soon as he saw Sammy. The large blue-green dragon nearly trampled over Dr Shivers, who jumped out of the way just in time.

'Are you in control of your dragon Sammy? Or do you need some of these?' said Dr Shivers, holding out his hand with two green pellets.

'I'm fine,' said Sammy. He was annoyed that Milly was giggling at him. He doubted if she would have any more control of Bubbles if she lived to be a hundred.

'Of course you are,' said Dr Shivers. He tossed the green pellets towards Kyrillan, who whipped his tail around to slap the pellets at the stone castle wall, where they disintegrated into thousands of pieces.

'That's not a very good start to the exam Sammy,' said Dr Shivers. 'Not having your dragon with you over the summer holiday seems to have made you rusty.'

'I'm not...' started Sammy.

Dr Shivers put a long grey finger on his grey lips. 'Prove it,' he whispered. I want you to show me, without touching, exactly where you would press to start the descaling process. I will give you a bonus point if you can tell me what the technique is called.'

Sammy pointed at Kyrillan's neck, just below his pointed ears. 'It's called the Domino Effect.'

Milly rested her hand on the same spot on Bubbles. A few scales dropped to the floor and Dr Shivers tutted.

'Tell me how you know your dragon is in good health. I will give you one point for every answer,' said Dr Shivers.

'By checking their teeth,' said Sammy. 'You check their scales for cracks, check for sores, check behind their ears and all the way down to their tail, avoiding the spikes. You check their toenails for breakages and also look at their eyes for any spots or redness.'

'Good,' said Dr Shivers. 'Very good indeed. Now, mount your dragons and demonstrate a controlled walk up to those trees, then fly back, landing smoothly. Sammy, you go first.'

Sammy rolled his eyes. This was so easy. He swung his leg across Kyrillan's back and sat on top of his dragon.

Kyrillan seemed determined to get away from Dr Shivers and set off at a quick trot.

'Slower Sammy,' called Dr Shivers.

Sammy dug his thighs into Kyrillan's scaly flank. He focussed his entire mind, visualising his dragon moving at a slower pace.

Kyrillan puffed a wisp of smoke in agreement and, to Sammy's relief, he slowed down as they approached the trees.

'Come on Kyrillan,' said Sammy.

Sammy squeezed his thighs again and kicked off. He gently pulled Kyrillan's neck skyward, feeling the rush of wind in his ears as his dragon's wings extended and a smile break across his face. Kyrillan's paws left the ground and with a swish of shimmering blue-green wings they were flying.

'Come on!' shouted Sammy. 'Let's go!'

But Kyrillan didn't seem to have any intention of going anywhere near Dr Shivers. He slowed down completely as he approached the castle courtyard and hovered, his thick wings beating cold air down onto Milly and the Dragon Studies teacher.

'Come down please Sammy,' said Dr Shivers, shielding his face from the dust Kyrillan was generating.

'I can't!' shouted Sammy, digging his heels into Kyrillan and focussing on bringing his dragon back down to the ground.

Kyrillan gave a loud "hurrumph" and puffed thick grey smoke downwards.

'Go on Milly,' said Dr Shivers. 'Take your turn trotting to the trees and flying back. Let's see if you can do it any better than Sammy.'

Dr Shivers stepped away from the smoke and into the entrance of the Dragon Chambers. As soon as Dr Shivers was out of sight, Kyrillan landed gracefully, folding his wings into his side.

Sammy leaned forward. 'Don't you like Dr Shivers?' he asked, whispering into Kyrillan's ear, annoyed his dragon's smoke breathing finale would cost him marks.

'You'll need more practice if you want to be one of those Dragon Knights,' said Dr Shivers, his voice echoing from the Dragon Chambers.

Sammy kept quiet. He didn't trust himself to speak. Dr Shivers returned to the courtyard, keeping a safe distance from Kyrillan.

'When General Aldebaran Altair comes to select the next Dragon Knights from the Dragamas students he won't look twice at you Sammy Rambles. That awful performance was absolutely dreadful. Terrible. I've never seen anything like it.'

Sammy kicked the cobbled courtyard floor. 'I haven't seen my dragons since the summer.'

'Dragons is it?' sneered Dr Shivers, over-pronouncing the "s" sarcastically. 'Well, I hope you treat them better than you treat Kyrillan. The Shape won't need to kill dragons, you'll do it for…woah!'

Dr Shivers ducked as Milly came flying past them at a rate of knots. Her dragon hit the castle wall nose first and catapulted Milly head over heels into the Rhododendron bushes that grew outside the entrance to the Dragon Chambers. Milly screamed and Sammy rushed forward to help her.

'Never laugh at the misfortunes of others Sammy. It could just as easily have been you,' said Dr Shivers.

'I wasn't laughing,' protested Sammy. 'Are you ok Milly?'

'I'm fine,' giggled Milly, emerging bedraggled from the large Rhododendron bushes, pink flowers falling from her ruffled hair. 'That was amazing!'

Sammy raised his eyebrows. 'Did you hit your head?'

'She seems to have finally come to her senses,' said Dr Shivers. 'Perhaps next year we'll see her without those ridiculous high heeled boots and a with a little less glitter.'

'Glitter is for babies,' said Milly, brushing her cheeks.

'So is crying,' said Dr Shivers unsympathetically. 'Wear the glitter if you like but just not in my classes and get yourself to Mrs Grock's. You're in a right state.'

Milly pouted and shook her head. 'I really don't need to see Mrs Grock,' she protested.

'You're going whether you think you should or not,' said Dr Shivers firmly. 'Take these exam question papers and complete them there. Yes, you too Sammy. I've had enough of the pair of you. You're both useless. We'll see if Mrs Grock still thinks you can be Dragon Knights after this! Ha!'

Sammy stood up straight and looked Dr Shivers right in the eye. 'I will be a Dragon Knight one day.'

Dr Shivers laughed. 'Maybe you will. Maybe you won't. Go to Mrs Grock's house and leave both of your dragons here please.'

# CHAPTER 10

# SAMMY'S DRAGONS

Sammy pushed past Milly, thrusting his hands deep into his trouser pockets. It wasn't fair. Dr Shivers knew he hadn't been able to visit his parents' dragons over the summer while he had been in Switzerland. If only his parents could see dragons, he wouldn't have any of these problems.

Kyrillan blew grey smoke rings affectionately in his direction as Sammy stomped off. Dr Shivers swung a rope around Kyrillan's neck and then a second rope around Bubbles's neck and he led the two dragons down into the Dragon Chambers.

Sammy slowed down as it started to drizzle with rain and Milly caught up with him.

'You might have waited,' said Milly, holding her hand over her head to stop the rain dripping on her hair.

'Whatever,' said Sammy, still annoyed at Dr Shivers for telling him he couldn't be a Dragon Knight.

'Kyrillan really likes you,' said Milly. 'He's just not good around Dr Shivers for some reason. Hey, wait for me!'

Sammy stopped outside Mrs Grock's gate. 'What?'

'It's raining,' said Milly.

'So?' asked Sammy, wondering if Milly had gone mad.

'So, you should let ladies go first. That's what gentlemen do. My Daddy is a gentleman. He thinks I'm a princess.'

Sammy snorted and pushed Milly forward. 'Mrs Grock had better be in.'

'Well she can't cure grouchiness,' snapped Milly. 'You're just like the rest of the boys. I can't see why Dixie liked you at all!'

Sammy jerked to a stop at the front door. He felt his cheeks suddenly going hot and pink. 'Dixie isn't here anymore,' he whispered.

'She'll be back,' said Milly. 'It'll take more than that smelly Dwarf man to...'

'What?' demanded Sammy.

'Nothing. It's just something Jock said to me. He liked Dixie as well and he's a Dwarf.'

'Well don't tell me then,' snapped Sammy. He rapped twice with his fist on the green front door and poked a sticking-out newspaper through the letterbox while they waited.

After a few minutes, Sammy knocked on the door again. He leaned close to the door to see if he could hear anything.

'It doesn't look like she's in,' said Sammy.

'Let's make a wish,' said Milly, pointing to the stone well in the corner of the cottage garden.

'I didn't think you believed in making wishes,' said Sammy.

'Um...well, I don't really believe in making wishes.' Milly looked embarrassed. 'It's just, well, making that wish worked for you didn't it. You put wrongs to rights.'

Sammy snorted loudly. 'Hah! That's why so many dragons are dead. That's why Alfie Agrock got the Angel of 'El Horidore. That's why Dixie is missing! Some good my wish did!'

Milly put her hands on her hips and stared at Sammy obstinately. 'Well, I'm going to make a wish,' she said in a firm voice. 'I wish you'd be happy and I wish Dixie would come back and I wish Daddy would buy me a pony and a car when I'm older and…'

'Shut up!' snapped Sammy, hammering on the door. 'If you're not going to let us come in just say so!'

He kicked the door hard with his right foot and it sprung open straight away.

'Ugh,' groaned Sammy, rubbing his toes.

'It was open all along!' Milly giggled and adjusted her pink hair slides. 'That's really funny!'

Sammy stepped into Mrs Grock's front room. It looked the same as it had when he had last been inside her house. The large rectangular lounge was dimly lit by a handful of green candles in silver holsters attached to the wall.

He could see the large bookshelves laden with ancient books containing recipes for herbal remedies and medical advice. He saw the well-read copy of "Cuts, Bruises and Broken Bones" and remembered the first time he had used the healing remedy to help Serberon.

There was a small gap on one of the other shelves which Sammy remembered was where Mrs Grock had found and lent him a copy of Helana Horidore's book called "The Angel". Sammy remembered the fate of the book which had disintegrated during the confrontation with his uncle two years ago.

On his right was the large purple three-seat settee facing the alcove with the stone fireplace and a fire roaring in the grate. A large copper pan was suspended above the fire, hanging by its looped copper handles.

For a moment Sammy was mesmerised by the flames and the occasional spark that flew onto the stone hearth. Then he remembered why he and Milly had been sent to Mrs Grock's house and the exam papers they still had to complete.

'Hello?' called Sammy, stepping further into Mrs Grock's lounge to see if anyone was home.

'Let's just sit and wait,' said Milly and she headed for the sofa nearest to the fire. 'Look, she's in the middle of making a potion.'

'Leave it alone, Mrs Grock will be back soon,' snapped Sammy, annoyed with himself for still being angry. 'I'm going to check on my parents' dragons.'

'Oooh,' said Milly, her eyes large. 'Are they here? Can I see them?'

'If you want,' said Sammy. 'They're really big. They've got big teeth.'

Milly flopped onto the sofa with a worried look on her face. 'Maybe you'd better see them by yourself after all.'

Sammy shrugged and made his way to the storeroom. To his surprise, both the storeroom door and the trapdoor leading to the steps into the underground chamber were wide open. He created a small fire to guide the way and started making his way down the stone steps. After only two steps, the fire went out.

'Who's there?' asked a suspicious voice.

Sammy peered into the darkness and saw that the voice belonged to Professor Burlay. Not only that, but Professor Burlay was holding Mrs Grock in a passionate embrace.

'You shouldn't be spying on us,' said Professor Burlay, looking rather embarrassed.

'Ooch John, he's probably just come to see these,' Mrs Grock pointed to the sleeping dragons. 'I was just checking on them myself when John turned up.'

'You can see for yourself Sammy, they're all fine, we've just been, um,' Professor Burlay looked at Mrs Grock and burst into an infectious laugh.

'We'd best get back upstairs,' said Mrs Grock, touching Professor Burlay's arm. 'Are you alone Sammy? Dixie isn't with you, is she?'

'She hasn't come back to Dragamas,' said Sammy, his voice cracking. 'She's still missing.'

'Milly is here though,' said Professor Burlay. 'I have seen it in the stars. There was an accident in Dr Shiver's Dragon Studies exam. He's making her try too hard.'

'She crashed her dragon,' said Sammy.

'Then she'll need some of this,' said Mrs Grock, pulling a bottle out of her apron pouch. 'I'll go and give this to her and you take as long as you need to check your parents' dragons Sammy, but I assure you, they are being well looked after.'

'Thanks,' said Sammy. He created a new fire and climbed down the remaining stone steps, his footsteps echoing in the chamber.

Professor Burlay slapped Sammy on the shoulder. 'Don't worry, your dragons are all being very well looked after here.'

For his own peace of mind, Sammy checked each of his three dragons thoroughly and methodically. He was aware of Professor Burlay watching him as he touched each dragon's eyelids to check for lack of sleep.

Sammy examined the colour and shape of their scales and gently lifted each talloned foot to check for any splinters or cuts. He checked the dragons' nails were strong and yellow-white and not loose or chipped.

'You'll make a good Dragon Knight soon Sammy,' said Professor Burlay approvingly. 'You've got a good way with dragons. They trust you.'

'Thanks,' said Sammy, stroking Paprika's orange nose. 'I just wish my parents could see them.'

Professor Burlay nodded. 'Are you done? Mrs Grock should be finished looking after Milly by now.'

Although he would have liked longer with Cyngard, Jovah and Paprika, Sammy nodded and put out his fire.

'Commander Altair tells me you're doing very well in his Armoury lessons,' said Professor Burlay. 'You'll definitely have a good chance of being chosen to work for the Snorgcadell next year. If that's what you want?'

'Yeah.' Sammy unravelled himself from Cyngard's tail and followed Professor Burlay up the steps into the storeroom.

'You're as good as new,' he heard Mrs Grock telling Milly. 'Use this whenever you need to be near your dragon and it will calm you down.'

'We don't want any more accidents,' agreed Professor Burlay. 'I'll escort you both back to the castle. I don't want any more mischief finding you.'

They left Mrs Grock tending to her potion by the fire and walked back through the grounds to the castle.

'Right,' said Professor Burlay as they reached the courtyard. 'I'll leave you here. You've got your Ancient and Modern Languages exam next, haven't you?'

'And Alchemistry and these Dragon Studies exam papers,' said Sammy. 'Dr Shivers told us we have to answer all the questions if we don't want to be put down a year.'

Professor Burlay smiled. 'Best of luck,' he said, tapping under his chin. 'I'm sure you'll both do well.'

'I'm not,' grumbled Milly when Professor Burlay was out of earshot. 'You'll help me with these questions, won't you Sammy? I don't want to stay down a year. Daddy thinks it would be such a disgrace.'

'Where do we need to go for Ancient and Modern Languages?' asked Sammy, losing patience.

# CHAPTER 11

# MORE EXAMS

There was a loud sizzle behind them and Miss Amoratti appeared. She was dressed in a smart two-piece grey striped pinafore jacket and matching skirt, with a crisp white shirt underneath and a large, knee length, grey overcoat over the top. The overcoat had an electric blue coloured rose in the top buttonhole that perfectly matched the electric blue streaks running through her jet black hair.

'Good evening,' said Miss Amoratti.

'Arug eventa,' beamed Milly.

'Indeed,' said Miss Amoratti, raising one of her sharp black eyebrows. 'Classroom four is free,' she said briskly. 'We will commence your examination in room four.'

However, after a brisk walk, room four, on the same level as the underground mines, turned out to be flooded.

'Drat!' exclaimed Miss Amoratti. 'We will try room fourteen instead. Do either of you know how to say fourteen in Elvish?'

'It's d'tor in Troll,' said Sammy helpfully.

'I didn't ask for it in Troll,' said Miss Amoratti. She swept the trail of her long skirt over her arm and hurried up the flight of stairs.

Room fourteen on the first floor was both dry and vacant. Rows of wooden desks with wooden chairs tucked neatly underneath faced a large teacher's desk with a plush looking executive leather chair that immediately caught Miss Amoratti's eye.

Directly in behind the teacher's desk was a large blackboard with a layer of chalk dust that hadn't quite been fully erased from the last lesson. The room had a faint musty smell, as though it wasn't used very often.

'This will do,' said Miss Amoratti, sitting herself down in the executive chair and spinning herself around and around.

When the chair stopped spinning, she took a small cassette player and bottle of electric blue nail polish out of her overcoat pocket and placed the items in the middle of the teacher's desk.

Miss Amoratti pointed to the front row of desks. 'Find yourselves a seat away from each other and then you will listen to the tape and write down the translation. Some phrases will be in Troll, some will be in Dwarven and some in the human tongue.'

'That won't need translating,' muttered Sammy.

Unfortunately, Miss Amoratti overheard him. 'Well Sammy, you had better get those questions all right then. I used this tape when I taught at DumCavaht, the only Dwarven school in the world,' Miss Amoratti added. 'At DumCavaht I was Pina-Cohoncha. In the human tongue, that means I was the Headmistress.'

'Is that one of the questions?' asked Sammy. He was bored already and had a suspicious feeling that the exam was going to be a sham.

'Of course not!' said Miss Amoratti looking shocked. She started the tape almost before Sammy and Milly had sat down and laid out their pens, pencils and paper.

'Welcome to Advanced Ancient and Modern Languages where we will be conducting a four-hour oral translation exam,' said a husky male voice interrupted every few seconds by a faint crunching as the cassette player churned the tape to play the next words.

Sammy leaned forward as the voice went on to explain the rules and regulations and then the exam started.

'Write down the human equivalent of the numbers twelve to fifty-four...write down the phrase "it's cold this morning" in Troll...write down how you would greet someone in Elvish...write down...write down...'

Three hours and fifty-nine minutes later, Sammy put down his pencil (his pen had run out of ink in the second hour and even the pencil had needed sharpening four times already). Milly had fallen asleep a long time ago, her pen twitching occasionally when the voice paused.

'Pens down,' said Miss Amoratti, putting her feet down off the teacher's desk and blowing on her freshly painted bright blue nails. 'I can't be bothered to check your papers. You will both pass with sixty-six per cent. Congratulations!'

'That's not fair!' exploded Sammy. 'I was trying really hard in that exam. If you're not even going to check our papers then why did we bother turning up?'

'Can you say that in Troll?' asked Miss Amoratti sugar sweetly. 'I have been watching you both and neither of you will excel in this subject. I consider sixty-six percent a very fair mark, especially considering your alternative is to repeat the third year at Dragamas.'

'I want you to mark our papers properly!' demanded Sammy.

'Very well,' Miss Amoratti smiled showing her perfectly white teeth. 'I will give you both seventy-five percent. Is that better?'

'Can't you give us eighty-five percent?' asked Milly hopefully. 'My Daddy said he'd buy me a pony if I do well in my exams.'

Miss Amoratti nodded. 'Very well, eighty-five percent, but make sure you both try harder in the summer. I won't be so generous next time. Now, please run along, I have a lesson plan to make up.'

'That shouldn't take long,' muttered Sammy as he followed Milly, who, despite her ridiculously high heeled shoes, was giggling and skipping out of the classroom.

'Eighty-five percent!' squealed Milly. 'Daddy will buy me a pony at Christmas!'

'You know it's not a real mark,' said Sammy, feeling extremely exasperated as she repeated it for the third time. 'I tried really hard in that exam and you just fell asleep! I might have got more than eighty-five percent for all she knows!'

Milly stopped skipping and looked earnestly at Sammy. 'You might have got less. Getting eighty-five percent in Ancient and Modern Languages is really good.'

'But it's not real!' exclaimed Sammy. 'Your Daddy won't be very pleased when he's bought you a pony and he finds out it's a fake mark, will he?'

Milly stopped in her tracks, her blue eyes painfully wide. 'You won't tell him Sammy, will you?'

Sammy shrugged. 'Whatever.'

'Promise me,' begged Milly, her blue eyes almost jumping out of their sockets. 'Promise me you'll never, ever tell him. Never, ever…'

'Fine,' said Sammy, glad they had reached the North Tower common room. He headed for the boys' staircase as the grandfather clock chimed the late hour. 'I'll see you tomorrow.'

Sammy looked back just before he turned the corner in the spiral staircase. Milly was using a small pocket mirror to apply some sort of makeup to her lips and cheeks. Sammy shook his head.

'Girls,' he muttered to himself and went up to bed.

The following morning Professor Sanchez's Alchemistry exam went rather well in Sammy's opinion. He successfully turned a large jam jar of pennies into a gold watch. Milly turned hers into a statue of a gold pony, which earned her a rare smile from Professor Sanchez.

'It looks like some of your glitter has rubbed off on your Alchemistry abilities Milly,' said Professor Sanchez.

Then with a tap of her staff on the desk, Professor Sanchez expertly dissolved both the pony and the watch into two puddles of gold and then back into the pennies which she conjured back into their jars.

'Congratulations, you have both passed your third year Alchemistry exam,' said Professor Sanchez. 'Milly, you have achieved seventy-seven percent and Sammy you have achieved seventy-one percent.'

'How much did Simon get?' asked Sammy.

Professor Sanchez blushed. 'Simon excels in my subject. He achieved ninety-eight percent in his exam.'

'That figures,' muttered Sammy.

'A word of advice Sammy, I'd watch who my friends were if I were you,' said Professor Sanchez cryptically as she ushered them out of the Alchemistry classroom and closed the door briskly behind them.

'I got more marks than you,' Milly grinned. 'I think Professor Sanchez likes me.'

'Whatever,' grumbled Sammy. 'I'm going to check on Kyrillan.'

'I'll come with you,' said Milly enthusiastically.

'No thanks.' Sammy stormed off, ashamed of himself, knowing he'd been mean to Milly because he wanted the better Alchemistry mark.

# CHAPTER 12

# JACOB'S FUNERAL

Saturday came almost too soon for Sammy's liking. At half past five in the morning, the alarm on his wristwatch beeped near his ear and woke him up.

He fixed his eyes on a patch of dirt on the tower room ceiling and wondered if it had come from a water bomb or a trick pellet and then he thought about the funeral he'd been asked to attend.

Darius rustled his curtain. 'Are you awake Sammy?'

'Just about,' said Sammy, sitting up in bed and rubbing the sleep out of his eyes.

'I can't sleep,' complained Darius, swinging back the curtain. 'How do I look? Do you think this will be alright?'

Sammy looked at his friend. Darius was fully dressed in shining black shoes, black trousers, crisp white shirt and he had turned his school tie inside out so that only the black silk lining was on show.

'Am I smart enough?' asked Darius, adjusting his tie and retying the knot several times.

'What are we supposed to wear?' asked Sammy. 'I've never been to a funeral before. Did Dr Shivers say what we're supposed to wear?'

Darius looked sheepish and held out his hand. 'Dr Shivers gave me this yesterday. I was supposed to give it to you but because you were re-taking the Alchemistry exam I couldn't give it to you. Then it got too late and I forgot.'

Sammy looked at the sapphire glowing in Darius's palm. 'Our fourth year gemstone,' whispered Sammy, taking the stone out of Darius's hand. It felt warm and powerful.

'Yeah, we just add it to the end of our staffs, the same as with the other gemstones. Oh and Dr Shivers said we should just wear our school uniform to Dixie's Dad's funeral. He reckons there won't be that many people there anyway.'

'Dixie should be there,' said Sammy, swapping his pyjama top for a plain t-shirt and long-sleeved white shirt over the top.

'I'm going to get Nelson from the Dragon Chambers. Do you want me to get Kyrillan for you?'

Sammy nodded, wrestling with his tie to pull it inside out so it was black instead of green.

Darius let out a giggle. 'Do you want any help with that?'

Sammy laughed. 'Yes! I can't get it the right way round.'

Darius took the tie and with a complicated twist of his fingers the green fabric disappeared and he gave Sammy back a black tie which Sammy quickly tied around his neck and they were both ready to go.

Downstairs in the Dragon Chambers, Kyrillan seemed to sense it was an important occasion and he trotted out on his own accord, his scales licked clean and sparkling in different tones of shimmering blues and greens in the pale half-light of the early morning.

'He's beautiful,' sighed Darius. 'Nelson's scales are just navy blue from head to tail.'

Sammy didn't disagree. He knew he had a special dragon, regardless of its shape or colour. Even his dragon's name, Kyrillan, meant strong and wise. He wondered for the first time whether it was in Dwarven, or Troll, or whether there was a whole other language for dragons that he hadn't heard of.

'Have you ever seen a dead body?' asked Darius.

Sammy shook his head. He hadn't.

'You don't want to, if you can help it, because they're so...lifeless! Darius erupted into a fit of hysteric giggles. 'Get it!'

Sammy grinned, wondering if it would be so bad after all. Taking care of his pristine school uniform, Sammy climbed onto Kyrillan's back and nudged his dragon to start walking.

'Race you to the gate!' yelled Sammy, kicking Kyrillan's flanks gently to encourage his dragon to take off.

Darius jumped onto Nelson's back and within seconds they disappeared into a silver teleporting mist.

'Cheat!' yelled Sammy, urging Kyrillan to spread his wings and fly towards the Dragamas front gates.

Darius wasted no time telling him it was forty-five seconds slower to fly to the gates than to teleport there.

Commander Altair was alone at the gates waiting for them. He was dressed equally sombrely in a black shirt tucked into black jeans with his familiar black belt studded with the three silver stars.

'You'll ruin those trousers,' tutted Commander Altair. 'Didn't you get my message to wear jeans?'

Sammy and Darius shook their heads.

'No matter. There's no time to change now. We'll have to fly fast as it is. The funeral starts in a few minutes.'

'What's the point of bringing dragons if we're going to teleport?' grumbled Sammy.

Commander Altair pointed to a hill in the distance. Sammy could just make out a small building and a wisp of smoke on the horizon.

'The funeral is being held at the Church of a Thousand Graves,' said Commander Altair. 'You can't teleport there.'

'There will be a thousand and one today,' said Darius, grimacing. 'They'll have to change its name.'

Commander Altair laughed out loud and kicked the flanks of his rustic red dragon. The dragon took slow steps forward then spread beautiful red wings with silver streaks.

Within seconds, Commander Altair was in the air and flying. Sammy and Darius took off on their dragons and soon they were flying one on either side of their Armoury teacher.

'The church is named after King Serberon's Dragon Knights,' said Commander Altair, raising his voice so Sammy and Darius could hear him above the sound of the wings. 'They are the first thousand men he personally appointed to be Dragon Knights, preserved in time. They are sleeping until they are needed. That's why it is called Church of a Thousand Graves. The Dragon Knights aren't dead, they are sleeping, but their sleep could be forever which is why they called it their graves.'

Sammy nodded, taking in every word. It made sense for the great King of the Dark Ages to have a timeless army that could one day be called upon to save the world.

'I'm surprised Dr Shivers hasn't told you this in your Dragon Studies lessons,' said Commander Altair, laughing. 'Perhaps you haven't listened!'

'We do listen!' said Sammy indignantly, wondering at the back of his mind if he had missed this important information in a Dragon Studies lesson.

As they flew higher and higher, the wind beat against Sammy's face in an exhilarating rush of cool air that took his breath away.

Dragamas Castle suddenly seemed very small and a very long way down. Sammy wondered whether anyone had fallen off a dragon from this great height and lived to tell the tale.

'We would catch you Sammy!' yelled Darius, tapping the side of his head, making the sign to show he had read Sammy's mind.

'Keep your eyes straight ahead and your knees tight together,' shouted Commander Altair. 'We're nearly there!'

Sammy looked behind him. Dragamas was now as much of a speck in the distance as the church had been from the school. He turned to face forwards as Commander Altair had instructed and looked at the building looming in front of them.

The Church of a Thousand Graves was a typical small English church with a grey slate roof and a tall bell tower with bronze bells of different sizes. The bells were playing a soothing melody that Sammy vaguely recognised the tune from the bells in the church in his hometown of Ratisbury.

The bronze bells rocked back and forth as Sammy, Darius and Commander Altair approached the church. They landed their dragons one after the other in a walled garden full of brightly coloured flowers.

In amongst the roses, snowdrops and daffodils were headstones and tombstones. There were carved stone angels and enamel plaques with names written in neat lines.

Cherry trees in late blossom hung across a white pebbled path in a floral archway, guiding them to the entrance. Pink petals which had fallen from the trees were scattered like confetti on the white pebbled path.

Soft singing came from within the double oak doors and Commander Altair frowned as he tied his dragon's harness to an iron loop beside the door. 'We're late,' he muttered.

'Dixie's Dad isn't going anywhere,' sniffed Darius, dabbing his eyes and nose. 'Darned cherry blossom setting off my hayfever.'

Sammy nodded, not quite sure if it was the real reason for Darius's red eyes. Despite his jokes and humour, Sammy could tell his friend was upset.

Commander Altair held the door open and Sammy ducked inside, his eyes quickly getting used to the darkened room.

Inside, the Church of a Thousand Graves wasn't very big. Sammy's eyes were drawn initially to a grand, white table clothed altar at the far end of the church.

Four green haired figures dressed in black were kneeling in front of the altar. Sammy recognised Mrs Deane, Serberon, Mikhael and Jason instantly.

Behind Dixie's family were what looked like several hundred people, presumably all family and friends, sitting sombrely on wooden chairs in rows behind them. They were all softly murmuring the words of a hymn that Sammy didn't recognise but he found the melody as soothing as the sound of the bronze bells outside.

In the front rows were several other green haired people and Sammy followed Commander Altair up the central aisle. Suddenly, he felt very small in the crowd. Darius stuck close behind them. For once, he had nothing to say.

Sammy recognised Sir Ragnarok and General Aldebaran Altair in the front row. They were wearing long green velvet robes and were sitting next to a large bulky man with green hair who was also dressed in a green velvet robe.

Commander Altair led Sammy and Darius to two empty seats in the second row, behind the green haired people.

'I'll catch up with you later,' whispered Commander Altair as the hymn came to an end. 'The words are in these,' he gave them small black leather-bound prayer books, 'and don't get into any trouble. You're representing Dragamas in front of some pretty big names,' he added, nodding towards his father, General Altair, and the bulky green haired man at the front. 'Be good!'

Sammy nodded and opened the prayer book, grateful when a small wizened green haired woman dressed in black, who looked like she was in her nineties, pointed out the right page for him.

'Arug shura,' she whispered.

'Arug shura,' replied Sammy, getting a buzz when she smiled at him. His pronunciation of the Troll words must have been correct.

'Insurlam vac a'salom ahu meeten sivec pleur undretakov,' said the old lady.

Sammy looked blankly. His Troll wasn't that good.

'A pity we don't meet under better circumstances,' she translated, registering his blank look.

Sammy nodded gratefully.

'I am Dixie's Grandmother,' said the old lady.

'How did you...' started Sammy.

'She talks of you,' whispered the old lady as a new hymn started and everyone around them started singing. 'You are too young to be one of my grandsons' classmates so you must be Dixie's friends, Sammy Rambles and Darius Murphy.'

Sammy cringed. 'We're just friends.'

The old lady nodded knowingly. 'That's how it starts,' she chuckled. 'Dixie speaks highly of you. Why, just this morning, she wished you would be with her.'

'How?' demanded Darius, a little loudly and some of the greenhaired people turned and stared at him.

The old lady pointed to her ears. 'It's there, faintly, but I can hear her voice. My precious Dixie. Maybe you need to listen if you are to see,' she said quietly. 'Jacob was my son and you are my granddaughter's friends. You must find her now he cannot.'

'I promise I will find her,' whispered Sammy.

Tears formed in the old woman's eyes and she clasped Sammy's hands. Without any words, she turned and shuffled towards the altar as the hymn drew to a close, a posy of pink flowers clasped in her wrinkled hands.

'You're not serious,' hissed Darius. 'She's crazy! A mad old bat! Very sweet but totally off her rocker!'

'You can hear people's thoughts,' whispered Sammy. 'We should try it. Maybe we could use our amber gemstones to make it stronger?'

'Look where that got you,' hissed Darius. 'What's really important is here and now. Dixie may never come back.'

'Cover for me,' whispered Sammy, excusing himself as he ducked out of the row of seats and slinked his way to the back of the church, through the thick oak doors and out into the grassy graveyard.

# CHAPTER 13

# SAMMY'S PROMISE

Sammy found Kyrillan curled up on the grass next to Commander Altair's dragon and Nelson, in the exact spot where he had dismounted.

It looked as though Kyrillan had fallen asleep as the blue-green dragon raised his sleepy eyelids and blew a faint wisp of smoke as Sammy approached.

Sammy knelt down and stroked his dragon's nose. 'It won't be long Kyrillan,' Sammy whispered and Kyrillan let out a quiet hurrumph and closed his eyes.

A noise made Sammy look up and he caught a shimmer of scales behind a silvery grey tombstone in the shape of an angel.

Two small green haired boys were throwing some of the white pebbles from the path at a pale orange dragon. The stones hit the dragon with a clink against its scales and the dragon was whimpering in pain.

'Oi!' yelled Sammy, leaping to his feet. 'Stop that!'

The boys looked around. They laughed at him and one of them threw a white pebble at Sammy.

'Stop it!' yelled Sammy. 'You don't treat dragons like that!'

'Meeten vatar,' laughed one boy. 'Vatar! Vatar! Vatar!'

'Vatar,' agreed the other boy.

'Sien!' shouted Sammy, alarming himself how natural "no" sounded in Troll. 'Sien!'

'Sien vatar?' asked one of the boys, scratching his green haired head.

Sammy stomped over to them. 'That's right,' said Sammy, grabbing the boy by his shirt collar. 'Sien vatar.'

'Ka!' said one of the boys.

'Ka vatar!' shouted the other boy.

'Sien,' said Sammy, pushing them away from the pale orange dragon thinking Miss Amoratti would be impressed with his Troll. He looked at the orange dragon, who stared with a bloodshot eyeball back at him.

'Sien vatar,' repeated Sammy and the dragon blew an orange smoke ring at him, thumping its bleeding tail on the hump of a raised grave.

The thumping got louder and Sammy realised the dragon was thumping in time with the church bells. Sammy felt a cold north wind blow icily across his back. It ran down the back of his blazer, finding its way up his sleeves and up his collar.

Sammy bent a little closer to the pale orange dragon, remembering he had some of Mrs Grock's healing potion that he carried with him at all times. He unscrewed the top of the small bottle and spread a few drops of the foul smelling liquid onto his fingers.

The dragon licked the solution off his fingers with a thick rasping tongue. It swished its tail and the blood disappeared. The dragon's scales grew visibly brighter with every drop it drank.

Sammy smiled, pleased with the results, when suddenly he was jerked to his feet by the scruff of his neck.

'Sien vatar,' barked a female voice.

'Mrs Deane?' asked Sammy, spinning round and clutching his staff, ready to see who had got hold of him.

'Oooh,' said Mrs Deane, releasing Sammy as soon as she recognised him. 'I thought you might come today. I didn't see you at the service.'

'I was in there,' said Sammy. 'I came outside to...er...to try something,' he added lamely.

Mrs Deane nodded. 'I don't blame you Sammy,' she said reassuringly. 'Funerals are difficult things.'

'No, it was Dixie's Grandmother,' Sammy tried to explain, 'she said I should listen. I was just coming out to get Kyrillan so I could use his power to help me, when I found two boys attacking this dragon.'

'Don't you think we've all tried that already?' asked Mrs Deane and to Sammy's embarrassment she started to cry, green crystal tears flowing down her cheeks.

Sammy rifled in his pocket and offered her a dirty handkerchief. 'She said...'

'Jacob's mother lives in another world,' interrupted Mrs Deane. 'Most people have stopped entertaining her and tell her she's barking mad to her face. Never trust the elderly Sammy. You never know what they'll do or say next.'

'Is this your dragon?' asked Sammy, pointing at the pale orange dragon that he had restored to health after the attack from the boys with the pebbles. He was keen to change the subject.

Mrs Deane nodded vigorously. 'Yes she is and those boys are my nephews, Van and Cyder. Thank you for helping her. They boys are too young to know any better.'

'What's "vatar"?' asked Sammy, stroking Mrs Deane's dragon. 'The boys said it when they threw the stones.'

Mrs Deane looked up, her face very serious. 'Vatar is the Troll word for death, dying or dead, depending on the context. It comes from the word "vat" which means "end".

'So they were trying to kill your dragon?' asked Sammy in amazement. 'Why would they do that?'

'Quite possibly,' said Mrs Deane dismissively. 'Oh, don't look like that Sammy. You'll see far worse before you get to my age. It's lucky you were here to stop them otherwise I'd have to walk home. With my Jacob dying trying to save dragons it won't hurt to see one of them suffer in return. A debt paid, don't you think?'

'No!' exploded Sammy. 'Sien! If all the dragons die, then the Shape will have won!'

'And would that be such a bad thing?' asked Mrs Deane, looking into the distance. 'Sometimes what we protect ourselves against may be the cure for the disease. Maybe my Jacob would still be alive.'

'No,' whispered Sammy. 'We need dragons. They'll help us find Dixie.'

Mrs Deane laughed. 'I used to be like you once. But just look at how many people will walk home from Jacob's funeral today. That will show you how many dragons are left. They are all being pulled towards Dragamas. All called by the Angel of 'El Horidore. They'll all be slaughtered by the Shape.'

Sammy put his hand on Mrs Deane's broad shoulder. 'We'll find Dixie. I promise you, we'll find her.'

'Thank you. I know you mean it,' whispered Mrs Deane, clutching awkwardly at Sammy's hand. 'Come with me. The hardest part is yet to come.'

'Ok,' said Sammy and he walked with Mrs Deane back into the Church of a Thousand Graves and down the central aisle.

He walked past Darius, past the rows of green haired Troll relations, past Sir Ragnarok, General Aldebaran Altair, Commander Altair and the huge Troll man sitting with them. The Troll man raised his eyebrows as if he was surprised to see Sammy.

Mrs Deane led him up to the very front of the church. She stopped at the white table clothed altar next to Serberon, Jason and Mikhael, who looked equally astonished to see him.

'Hey Sammy,' whispered Serberon.

Sammy nodded to Serberon, alarmed as Mrs Deane waved her arm in the air for the congregation and choir to cease singing in mid-hymn.

'This is Sammy Rambles,' announced Mrs Deane, her voice clear as a bell, the sound resonating into every corner of the church.

Everyone stopped singing and turned to look at them. Sammy looked at his feet, wishing the ground would swallow him up.

'Sammy Rambles is a friend of my daughter, Dixie, who is missing. Sammy Rambles promises he will find her for me.'

'And bring the dead back to life in the process,' muttered Serberon.

The congregation clapped and cheered. Sammy stared harder at his feet.

'Let us seal the past!' shouted Mrs Deane, throwing aside the white tablecloth on the altar to reveal a wooden coffin underneath.

Mrs Deane opened the lid of the coffin and dropped a small object inside. 'Goodbye Jacob, we will meet again!'

Sammy cast a quick look into the coffin as Serberon, Mikhael, Jason and Mrs Deane stood holding hands beside it and he gulped.

Jacob Deane had been a huge solid Troll man with grey green skin, tufts of dark green hair, wide sunken green eyes and a kind smile, just like Dixie's. But there were slashes of blood around the collar of his white shirt where his throat had been cut many times.

'Holy dragon,' whispered Serberon. 'What has he done to him?'

'Murdered,' said Mikhael, resting his hands on the side of the coffin.

Sammy bit his tongue and pinched his fingers. There was a lump the size of a rock in his throat.

'It's so final,' whispered Sammy.

'He's gone, we might as well be dead,' said Serberon, wiping green tears that looked like limeade falling from his eyes.

Sammy found himself engulfed in a hug from Mrs Deane's wide arms.

'Be strong boys,' said Mrs Deane bursting into tears.

Commander Altair, General Altair and the Troll man from the front row came up to the coffin. They were holding handfuls of silver scales which they scattered over Jacob Deane's body. Two scales covered his eyes and as more silver scales were poured into the coffin they soon enveloped him so that only his toes and tufts of green hair showed. They he disappeared completely.

As soon as Jacob Deane's body was covered entirely, the coffin started lowering itself slowly down inside the altar. When it was out of sight, Mrs Deane replaced the white tablecloth over the top.

Sammy found he had tears prickling in his eyes. Standing next to Serberon, Mikhael and Jason and watching the coffin disappear into oblivion, crying didn't seem such a bad idea, but Commander Altair pulled him aside.

'That was a kind thing you just did,' said Commander Altair.

'It's ok.' Sammy coughed back his tears, trying to make his voice sound normal.

'Jacob Deane was a good man,' said Commander Altair, resting his hands on Serberon's shoulders. 'He was proud of his sons and his daughter.'

'Dixie should be here too,' said Serberon. 'Why hasn't she come back?'

Sammy backed away, feeling uncomfortable among the grieving family. He sought out Darius who had moved from his seat and was standing by one of the stained glass windows. With the ceremony over, the congregation of people were starting to drift away.

'Have you seen the people in the windows watching us?' asked Darius.

Sammy frowned. 'No? What people?'

'Look,' hissed Darius, pointing behind him at a large stained glass window of a shadowy man standing upright on the back of a silver dragon.

'Is it a ghost?' whispered Sammy.

'Have you been crying?' asked Darius.

'No,' lied Sammy.

'It might be a ghost,' said Darius. He pointed at the other windows around the room. 'There are more, but you can't let them know you can see them.'

'What?' asked Sammy, spinning around to look at the window.

'No!' Darius clutched Sammy's shoulder. 'It takes ages to see them again. You have to look sideways at them.'

After a few seconds, Sammy saw the faintest wisp of silvery grey smoke in the window at the front of the church.

'Do you think it's Dixie's Dad's ghost?' asked Sammy, stepping aside to let some green haired people walk past him on their way out of the church.

'Maybe,' Darius nodded. 'Did you try listening outside?'

Sammy shook his head. 'There were these boys throwing stones at Mrs Deane's dragon and then Mrs Deane came outside so I didn't have the chance to try it.'

'You couldn't do it,' laughed Darius. He mimicked Dr Shivers's voice. 'Some Dragon Knight you'll be!'

Sammy froze. He gripped Darius's sleeve. He had suddenly seen silver people in all of the windows. They were glowing with a pink halo around them.

'Do you see that?' whispered Sammy, his voice shaking.

Darius nodded, his mouth wide open. 'They're King Serberon's Knights.'

Sammy looked around. The church was deserted. Mrs Deane, Commander Altair, everyone, including Jacob Deane's coffin and the altar were gone. The figures in the windows moved around, hissing amongst themselves, pointing, staring and frowning down at them.

'Run!' yelled Darius, yanking Sammy down the aisle by the hand.

Sammy obeyed. He could feel the same icy breeze send goosebumps up and down his body from his head to his toes. They clambered over the chairs, aware that the ghostly figures were leaping down from the windows with staffs in their hands.

Darius flung open the double oak doors at the entrance to the church and they bumped straight into Commander Altair, who was staring at his watch.

'What do you think you're doing?' asked Commander Altair.

'Shapes,' puffed Sammy. 'In the windows.'

'Look,' said Commander Altair, thrusting his watch in front of Sammy and Darius.

Sammy saw the watch face turn into an oilslick with ten green dots where the numbers would usually be and two white dots in the middle.

'You have meddled with things far beyond you,' said Commander Altair.

'So what?' asked Darius. 'So what if there are ghosts in there?'

Commander Altair dragged both his hands through his corn coloured hair. 'They're not just any ghosts. Leave this to me. You'd best get back to Dragamas. I'll handle it,' he said, pushing open the wooden doors and disappearing inside.

'Do you think we're in trouble?' asked Sammy as the doors closed behind him.

Darius nodded. 'Lots of trouble. They probably were King Serberon's ghosts or something!'

Sammy felt shivery again and was glad to step into the sun. He checked his own watch. It was nearly ten o'clock.

'Shall we try listening for Dixie at Dragamas?' asked Sammy. 'We could use all of the dragons at the school to make our power stronger.'

'Ok,' said Darius, but he didn't look too sure about the idea. 'Maybe some other time.'

'Don't you want Dixie back?' asked Sammy.

Darius swung himself up onto Nelson's arched back. 'Of course I do, but, well, it's been nice without her tagging along. I'm sure she'll come back eventually.'

'You've given up as well,' said Sammy, laying his blazer over Kyrillan's back to protect his school trousers from chaffing. 'I've promised Mrs Deane I'll find her.'

'I'm sure you will,' said Darius. 'I was just saying it's been nice without her tagging along to everything.'

'I've made a promise to find her,' said Sammy and he kept whispering this to himself and Kyrillan all the way back to Dragamas.

Jock was waiting for Sammy and Darius at the school gates. He was flying on Kiridor, round and round in circles.

'Come on!' yelled Jock. 'There's a Dragonball match going on and we need you to play!'

Sammy didn't need telling twice. He loved Dragonball as much as Dixie and quickly forgot about the funeral and the ghostly figures in the church windows as they flew up the castle driveway to the Dragonball pitch.

Sammy spend the next six hours ruining both his blazer and school trousers in a series of severe attacks against the second and third years. The fourth years on their older, more experienced, dragons won the game with conviction.

'We won,' sighed Sammy as he lay down on the grass with his classmates and their dragons outside the Gymnasium several hours later. 'Now we just need to beat the Shape.'

'And save all the dragons,' added Toby. 'That'll be easy!'

CHAPTER 14

# TERRIBLE NEWS

Several weeks later, Sir Ragnarok marched into the morning assembly in the Main Hall holding a large black scroll. He paused to rest a hand on Sammy and Darius's shoulders before taking his place in the centre of the teachers' table at the front of the hall. He waved his hand for silence.

'Students of Dragamas, I bring sad tidings,' said Sir Ragnarok, unrolling the large scroll.

'Dragamas is going to shut?' asked Gavin, looking hopeful and crossing his fingers.

'Sad news about a former Dragamas pupil who found the pressures of life and recent events overwhelming to the extent that he sought and succeeded in taking his own life.'

An audible gasp rippled through the hall from the first year table right the way through to the fifth year table. Every student hung onto each and every word.

'Some of you will remember him, perhaps in particular if he was your mentor or a close friend. His loss comes at a particularly sad time after the loss of his father and the abduction of his younger sister…'

'Serberon,' whispered Sammy. 'No.'

'…who was taken at the end of last term. Our thoughts and prayers are with his two brothers and his mother. His name was Serberon Edvard Igor Deane. May his troubled spirit find peace. Let us hold a minute of silence for him,' finished Sir Ragnarok and he closed the scroll.

Sammy closed his eyes and his mind was filled with flashbacks of Serberon laughing, Serberon teasing him, Serberon with Mary-Beth, Serberon giving him the soft toy lion, the fun they'd had playing Dragon Questers, Serberon teaching him Dragonball tactics, Serberon attacking him, telling him to look out for Dixie and protect her, Serberon luring him into the Great Pyramid, Serberon wanting Sammy to join the Shape.

The sixty seconds passed quickly and Sir Ragnarok broke the silence.

'If anyone is in a similar situation, or would like to talk through any issues, please see your Housemaster, or at the very least, discuss things with your mentor, who can talk through issues with you. Please do not think this is the answer. There are many better ways to die. Old age is my choice.'

Sammy looked down at the triangles of toast and the bowl of cereal he had chosen for breakfast. He was unable to eat anything as his stomach was churning at the news.

Dr Shivers approached the fourth year North table handing out black leaflets with white writing on both sides.

'It's a terrible waste of life,' said Dr Shivers briskly. 'He was so young, so very talented, and there was so much he could have achieved.'

Sammy looked at one of the leaflets over Darius's shoulder. They appeared to be offering counselling services with Miss Thosewa Left, a bereavement counsellor from Gravesend in Kent.

'That's got to be a joke,' snorted Darius.

'I'm going,' said Milly. 'Mummy says…'

'La la la!' shouted Gavin, sticking his fingers in his ears. 'No one cares Milly. Shut up!'

'You'll come to counselling, won't you Sammy?' Milly looked imploringly at him.

'Uh, I wasn't, uh, no,' Sammy stumbled over his words.

'Fine!' stormed Milly, clutching Holly and Naomi's hands. 'I was only thinking of you. Serberon was your mentor, wasn't he?'

Sammy nodded. 'But I don't need to see anyone. I'm ok. I've…'

'Sammy wants to find Dixie,' interrupted Darius. 'He doesn't want to go to some therapy session with you!'

'Oooh Sammy,' said Gavin, grinning mischievously. 'You kept that really quiet! Is Dixie your girlfriend?'

'Shut it!' said Sammy. 'Have you got any ideas for a Halloween costume this year?'

'Ghosts as usual,' said Toby, winking at Gavin. 'We've found a way to make our sheets glow in the dark.'

CHAPTER 15

# HALLOWEEN PREPARATIONS

On October the 30<sup>th</sup>, the night before the annual Dragamas Halloween party, Sammy spent the evening with the fourth year North boys in their tower room preparing their costumes.

As promised, Gavin and Toby had supplied large white sheets and fluorescent snap tubes that, once broken, gave off an eerie, iridescent glow.

Using a pair of long handled dressmaker scissors, thick white cotton and a metal needle Darius had borrowed from Naomi, Sammy cut a half-moon shaped hole in the middle of each sheet and then two more holes in the half-moon part for their eyes.

This was so they could put the sheet completely over their heads, or push it back like a hood if it got too hot, or if they wanted to eat something or drink something.

Sammy also roughly stitched the edges of the sheets so it created two sleeves for them to put their arms through and when he was finished, he was quite pleased with the result.

Gavin had taken several large bottles of tomato ketchup out of his school rucksack and was busy squirting dollops of "blood" onto the costumes.

'I nicked these from the kitchen,' said Gavin with a big grin. 'I'll take them back tomorrow.'

'It's a good job Dr Shivers doesn't know you stole the ketchup,' said Darius, putting his red stained sheet over his head. He licked his sleeve where Gavin had splashed a large red dollop of ketchup. 'Mmm, mmm. We can eat off our costumes if the food is rubbish!' said Darius, exploding into a hysterical fit of the giggles.

'We'll also need masks,' said Gavin. 'How can we make masks?'

'Face paint,' suggested Toby. 'Hey Sammy, will you hurry up stitching the sleeves!'

'I've already finished them,' said Sammy, pulling open the curtain between their beds. 'What's that?' he asked, spotting an envelope and some money on Toby's duvet.

'Nothing,' said Toby, looking embarrassed. 'I'm just sending a tenner to some charity to help fight the Shape.'

'Oh, you're helping "fight" the Shape now, are you?' demanded Sammy.

'You know we are,' said Toby testily. 'Our world doesn't exist without dragons. We're Dragonfolk. Dragons are our way of life.'

'Without them we are nothing,' added Jock. 'We would just be normal human beings.'

'You'll never be human,' scoffed Gavin. 'Try this on and shut up.'

'You shut up,' retorted Jock, picking up his pillow. 'Do you want a fight?'

'I'm going to bed,' said Sammy, handing Toby the last of the Halloween sheets. He drew his curtain and listened for a moment as Jock and Gavin destroyed their pillows before closing his eyes and falling fast asleep.

The following morning, Sammy woke to a frightful gory face painted on a white sheet with spots of red blood all over it, just inches from his nose.

'Boo!' shouted Gavin, waking everyone up, except for Darius, who had already gone down to the Dragon Chambers to check up on the dragons as part of his Dragon Minder duties.

'Boo to you too,' said Sammy, pushing Gavin away. 'Do you know what time it is?'

'It's Halloweeeentime!' shouted Gavin. 'Party! Food! Girls!'

'Dixie won't be there,' said Toby, winking at his brother. 'You can't expect Sammy to get excited without her there.'

'Or me,' said Jock. 'I like her too!'

'Bunch of freaks,' said Gavin. 'Has everyone got their snap lights for tonight?'

'You need to grow up,' snapped Jock.

'Have you looked in the mirror?' laughed Gavin. 'You need to grow at least two feet to be half as tall as me and Toby.'

Jock's eyes narrowed. 'You got a problem with me?'

'Ooh, so scared,' Gavin pushed Jock's head with his hand. 'You...ug...' Gavin froze as Jock released a blast of ruby red lightning.

'Short but sweet,' said Jock, keeping his hand on the ruby at the end of his staff. 'May the best Dwarf win.' He turned to Sammy. 'You're not really interested in going out with Dixie are you Sammy?'

Sammy surveyed the frozen bodies in the tower room to check who had fallen under Jock's spell. Gavin and Toby were rock solid but Darius seemed to be ok.

'Uh, I don't know,' said Sammy, reaching for his own staff to release Gavin and Toby.

'Sorted!' Jock grinned triumphantly. 'When she's back I'll have her as well as her dragon.'

'How do you know when she'll be back?' interrupted Sammy.

Jock tapped his nose. 'I've got connections.'

'Pah!' snorted Darius. 'The only connections you've got in your family are water and electricity.'

'Two more than you,' retorted Jock.

'We've got electricity,' argued Darius.

'Liar!' shouted Jock.

Sammy reached for his ruby to undo Jock's freezing, which had caught Gavin and Toby off guard.

Darius shoved his hands in his pockets. 'Why don't you come to mine this Christmas, you too Sammy. I want to show you for real. We have got electricity!'

'Fine.' Jock grinned and rubbed his ruby crystal. 'Unless I get a better offer.'

'I'm going to kill you Dwarf breath!' yelled Gavin, suddenly unfrozen and back to normal. 'I'm getting better at Gemology. You won't be able to do that next time!'

With an evil grin, Jock unpocketed his ruby and sent a blinding red glare bouncing around the tower room.

Sammy felt his knees weakening. 'I must keep practicing,' he muttered, grabbing Jock's wrist. 'Come on, we're supposed to be helping with the food.'

Jock nodded and with one last flash of his ruby that brought Gavin to his knees, he covered the red stone and put it away.

'We're going to have pumpkin pies,' giggled Darius. 'I can't believe we ever thought they were cool.'

'Or these stupid costumes,' said Gavin.

'You liked them yesterday,' said Toby. 'I think they look awesome!'

'You're easily pleased,' scoffed Gavin.

'Sammy likes them,' protested Toby.

'Sammy would,' came Gavin's muffled reply as he swung the heavy linen sheet over his head. 'Do we have to wear these all day?'

'I don't think Dr Shivers would like that,' giggled Darius. 'Turn on the snap light.'

Gavin reached inside his costume and there was a loud snapping sound and an eerie purple iridescent glow appeared around Gavin's waist. The light projected up to Gavin's cut out eyes and made the ketchup stains turn a murky brown.

'I'm Dracula's ghost,' giggled Gavin. 'I'm gonna suck some blood!'

'Cool,' said Sammy, a little sarcastically. He was starting to tire of Gavin's sudden mood changes.

'Blooood!' yelled Gavin. 'Suck some blooood! Yeehah!' he let rip a blood curdling yowl.

'Shh!' hissed Darius. 'You'll bring Dr Shivers up here and we'll lose some stars!'

Sammy turned around cautiously. He was half expecting gaunt and ghostly Dr Shivers to be standing at the tower doorway. But he wasn't and Sammy scooped up his rucksack and books and together with Darius, he ran out of the tower room and down to their Gemology lesson.

Inside room seven, Mrs Hubar eyed them suspiciously. It wasn't every day students dressed up as ghosts charged into her classroom. She waved them into their usual seats at the North table and waited for the other students to arrive.

Sammy noticed Mrs Hubar was rolling several lumps of blue-green draconite in her hands, cracking them together like dragon bones. She had prepared a test on their new sapphire gemstones.

'Jock, please stand at the front,' said Mrs Hubar, beckoning for her son to come forward. 'I would like you to demonstrate how we use the sapphire to protect an object, or a person, or an area.'

Jock stood up straightaway with a broad grin on his face. Sammy knew he found these lessons very easy, which wasn't surprising as his mother was the Gemology teacher.

Sammy watched with interest as Jock extended his staff and rubbed his hand over the blue stone at the end.

As Jock's swarthy fingers touched the sapphire, a small cyclone of rainbow coloured oilslick mist was conjured out of thin air.

Jock held the mist steady using his right hand and moved the oilslick mist over to the North table and held it over his pencilcase.

Sammy gasped as the pencilcase vanished from sight. One moment it was there and the next moment it had gone.

Jock ran his hand back over the sapphire and although the oilslick coloured mist disappeared, the pencilcase was absolutely nowhere to be seen.

'Very good Jock,' beamed Mrs Hubar. 'Now, please bring the object back into view.'

Jock held his sapphire close to where the pencilcase had been and slowly it came back into view.

'Stop!' said Mrs Hubar when half of the pencilcase had materialised. 'Let me show the class how only the person who created this protection can break it. Simon, would you be so kind to attempt this?'

From his seat at the East table, Simon Sanchez shook his head. 'There is no point,' he said, shaking his head.

'I'll do it!' shouted Gavin, producing his staff from within his ghost costume. 'I'll get his pencilcase back!'

Mrs Hubar laughed. 'Take that ridiculous costume off first Gavin! Whatever next!'

Gavin lifted the hooded bloodstained sheet over his head and held out his staff. He covered his sapphire with the palm of his hand.

'Reappear!' yelled Gavin. 'Magica!'

Toby stood up next to his brother, cheering him on. 'Come on Gavin! Get it back! You can do it!'

Gavin frowned as he concentrated on the sapphire stone at the end of his staff. The whole class were watching closely. Out of the corner of his eye, Sammy saw Jock, Simon and Amos grinning.

'The oilslick protection can only be removed by the person who put it there,' said Simon.

'Or when it wears off by itself,' added Mrs Hubar. 'It is a strong but temporary protection or shield. If you want something or someone to be protected for longer then you must reapply the sapphire at regular intervals. Well done Simon. I will award you two stars.'

Mrs Hubar sent two silver stars spinning out of the Gemology classroom. Sammy mentally added them to the totals and suspected East would win the most house points and the trophy this year.

Jock waved his staff over the pencilcase and it reappeared completely. He pointed the crystal tip of his staff at Gavin. 'Bet you wish you could do that!' he said mockingly.

'Hah!' said Gavin, flicking his staff up towards Jock's nose. 'I'll make you disappear!'

'Not today, thank you,' said Mrs Hubar, shielding Jock from Gavin's staff. 'Please write this experiment up with the title "Making objects disappear and reappear using sapphires", thank you.'

Sammy took his pen and paper out of his rucksack. It didn't look as though Mrs Hubar was going to let anyone else practice creating the oilslick to make things disappear and reappear again today.

The lesson dragged extremely slowly, with Mrs Hubar drifting amongst the tables checking on their work and making suggestions for improvement.

As soon as the end of the lesson bell started chiming, Sammy threw his pen and paper into his rucksack. He was desperate to get back to the boys' tower room to practice making objects disappear with his sapphire.

# CHAPTER 16

# HALLOWEEN MISADVENTURES

After several hours of very limited success, Sammy had only mastered how to create a semi-transparent oilslick. It was nothing like the non-see-through oilslick Jock had created in the Gemology lesson.

Sammy found he could move the oilslick he had created around using just his staff and directing it with his mind. However, it was completely useless as he could still see the pennies he was trying to hide and protect.

In frustration he knocked the stack of pennies onto the floor. They clattered onto the stone floor and rolled away under the bed. Sammy didn't bother to pick them up.

In fact, as Sammy lay flat out on his bed wondering what had gone wrong with his experiment, he was extremely glad to see Jock and Darius bursting into the tower room as they returned from the Dragon Chambers.

'Look what Naomi gave him!' shouted Jock, pulling down the top of Darius's sheet costume.

Sammy peered at the red lump on Darius's neck. 'What on earth is that?'

'It's an everlasting kiss,' said Jock. 'I'm gonna give one to Dixie.'

'Naomi gave me one and I gave her one,' grinned Darius. 'It was in the Dragon Chambers, behind the water basins.'

Sammy stared. 'Did it hurt?'

'No, you just suck, like this,' Darius demonstrated by sucking noisily on the back of his hand.

After a couple of seconds, Darius held up his hand showed Sammy and Jock a small red mark.

'Dixie's gonna get my first everlasting kiss,' said Jock. 'My Mum knows where she's gone.'

'Where she's been taken,' corrected Sammy. 'How come you know so much about Dixie all of a sudden? Is your Mum in the Shape?' he snapped.

'Oooh yeah,' said Darius. 'She's a Dwarf isn't she, like Dr Lithoman and she was in the Shape.'

'Yeah right!' scoffed Jock. 'Are you saying all the Dwarves want all the dragons dead? Is that it? I don't think so!'

'Your Mum's helping Sir Ragnarok to store all the draconite, isn't she?' added Sammy. 'Maybe we should go back to the library and see if we can find out any more about the Stone Cross. The Shape want to rebuild the Stone Cross with draconite to give them invincibility and immortality.'

'I'll help,' said Jock. 'I know the library inside out.'

'Ok,' said Sammy. 'Let's get changed first, otherwise Mrs Skoob will never let us in!'

In fact, Mrs Skoob was about to close the library when Sammy, Jock and Darius burst in and demanded to know where to find books about the Stone Cross.

'You can try the History section,' said Mrs Skoob, pointing them towards the shelves in the furthest, darkest and dustiest, corner of the library. 'However, please don't dawdle. I have things to do.'

Sammy, Darius and Jock ran to the History section. Mrs Skoob threw up her arms in despair.

'Don't run!' squawked Mrs Skoob. 'This is a library not a racing track!'

'You said not to dawdle!' Jock shouted over his shoulder and Darius collapsed in a fit of giggles that went echoing around the quiet library.

Sammy scoured the bookshelves in the History section. There were hundreds and hundreds of dusty leather bound books that looked as though they might be helpful. The books were neatly stored alphabetically by author in tall wooden bookshelves.

The bookshelves towered over a long wooden study table that ran down the middle of the History section. There were high-backed wooden chairs, with padded purple velvet cushion seats, tucked neatly under the table.

'We'll never get to read all this lot,' complained Sammy, shovelling a pile of books onto the study table. A cloud of dust erupted and he sneezed. He pushed aside an empty packet of crisps and sat down on one of the padded seats.

Jock picked up a book with a picture of a large golden dragon coming out of some orange and yellow flames on the front cover.

'That looks interesting,' said Darius, leaning over Jock's shoulder. 'The Fires of Karmandor.'

'We're supposed to be looking at things about the Stone Cross,' said Sammy crossly. 'We can look at golden dragons another day.'

Jock and Darius exchanged looks and both erupted into laughter.

'Quiet please!' screeched Mrs Skoob. 'Please keep noise to a minimum in my library!'

It soon became clear that Darius and Jock weren't going to take the research seriously and Sammy snapped the book he was reading shut with a loud bang.

'Let's borrow some of these,' said Sammy, seeing Mrs Skoob marching towards them. 'We can do some research and bring them back.'

Mrs Skoob was very reluctant to let any books leave her library but she conceded to allow Sammy, Jock and Darius to borrow three books each after a little persuasion.

'We'll bring them back,' promised Darius.

'You had better bring them back,' grumbled Mrs Skoob, pushing her glasses up her nose and making copious notes of which books they were borrowing and the condition they were borrowing them in.

As Sammy, Darius and Jock returned to the North Tower fourth year boys' room, Gavin met them at the door. He handed each of them their own snap tube so they could light up the inside of their costume. Gavin had already snapped the tubes and these ones glowed with an eerie bright green light that reminded Sammy of the colour of Dixie's hair.

'This is going to be so much fun!' shouted Gavin, jumping up and down wearing his gruesome bedsheet. The green light from his snap tube lit up his whole costume making him look like a ghostly Troll.

Sammy looked at the arrangement of bedsheet ghost costumes Toby was handing out for the Halloween party. It looked as though he and Gavin had liberally sprayed more ketchup on the bedsheets than before.

Sammy took his ghost costume from Toby and slipped it over his head. It was much more claustrophobic than he remembered. He could hardly breathe.

'You've put your head through one of the sleeves!' said Darius bending over double with infectious giggles.

'Help me out!' laughed Sammy, contorting himself trying to manoeuvre inside the bedsheet and blinding himself with the green light.

Still laughing hysterically, Darius helped Sammy to rearrange himself.

Sammy stuck his head out of the right hole and gasped for air. 'That's better!'

'Hurry up!' shouted Gavin, leaping from bed to bed around the tower room. 'It's time to party!'

Sammy found it hard to walk with the large bedsheet trailing behind him. He kept standing on the edges and slipping as the material stayed put while he tried to step forward. He clung to the handrail as they went down the two flights of stairs to the North common room.

Along with the other North students, who were equally dressed in frightening Halloween costumes, they spent the time waiting for Dr Shivers, who was coming to escort them to the Halloween party, trying to guess who was who underneath the face paint, prosthetics and bulky costumes.

When Dr Shivers finally arrived, Sammy thought he could recognise everyone in the North house. He agreed with Gavin that their costumes with the light up snap tubes were by far the best.

'Happy Halloween!' said Dr Shivers, poking his head around the common room door.

Sammy gasped, hardly recognising his Dragon Studies teacher as Dr Shivers flounced into the room wearing none other than a vampire outfit, with a long black cape flowing behind him.

Dr Shivers seemed to have made a tremendous effort with his costume this year. Sammy noticed he had swapped his serious grey suit for a black tuxedo with a white shirt and black bowtie. His face was painted even paler than his usual translucent skin and when Dr Shivers opened his mouth, long white fangs protruded from his gums.

'Come with me,' said Dr Shivers, the fangs giving him a slight lisp. 'I shall escort you to the Main Hall where the Halloween feast shall commence.'

Sammy shuffled forward, his ghost costume slowing him down. The North students marched boisterously down the castle corridors, talking and laughing and looking forward to the feast.

Dr Shivers held open the double doors into the Main Hall. Sammy peered into the orange tinged darkness. Sir Ragnarok had turned the hall into a giant pumpkin again and fleshy fruit spread from wall to wall.

They squelched into the Main Hall, where students from the South, West and East houses were already congregating and were dressed in equally macabre outfits. There were students dressed as witches and wizards, cats, toads, spiders and vampires.

Lots of students had also come as ghosts and Sammy felt like he and the other fourth year North boys had the best ghost costumes as theirs were glowing with the green snap tubes Gavin had organised.

As Sammy's eyes grew used to the dim orange light, he could see signs of the traditional Halloween feast spread on the house tables. This year, perhaps because he was older, it seemed tacky with trails of cobwebs dangling a little too realistically into the food.

Unlike in previous years, a sickly orange juice potion dyed green was all there was to drink. The large glass jugs were full to the brim of the lumpy liquid and no one seemed brave enough to try it.

Next to the jugs were hand-shaped skeleton bones clasped around the usual glass tumblers and plates piled high with Halloween themed food. There were also lots and lots of pumpkins with candles inside providing the majority of light in the room.

Sammy helped himself to a large slice of pumpkin pie. He broke the slice into two pieces, eating half himself and putting the other half into a black serviette, which he stuffed into his jeans pocket underneath his bedsheet ghost costume, intending to take it to the Dragon Chambers later as a treat for Kyrillan.

After just a few minutes, Sammy found himself annoyed at the first years, who were tearing up and down the Main Hall pretending to be bats, dressed from head to toe in pitch black flowing gowns.

'Watch where you're going,' snapped Sammy, as they ran past him for the third time.

'Come on Sammy!' yelled Gavin, raising one of the skeleton hand-shaped glasses and taking a large swig of the foul looking liquid. 'Let's get them!' he shouted, storming after the first years making bloodthirsty howling noises.

Sammy picked up the hem of his bedsheet costume and ran after Gavin, stopping short as Gavin grabbed a small boy dressed as a bat by the scruff of his tiny neck.

'Give us your money then,' demanded Gavin. 'Or whatever you've got.'

Sammy reached for Gavin's illuminated shoulder to pull him back.

'What are you doing Gavin?' demanded Sammy, completely shocked at his friend's behaviour.

The first year took advantage of Gavin releasing his grip and spat in his face and stamped hard on their toes.

'Stuff you!' said the first year bat boy, ripping himself free.

Gavin's eyes swelled up inside his ghost costume. 'Dirty little...'

Sammy rubbed his toes. 'You deserved it! What's got into you Gavin? You never used to be like this.'

Gavin shoved Sammy away. 'What do you care? You're just like the rest of them.'

'The rest of who?' Sammy asked the empty air as Gavin whisked himself into the crowd of nearby students and out of sight.

Sammy made his way back to the North table. He was shaken at Gavin's treatment of the first year.

'Oi! Sammy! Come here! We've saved you a seat!'

Sammy spun around. Nigel Ashford, the boy in the third year he was supposed to be mentoring was waving his old toy lion at him.

'Come on Sammy! We're doing an initiation ceremony,' said Nigel, his voice still excitable and squeaky.

Sammy watched as Nigel gave the toy lion to a small blond haired boy in the first year and then nodded to one of his classmates.

He held back a laugh as Nigel's friend picked up one of the large jugs of the lumpy green coloured orange juice and poured it over the head of the first year, who promptly burst into tears.

'You're in!' said Nigel, thumping the first year on his back. 'You're in our club, the Passage Spotters!'

'The what?' asked Sammy. 'The Passage Spotters was our idea. Not yours.'

Nigel Ashford shrugged. Gavin in your year suggested it and Jock said his Mum said it was ok as well. We're a new club and we get money off people. So we can get stuff, you know, for the Shape. I've sent fifty pounds so far.'

'For the Ssshape?' Sammy stuttered like he'd been punched in the back himself.

'Yes,' said Nigel. 'My Dad says we should accept our fate. The dragons' days are numbered and it is time for a new King and a new way of life. Besides,' he added, 'everyone outside of the Dragon World gets on ok. Why shouldn't we just get rid of all our dragons and join them?'

'The Shape are just speeding up the inevitable,' said the boy with the lion. Lumpy green gunk dribbled out of his hair and down his face but he didn't seem to notice.

'That's because the Shape are evil murderers who stop at nothing to get what they want,' said Sammy in a low, choked voice. 'They don't care if it's humans, Trolls or dragons they kill.'

'But look at their power,' Nigel smiled, his eyes bright. 'Look at Gavin and Jock. Look what they can do. Look at their power to do things. That's why I wanted to be a Dragon Minder,' he added, holding up his green eyed Dragon Minder pin that was attached to his costume.

'It's fake power,' said Sammy. 'It's bullying. Gavin changes his mind about dragons like the weather. One minute he wants to save them and the next minute he wants to kill them! Anyway, who wants to have control over everything?'

Nigel's eyes glazed over. 'I do.'

Sammy threw his hands into his pockets in despair, remembering too late that he'd stored the sticky slice of pumpkin pie in there for Kyrillan. Pumpkin juice oozed onto his fingers.

'Grr,' muttered Sammy to himself, then he turned to the boys in front of him. 'The Shape will be defeated,' he announced and his dramatic statement was met with high pitched cackles from Nigel and his gang.

Sammy stomped off. 'Did you know Gavin's funding the Shape?' he demanded to Toby when he found his classmate a few minutes later.

Toby was playing crisp stackers with Darius and they each had tall piles of crisps balanced precariously on their tongues. Milly and girls from the fourth year were watching and cheering them on.

Toby removed the crisps, his face pale. 'That's why I sent my pocket money to fight the Shape. I want to keep Puttee. I want to fly and do magic.'

Those weren't the reasons Sammy was looking for but he accepted them anyway.

'We have to stick together,' Sammy informed his friends. 'We have to fight the Shape. Who's in?'

Darius raised his hand. 'I'm in,' he mumbled, his tongue loaded with about twenty crisps.

'I'm in too,' giggled Milly mischievously flicking Darius's stack of crisps so Toby would win.

'Cheat!' snapped Darius, kicking the fallen crisps under the North table. 'You're in too Naomi, aren't you?'

'Sure,' Naomi nodded and blew Darius a kiss across the table.

By the time Sir Ragnarok arrived, it was ten to midnight and they were escorted back to the North Tower by a dishevelled and giggling Professor Burlay and a strictly disapproving Dr Shivers, who was still dressed as a ghostly vampire.

'Good night boys,' said Dr Shivers, taking out his fanged teeth. He divided the boys and girls and sent them up their respective towers. 'No more nonsense,' he added firmly, swaying a withered pumpkin lantern, 'until next year.'

CHAPTER 17

# RESUSCITATING A DRAGON

Less than three weeks after the misadventures of Halloween and the shock of finding out not only that some of his friends were funding the Shape but that others were collecting money to stop them, Sammy found himself wishing, not for the first time that he had failed his third year exams and been allowed to stay down a year.

Things were tense among the fourth year North boys. Toby was trying to match Gavin penny for penny with the money Gavin was sending to the Shape against his own fund he was raising to save the dragons.

Gavin seemed to have let the power of being in charge of the Passage Spotters go to his head. His new hobby was taunting Jock over the death of his dragon, Giselle.

Toby kept getting on the receiving end of Jock's punching, kicking, scratching and spitting as he tried to protect his twin brother. Gavin didn't seem grateful at all for Toby's help and spent all his time thinking up new insults to annoy and upset Jock.

Sammy joined Darius whenever possible to check on the dragons under the castle. It had unsettled him finding out that Nigel Ashford had been made a Dragon Minder. He found himself feeling anxious every time he saw Nigel throw down food for the third year dragons.

On one particularly horrible day, four dead dragons materialised in the castle courtyard. Sammy happened to glance out of his dormitory window and saw the gruesome spectacle as the dragons arrived one by one.

They were all gigantic adult dragons, the size of double decker busses. There was a large blood red dragon, an orangey-yellow dragon, a deep sea blue dragon and an emerald green dragon with sparkling scales. Four enormous motionless shapes that were taking up most of the space in the courtyard.

Within moments of the dragons arriving, Dr Shivers appeared with the fifth year students. Moments later, Professor Burlay appeared at the tower room door and summoned the fourth year students to watch.

Dr Shivers divided the students into their houses and let the ten fifth year students per house dissect one dragon each as a macabre Dragon Studies lesson project while the fourth year students stood back and watched.

Sammy held his breath as he watched the fifth years unsheathe sharp knives and strip the dragons of their scales. Piles of red, yellow, blue and green scales were stacked beside each dragon carcass. The dragons were then morbidly gutted by the fifth years. Flesh was cut away from the bones and there was a stench of death in the air.

After a few minutes, there was a cry of "draconite!" and Sammy's stomach lurched and he ran into the Dragon Chambers clutching his stomach.

Sammy bent double over what looked like a bucket of muddy water and threw up. When he'd emptied his stomach of its contents, he noticed a pair of black boots belonging to someone standing next to him.

'I'll thank yer not to be chuckin' up in me fermenting cider Sammy,' growled Captain Firebreath, hoiking Sammy up by his collar and throwing him unceremoniously out of the Dragon Chambers.

When Sammy returned to the courtyard, everyone was gathered around the East students. They had managed to resuscitate their dragon and keep it alive. Amongst the death and destruction of the other three dragons, Sammy felt a warm glow. One dragon had been saved.

Sammy noticed that Dr Shivers had collected the three draconite stones from the three dead dragons and concealed them in his suit jacket pocket.

'Well done,' said Dr Shivers. 'This is an incredible achievement. I will award the East house five hundred stars. Class dismissed.'

All the students in the East house gave each other high-fives and cheered loudly. Five hundred stars was the most stars that had ever been awarded in one go.

With a noisy hustle and bustle, the students left the courtyard. Some of them stopped to pick up the brightly coloured dragon scales and others hurried away to their next lesson. Sammy checked his parchment timetable. Ancient and Modern Languages was next.

Up in the Ancient and Modern Languages classroom, Miss Amoratti seemed to be in an unusually good mood.

'Good morning fourth years,' said Miss Amoratti tapping her wooden ruler tunefully on her desk. 'I hear a dragon has been resuscitated this morning.'

'Yes!' shouted out Gavin, as though he alone had been responsible for the revival. 'The East house got five hundred stars!'

Miss Amoratti gasped and tapped her ruler on her wrist. 'I feel that you all played a part in this event,' she said, nodding vigorously, the blue streaks in her hair bouncing as if they agreed with her. 'I shall award every fourth year student twenty-five stars each.'

Sammy shook his head. Miss Amoratti was very strange in the way she awarded stars and marks compared with the other teachers.

Miss Amoratti waved her staff above her head and dozens of silver stars burst from the end. They flew around the room, circling high above everyone's heads. After just a few minutes, the ceiling was shimmering with silver stars.

'Go on!' said Miss Amoratti, waving her ruler at the stars. 'Why won't you leave the classroom?'

Darius let out an explosive giggle and stood up, waving his staff, trying to help. Within seconds, everyone was on their feet with their staffs, trying to guide the stars.

Eventually, Naomi suggested opening a window. She reached up to the clasp and pushed one of the tall classroom windows open.

There was a loud whooshing as the silver stars realised they could escape out of the Ancient and Modern Languages classroom. They chased each other out into the fresh air, taking the shortest route to the noticeboard in the Main Hall.

'Close the window please Naomi,' said Miss Amoratti, putting a shawl around her shoulders. 'It's rather cold in here. I don't know how you coped outside this morning in the courtyard trying to resuscitate that dragon. Now we can begin the lesson and I would like you to use the Troll language please.'

Sammy had to stop himself giggling when Darius leaned across and whispered a suggestion that the dragon had been given an everlasting kiss.

Darius pulled down his shirt collar and showed Sammy his latest everlasting kiss. It looked rather red and sore with deep toothmarks that had not quite broken Darius's skin.

'She was a bit rough,' whispered Darius. 'But it's cool, isn't it?'

Sammy leaned closer to inspect the marks. He nodded, even though he wasn't sure he wanted one himself.

'Pay some attention Sammy,' barked Miss Amoratti. 'Your mother works in the bank so you have lots of money to pay with,' she chuckled.

'Sien, Miss Amoratti,' said Sammy, answering in Troll as she had instructed.

'Ka insurlam, yes indeed,' said Miss Amoratti. 'No doubt you will talk only in Troll now that you have mastered its grotesque tongue.'

'It's not gross,' shouted out Jock. 'You don't know what you're talking about.'

Miss Amoratti frowned, deep lines appearing in her pointed face, and raised her staff, firing tiny black chards of charcoal-like material at them.

Sammy stood up straightaway. Simon Sanchez stood up next to him and together they blocked the pieces of black chards with a joint net of blue sparks using their sapphire gemstone.

Miss Amoratti looked totally taken aback as the net of blue sparks captured and extinguished the black chards.

'Well, at least you pay some attention in your other classes,' said Miss Amoratti quietly.

Sammy knew she was making mental notes about this and he was grateful when the bell outside classroom fourteen chimed loudly and the lesson ended.

CHAPTER 18

# THE ART OF LISTENING

Sammy folded up his staff and packed his rucksack at lightning speed. He ran from the Ancient and Modern Languages classroom, down the corridor and down the stone stairs.

He made a quick detour to the school canteen to collect some sandwiches, an apple and a bar of chocolate, then ran to the library.

Inside the entrance of the library, Mrs Skoob was sitting at one of the long wooden tables. It looked as though she was teaching a group of first years how to bind books.

Sammy didn't stop. He skilfully smuggled the food past Mrs Skoob and the first years and he sat, out of sight, on one of the padded chairs in the dusty History section.

Sammy took a bite out of the apple as quietly as he could and began his research on the Stone Cross and the art of projection and listening.

He had convinced himself, after Jock's teasing, that Dixie was still alive and he was sure, with a bit of research and practice, that he would be able to find her using the special listening technique he had heard about from Dixie's grandmother.

Sammy opened the first book he had borrowed. It was one Jock and Darius didn't know about but it had looked as though it would contain everything he needed to know about how to train your mind to listen for things that were extremely quiet or where the sound was initiated a long way away. The book was called "The Art of Listening" by E. Coute.

Sammy read slowly through the pages, searching for tips and wondering if he was wasting his time. It seemed that only he, Darius and Jock were convinced Dixie would return on her own. Everyone else seemed convinced she would be discovered in a ditch.

Sammy turned the page and looked at a series of diagrams with cartoon style drawings of people. They were showing the best positions to sit or stand, depending on whether you were listening for something that was nearby or hundreds of miles away.

Sammy copied one of the sitting down diagrams and pressed his right hand against his ear in a cup shape. He was going to make sure he'd tried everything he knew to try to bring Dixie back himself.

It seemed to be quite successful. Sammy found he could hear everything Mrs Skoob was saying to the first years. But they were only at the other end of the library.

Frustrated, Sammy closed "The Art of Listening". He scoured the History section bookshelves and picked out a handful of books that looked interesting. He unwrapped his sandwiches and took the first book off the pile. It was called "The Stone Cross" and had a pencil drawing of the familiar Celtic wheel cross on the cover.

About an hour later, Sammy was just finishing the last mouthful of his chocolate bar when Darius came into the library.

Darius slung himself into the seat next to Sammy and pulled his shirt collar almost down to his elbow. Sammy gasped. Darius had fresh teethmarks on his lower shoulder.

'We're doing other stuff,' said Darius, grinning wickedly at Sammy, but he would say no more.

'I've found three more books on the Stone Cross,' said Sammy, 'but only this one seems to have the right sort of stuff in it.'

'Let's have a look!' Darius snatched the book away. 'Wow! Look at the pictures!'

Sammy nodded. Even though the pictures were black and white pencil drawings, they were very detailed. Every line was hand drawn and it was very effective.

'It's the Stone Cross, as it was in King Serberon's reign. It says here it was the last time the Stone Cross was intact,' said Sammy, reading the lines below one of the pictures.

'It's never been intact,' scoffed Darius, scattering a handful of green foil-wrapped chocolates on the table to share. 'If it had been intact then the Shape wouldn't be trying to fill it with draconite.'

'It says in this book that the Stone Cross is an ancient monument to mark the place where the first dragon was born...' said Sammy.

'Yeah right,' interrupted Darius. 'If it was the "first dragon", how could it be born?'

'Maybe it means Karmandor?' suggested Sammy. 'He's supposed to be a powerful dragon.'

'I wonder when his bones will get here,' Darius giggled loudly, earning himself a furious "tut" from Mrs Skoob. 'He was supposed to be huge, like...this big,' Darius held his arms outstretched. 'Bigger than this whole library!'

Mrs Skoob scuttled over to the History section, her eyes blazing. 'Noise! You're making too much noise!' she squawked, her eyes bulging as she saw the apple core, sandwich papers and chocolate wrappers. 'Food in my library is not allowed! Out!' she hollered. 'Both of you! Get out now!'

'North Tower Fourth Year Boys' Room!' shouted Sammy. He grinned at Mrs Skoob, grabbing the books in one hand and Darius's shirt sleeve in the other.

'Walk!' Mrs Skoob screeched in Sammy's ear.

But it was too late as Sammy, Darius and the books about the Stone Cross vanished in a gold teleporting mist.

CHAPTER 19

# SAMMY'S VISIONS

Sammy and Darius sent Gavin flying as they appeared out of thin air in the fourth year North Tower boys' room.

'Oi!' yelled Gavin.

'Sorry,' said Sammy and Darius together and burst into hysterics at Gavin's indignant face.

'Can't you just walk in here like everyone else?' demanded Gavin. 'How did you get here Darius? You can't teleport without a dragon any more than I can.'

'Since when can you teleport with a dragon?' retorted Darius. 'Just last week, you said the best you could do was send coins from one side of the room to the other side.'

'Coins?' asked Sammy, thinking back to his practice with his sapphire, bringing things in and out of view.

'Just because you can do it already, some of us have to start somewhere,' snapped Gavin.

'I didn't mean it like that,' said Sammy.

Gavin shrugged and frowned at the pile of coins on his bed.

'If all the dragons are going to be dead then we've got to learn how to do things the old way,' said Gavin.

'With our staffs and gemstones?' asked Sammy.

'Older,' said Gavin, frowning harder. 'Without anything. No crystals. No staffs. Nothing. You know, the stuff you do sometimes Sammy.'

'The stuff I do sometimes...' started Sammy, putting the books he was carrying on to his bed.

He had a brief thought that Mrs Skoob wouldn't be pleased he and Darius hadn't checked the books out of the library. Then he remembered Professor Preverence, the teacher he had met in his first year who had tried to teach him skills without using his staff. Even Commander Altair frequently told him that things could be done using his mind alone.

Sammy waved his right hand at the pile of coins on Gavin's bed. He scrunched up his fingers into a tight fist and suddenly, he felt an electric pulse trigger inside him.

Slowly, Sammy released his fingers and pointed his hand at Toby's bed.

'Go!' Sammy whispered inside his head.

The boys stared as one by one the coins gathered together in a stack. They lifted off Gavin's duvet and arced like a rainbow and flew over to Toby's bed. Sammy gasped as the coins clattered into separate piles of shiny coins organised neatly by denomination.

'That's so cool,' said Darius, shaking his head in disbelief. 'How did you do that?'

Sammy shrugged, secretly pleased with the result. His fingers had stopped tingling the moment the coins landed on Toby's duvet.

'You're not supposed to see the coins move,' said Gavin. 'Try it again!'

Sammy waved his staff. The sapphire glowed and the coins vanished completely.

'Oi! Bring them back!' demanded Gavin. 'They're mine!'

Sammy clutched his staff. He focussed hard, seeing in his mind's eye, the invisible coins in transit. He dragged his staff across to Gavin's bed. The sapphire glowed even brighter and the coins reappeared in a wavering tower.

'Are you giving these coins to the Shape?' asked Sammy suddenly. 'Did you steal these coins from the first years? Are they what you've got for your stupid Passage Spotters gang?'

Gavin knocked over the coin tower and poked Sammy in the chest.

'What I do with my money is none of your business,' retorted Gavin.

'You're not giving them to the Shape,' said Sammy, raising his staff.

Gavin lunged, knocking Sammy off balance. 'It's not my choice,' said Gavin, his voice cracking. 'The dragons are going to die anyway. I'm just not going to be left behind with nothing.

Sammy took Darius's hand and got back on his feet. 'We can help you,' said Sammy. 'Tell us, who's making you do this?'

Gavin shook his head. 'You'll find out soon enough. She said if I told anyone then I'd die a Troll's death and that's never gonna happen.'

'What do you mean?' asked Sammy.

Gavin raised his staff and waved his sapphire, which was glowing bright blue at the tip. He marched out of the tower room.

'Don't come after me,' said Gavin, attempting to fling a half-hearted oilslick at the tower doorway behind him.

The oilslick bounced off and started sliding down the tower stairs after Gavin. Darius let out a giggle and Sammy shook his head in despair.

'Who do you reckon it is?' asked Darius. 'Could it be Miss Amoratti? She hates Trolls.'

'Dunno.' Sammy frowned and scratched his head. 'I guess whoever it is, Sir Ragnarok will probably find out about it. Come on, help me look at the Stone Cross.'

'Fine,' conceded Darius. 'Pass me that book. The one called "The Stone Cross" and I'll see if it's got anything interesting in it.'

Sammy handed Darius the book with the Celtic wheel cross on the cover. Darius opened it straight in the middle pages, which were yellow with age and crumbling slightly.

'We already know that the Stone Cross was put there by King Serberon,' said Darius.

'Hey,' interrupted Sammy, 'do you think maybe Karmandor was the first dragon?'

Darius frowned. 'Maybe. The first dragon had to come from somewhere.'

'The stars?' asked Sammy. 'Maybe Karmandor came from the stars?'

'Yeah, maybe,' said Darius, engrossed in the leather bound book. 'Hey! There's a bit here that says Karmandor was a female dragon!'

'No way!' Sammy snatched the dusty book from Darius and a couple of pages fell out. 'A female dragon!'

'That's what it says here,' said Darius, pointing to the words on the page. 'She must have been a really special dragon with all the wars that went on. Imagine having a dragon on your side. You'd be invincible.'

'It says it was enchanted magic,' added Sammy. 'That might be helpful in our Dragon Studies exams.'

Darius leaped up and punched the air. 'That's it!' shouted Darius. 'Karmandor is an enchanted Princess!'

'No way,' Sammy laughed. 'That's impossible!'

'Look!' insisted Darius, pointing at one of the pictures in the crumbling book. 'Look at that woman behind King Serberon and Helana Horidore, she's...'

'Just some peasant,' said Sammy. 'Look, there are dozens of peasants in the picture.'

'But look at the way King Serberon is looking at her,' said Darius. 'He loves her.'

'It's just the artist's impression,' scoffed Sammy. 'If it was a photograph I'd believe you.'

'His first true love,' said Darius dreamily. 'Maybe King Serberon transformed her into a dragon?'

'Yeah and then Helana Horidore lured her as a dragon into the forest?' asked Sammy, rolling his eyes.

Darius looked sideways at Sammy. 'You reckon?'

Sammy laughed, sifting through the coins Gavin had left on his bed. 'Who knows.'

'No, seriously,' said Darius. 'You're on to something there. We should ask Dr Shivers about it in our next Dragon Studies lesson.'

'Or we could ask Mrs Grock,' said Sammy. He was keen to avoid speaking to Dr Shivers at the moment.

'Oh yeah, I forgot, Dr Shivers puts you in these trances,' said Darius, goggling his eyes in a mock hypnotic stare. 'Sammy, you are getting sleepy. You will see the Stone Cross. Tell me, how much is there left to do?' said Darius, mimicking Dr Shivers's harsh gravelly tone of voice.

A shadowy figure swam in behind Sammy's eyes. 'Aaagh!' screeched Sammy. 'Stop it!'

'What?' demanded Darius, his voice sounded echoing and distant. 'Sammy? Are you ok?'

Sammy gasped. 'Dixie,' he whispered, passing out on the bed and sending the coins scattering.

'Sammy?'

Sammy sneezed, jerking his eyes wide open. He lurched forward, catching his nose in the makeshift fan Darius seemed to be using to rouse him. 'Aatchoo!'

'What's wrong with you?' asked Darius, looking unusually concerned. 'All I said was...'

'No,' gurgled Sammy. 'It's the voice. Dr Shivers. Inside my head. I saw Dixie. She's in an underground room. Stone walls. Chains. Dragons.'

Darius passed Sammy a glass of cool water. 'Slow down and drink this,' said Darius, holding his hand up against Sammy's forehead. 'You're burning up!'

'Thanks,' gasped Sammy, downing the water in one long gulp that blocked his airway and made him cough. 'Try doing it again!'

'No,' said Darius firmly.

'Do it again Darius, please...' begged Sammy. 'I have to see where Dixie is.'

'Are you sure?'

Sammy nodded, bracing himself.

Darius put on his Dr Shivers voice. 'You are getting sleepy...you will see the Stone Cross...this is stupid.'

'Go on,' encouraged Sammy, closing his eyes.

'Find the Valley of the Stone Cross...this isn't working...where the Shape are rebuilding...the cross...;

Sammy opened his eyes. 'You're right,' Sammy conceded. 'You can't force it. I'll try and draw you the room I saw in the vision.'

Darius reached for Sammy's hand. 'Hold my hand and project it into my mind instead.'

'Can't you just see it anyway?' asked Sammy.

'Not like you and Dixie,' said Darius. 'We need a physical bond, uh, connection, you know. I've read about it in Alchemistry, honest. You project your thoughts along the energy lines. Some people can do it over long distances but otherwise you need to have a physical contact to transfer thoughts, like holding my hand. Try it if you don't believe me!'

With some misgivings, reluctantly, Sammy held out his hands with his palms facing Darius. A lightning bolt seemed to fizz inside his head. The current ran down his body, electrocuting his hands in the same way he had experienced lifting the coins and transcribing lesson notes from textbooks to paper.

'Woah,' moaned Darius, clutching his head. 'That's some room they've got Dixie in. It's like a zoo. There must be a hundred dragons!'

Sammy felt pale and drawn but he didn't faint. 'You don't get dragons in a zoo,' he said, trying to laugh.

'You do in the Dragon World,' said Darius, grinning. 'Are you sure you're ok Sammy?'

Sammy nodded. 'I don't think I want to do that again in a hurry. Have you got any idea where it was?'

Darius shook his head. 'I've got no idea at all. It was somewhere really dark. Maybe it was underground?'

'At Dragamas?' asked Sammy.

'Further away.' Darius scratched his head. 'Maybe it was London? They have lots of dragons in London.'

'No!' said Sammy suddenly. 'She's got to be here! The Angel of 'El Horidore called all the dragons to Dragamas. So, if we saw dragons with Dixie in the underground room, she's got to be here too!'

'But we took dragons out of Dragamas when we went to the funeral,' said Darius.

'No we didn't, we just took them to the edge of the circle around the school,' said Sammy, pointing to one of the maps in the cover of the book. 'The Church of a Thousand Graves is where King Serberon and Helana Horidore got married.'

'In the grounds of Dragamas Castle?' asked Darius, disbelievingly.

'It makes sense!' said Sammy enthusiastically. 'That's how we could fly to the church. I wondered that when we got back. If the Angel of 'El Horidore is pulling all the dragons to Dragamas then…'

'…it makes sense that we couldn't go far outside the school grounds,' finished Darius, his eyes shining.

'It says the Church of a Thousand Graves was formerly called the Church of a Thousand Groves, orange groves from when the church and the castle were at the centre of the land,' said Sammy.

Darius whistled. 'That church must be ancient.'

'It was built in the Dark Ages,' said Sammy. 'It explains the ghosts in the windows.'

'Ooh,' whispered Darius. 'Commander Altair said those ghosts were King Serberon's Dragon Knights. He said they were preserved in time.'

'He said they were protecting something,' said Sammy, thinking things through.

'Like the Stone Cross!' shouted Sammy and Darius at the same time.

'They're the Knights of the Stone Cross,' said Darius. 'They'll come back to life when the Stone Cross is complete.'

'Or to stop it from being completed,' whispered Sammy. 'Maybe they'll protect our dragons.'

Darius laughed. 'I think we have to do that ourselves.'

'We could try to wake them!' said Sammy.

Darius let out an explosive giggle. 'And just how do you expect to do that?'

Sammy picked up his staff and touched the onyx, ruby, amber and sapphire at the end. The stones vibrated a little and gave Sammy an idea. 'Maybe if we went back to the church,' he suggested. 'Maybe we could wake up the Dragon Knights and they could help us fight the Shape and protect our dragons.'

'You want to go back to the church?' asked Darius.

'Yeah,' said Sammy, a little recklessly, the idea sounding much more dangerous when it was spoken out loud.

'Sure,' said Darius, without any hesitation. 'How about tomorrow after Dragonball. Then we'll already have Nelson and Kyrillan out of the Dragon Chambers so we won't need to ask Captain Stronghammer or Captain Firebreath for permission to take the dragons.'

'It's my fourteenth birthday tomorrow,' said Sammy, a shiver running up his spine. 'Are you sure?'

Darius stood up, holding his staff above his head. 'Are you scared?'

Sammy matched his stance, his gemstone crystals shining and casting rainbows around the room. 'No.'

'Then it's sorted. I'm a Dragon Minder so I'll put all the dragons except ours into the Dragon Chambers with Naomi after we've finished playing Dragonball,' said Darius, 'and then we'll all go.'

'You can't bring Naomi!' exclaimed Sammy.

'She'll think it's suspicious,' said Darius. 'She might tell Dr Shivers and then none of us will be able to go.'

Sammy shook his head in defeat. He was sure that Darius had other reasons for inviting Naomi.

'Fine, tomorrow night, the three of us will go to the Church of a Thousand Graves,' said Sammy, shielding his eyes against the sun and looking up at the tiny building on the horizon.

He took a step back as Jock teleported himself into the tower room.

'You going somewhere?' asked Jock, picking up a book from his bedside table.

'No,' said Sammy, at the same time as Darius said 'like we'd tell you!'

Jock raised his hands in surrender. 'Fine! I've got bigger things going on anyway. See you later.' Jock shimmered and vanished in a grey teleporting mist.

'Weird,' muttered Darius, scooping up his Alchemistry textbook entitled "Foolsgold" by "Ron Pirate". 'Have you read this rubbish? I can't believe we're supposed to be able to turn some base metal into gold by the time we leave here. What use is that when all I want to do is heal dragons?'

'We'd best get talking to these ghosts tomorrow,' Sammy muttered grimly. 'Otherwise there won't be any dragons left to heal.'

CHAPTER 20

# SHADOWS IN THE WINDOWS

After an exhausting Dragonball match, Sammy was almost too tired to dismount, let alone think about flying to the Church of a Thousand Graves.

During the match, Jock had annoyingly placed himself between Sammy and Darius, trying to listen to their plans at every opportunity.

'Come on,' teased Jock. 'Let me and Kiridor come with you. I know where you're going.'

'No you don't,' snapped Darius, with bad timing as at that exact moment Naomi flew down to meet them.

'Are you ready?' asked Naomi. 'Shall we go?'

'Just need to sort something out first,' said Darius, pointing behind his back at Jock.

Naomi grinned and nodded. 'Will you help me put the dragons to bed tonight Jock? You're always on about helping and how much you wish you were a Dragon Minder this year.'

'I…well…Darius is a Dragon Minder…why doesn't he want to do it…oh, ok,' Jock gave in.

Sammy grinned. He knew Jock was torn between following him and Darius and being allowed to help in the Dragon Chambers.

'I'll report this to Dr Shivers,' warned Jock, shaking his fist as Sammy and Darius launched into the air on their dragons' backs and soared high above him.

A few minutes later, Naomi caught up with Sammy and Darius. She was flying furiously on Quentina, her royal purple and green speckled dragon.

'Slow down!' shrieked Naomi. 'Wait for me!'

'That was quick,' said Sammy, grinning as he heard Darius project that he'd missed Naomi and her mushy reply saying she'd flown as fast as possible to be with him.

Under the cover of dusk, they flew beyond the school gates, across the fields. The Church of a Thousand Graves loomed in the distance, growing larger as they drew nearer.

Landing in the graveyard wasn't as easy in the darkness as it had been in the early morning sunrise. Dusk breathed a dark mist around them. One by one, Sammy, Darius and Naomi landed their dragons near the church doorway.

Sammy jumped down off Kyrillan's back and lit a small fire. Using his mind, he held the fire close to the end of his staff while he tethered Kyrillan, using his harness reins, to a small iron ring in the wall.

'Are we really going in?' asked Naomi, dismounting from Quentina and securing her dragon to an iron ring next to Kyrillan.

'Yeah,' said Darius. 'But there's nothing to worry about,' he added, dismounting from his seat on Nelson's scaly back. 'I'll look after you.'

Sammy grinned. Naomi was super-tough. It was more likely to be her looking after Darius than the other way around.

'Oi Sammy Rambles!' giggled Naomi, tapping her left ear. 'I heard you thinking that!'

Naomi marched on ahead and pulled at the church door. It opened straightaway.

'It's not locked!' Naomi cried out in surprise.

'They were expecting us,' whispered Sammy.

Darius laughed. 'It's not locked because there's nothing worth nicking, except maybe a few chairs.'

'Shh,' hissed Naomi. 'Have some respect.'

'Darius doesn't believe in…' started Sammy.

'Shh.'

'What?' demanded Sammy.

'Can't you hear it?' asked Naomi.

Sammy stopped in his tracks and the crunching noise of him walking on the white pebbled path stopped as well.

The wind faintly rustled amongst the remains of the autumn leaves in the cherry trees but otherwise everything was silent.

Darius paused from tethering Nelson to one of the iron rings and looked expectantly at Naomi.

'What?' asked Darius. 'What can you hear?'

'Crying,' said Naomi. 'Can you honestly not hear it?'

Sammy shook his head.

'It's female,' said Naomi, cocking her head through the doorway and into the church. 'Definitely female crying.'

Sammy glanced at the floor. As he had expected there was an iron grill that Naomi had crossed. In the darkness he thought her voice sounded strange and distorted.

Now he knew she was standing half-in, half-out of the grill's protection. Sammy gently pushed Naomi forwards into the Church of a Thousand Graves and stepped in after her, taking his staff and the small fire into the church.

'Hey! Where did you go? Who turned out the light?' shouted Darius.

Naomi clicked her tongue. She reached out, grabbed Darius's arm and pulled him through the doorway.

'Cattlegrid,' whispered Sammy, holding the fire above his head so the light spread further into the dark room.

'Oh,' whispered Darius.

'Are those the windows where you saw the people?' asked Naomi.

Sammy nodded, staring up at the hollow grey shadows in the long grey walls. Even the oak beams and arches supporting the roof seemed grey. Everything looked grey.

Between the small light of the flames from his fire and the pale moonlight, the church was a deathly dark place. It was pitch black in some of the far corners. Very spooky. For a moment, Sammy wondered why they had come.

As his eyes grew used to the firelight, Sammy noticed there were tiny flickers of light coming from the direction of the altar at the front of the church. He stepped slowly towards them, sending part of his fire ahead of him to light the way.

Darius and Naomi tiptoed behind him and when they reached the altar, they found four coloured candles were lit. There was a red candle, a blue candle, a yellow candle and a green candle.

Sammy jumped as both his fire and three of the candles went out in a sudden gust of wind. Only the green candle was left still burning. He noticed the green candle's flame was also tinged with murky green.

'Green fire,' whispered Sammy.

'Are you ok?' whispered Darius. 'I don't think the Knights are here tonight.'

'To knight,' giggled Naomi. 'There are eight windows and not even one knight, apart from the night that's outside.'

Darius laughed and put his arm around Naomi's shoulders. 'Come on Sammy. There's nothing here. Let's go.'

Sammy held up his hand. 'Let's wait Darius. It took a few minutes to see them before.'

'We have come to see the sleeping Dragon Knights,' said Darius, putting on an impression of Professor Sanchez, merging with Miss Amoratti, Dr Shivers and Professor Burlay. 'We want to see Trolls. What are you doing Samuel? There are strange things in the stars tonight!'

'Stop!' hissed Sammy. He peered into the darkness beyond Darius, his heart wedged in his throat. All of the windows were glowing silver.

'Woah,' said Darius. 'Look at that!'

Naomi screamed. She turned and ran up the central aisle and out of the church as if the wind was carrying her.

'Girls! She's such a scaredy-cat...' snorted Darius, his voice dying out as suddenly there was a lot of strange noise coming from the windows.

Voices started saying things in their ears but Sammy didn't immediately recognise the words. Darius clung like a limpet to Sammy's right shoulder.

'They're calling you,' whispered Darius.

Sammy nodded. He could hear them.

'Sammy, Sammy, Sammy Rambles,' said the voices and there were shadows forming slowly into the shapes of people at the silver glowing windows.

Sammy switched to hold his staff in his left hand and picked up the green candle.

'I am Sammy Rambles,' said Sammy, using the bravest voice he could muster.

'Sammy, Sammy, Sammy,' said the voices, that were now belonging to ghostly figures wearing suits of armour.

Darius clung harder, his fingers gripping so hard they almost pierced Sammy's skin. His terrified eyes were almost luminescent in the green light of the candle.

'We have waited for you to return to the Church of a Thousand Graves,' said the voices in unison. 'You will bring her back.'

Sammy nodded, glad they had finally spoken in a language he could understand.

There was a sudden burst of red and blue light and Sammy froze. Coldness seeped through his clothes and it felt like ice was pouring into his skin.

He could move slowly, but there was now a red halo around the church door, which was covered in an oilslick. Neither he, nor Darius, were going anywhere in the near future.

'Dixie's already coming back,' Sammy whispered to Darius. 'Jock said so.'

Darius nodded, his jaw wide open, his eyes glistening. 'She's coming back,' he whispered. 'But I don't think they mean Dixie.'

One of the shadowy figures in the window closest to Sammy and Darius glowed more brightly than the others. It looked like it was a huge man dressed in silver armour.

'Karmandor, my Princess Karmandor,' said the huge man in the window. 'My beautiful daughter. You said you would find her Sammy Rambles. We willed you to return here and here you are. You will bring her back.'

Sammy gripped Darius's sleeve as the grey shadow man floated down from the window. It took everything he had to stop himself from screaming and running out of the door like Naomi. The ghost was an enormous Troll.

CHAPTER 21

# THE KINGS OF THE DARK AGES

The ghostly Troll stopped a few feet away from Sammy and Darius, a sad frown was etched on his huge face.

'I have frightened you,' he said in a gentle voice. 'Allow me to introduce myself. I am King Segragore of the North. I am the Supreme General of the Snorgcadell and, of course, I am Princess Karmandor's father.'

Sammy's jaw dropped lower than Darius's jaw as he stared at the huge grey Troll man with his large hooked nose, thick jaw, kind green eyes, thick treetrunk body and gigantic hands. He looked very old and he had a long grey warrior beard stretching halfway down his silver battle armour breastplate. A band of gold and jewels was resting on his head of shoulder length grey hair. He seemed sad, as though he was carrying some hidden burden.

'Karmandor's father,' whispered Darius, his teeth chattering loudly. 'Karmandor the dragon's father.'

King Segragore looked at Darius and frowned. 'Who are you boy?' he demanded.

'I'm Darius,' whispered Darius, his knees knocking together and his voice quavering.

King Segragore nodded. 'We have waited so long for this day. We will put wrongs to right.'

Sammy felt his heart lurch. 'Put wrongs to right. That was my wish,' he whispered.

'And the wish of every Dragon Commander who has gone before you,' said King Segragore smiling and pointing his wispy hand towards the other windows.

Sammy looked at the windows and gasped. Where there had just been a silver glow, there were now hundreds of faces peering into the dark church. It felt like they were watching him and waiting for something to happen.

'We will succeed,' said King Segragore. 'I see the green candle is still lit. You have chosen Earth.'

Sammy looked at the green candle in his right hand. 'Green is North where we come from. At Dragamas. Darius and me, we're in the North house.'

King Segragore laughed, a deep rich laugh that filled the church. 'North is it now. In my day, they were called by their true names of Earth, Air, Fire and Water. It is also a clue Sammy Rambles. In the earth is where you will find your friend. She is underground, below this very building. I will help you find her. Then you will help me find my Karmandor.'

'Sir Segragore,' Sammy started hesitantly.

'King Segragore,' corrected King Segragore, adjusting the band of jewels on his head.

'Uh, King Segragore,' said Sammy, looking down at his feet. 'We don't know where Karmandor is,' he paused and took a deep breath, 'but we do need to find Dixie. I promised her Mum we would find her.'

'And the whole congregation of Trolls who were here as well. Alas, that would have been a fine day for my Troll

162

Princess to marry King Serberon in this very church,' King Segragore sniffed loudly, as though he was close to tears and trying not to show it. 'But, it was not meant to be.'

'He was going to marry her?' asked Darius in surprise.

King Segragore narrowed his brow. 'We are used to your prejudices. She was a Troll, a fine young woman and rightful heir to all of Samagard's lands.'

The shadows in the windows nodded their agreement, whispering faintly amongst themselves.

'Old Samagard,' whispered Darius.

'What happened?' asked Sammy, feeling completely in awe of King Segragore.

The Troll King sighed. 'To my Karmandor, it wasn't just an arranged marriage to join our lands. It was a marriage for love. She loved Serberon and he worshipped her. He asked for Karmandor's hand without mentioning land,' said King Segragore proudly. 'Then "she" came along and spoiled things,' he added bitterly.

'How?' asked Sammy. He was growing less and less afraid of the Troll King in front of him every second.

'I would like to leave "that" buried in the past,' said King Segragore, sniffing loudly as though Sammy's question had unsettled him. 'It was a dark day in the Dark Ages. She wove an enchantment to turn Karmandor's skin into scales. She made her arms wings and her hands claws. She turned my daughter, my only child, into a dragon.'

'A dragon?' gasped Sammy.

King Segragore nodded. 'King Serberon kept my daughter in her dragon form at the castle and they flew everywhere together until "she" appeared. Even as a dragon Karmandor's scales were beautiful. They were pure gold, just like the golden sun. That's when King Serberon created the motto, which I'm sure you know well.'

'Validus Aureus Draco,' said Sammy, nodding. 'It means Mighty is the Golden Dragon. Who was "she"? Who turned Karmandor into a dragon?'

King Segragore spat on the floor. 'She was called Helana. We called her "hell" and hell she was.'

'Helana Horidore?' asked Sammy. 'King Serberon's wife? The woman he made the Angel whistle for?'

'She is pure evil,' said King Segragore. 'She is a witch woman. She kidnapped my dragon daughter, sabotaged our plans of a united kingdom and...' King Segragore broke down, '...and she made my daughter a common tool for her bidding between the worlds.'

'Why would she do that?' asked Darius. 'It doesn't make sense.'

'A puritan,' spat King Segragore. 'She wanted men and Trolls kept apart. She slowly made the people turn against Karmandor, then she changed my daughter from a Troll to a dragon while Karmandor was about to bear the heirs of our future kingdom.'

'King Serberon created the Stone Cross to mark where it happened,' said Darius. 'We've read about that.'

'And even the Angel wouldn't work. It was a gift to Helana Horidore for her wedding,' spat King Segragore. 'But she never blew the whistle so the dragons never came.'

'You created the Angel of 'El Horidore hoping Helana Horidore would use it and it would call Karmandor out of where she was hidden?' asked Sammy. Pieces of the jigsaw were coming together and it was all starting to make sense.

'In the Forgotten Forest,' said King Segragore. 'Helana Horidore put Karmandor in there. In my time, no one ever walked out of the forest alive.'

'The Shape blew the Angel,' interrupted Darius. 'So Karmandor will have to come out, won't she?'

'It was a long, long time ago,' said King Segragore sadly. 'Perhaps the sound of the Angel will take longer to penetrate, especially if she is deep in the forest. We have seen many dragons overhead recently, but no gold dragons. Nor blue-green dragons.' King Segragore smiled. 'That was the colour of Karmandor's children, they were all going to be blue-green dragons. I've been told it is sometimes called "draconite blue". Do you boys know about draconite?'

Darius nodded and gave a text book answer. 'Draconite is the magic stone inside a dragon's brain which gives a dragon special powers.'

King Segragore nodded. 'Kyrillan, Kiridor and Kelsepe. That's what King Serberon told me my grandchildren would have been called.'

'Oooh,' said Darius, sending a chill down Sammy's neck.

'My dragon is blue-green,' said Sammy. 'He's called Kyrillan.'

'Oho!' said King Segragore, his green eyes wide. 'Is he here?'

'Yes,' said Sammy warily. 'He's outside.'

'Then you must show me,' said King Segragore firmly. 'Show me your dragon. I want to see him.'

Sammy nodded. He put the green candle back on the altar and led the way to the church door. He was a little unnerved as more of the shadowy Dragon Knight ghosts flew down from the windows and followed at a short distance behind King Segragore.

Outside, Kyrillan, Nelson and Quentina were playing a game of puffing grey smoke rings, like quoits, over the headstones. Naomi was guiding the rings away from the graves with her staff.

'I heard everything,' said Naomi, collapsing against Darius's shoulder. 'Kyrillan is a direct relation of poor Princess Karmandor.'

King Segragore peered at Kyrillan, gliding around the dragons and inspecting them. Kyrillan obligingly blew two more smoke rings. One smoke ring wafted over to one of the grey ghostly shadow men and he coughed as it swept through his ghostly body and out of the other side.

'Kyrillan means strong and wise,' said King Segragore thoughtfully. 'Tell me dragon, has your master treated you well? He will free you soon.'

Sammy felt a knot twist in his stomach. As much as he wanted Karmandor's sons and daughter to be free, he didn't want to lose his dragon. How many fourteen-year-old boys were there in the country who had a dragon for a pet?

'He'll always be in that form,' muttered King Segragore. 'It was done with two-layer magic, "she" saw to that, however, with my Karmandor, if she was here…we found the cure soon after she was lost in the forest. It nearly killed you, didn't it Serberon. To have the cure in our hands but to have lost Karmandor in the Forgotten Forest.'

Sammy spun around. A tall human ghost, dressed in shining silver armour and wearing a similar band of jewels on his head stood imposingly next to King Segragore.

Sammy felt almost compelled to drop to one knee but he stood up straight and lowered his eyes.

'We are indebted to you Sammy Rambles,' said the man and Sammy realised he was the shadow man who had just been entangled with Kyrillan's smoke ring.

'I am King Serberon of the South,' said the man. 'I am son of King Samagard the Shape Shifter, grandson of King Lariston the Lenient.'

'Sir Ragnarok's cat!' said Sammy and Darius together.

'Indeed,' said King Serberon, frowning. 'It was his idea of a misadventure gone wrong, I believe. Does he still have a liking for mince pies?'

Sammy nodded. It was surreal standing in the graveyard in the dead of night with these huge figureheads of times gone by.

'We promised you that we would help you find your friend and we will deliver on our promise. But you in turn have your debt to fulfil,' said King Serberon sternly. 'You will ensure that when my bride, King Segragore's daughter, our Karmandor, when she awakens, you will bring her here so we can undo what has been done. Then she can become Queen Karmandor like I wanted so many years ago.'

Sammy nodded. 'I promise.'

'We promise too,' said Darius and Naomi nodded her agreement of the King's request.

'We will find her for you,' said Sammy.

'Thank you.' King Serberon smiled. 'I have been very foolish throwing away my happiness and the peoples' best interest by listening to a witch woman, but I hope there will be a chance to put things right again.'

'Your friend is this way,' said King Segragore and the ghostly king led the way back into the church, up the darkened aisle to the altar and he lifted up the lid.

Remembering the last time he had looked into the altar, Sammy grimaced, using as little of his eyes as possible to look inside, hoping Dixie's father was no longer in there.

'It's empty,' King Segragore reassured him.

Sammy squinted into the altar. To his relief, instead of Jacob Deane's grey-green Troll body, a striped shadowy floor lay at the bottom of the altar.

'Get in,' commanded King Serberon.

# CHAPTER 22

# DIXIE'S DUNGEON DRAGONS

Sammy exchanged looks with Darius and Naomi. He suddenly felt nervous. There was a long pause. Eventually Sammy took the plunge and volunteered.

'I'll go in,' said Sammy. 'If I'm not back soon, or if I shout for help, come in after me.'

Darius nodded and linked hands with Naomi. Sammy stepped up onto a conveniently placed ledge at the side of the altar. Up close, he could see the altar was ornately decorated with white marble statues of ever-watching angels. They were all exquisitely carved with stern faces and they were holding various weapons.

Some of the angels were carrying sharp swords and crested shields. Others held long bows and had sheaths of arrows over their shoulders. It was as if they were guarding the hidden entrance.

Sammy stepped gingerly onto the ledge and found he could see black and white striped marble steps inside the altar. He gripped the edge of the altar wall and prepared to lower himself into oblivion.

King Serberon laughed. 'It is an illusion Sammy. Surely you've seen these before?'

Darius peered into the altar. 'It looks solid to me.'

Sammy nodded. 'What's down there?'

'We'll show you,' said King Segragore, elevating himself effortlessly into the altar. 'Your friend has seen much in her time here and you have certainly put some pieces of history together for us tonight.'

King Serberon followed King Segragore. The ghostly kings floated their way down a finely cut set of steep rectangular steps.

'Watch your head,' advised King Segragore, then he stuck his own head inside the rocky wall. 'Ha ha!'

'Be on your guard, friend,' said King Serberon. 'I fear this night's magic is far from over.'

'Magic?' asked Sammy, twisting around to look at King Serberon.

'Yes Sammy Rambles,' said King Serberon. 'More than fate or destiny has brought you here tonight.'

Sammy shivered, hardly taking comfort in the thought that he was stepping down into who knew where, with who knew who. The bodies of the two warrior kings could simply dissolve at any time of trouble but he could be stepping into unknown danger.

After fourteen steps, Sammy reached the bottom. He reached for his staff, ready to defend himself.

'She is within this room,' said King Serberon. 'Use your light sparingly, for all is not as you may expect.'

Sammy nodded. He felt nervous but raised his staff and cautiously lit a small fire, which he controlled and moved it around the room to see what he was dealing with.

The chamber under the altar seemed to extend the entire width and length of the church. There were dozens and dozens of brown sacks filled with grain and he could see the faint eyes of a dragon and the gleam of scales glowing beyond them.

Sammy made the fire a little brighter and he saw a giant orange and yellow dragon, fast asleep and snoring, with its tail tightly coiled around some of the sacks of grain. One step forward and he would have walked into the dragon and disturbed it from its slumber.

In the far corner, he saw a huddled shape he had first dismissed as another sack of grain, but in the brighter light, he could see more clearly.

'Dixie?' Sammy whispered as loudly as he dared.

The shape stirred and there was a clanking of chains.

'Who's there?' came a quiet, suspicious whisper. 'You'll wake them up.'

'It's me, Sammy,' said Sammy, projecting the words without making any sound. 'I've come to rescue you.'

The chains clanked again and Sammy could see that the huddled shape was in fact Dixie, if not a little thinner and paler than he remembered.

'Are you ok?' asked Sammy, feeling stupid as the words left his mouth. She had been kidnapped by the Shape for months. Of course she wasn't ok.

Dixie rattled the chains, projecting to him that she could only move to the sacks of grain. She shuffled over and Sammy gasped at her bruised face and her arms cut and coated with dried black blood.

'What happened?' whispered Sammy.

'It was Alfie,' Dixie whispered back. 'I got him too. Is that Darius with you?'

Sammy looked behind him. King Serberon and King Segragore were there but they had stopped looking ashen and grey. King Serberon had pale pink and fleshy skin under his silver armour and King Serberon had thick green skin under his silver armour. Sammy jumped. They looked very real.

'Down here, we are almost real,' explained King Serberon. 'Miss, allow me to introduce ourselves. I am King Serberon of the Dark Ages. I am King of the South.'

'And I am King Segragore of the North,' said King Segragore. 'I am Karmandor's father.'

'Hullo,' said Dixie, rubbing a cut on her forehead. 'Have you come to see the Stone Cross?'

'Is it here?' asked Sammy. 'Never mind that for now, we have come to rescue you.'

'Hah!' snorted Dixie. 'Look! I'm needed here.'

'What?' exclaimed Sammy. He checked his watch. It was nearly midnight and when he changed the setting, he was only one of two green dots on the Directometer. Apparently it wouldn't show the ghosts and Darius and Naomi were too far away.

'Look around,' said Dixie, swinging her arms as far as the chains would allow. 'Dragonlings. Five of them. They were born yesterday and they need me. Besides, you can't cut the chains,' she held up her wrists which were bound in black iron chains which extended to solid loops in the wall.

'What about Kiridor?' demanded Sammy. 'He needs you too!'

'Jock's got him now,' said Dixie, her mouth twisting into a grimace. 'That's what he told me.'

'Has Jock been here?' asked Sammy.

Dixie shook her head. 'He's supposed to have passed on my messages. I've been talking to him using the art of listening. I used all these dragons to make the signal stronger.'

'I tried listening as well,' said Sammy. 'I was here as well but I never realised you were underneath the Church of a Thousand Graves all along.'

'You were here?' asked Dixie, looking at him keenly with her bright green eyes.

'Uh, yeah, I was here,' said Sammy.

Dixie frowned. 'Why?'

'Dixie, no,' said Sammy, not wanting to say the reason out loud.

'Were you at the funeral?' asked Dixie. 'I know my Daddy's dead.'

There was an awkward silence and Dixie faked a cough to hide the green tears falling down her cheeks.

'He came down here in his coffin. Then the dragons burnt him to ashes,' choked Dixie, pointing at the wall opposite them.

Sammy followed her outstretched hand. There was a powdery pile of black soot. It looked as though many bodies had been burnt over the years.

'He burns dragons as well,' said Dixie coldly. 'I've been protecting Wild-Eye, the orange and yellow dragon. She's the one who had the dragon pups I'm looking after.'

'Do you mean Alfie Grock?' asked Sammy. 'I mean Alfie Agrock, that's his real name. Grock was just his Dwarf name.'

'Agrock,' said Dixie thoughtfully. 'That fits with your theory. He would be the "A" in the Shape. So we've had Eliza Elungwen, Peter Pickering, Alfie Agrock and he knows Jock's Mum.'

'Helana Hubar,' finished Sammy. 'She must be the "H" in Shape.'

'So that's why Jock didn't pass on my messages,' said Dixie, stamping her foot in anger. 'You were never supposed to find me. His Mum's in the Shape. You can't tell Jock. He'll be devastated.'

'Fine,' said Sammy, taking one of Dixie's hands and finding it cold and slimy.

'Dragon gunk,' apologised Dixie, releasing her hand and wiping it on her jeans. 'Alfie Agrock wants to lay the last piece of draconite in the Stone Cross. That's why he's kept these dragons here, so he can have the last dragon and take the last piece of draconite...oh no! Shhh!'

'What?' whispered Sammy.

'He's coming back. You have to go.' Dixie shook her head at Sammy. 'You can't help me tonight. You have to go. I can take care of myself. I'll see you soon. I promise.'

From behind the pile of soot there was the creaking sound of a hidden door opening. Sammy looked around. King Serberon and King Segragore had stepped back out of the light and were dull grey shadows again. They floated in front of Sammy, watching and waiting.

'I'll come back for you,' Sammy projected at Dixie without making a sound.

Dixie smiled, holding her staff firmly her hands. 'Bye Sammy,' she projected back at him.

Sammy paused trying to catch a glimpse of the man coming through the underground doorway.

'I see you've had visitors,' a deep voice barked in the darkness.

Sammy recognised the deep, sinister voice straightaway. It belonged to Alfie Agrock, Mrs Grock's former husband, the Dwarf, the Dragon Knight, the killer of Dixie's father and the man they had identified as the "A" in the Shape.

'You'll pay for that,' shouted Alfie Agrock.

The chains rattled and Dixie screamed. Sammy lurched forward to help her but he didn't dare run through the ghostly body of King Serberon who was blocking his way.

'We will protect her,' said King Serberon.

King Segragore nodded. 'Woooh!' he laughed and floated into the underground room, his body returning to flesh inside the chamber.

'What the!' squawked Alfie Agrock. 'Get away! Get away from me!'

Sammy relaxed. King Segragore of the Dark Ages had this in hand. He darted back up the steps, taking a quick backwards glance at the doorway where Alfie Agrock had entered the chamber.

The doorway opened out into a green valley dotted with houses and there was a gleaming Celtic stone cross on the horizon.

'The Dark Ages, the past, it's all underground, buried very deeply but it surfaces from time to time, when it is called upon,' said King Serberon, following Sammy up the stone steps. 'My Knights and their families, we live down here in our human form and turn to ghosts when we venture above ground,' he gazed at his silvery grey arm. 'It's an interesting state to be in, but we can see the beginning and the end.'

'What must I do?' asked Sammy. 'How will it end?'

King Serberon looked sternly at Sammy, his grey sword drawn, implying that death held the answer. 'Do you really want to know?'

Sammy paused. Darius and Naomi were above him at the top of the steps. He could see them, but, they were locked in a deep embrace and couldn't see him.

'No Sir,' said Sammy. 'I have things to do here. I have to save Dixie,' he added quietly.

King Serberon nodded and sheathed his sword. 'You'll make a fine Dragon Knight one day, and your girlfriend too. She has a natural touch, a kind hand and a strong will. With our help, she will return to you.'

'Is she...' Sammy faltered, the words too difficult to say.

'She is alive of course,' said King Serberon brightly. 'Although I wouldn't like to see her in that dungeon indefinitely. Isolation does funny things to you, if you're not careful.'

Sammy nodded and climbed up the last step. He swung himself out of the altar, closing the lid tightly shut behind him.

'Hi Sammy!' Darius leaned over Naomi's shoulder. 'We were just wondering when you'd be back.'

'Well here I am,' said Sammy, angry that they didn't seem to have missed him at all.

'Can we go now?' asked Naomi, showing off the everlasting kiss on her shoulder Darius had just given her. 'I want to get back to Dragamas.'

Sammy nodded, hardly trusting himself to speak. He watched as King Segragore floated up through the lid of the altar and then the two ghostly kings of the Dark Ages accompanied him, Darius and Naomi out of the church and into the graveyard.

It wasn't until they said goodbye to King Serberon and King Segragore and they were untying their dragons from the iron rings that Naomi stopped and looked at Sammy.

'Well, did you find her?' asked Naomi as she climbed onto Quentina's back.

'Yeah,' said Sammy coldly and said no more until they got back to Dragamas.

When they landed in the castle courtyard outside the Dragon Chambers, Sammy slid down Kyrillan's scaly side and teleported up to the tower room, where he sat, red eyed from crying, until Darius walked in through the open tower door.

'I put Kyrillan away for you,' said Darius, whipping open the green velvet dividing curtain. 'Are you ok? You know, downstairs, I, uh…sorry we didn't ask about Dixie first.'

Sammy stood up. 'It's ok. It's just...down there, she's been hurt and she's chained up. We have to go back there and get her out.'

'You really like her, don't you,' said Darius, smiling. 'She cares about you as well. That's more than I'll ever have with Naomi.'

Sammy looked at Darius in surprise. 'But you're really close. You'll probably get married one day.'

'It's for the cameras,' grinned Darius. 'It shuts Gavin up, doesn't it? Naomi and me, we've got an arrangement.'

'A what?' asked Sammy.

'An arrangement,' repeated Darius. 'She likes it to look like she's got a boyfriend, that's all. I know that. As soon as the summer comes, she'll break up with me and go her own way. She fancies someone back home.' Darius shrugged. 'Dixie's perfect for you.'

Sammy laughed. 'I don't see her like that. She's just been there for me a bit.'

'A lot!' giggled Darius. 'The Shape would have got you ages ago.'

'Oh yeah?' asked Sammy.

'Yeah,' said Darius. 'Hey, do you reckon Jock did get Dixie's messages and his Mum's involved in the Shape?'

Sammy poked his head around the adjacent dividing curtain to check that Jock was asleep.

'Mrs Hubar is getting all the draconite,' whispered Sammy. 'There's nothing to stop her or Jock taking the draconite to the Church of a Thousand Graves, down the steps under the altar and through that door to the Valley of the Stone Cross.'

'Nothing at all,' said Darius, yawning widely. 'We'll sort it out tomorrow.'

## CHAPTER 23

# YOU CANNOT ALWAYS BE RIGHT

Sammy woke with butterflies in his stomach. Somehow, accusing Gemology teacher, Mrs Hubar, Jock's Mum, who was also Sir Ragnarok's friend, seemed less appealing and more daunting than even visiting the Church of a Thousand Graves the night before.

Darius poked his head around the green velvet dividing curtain.

'Go and see Sir Ragnarok at breakfast,' said Darius. 'There should be time after breakfast and before our first lesson.'

'Are you trying out for the Dragonball team?' asked Toby, sticking his head around Sammy's other dividing curtain. 'Mr Cross wanted our names yesterday. I put you both down. Hope that's ok. Gavin isn't bothering. He says there's no point, if, you know...all the dragons are dead.'

Sammy nodded. 'We'll be ok. As long as our dragons are still alive.'

'Unless Mrs Hubar gets them,' said Darius darkly.

'What's your problem with my Mum?' demanded Jock, appearing behind Toby and ripping open the curtain.

Sammy ducked as Jock launched a pale cloud of red mist. He grabbed his uniform and sprinted down to the bathroom, unconsciously jumping down the stairs two at a time. He washed quickly, borrowing some funny smelling shower gel someone had left behind, dried off and got dressed at record speed.

Sammy straightened his tie in front of the mirror, checking himself against his reflection. He noticed someone had written "Validus Aureus Dragon" in pencil above the mirror.

'Validus Aureus Draco,' Sammy muttered to himself, scrunching the water out of his flannel. 'Mighty is the Golden Dragon. Karmandor is the golden dragon. She's related to Lariston, Sir Ragnarok's cat...Sir Ragnarok. I'll see him at breakfast,' said Sammy, packing up his wash things and psyching himself up for the hard conversation.

Downstairs, the Main Hall was filling up with North, South, East and West students. Everyone was sitting at the tables, chatting with friends and waiting to be allowed to eat. The Dragamas twin-tailed "D" crest shone down from the ceiling.

Sir Ragnarok sat in his chair in the centre of the teachers' table. He was frowning and looking at Professor Burlay and Commander Altair, who were next to him. Sammy noticed they were all looking at a large crystal globe with stars floating around its surface.

'Good morning students of Dragamas,' said Sir Ragnarok and everyone stood up promptly. 'I would like to draw your attention to the number of stars each house has achieved and to congratulate the East house for winning five hundred stars for reviving a dragon that we believed had been killed by the Shape.'

Sir Ragnarok pointed at the four noticeboards which collected the house stars. He waved his hand and gave the signal that the students were allowed to choose exactly what they wanted for their breakfast.

Soon the hall was filled with popping sounds as the chosen food materialised on the plates.

Sammy looked at the number of gold and silver stars on the noticeboards and they seemed fairly evenly matched. He wasn't interested in collecting stars. It was much more important to fight the Shape and to bring Dixie back.

While plates of toast, bowls of cereal, fresh fruit and jugs of milk and jugs of orange juice filled the gaps on the tables, Sammy focussed on Dixie in the chamber under the Church of a Thousand Graves. He took a bowl of cereal and two slices of toast and ate slowly in unusual silence.

'Is everything all right?' asked Milly, as Sammy poured orange juice over his toast.

'I guess so,' muttered Sammy, taking a bite and spitting out the soggy toast.

'Let me help,' said Milly, giggling and helping herself to the last slice of white toast. She took the knife out of Sammy's hand and buttered the toast, adding a dragon hand drawn with marmalade on top.

'Thanks,' grinned Sammy, taking a large bite just as the end-of-breakfast bell sounded.

'I'll save you a seat in Alchemistry,' said Milly, setting off for the lesson with Holly and Helana.

Jock and Gavin giggled as the girls left the table. They followed a short distance behind them. Toby frowned and walked off by himself.

'I'm going to check on our dragons,' announced Darius, winking at Naomi.

Naomi pushed her chair back and followed Darius, giggling as they linked hands.

'Fine, I'll speak to Sir Ragnarok myself,' muttered Sammy, finding himself alone on the fourth year North table.

Sammy marched up to the teachers' table. The Main Hall was emptying quickly. He waited until Professor Burlay and Commander Altair had finished showing Sir Ragnarok their globe.

'Interesting,' said Sir Ragnarok. 'You say the stars are fading?'

'Is it the Dragamas Constellation that's fading?' asked Sammy. 'Are all the dragons dying?'

Professor Burlay covered the globe with his hand and it vanished from sight. 'There's no need to worry like that Sammy,' he said briskly.

Commander Altair nodded. 'We think we've found out how to stop it.'

'Keep up the good work,' said Sir Ragnarok, smiling. 'Now, Sammy, what can I do for you?'

'It's about Dixie,' said Sammy, and he felt Commander Altair jerk towards him. 'We've found her. She's under the Church of a Thousand Graves. The Stone Cross is there too.'

Sir Ragnarok stroked his beard and tightened his cloak. 'Under the Church of a Thousand Graves you say? Well, well, well.'

'She's a prisoner down there,' said Sammy. 'Alfie Agrock is keeping her a prisoner. He's there too.'

'Well, well, well,' repeated Sir Ragnarok. 'Thank you Sammy.' He turned to Commander Altair. 'Orion, I trust you can handle this?'

Commander Altair nodded. 'I'll raise my father and the Snorgcadell. We can get her out within the hour.'

'I'll speak with Elsie,' said Professor Burlay. 'She can make some space in her hospital beds.'

'Dixie won't leave,' said Sammy. 'She's looking after some dragonlings. Alfie Agrock has kept some dragons for himself.'

'So he thinks he can lay the final piece of draconite on the Stone Cross,' said Sir Ragnarok, shaking his head. 'Not while I'm the Headmaster of Dragamas School for Dragon Charming.'

'We'll handle this from here, thank you Sammy. You have kept your promise to Dixie's mother,' Commander Altair smiled. 'You will be a good Dragon Knight one day,' he added softly.

'Was there something else?' asked Sir Ragnarok, motioning Professor Burlay and Commander Altair away.

'Uh, yeah,' said Sammy, twisting his hands into a knot as he found the courage to say the words. 'I think Mrs Hubar is in the Shape.'

Sir Ragnarok took a deep breath, his sea blue eyes narrowing to thin slits.

'Mrs Hubar and I grew up together,' said Sir Ragnarok softly. 'We have been friends all our lives. There is no one I would trust more to help save dragons. I am even trusting her with the draconite we find. No, Sammy, this time I am afraid you are trying to help too much. You cannot always be right.'

'So what's she done with the draconite?' asked Sammy, his heart beating fast in his chest. 'Has she put it on the Stone Cross?'

Sir Ragnarok sighed deeply. 'You are aware I do not have to explain myself to you Sammy, but to prevent wildfire rumours which would badly affect young Jock, I shall explain.'

Sir Ragnarok paused and wound a silk handkerchief around his fingers. Sammy leaned forward, eager to hear the explanation. He could feel his temperature rising. Sir Ragnarok didn't seem to be listening to him.

'Mrs Hubar has helped crush the draconite into a fine powder which we are feeding to the remaining dragons with their daily food,' continued Sir Ragnarok. 'It will prevent the Shape from obtaining the draconite and it will enhance the powers of the dragons we have left.'

Sammy couldn't contain himself. 'Prove it!' he exploded. 'You're wrong! She's taking the draconite to Alfie Agrock. They're rebuilding the Stone Cross. She hasn't fed any draconite to any of our dragons!'

Sir Ragnarok pursed his lips, his blue eyes burning the colour of draconite itself.

'This will be the end of the matter,' he roared, raising his staff. 'One thousand stars from North! You shall be excluded from the Christmas break and lose the right to go to the lands above the school until you show me some respect. Now get out of my sight!'

CHAPTER 24

# MAKING GOLD

Biting deep into his tongue, Sammy teleported to the Alchemistry corridor. Professor Sanchez's lesson had already started and he lost five more stars for being late.

'You are not usually late,' said Professor Sanchez, looking keenly at Sammy. 'Perhaps you have been in trouble.'

Sammy felt her reading his mind and he didn't have the strength after being shouted at by Sir Ragnarok, or the inclination after receiving the enormous punishment, to stop her.

'I see,' said Professor Sanchez, after a few moments. 'You cannot always be right. However, let us see how you perform in my class and perhaps I will award some stars to my best students.'

Sammy slumped into the empty chair by the window that Milly had saved for him. Outside it was quite sunny and Sammy wished he was anywhere else but in the classroom.

'Thanks for saving me a seat,' said Sammy, trying to ignore Darius and Naomi giggling directly behind him.

'That's ok,' Milly smiled at him, the glitter blusher on her cheeks sparkling in the sunlight.

Professor Sanchez walked around the desks and dropped a silver coloured paperclip in front of each student.

'In today's lesson, I would like you to turn your paperclip into something else,' said Professor Sanchez. 'I will award gold stars to the very best students.'

Still ignoring Darius and Naomi, Sammy focussed on his paperclip. He held his staff over the metal and watched as the paperclip dissolved into a puddle of grey silver.

'Very good,' said Professor Sanchez, leaning over Sammy's shoulder. 'Perhaps we have an Alchemist in my class.'

Sammy looked around. Milly was waving her staff over her paperclip but nothing seemed to have happened. Darius's paperclip looked like it was kissing Naomi's paperclip. Jock's paperclip was three times bigger than normal and Simon Sanchez's paperclip had turned bronze.

Professor Sanchez moved to the front of Sammy's desk and picked up his grey liquid using her staff.

'The nectar of the Gods,' whispered Professor Sanchez.

'The what?' asked Peter Grayling, leaning across Milly's desk to have a better look.

'Gold,' said Professor Sanchez. 'With the quicksilver Sammy has created we can produce pure gold. Watch…'

Sammy leaned closer, aware everyone was standing up and circling his desk, craning their necks to get a better look.

Professor Sanchez held the drips of grey liquid, that had once been his paperclip, dramatically in mid-air. She dropped the drips behind her hand like a magician and the drips came out the other side like liquid sunshine.

'Wow,' breathed Sammy as the droplets of gold fell with a "splish" onto his desk.

'The gold is perfect,' said Professor Sanchez, beaming and pointing to the yellow droplets.

Sammy noticed that Professor Sanchez was wearing multiple gold accessories today. She wore a large gold watch, a thick gold pendant in the shape of a dragon, gold hoop earrings, a gold hair comb, several gold rings on her fingers and gold bracelets dangling from her wrists. Today, he thought, it seemed the Alchemistry teacher was wearing more jewellery than Milly.

'It is easy,' said Professor Sanchez and Sammy knew she had read his mind again. 'I will show you!' she laughed and joined the gold droplets into a delicate bracelet that she gave to Milly.

'Thank you!' gushed Milly. She put the bracelet on her left wrist and held it up for the class to see.

Later in the lesson, Sammy overheard Milly telling Naomi that the bracelet was really special because it had been made from his paperclip. Sammy noticed Naomi's paperclip had turned a pale shade of green.

After Alchemistry, Sammy followed the fourth years up to the Armoury classroom. Rather than Commander Altair standing by the blackboard ready to take the class, they found Mr Synclair-Smythe standing there instead.

'What are you doing here?' demanded Gavin.

'Where's Commander Altair?' asked Peter Grayling.

'Rescuing Dixie, hopefully,' said Sammy, really quietly under his breath so that no-one could hear him.

'Questions, questions,' said Mr Synclair-Smythe irritably. 'Sit down quickly and quietly please. We have a lot to cover in Commander Altair's absence. Please take out some writing paper and pens and I will dictate the notes Commander Altair has given me for this lesson.'

Half an hour into the dictation, Sammy wished he was ambidextrous. His right hand was burning in pain from gripping the pen tightly. He looked at the illegible scribble and sighed. Perhaps he could copy some of the notes off Milly or Darius, who both had neater handwriting than him, later on.

Another half an hour later, the end of the lesson bell chimed above the classroom door.

Sammy threw his pen on the desk and rubbed his hands trying to get the circulation going again.

'I'm surprised you haven't been taught projection,' said Mr Synclair-Smythe. 'We could have wrapped this up in ten minutes and spent the remainder of the lesson doing some metalwork.'

'What metalwork?' yelled Gavin from the back of the class. 'Do we get to make metal stuff?'

Mr Synclair-Smythe nodded. 'You will all have the opportunity to make a variety of items from swords and knives to shields and harnesses.'

Naomi raised her hand. 'Girls as well?' she asked.

'Of course,' said Mr Synclair-Smythe.

Milly groaned loudly. 'I don't want to do metalwork,' she grumbled.

'Usually you would have done some metalwork already,' said Mr Synclair-Smythe. 'The fourth years I used to teach were extremely competent in Metalwork, Archery, Alchemistry, Mind Reading and Projection. Despite having a Commander of the Snorgcadell as your tutor, you seem to know very little.'

'Commander Altair taught us self-defence, not some dictation,' scoffed Simon Sanchez. 'We are good students. We will make the best weapons you have ever seen.'

'That remains to be seen,' said Mr Synclair-Smythe dismissively. 'Now hurry, or you shall be late for your next classes.'

'It's lunch next,' laughed Gavin. 'You couldn't mind read that!'

Mr Synclair-Smythe sidled up to Gavin and Sammy caught snippets of the conversation.

'...but don't for one second think I don't know what you and your petty gang are up to...' said Mr Synclair-Smythe, holding open the classroom door to let the fourth years out into the corridor.

'Oooer,' giggled Gavin.

'Gavin's in trouble!' laughed Jock.

Gavin raised his staff. The four coloured gemstones at the end sparkled and cast rainbows on the corridor walls.

'Stinky Dwarf breath,' muttered Gavin, stomping off.

# CHAPTER 25

# EMERALDS

In the Main Hall, Captain Stronghammer and Captain Firebreath were passing round huge glass jugs filled to the brim with orange juice.

As it was nearly Christmas, each jug of orange juice had green Christmas tree shaped ice cubes. The jugs of orange juice were in various shades of green, depending on how much they had melted.

Darius was the first student on the North table to spot that when each ice cube melted there was a tiny toy hidden in the ice.

'Look!' exclaimed Darius. 'The ice cubes have got things inside them!'

Everyone on the fourth year North table surged forward and fought to dig out the ice cubes from the orange juice. The jugs went flying, soaking the snowflake patterned tablecloth.

Sammy grasped one of the ice cubes that was making its way down the table. He held it in his hands to warm it up and melt the ice and a tiny orange plastic aeroplane appeared. It was a bit like getting the toys inside Christmas crackers.

Sammy noticed Milly's ice cube had a pair of tiny pink heart shaped earrings that she inserted into her pierced ears. He must have looked a little too long as Holly nudged Milly and she grinned and looked away.

Sir Ragnarok had arranged different flavoured hot pies with vegetables for lunch. Sammy found he'd been given a steak pie and he devoured it as he was really hungry after the stressful morning. He ate quickly and scooped up the last of the gravy with his knife.

Almost before he had finished, Captain Firebreath, accompanied by two other Dwarves wearing spotless white aprons tied over their dungarees, took the empty plates and loaded them onto large metal trays.

'Should be mining us should,' grumbled one of the Dwarves.

'Uh huh,' agreed the other Dwarf, laying out plates filled with brightly coloured yellow and orange cheese and piles of thin biscuits for dessert.

'All right Jock,' growled Captain Firebreath.

Jock nodded. 'It would be better if the dragons could use their magic to clear the tables, wouldn't it?'

'Well,' said Captain Firebreath, leaning close to the fourth year North table. 'You didn't hear it from me, but Sir Ragnarok is expecting some visitors in that department.'

'What would you know?' demanded Gavin. 'You're just a slave.'

Captain Firebreath glowered at Gavin. 'One day, yer'll be sorry fer that remark. Maybe not today, huh?'

'Huh,' scoffed Gavin. 'You wait until my Dad hears about this. He'll get all you Dwarves sacked!'

'Like that's gonna happen!' snapped Jock, standing up and raising his fists. 'My Dad will sort your Dad out.'

Gavin stood up with his fists raised. 'Come on then Dwarf breath!'

Dr Shivers swept up to the fourth year table. 'That's hardly the Christmas spirit boys. Hurry up or you'll be late for Dragonball. You might as well enjoy it as it will be your last game before Christmas. Sammy, would you see me for a moment please?'

Sammy picked up a handful of yellow cheese and a few biscuits and followed Dr Shivers out of the Main Hall.

'I understand you will be staying with us at Dragamas over the Christmas holiday,' said Dr Shivers.

Sammy nodded. 'Sir Ragnarok said...'

'I am aware of your accusation,' interrupted Dr Shivers, 'however, I am here to discuss your sleeping arrangements. Since you will be the only North boy staying at Dragamas, in fact you are the only North student staying at Dragamas, you will be asked to stay in the East Tower. Sir Ragnarok wishes to save on the heating bill.'

'No!' moaned Sammy. 'Can't I stay in our tower?'

Dr Shivers shook his head. 'Mr One-Four will be good and stay where he is told.' He opened his hand and held out four emerald crystals. 'Happy birthday Sammy.'

Sammy gasped and took the four stones, each no bigger than his fingernail. 'Thank you,' he murmured as Dr Shivers left him in a cloud of grey teleporting mist.

It was bitterly cold on the Dragonball pitch. The weather was turning from the bright morning sunshine to a sky filled with heavy rainclouds threatening to burst at any moment.

The flame coloured leaves of Autumn were slushy underfoot and the bare tree branches seemed to sway in support, almost like cheerleaders, as the students shunted the black leather balls from one end of the grass pitch to the other.

Riding on Kiridor, Jock played as goalkeeper for North, circling the goal and keeping out as many balls as he could.

At the opposite end, Peter Grayling played as goalkeeper for the West house. The game had just started as the first few spots of rain fell. Within minutes, it became a deluge with droplets the size of marbles firing down and bouncing on the grass.

Wearing his navy tracksuit with the zip done up to the collar, Sportsmaster Mr Cross ran for cover. Within seconds of the rain starting, he was refereeing and keeping score from the cosy warmth of the Gymnasium foyer.

Despite the cold rain splashing into his eyes, Sammy easily scored goal after goal after goal with Kyrillan's help. The blue-green shimmering dragon seemed to know exactly when to flick his tail and smack the ball over Peter Grayling's head and into the back of the net.

Sammy counted twelve goals scored personally by himself and Kyrillan. This took the North house up to fifty goals against the West house, who had only scored seven goals and most of those, in Sammy's opinion, were flukes.

'Next game!' Mr Cross called out of the Gymnasium window. 'North off! East on! I'm looking for the best players to put in my Dragamas Dragonball team.'

Sammy flew down on Kyrillan. He sat on his dragon's back under the trees at the edge of the Dragonball pitch and watched as Simon Sanchez on his great black dragon lurched between the West students and their dragons. Simon was becoming a very good Dragonball player and Sammy saw him score three goals back to back.

'Good goals Simon!' roared Mr Cross, raising his voice above the wind and the rain. 'Play on!'

Just as Sammy was losing the feeling in his fingers from the cold, Mr Cross shouted for the North students to return to the pitch and play against the South students.

Drenched by the foul weather and bruised by foul play, Sammy was grateful when they were allowed back into the Gymnasium to have a hot shower and get changed back into their school uniform.

He was even more grateful when Mr Cross finished his summary of the match and told the Dragon Minders to return the dragons to the Dragon Chambers.

It wasn't until the North students were back in the North common room and Dr Shivers handed the fourth years mugs of steaming hot chocolate, or tea or coffee for those who didn't want hot chocolate, that Sammy finally felt warm again.

Dr Shivers stayed in the common room, checking homework and answering Dragon Studies questions for the fourth years and the other North students as they returned from lessons and other activities.

The Dragon Studies teacher also spent half an hour with Milly and the other North fourth year girls playing Dragon Dice and he seemed genuinely interested in learning the rules of the game.

Later in the evening the bell rang for bedtime and the students packed up their books and toys and started moving towards either the boys' staircase or the girls' staircase.

Dr Shivers stood up and went to the boys' staircase as Sammy went to go upstairs. Sammy stopped at the bottom stair and waited for Dr Shivers to speak to him privately.

'Have you used the emerald stones?' asked Dr Shivers quietly. 'They are a gift to you. They should offer you an advantage when the time comes.'

Sammy shook his head. 'Not yet,' he said equally quietly and he marched upstairs behind Jock, Darius, Gavin and Toby quickly to avoid any further questions.

In the tower bedroom, Sammy settled down in his bed. He was tired and a little bit cold. He wished he had Kyrillan's warm, dragon body to cosy up against. In the bed next to him, Darius was snoring gently.

Toby's desk light was still on and Sammy guessed he was staying up late to write letters to rally support to fight against the Shape.

Earlier, when Gavin wasn't listening, Toby had confided that the letters had been stamped by General Aldebaran Altair at the Snorgcadell with the official gold seal.

Sammy didn't know if this would help convince people to fight the Shape, but he was impressed how much effort Toby was putting into the campaign.

CHAPTER 26

# FIRST KISS

On the evening before everyone else was going home for the Christmas holiday, Sammy was sitting in the fourth year North boys tower room with Jock and Darius. They were finishing wrapping Christmas presents and talking non-stop about dragons.

'You'll love it Jock,' said Darius enthusiastically. 'We get to see dragons from all over the world!'

'It sounds amazing!' said Jock. 'We'll be able to see all the dragons that are left in the world.'

'You can help me and my parents with everything they do to heal dragons. I wish you were coming with us as well Sammy,' said Darius.

'Yeah, it's a shame Sir Ragnarok banned you from going anywhere,' added Jock. 'What did your parents say about it?'

Sammy ignored Jock's question and concentrated on finishing wrapping the Christmas presents he'd bought for the fourth year North boys. He tied small labels with each boy's name around each present and packed away his scissors and sellotape.

Darius got out a large picture book and started telling Jock about all the dragons his parents had helped to heal. Sammy felt uncomfortable. He'd had more than enough of listening about the amazing Christmas holiday Jock and Darius were going to have.

Sammy put the four presents on the chest of drawers beside each of his roommates beds and excused himself.

'I'm going to the library,' said Sammy. He carefully picked up a small pink box which had arrived in the school post that morning.

The pink box contained a small but expensive charm bracelet Sammy had ordered from a jewellery catalogue. He was going to give it to Milly and he had found out from Naomi where he was most likely to find her.

Naomi's advice was to check for Milly in the library, where she had said Milly would be hiding away from the last minute preparations to ensure their dragons would be comfortable during the Christmas holiday.

Sammy held the small pink box tightly and pushed open the library door. He had an excuse ready for Mrs Skoob, should she ask, that he had forgotten a text book that he needed to borrow over the Christmas holiday.

As it turned out, he needn't have worried since the library was completely deserted, except for a small light in the farthest cubicle.

Sammy padded, soft-footed, on the thick carpet, down to the end of the central aisle and into the end cubicle surrounded by tall bookshelves.

As Naomi had reliably informed him, Milly was there, alone, practicing making things disappear and reappear with her staff. She held her staff in her right hand and was sweeping it over a pile of handwritten notes.

'Hi Sammy,' said Milly, looking up from her notes. 'I think it's working. I'm getting the hang of it, look.'

Sammy watched as the handwritten notes disappeared in a pale blue haze and then re-appeared at Milly's command.

'It's so much easier when I do it on my own,' said Milly. 'There's less pressure.'

Sammy nodded. He totally agreed. It was much less stressful practicing alone, usually sitting at his tower room desk with coins or other small objects.

'If you hold the staff higher up, it works better,' said Sammy.

He rested his hand on top of Milly's hand, guiding her soft fingers smoothly up the wooden staff towards the crystals at the top. He felt a jolt in his stomach and Milly's staff quivered.

The notes disappeared and Milly giggled. Her eyes were really pale blue, Sammy noticed. He was so close he could count the freckles on her nose and spot the flecks of glitter in her mascara.

He leaned closer, feeling her breath against his face. She was beautiful. He wanted to kiss her. He had found what Darius had described as "The Moment". Sammy tipped his head gently to his left and pressed his lips close to Milly's.

Two seconds later, although it could easily have been ten seconds, or thirty seconds, Sammy opened his eyes, a warm glow in his stomach. Milly was smiling shyly. She must have liked it too.

It can't have been that bad, Sammy thought, staring suddenly, as he saw a small shadow in the cubicle entrance. The glow faded to a guilty burden like lead and he breathed in sharply.

'Dixie,' gasped Sammy. 'What are you doing here?'

Milly spun round on her heels, her arm resting on Sammy's shoulder. 'Dixie! You're back!'

Dixie nodded, her eyes dull with green tears forming in the corners. She had a plaster under her right eye and her left wrist was tied in a white cloth bandage.

'Hi Sammy,' said Dixie, in a small faraway voice. 'I was going to ask if you'd like to come to my house for Christmas. Sir Ragnarok gave me permission to ask you and he undid the thousand stars you lost, but it looks like you've got a better offer.'

Sammy shook Milly's arm off his shoulder a little rougher than he intended.

'Fine,' snapped Milly. 'My parents are probably here now anyway. You can have her now she's back. It was rubbish anyway. Have the stinking Troll. I'll spread it around the school and no one will speak to her.' Milly pushed roughly past Dixie, knocking her into a bookcase.

'I don't mind,' started Dixie, the hollow, beaten look back in her eyes. 'Commander Altair rescued me and the five dragon pups. Alfie Agrock killed Wild-Eye. I'll see you next term. Go and patch things up with Milly.'

Sammy fumbled with Milly's staff. He realised her handwritten notes were still invisible.

'I'd better, uh, take this back to her,' said Sammy, raising the staff awkwardly.

'Wait,' said Dixie. She held his shirt sleeve and took a green rock out of her pocket. 'Commander Altair gave me this. It's our emerald gemstone crystal for next year. It's really advanced. Watch this.'

Sammy watched open mouthed as Milly's notes came back into view.

'You can give her these back as well. Bye Sammy,' said Dixie, a cool grey mist enveloping her from head to foot.

Both Dixie and the green emerald disappeared. When the mist cleared, Sammy was alone in the library and the bell was chiming in the corridor outside.

CHAPTER 27

# WELCOME TO EAST

Sammy picked up Milly's staff, her handwritten notes and the small pink box with the expensive charm bracelet he had forgotten to give to her. He teleported from the empty library to the North common room where he found Professor Burlay cleaning the study tables and tucking the chairs neatly underneath.

'Hello Sammy,' said Professor Burlay. 'Is everything all right?'

'Please could you put these things in Milly's room,' said Sammy, avoiding Professor Burlay's question. 'She left them in the library.'

'That was careless,' said Professor Burlay. 'I wonder why she would do that,' he added, blissfully unaware of the real reason why she had left the items.

'I need to get my stuff,' said Sammy, disappearing up the boys' staircase before Professor Burlay could ask anything else.

The fourth year tower room was empty. Gavin and Toby, Jock and Darius had all left for the Christmas holiday. Sammy quickly packed his staff, a few clothes, the Christmas presents left for him, his pillow and duvet and walked back downstairs.

Professor Burlay was busy fluffing the beanbags at the opposite end of the common room and didn't see Sammy slink out of the North common room door. In fact, no one saw him wandering down the corridor to the East wing, listening to the hollow sound of his own footsteps.

The castle was completely deserted. Even the school caretaker, Tom Sweep, was nowhere to be seen. Sammy had a fleeting bitter thought about how much fun Darius and Jock would be having travelling with Darius's parents in their brightly coloured minivan and how he had to share a pokey East facing bedroom with Simon Sanchez and Amos Leech.

Sammy turned a corner in the corridor and stopped at the imposing East tower common room door. It had the word "East' written on a plaque in Gothic scrawl. He kicked open the door and stomped inside, dragging his duvet behind him.

Although the East tower common room was ninety degrees to the right of the North tower common room, it seemed to be laid out in exactly the same way. To match the colour of the East house, the East common room was richly decorated with touches of yellow, gold and cream.

The fireplace was on the opposite wall compared with the North common room and the couches, instead of facing each other, were lined up with their curved backs snugly pressed against the curved tower wall with small round coffee tables dotted at regular intervals.

A long row of wooden desks and chairs ran down the middle of the circular room as a communal study area and there were curved bookcases overflowing with copies of the school text books.

Clutching his possessions, Sammy had the eerie feeling he was being watched and he scurried over to the dormitory staircases. He started climbing up the staircase with "Boys" written above the doorway.

'Oi! Sammy!' a voice shouted behind him. 'Sammy Rambles! Where are you going?'

Sammy spun around. Simon Sanchez and Amos Leech were standing by the other staircase doubled up with laughter.

'Are you sleeping with the girls this Christmas?' asked Simon Sanchez.

Amos snickered and pointed his staff at the words above the doorways, reversing the signs saying "Boys" and "Girls" back to normal.

'Ha,' Sammy forced a laugh and stomped back down the stairs.

'We are on the second floor,' said Simon Sanchez, holding out his hand. 'Welcome to the East tower.'

Sammy shook Simon's hand and got an electric shock. Simon and Amos almost collapsed laughing as Sammy dropped his duvet and Christmas presents.

Simon showed Sammy a small yellow dome concealed in his palm which had created the powerful current.

'When your hand touched my hand you got zapped!' said Simon, clutching his side with laughter.

'Very funny,' muttered Sammy.

'It's just a joke,' said Amos, grinning. 'We got lots of them from Simon's cousin. The envelope they arrived in was covered in the stuff!'

'We had to open it with our eyes,' said Simon, demonstrating by picking up Sammy's Christmas presents and dropping them on the floor, simply by looking at them.

As one of the parcels hit the floor, it unwrapped itself. As the wrapping fell away, Sammy recognised the box of chocolate snowmen he had been given by Darius.

'We will share these, yes?' asked Simon.

'Whatever,' scowled Sammy. 'Just let me get my stuff upstairs.

Amos led the way up the boys' tower staircase. He walked past the first doorway which had "Fifth Years" written on a plaque on an old wooden door with iron bands.

From the fifth year dormitory upwards, the stone floor was covered in a thick mustard yellow carpet that swallowed their footsteps.

Oil paintings and photographs lined the walls as they climbed upwards. Each painting or photograph showed the achievements accomplished by students from the East house in the past.

There were photographs of students in gold gowns picking up certificates and paintings of East students flying their dragons.

Further up, Sammy saw a picture of Amos being handed his East house school tie by Professor Sanchez. He remembered how happy Amos had been to swap houses from North to East.

They stopped outside a narrow door with the words "Fourth Years" written on a plaque. Sammy noticed lots of photographs had been taken with an instant camera and pinned to the oak panels. It reminded him of Darius's pocket television which could also take photographs.

'This is our room,' announced Simon, holding his arm outstretched to welcome Sammy inside.

'You first,' said Sammy, feeling rather suspicious.

'You go first,' said Amos. 'You're our guest, you must go first,' he added, exchanging a sly glance with Simon.

Sammy took a deep breath and kicked the door open with his foot. He just stepped back in time as a torrent of ice cold water sploshed down from an upturned bucket.

'Sammy is good!' cackled Simon. 'I said this wouldn't work!'

'Hah!' said Amos. 'Wait until he sees the rest of it!'

Sammy surveyed the room, which was very similar to the fourth year North boys' room. He sat down on an empty bed that had his name scribbled, and spelt wrongly, on a sheet of white paper and sellotaped over someone else's bed plaque.

He felt the bed move slightly underneath him and he stood up and turned back the duvet cover.

'Dragon dung!' exclaimed Sammy. 'You've put dragon dung in my bed!'

'Just a joke!' said Amos, high-fiving with Simon and howling with laughter.

Sammy was glad he'd thought to bring his own bedding. Who knew what else Simon and Amos had thought up to make his stay as horrible as possible.

Sammy tried to open the drawers in the chest of drawers beside the bed and found them held shut with a blue oilslick. Even the study desk had been tampered with, using upturned drawing pins to hurt him, had he wanted to sit down.

'Just a joke,' repeated Amos, tears falling out of his eyes from laughing so much. 'Me and Matthew Iris did this for you!'

'Matthew Iris?' asked Sammy. 'I thought he was in West?'

'He sits with the West house in lessons,' said Simon. 'We don't like him much either.'

'I'm only here so Sir Ragnarok can turn off the heating in the North tower and my parents don't sue him for me catching pneumonia,' snapped Sammy.

Simon laughed. 'Then it is as well that you didn't get wet from the bucket of water! Besides, you are here for another reason.'

Amos pointed to a seascape oil painting above Sammy's bed. It was of a boat being struck by lightning. Underneath the painting, Sammy could make out some words. He squinted and it looked like it said "There are things for all reasons and reasons for all things."

Sammy looked further around the room. Amos had a picture on his share of the tower room wall with a sunrise over a valley. Under his picture, the inscription read "Under the sun we are one. We are someone."

'These paintings were created by my Grandfather,' said Simon. 'He was a great Seer. He painted his own death.'

Sammy looked again at the little boat being struck by lightning and shivered. There were no other paintings on the wall to examine, so he set to work remaking his bed. He scooped the soiled duvet carefully off the bed and into the laundry basket.

'I'm going to check on our dragons,' said Amos.

Sammy nodded, thinking "good riddance" and laid his green duvet and pillow on the bed he would be using over the Christmas holiday.

'You are here for a reason,' said Simon, coming closer to Sammy as Amos left the room. 'Sir Ragnarok wants something from us. We are the best chance he has to secure the future of dragons.'

'Yeah right,' said Sammy, not bothering to hide his sarcasm. 'How are we supposed to do that?'

'It's the truth,' said Simon, craning his head out of the door to make sure Amos had gone. 'You are friends with Jock Hubar, are you not?'

'He's North, but I don't know him that well,' said Sammy. 'He's spending Christmas with Darius.'

'You know things about his mother,' said Simon, opening the top drawer of the chest of drawers beside his bed. 'We have been taking the draconite from where she has been leaving it out for him. You know who I mean.'

Sammy gasped as he looked in the drawer. It was almost overflowing with highly polished blue-green stones. He saw the faint outline of a protective oilslick that he knew would be preventing anyone else from seeing the contents of the drawer.

'You must pretend you know nothing about this,' said Simon.

'But…' started Sammy.

'Sir Ragnarok will know the truth when it is time,' said Simon, pointing to his beetle black eyes. 'I can see it.'

'Great,' muttered Sammy, unable to take his eyes away from the glittering draconite.

Simon clutched Sammy's hands and Sammy received another electric shock. 'Promise me,' said Simon, trying not to laugh. 'You will tell no-one about this.'

'Fine,' said Sammy, rubbing his hand. 'But, surely Alfie Agrock knows that Mrs Hubar hasn't been delivering the draconite so he can use it to rebuild the Stone Cross?'

Simon's black eyes sparkled mischievously. 'We have been sending false messages. Dixie is also back, yes?'

'How do you know that?' demanded Sammy.

'Is she back?' asked Simon.

'Yes.'

Simon nodded. 'Then it will all be ok. Did she save the eyeball dragon? Did she save Wild-Eye?'

'Could you see Dixie?' demanded Sammy. 'Did you see her getting beaten up and you didn't do anything?'

Simon shrugged. 'She gave as good as she got. Besides, we could do nothing if we wanted to carry on collecting the draconite.'

'Unbelievable!' spat Sammy. 'I suppose you can do the listening without using your staff as well?'

Simon shook his head. 'Both Amos and myself, we need both the staff and the draconite to enhance our powers.'

Sammy took a final glimpse of the pile of brightly glowing draconite gemstones before Simon closed the drawer. With that much draconite, even someone outside of the Dragon World would be able to do anything they wanted. They could intervene in world events, predict lottery numbers and influence football match scores for years in advance.

'We are full of surprises,' said Simon, grinning and extending his hand, which no longer had the electric-shock device, to Sammy. 'Welcome to East.'

CHAPTER 28

# CHRISTMAS AT DRAGAMAS

Sammy slept soundly in Matthew Iris's bed. He had borrowed some of Simon's deodorant to use as a room spray to clear the pungent scent of fresh dragon dung from his sleeping area and he had left the tower room window wide open all night. It was cold but worth it to get rid of the terrible smell.

Amos had removed the blue oilslick from the bedside chest of drawers and Sammy had unpacked his things and put them away for the week.

Although Sammy was disappointed not to see any of the North students over the Christmas holiday, Simon and Amos made sure he had a good time.

After just a few days, Sammy felt as though he had been informally accepted into their clique. Amos had even made Sammy a dragon shaped Christmas card.

Sammy reciprocated by sharing the chocolate snowmen he had been given by Darius and masses of chocolate that came in a huge Christmas hamper he had been sent by his parents and baby sister Eliza all the way from Switzerland.

As he ripped open the Christmas card with a long letter from his mother resting on the top of the hamper, Sammy realised with a jolt that Eliza would be having her second birthday in the summer. It sounded as though she was growing up quickly and had started to talk and walk.

Sammy saved a handful of chocolate snowmen to share with Darius. He hoped Darius would like the set of three Firesticks Invisiballs he had left on Darius's bed as his Christmas present. He wondered if Darius would see them before accidentally sitting on them.

Sir Ragnarok put on a small feast for the small number of students staying at the school. Sammy sat at the East table for his meals and occasionally Professor Sanchez left the teachers' table and joined them.

There were Christmas crackers laid out for breakfast, lunch and tea. Sammy loved pulling the crackers with his new friends. The crackers exploded with loud bangs and shot streamers and tinsel all over the table and the floor.

The best prize Sammy won was a tiny golden dragon in a cracker he had pulled with Professor Sanchez when she joined their table for lunch one day. The cracker came with the prize as well as a silly joke and a golden paper hat which Sammy wore for the whole meal of roast turkey with all the trimmings.

The festivities continued with more turkey, tinsel and trimmings for the next few days. Eventually the large Christmas trees in the Main Hall started to drop their needles and the holiday was coming to an end.

After helping sweep up the last of the streamers and stuffing his pockets with the remains of their sumptuous New Year's Eve feast, Sammy felt very full and went back to watch the last of the fireworks from the East tower bedroom.

It was his last evening in the East tower and it really hadn't been too bad after all. However, as he packed the last of his belongings back into his rucksack, he thought it would be good to be back with Darius, Gavin, Toby and Jock again.

Sammy fluffed up his pillow for his last night and changed into his green pyjamas. He was just getting into bed as Simon and Amos returned, laughing and joking and making generally a lot of noise.

'You will keep your promise, yes?' asked Simon, as he and Amos fell through the door, a bottle of Captain Firebreath's cider bulging out from under Amos's jumper.

'Yeah,' said Sammy, yawning widely. 'Is that cider any good?'

'Try some,' giggled Simon and he conjured three pint glasses out of thin air. 'We have the nectar of the Gods here. My mother, she thinks the nectar is gold, but what does she know?'

'This is a good example to be setting Simon, no?' barked a voice from the tower door.

Sammy looked up. Professor Sanchez was standing in the doorway, holding a yellow candle with a faint yellow teleporting mist evaporating around her.

'Go away mother,' giggled Simon. 'We are partying!'

With a toss of her raven haired head, Professor Sanchez waved her arm at the cider bottle and it vanished.

Simon laughed and took out a green emerald from his pocket. Sammy reached for his emerald, noticing that Amos did the same. The cider re-appeared and Professor Sanchez clicked her tongue.

'Very well. You may keep it, but don't tell on me!' she laughed and Sammy wondered if she was a little tipsy herself.

'I am good,' laughed Professor Sanchez. 'Am I not allowed to enjoy the festivities? Two stars each from East!'

'Grr,' said Simon, as six black stars whizzed down the stairs. He took a swig from the bottle. 'She doesn't remember you are North!'

'Two stars is nothing,' said Sammy, grinning and pouring himself half a glass of cider. 'I once lost a thousand stars in one go!'

'That's nothing compared to what Jock will lose for trying to give the draconite to Alfie Agrock,' said Amos darkly.

CHAPTER 29

# AMOS KNOWS

On the second of January, the rest of the students began to arrive back at Dragamas from their Christmas holidays. Darius and Jock were back first and wasted no time telling Sammy what a fantastic holiday he had missed.

'The dragon was "this" big!' said Jock, holding out his hands as wide as he could stretch. 'Letticia got its heart going again and healed all the cuts on its paw.'

'Letticia is my Mum,' Darius explained. 'She brought seven dragons back to life over Christmas. They are probably being drawn here.'

'Yeah, by the Angel of 'El Horidore,' added Jock enthusiastically.

'Have you seen them?' asked Darius.

Sammy shook his head. 'It's been snowing here. We haven't really been outside.' He saw Darius look out of the tower room window.

Darius gave him a sideways glance, as if to say "has it really been snowing?" and "if it was snowing, why weren't you outside enjoying it as you love the snow?".

'How was it sleeping in the same room as Amos?' asked Jock. 'He's creepy and weird. Why would anyone "not" want to be in North?'

'It was Gavin and Toby,' said Darius. 'They...'

'Gavin and Toby what?' demanded Toby, bursting through the dormitory doorway armed with two sets of skis and a grey suitcase floating behind him.

'We're back!' yelled Gavin, leaping over the suitcase and bouncing into the tower room.

'Uh, nothing,' said Darius. 'We were just telling Sammy about our holiday. I took loads of videos with this,' added Darius, holding up his pocket television recorder.

'The dragon was "this" big!' said Jock, grinning at the twins. 'Where are you going to put those skis Toby?'

'Who cares?' Gavin yawned. 'Has anyone seen my staff?'

After a rummage, Toby found Gavin's staff wrapped inside the curtain next to Gavin's bed.

'It's really cold in here,' said Toby, sliding the skis under his bed. 'How did you manage Sammy?'

'I stayed in the East tower,' said Sammy, his mouth full of a chocolate snowman.

Gavin helped himself to one of the sweets in a bowl on Jock's bedside chest of drawers. 'Yuck!' he spat out a mass of chocolate into his hand. 'What did you want to stay in the East tower for Sammy? Have you gone mad?'

'Sir Ragnarok told me I had to stay there,' said Sammy.

'I'm going to check on the dragons,' said Darius. 'Are you coming Jock?'

'I'll come,' said Sammy.

Darius looked oddly at him and Sammy felt like an outsider. 'Uh, I was going to go with Jock.'

'We're "walking" downstairs,' said Jock, resting his arm around Darius's neck. 'Daz doesn't teleport.'

'It's ok, I've got some things to do,' Sammy lied and picked up a Gemology textbook.

'Right,' said Darius, looking awkward for a second. Then he recomposed himself. 'Come on Jock, I can't wait to see Nelson!'

'And Kiridor!' shouted Jock.

Behind his curtain, Sammy grinned. Jock obviously didn't know Dixie was back. He also thought twice about sharing the news about Simon and Amos collecting the draconite and storing it in the East tower. Normally he would have shared everything straight away with Darius.

Sammy waited for them to go and then he changed into his green striped pyjamas and listened to Gavin and Toby telling him all about their skiing holiday. The twins were exhausted and were asleep long before Jock and Darius returned from the Dragon Chambers.

Sammy gritted his teeth. He wished he had waited for Darius so they could have told Sir Ragnarok about Mrs Hubar together. Then he could have gone on the camper van holiday with Darius and Jock and dealt with how to accuse Mrs Hubar after the holiday. But then again, they had no proof for Sir Ragnarok about Mrs Hubar and Jock.

It was darker in the morning than it had been the night before. Sammy looked out of his tower room window and could hardly see anything. He shivered while he got dressed and when he went down to the bathroom to wash, he found the taps and the showers had completely iced up.

'It's just like it was at home,' giggled a second year boy that Sammy didn't recognise. 'We didn't have any water at all over Christmas.'

'Cool! No baths!' said his friend. 'What did you drink?'

'Cola, lemonade and we melted ice. Dad was happy because he could drink lots of brandy,' laughed the first boy.

Sammy turned to the second year boys. He was confused. 'Can't your parents' dragons just unfreeze the pipes and get the water running again?'

The second year stared awkwardly at him and burst into tears.

'His parents' dragons got taken, didn't they,' said the other boy accusingly. 'My parents' dragons are dead and my older sister's dragon. They're all dead, dead, dead!'

Sammy shuddered. 'I'm so sorry,' he mumbled. 'Sir Ragnarok will fix it.'

The second year boys seemed content, but Sammy doubted his own words. If what he suspected was right, then Sir Ragnarok might know more about the Stone Cross and the draconite than he had let on.

Further downstairs, in the Main Hall, Sammy walked into a huge crowd around the fourth year North table. As he got closer, he saw that Jock and Milly had their arms wrapped around Dixie and were begging her to re-tell her story.

'Go on,' encouraged Jock. 'Sammy doesn't know about it yet.'

Sammy caught Dixie's eye and shook his head. 'It's ok,' he said, smiling brightly and changing the subject. 'So, what did everyone do over Christmas?'

'Skiing,' said Gavin promptly.

'Sunbathing,' said Holly, showing off her tanned arms. 'In Mexico!'

'I went tractor driving,' said Milly.

There was a stunned silence.

'You what?' asked Darius, exploding into a giggle.

'That's cool,' said Sammy, noticing how closely Milly was sitting next to him.

'It would have been better if you had been there,' said Milly, winking at Sammy.

Dixie coughed loudly. 'Who's going to help me catch up with what I missed?'

Jock shot his hand up. 'Me!'

'Me too!' said Darius and Naomi in synchronisation.

In the hubbub, Simon Sanchez dropped a note into Sammy's lap.

Without anyone noticing, Sammy read the note at top speed. In Simon's slanting writing, it simply said "watch out, Amos knows you know about the draconite".

Sammy glanced at the East fourth year table. Amos looked coolly back at him, shaking his head from side to side. He raised his finger to his lips and Sammy felt a shiver run down his spine.

'Come on,' said Sammy. 'Armoury is our first lesson.'

# CHAPTER 30

# SIDE SPLITTING

Commander Altair was waiting for them in the upper Armoury room. He acknowledged Dixie with a smile and waved his hand for her to pick her seat anywhere she wanted in the classroom.

'This morning we will continue what you have been learning in Gemology about using your sapphire gemstones to make things disappear and reappear,' said Commander Altair. 'Tell me, what have you made disappear and reappear so far?'

'Coins,' shouted Gavin.

'And pencil cases,' added Jock.

Commander Altair nodded. 'That is all very good,' he said, 'however, today we will make bigger things disappear and reappear. We will be practicing how to make yourself become invisible!'

Commander Altair held the sapphire gemstone at the end of his staff in his right hand. There was a brief moment when the sapphire glowed bright blue and then, in an instant, Commander Altair was gone.

There was a gasp from the students in the West house sitting in the front row. Two seconds later, Commander Altair reappeared.

'It is like teleporting on the spot,' explained Commander Altair. 'We do not actually go anywhere. However, you can also extend the power so that it becomes the art of being seen here, when we are really here…'

Commander Altair seemed to take a step forward and a copy of his body walked forward in amongst the rows of desks.

The Commander Altair at the front of the class carried on talking, while the other Commander Altair stepped behind Sammy's chair and gripped his shoulders.

'For those of you seeking a career in the Snorgcadell, you may wish to pay close attention,' said the Commander Altair at the front of the class.

'This is a pre-requisite skill that you must be able to demonstrate to the Snorgcadell. It is both compulsory and obligatory,' said the Commander Altair behind Sammy's chair.

Sammy gasped as Commander Altair split into a third persona, who also continued the conversation.

'This is an advanced skill known as Side Splitting,' said the third Commander Altair. 'On occasion it can be life threatening, should one of your Side Splits fail to return.'

Simon Sanchez put up his hand. 'My mother can do this,' said Simon. 'She cooks while she cleans and does the gardening and marks our books. She does the work of ten women in one body.'

'What a body!' snickered Gavin. 'It would be better if she lost some of it.'

'You will regret saying that!' shouted Simon, raising his fist. 'I will make sure of it.'

'Whatever,' scoffed Gavin.

'Easy boys,' said Commander Altair, re-creating himself as the Side Splits returned to the front of the classroom. 'This lesson will only cover the theory of Side Splitting. Sir Ragnarok has changed the course material and you won't be allowed to do this for real until you're thirty at this rate.'

'Darn it,' Sammy heard Dixie projecting at Jock.

'I know,' he heard Jock project back at her. 'I'll show you how it's done,' Jock added, making Sammy's skin crawl until he heard Dixie's reply.

'It's ok,' Dixie replied without opening her mouth. 'I'll ask Sammy. He's already done it.'

Sammy's heart skipped a beat. Of course he had already done Side Splitting! That's what Dr Shivers had done to him through the visions he'd experienced. Dr Shivers had helped Sammy to leave the school and see the Stone Cross.

'Two stars for daydreaming Sammy,' said Commander Altair, 'and I'll see you at the end of the class.'

Amos sniggered and Jock turned around and mouthed, "she's mine".

Commander Altair handed round course sheets with a detailed flowchart showing the process of how the sapphire made objects and people disappear and what happened to the solid matter while it was invisible.

Sitting next to Gavin and Toby, Sammy studied his diagram and they looked up more information in their copy of "Defend Yourself", the fourth year Armoury textbook written by Commander Altair's father, General Aldebaran Altair, one of the most highest ranked Generals of the Snorgcadell.

On page thirty-six, they found the list of steps to copy into their notebooks and memorise about how to make items vanish.

'This is useful when hiding ammunition supplies in battle,' advised Commander Altair. 'You must remember to leave memorable markers so that you know where you have left them. Items only stay invisible under the sapphire protection for a certain length of time.'

On page thirty-seven there was a diagram of a leaf with a stone resting on top. Under the diagram was a description which read, "Snorgcadell sign for up to ten people with dragons and their campsite".

'Cool,' said Toby. He turned the page and there was another diagram with four stones resting on a leaf. 'Look, four stones means up to forty people and their dragons.'

Commander Altair nodded. 'If there is a white stone in the middle, then it means that some dragons have fallen.'

They looked through the next pages in the textbook and discovered other symbols used by the Snorgcadell to describe hidden campsites and how to represent stores of weapons and food.

Commander Altair went through other patterns that could be left to show how many Dragon Knights had passed through a particular town or village and on which day and at what time.

Sammy was so totally engrossed in the lesson that he barely heard the end-of-lesson bell chiming above the classroom door.

The classroom emptied almost instantly. Most students teleported out of the Armoury classroom and the room was soon filled with a thick teleporting mist.

Within just a few moments, Sammy and Dixie were the only students left and they stood together at the front of the class, both looking down at their feet and wondering what Commander Altair wanted.

# CHAPTER 31

# SAMMY'S KISS

Commander Altair gripped his staff. There was a flash of blue and he split into four versions of himself. Three Commander Altairs stood behind Sammy and Dixie and a brighter, real version of their teacher stood at the front.

'I have kept you both back to establish why you have fallen out,' said Commander Altair, looking concerned. 'It is so important that we stick together towards the end.'

'Sammy kissed Milly,' Dixie blurted out.

'The end of what?' demanded Sammy, looking firstly at Dixie and then at Commander Altair. 'It was just a little one, nothing heavy.'

Commander Altair smiled. 'Who you share your time with is your business Sammy, but remember what Dixie has been through and perhaps you could be more considerate.'

'She just appeared!' spluttered Sammy. 'Right in the middle of it!'

'I bet you wish I'd stayed in that dungeon, don't you?' snapped Dixie.

'No!' exclaimed Sammy. 'I'm glad you're back. I tried everything to find you and rescue you.'

'You just had bad timing, right?' Commander Altair intervened.

'Humph,' said Dixie. 'I got Sir Ragnarok to undo Sammy's punishments as well. Sammy could have stayed with me over Christmas instead of going into the pokey East tower with Simon and Amos.'

'Oh, yeah, that reminds me,' said Sammy.

'No way!' said Dixie and Commander Altair, reading Sammy's mind before he could say another word.

'Draconite!' exclaimed Dixie.

'In the East Tower?' asked Commander Altair.

'Yeah,' said Sammy. 'In Simon's chest of drawers beside his bed.'

'I shall inform Sir Ragnarok,' said Commander Altair, calling the extra Commander Altair personas back into himself. 'Leave this with me,' he added, dissolving into a gold teleporting mist.

'Do you reckon all of him has gone?' giggled Dixie. 'Was Milly a good kisser?'

'Yeah, I think he's all gone,' stumbled Sammy. 'Uh, what do you want to know about me and Milly for?'

'Checking out the competition,' said Dixie, grinning mischievously. 'Come on, let's go.'

Sammy followed Dixie into the corridor and they started walking towards the Ancient and Modern Languages classroom.

As they approached the classroom, Dixie grabbed Sammy's arm.

'I saw Miss Amoratti earlier,' said Dixie, 'and she's giving us a surprise test this morning. Do you want to skip it? Sir Ragnarok said I could take some time off, you know, after what happened to me. If I don't think I can manage certain lessons, then I can take them as study breaks.'

Sammy grinned and nodded. He turned around and sneaked down the back stairs with Dixie, weaving their way out of the castle and into the school grounds. They stopped at the remains of the den, where Dixie had been kidnapped.

Sammy sat next to Dixie on the treestump, which was now all that remained of their den.

'It seems funny, being here, after, you know,' started Sammy.

Dixie nodded. 'It looks ruined like my treehouse. That got destroyed as well. Over Christmas there was a huge storm and it blew the treehouse out of the tree. It shattered amongst Dad's potatoes,' Dixie gave a half-laugh and rubbed her eyes with her jumper sleeve.

Awkwardly, Sammy put his arm around Dixie's shoulders. 'So, what did happen to you?' he asked softly.

Dixie looked up, her eyes wide. 'Sir Ragnarok says I don't have to talk about it. I don't...I can't...;

Sammy gripped harder as Dixie buried her head against him.

'It's ok, I'm here for you. Don't worry.'

'I know,' whispered Dixie. 'It's just the things I've seen. The things he made me do. I can't...'

'With dragons and the Stone Cross?' asked Sammy.

Dixie nodded. 'I'll tell you one day, I promise.'

'It's ok, you don't have to say anything,' said Sammy.

'I want to,' said Dixie. 'Hey Sammy, there is one thing you can do for me.'

'What?'

Dixie pressed so close against him, he could feel her warm breath and she leant so close, her lips brushing against his.

'Kiss me,' she commanded and Sammy found himself obeying, his tongue reaching inside her mouth, exploring where he had only read about in magazines before that moment. He closed his eyes, pulling Dixie closer to him.

'How was that?' Sammy asked gently. 'It wasn't too rough was it?'

Dixie was smiling. 'It was better than my dream,' she whispered. 'You chased Nitron Dark on Kyrillan, then suddenly we were here and...'

'Cool,' said Sammy. 'Can we do it again?'

'Sure,' Dixie grinned. 'Then we'd better go to Ancient and Modern Languages. I don't really feel so bad I can't take the test.'

'We'll tell her,' Sammy kissed Dixie again, 'we've been practicing!'

'Mm,' agreed Dixie, ending the kiss with a warm hug. 'Please don't tell Jason or Mikhael about this yet. I want it to be special. I want you to myself.'

'Sure,' said Sammy, hoping for another kiss before they went back out of the cover of the trees. But Dixie had skipped on ahead. Sammy could hear her whistling some sort of "mission accomplished" march song and he grinned.

His grin faded as they met Jock at the castle doors. He had his hands on his hips and he didn't look pleased to see Sammy and Dixie together.

'Miss Amoratti sent me to look for you,' said Jock.

'It's more likely you were sneaking around,' spat Dixie.

'I came to look for you. I didn't want you to lose any stars,' said Jock.

'What about Sammy?' asked Dixie. 'Didn't you want him to lose any stars either?'

Jock shrugged, completely ignoring Sammy. 'Who cares?' said Jock, taking Dixie's hand. 'I'll look after you.'

Dixie looked down at Jock and shook her hand free. 'Sammy's looking after me. Oh, and you'll need to see Dr Shivers about getting yourself a dragon. I'm having Kiridor back.'

'Since when?' spluttered Jock. 'He's a male dragon. He needs a man looking after him.'

Dixie looked at her watch with the chewed strap. 'Since now. Ancient and Modern Languages classroom,' she said and teleported out of sight.

'You want to watch out Sammy,' Jock retorted. 'Us Dwarves get what we want.'

'Like your mother,' sniped Sammy. 'She'll get what's coming to her too.'

'What about my mother?' demanded Jock. 'You don't know nothing about my mother.'

'I know she's taking draconite to Alfie Agrock under the Church of a Thousand Graves,' said Sammy, ducking as Jock lunged at him.

'You don't know nothing,' repeated Jock. 'All the dragons are gonna die, then me and Mum, we're gonna have all the power in the world!'

'Ugh! Ancient and Modern Languages, chair next to Dixie,' gasped Sammy as Jock threw a punch in his stomach.

Luckily Miss Amoratti was writing on the blackboard and had her back to him when Sammy landed in Holly's lap and the whole classroom let out a surprised giggle.

'Sorry,' puffed Sammy.

'Watch where you're going then,' muttered Holly, moving up a seat so that Sammy could sit down without squashing her.

'What's so funny?' asked Miss Amoratti, turning around. 'Oh, Sammy, I see you've decided to join us. I sent Jock looking for you. Did he find you?'

'I'm here!' snapped Jock, landing half-in, half-out, of Miss Amoratti's wooden teacher's desk between a pile of text books and a large red apple.

'Oooh!' giggled Miss Amoratti. 'We'll have to get Mr Sweep to cut you out.' She looked sternly at the class. 'There will be no more teleporting in my classes please. Now, translate the words I have written in Troll back into Human please.'

'Good morning class. Today is Thursday. We will be learning the difference between the Light Ages and the Dark Ages,' muttered Dixie, translating perfectly from the board. She turned to Sammy and whispered, 'if these are supposed to be the Light Ages, I don't know…'

'No talking out loud,' said Miss Amoratti, taking a bite out of her apple. 'At the end of the translation, I would like you to write a short essay on the Dark Ages. The third years are doing a play at Easter on the Dark Ages that we will watch. Now, for your homework, please continue your essays and hand them in at our next lesson.'

Sammy translated the last word on the blackboard as the end-of-lesson bell chimed and the third years poured in for their Ancient and Modern Languages lesson. He was impressed as each student wished Miss Amoratti "Arug Shura" as they entered the classroom and wondered if they would get lots of extra stars awarded for the correct pronunciation.

Tom Sweep was the next to enter the classroom. He was sneezing violently and, to Sammy's surprise, the school caretaker was followed into the Ancient and Modern Languages classroom by none other than Sir Ragnarok himself.

'Let's undo this, shall we Jock?' said Sir Ragnarok with a smile and he held up his hand, which Sammy saw was concealing a small emerald which was casting a green glow.

Jock leapt free and Tom Sweep tapped the desk in several places to make sure no damage had been done. He spun Miss Amoratti's leather executive chair around and grunted that he was satisfied everything was as it should be.

'A cushion would be nice,' said Miss Amoratti, looking hopefully at Sir Ragnarok.

'Very well,' said Sir Ragnarok. He flicked his wrist and three fluffy purple cushions appeared out of thin air.

'Oooh, purple,' giggled Miss Amoratti. 'My favourite colour.'

## CHAPTER 32

# PINK BALLOONS

Gradually, the freezing cold, dark and misty mornings were replaced by warmer weather. Sammy woke early one Friday morning to find a pink balloon tied to the end of his bed. He sat up and, through a chink in his curtain, he could see that Darius and Jock had pink balloons tied to the end of their beds as well.

'Morning everyone,' called Sammy, pulling the pink balloon towards him. As the balloon got closer, he spotted a pink envelope tied to the end of the string.

'What's this rubbish?' came Gavin's voice from behind the green velvet curtain.

'It's for Saint Valentine's Day!' shouted Toby. 'It's the fourteenth of February today!'

'I've got a balloon!' shouted Jock, leaping out of bed and swinging back all the curtains. 'Dixie has sent me a Valentine's balloon!'

'We've all got pink balloons, Dwarf breath,' scoffed Gavin.

'Watch your mouth,' snapped Jock.

Toby reeled in his balloon, ripped open the pink envelope and pulled out a piece of pink paper.

'The balloons are from Professor Burlay!' exclaimed Toby. 'We're invited to his wedding!'

Sammy scrambled to open his own pink envelope tied to the balloon string.

'Professor Burlay is marrying Mrs Grock,' announced Sammy.

'She should really be Mrs Agrock,' interrupted Jock. 'She never actually married Uncle Alfie properly. She said the surnames were so similar, what was the point of changing everything?'

'What do you mean "Uncle Alfie"?' demanded Sammy. 'Since when?'

'Since I was born, stupid!' said Jock.

'Alfie Agrock? The Dwarf who stole the Angel of 'El Horidore, who kills dragons and kidnapped Dixie?' demanded Sammy. 'You're saying he's your uncle?'

'Must be another Alfie Agrock,' said Jock sarcastically. 'My mistake.'

'Liar!' said Darius. 'You're a big, fat, liar. I let you help with all those dragons at Christmas and your uncle is Alfie Agrock, the "A" in the Shape?'

Sammy bit his tongue. He knew first-hand what it felt like to have an uncle who was in the Shape.

'I got ten pieces of draconite at Christmas, didn't I?' said Jock. 'They were all given to my Mum.'

'Hah!' shouted Sammy. 'That's what you think!'

'What?' demanded Jock. 'I gave them to my Mum.'

Sammy focussed his mind on porridge and toast, desperately trying to conceal his secret. But it wasn't working and he could feel his thoughts spilling out for everyone to hear.

'The East Tower?' asked Darius. 'What does Simon porridge know about draconite?'

'Sanchez,' giggled Toby. 'Sammy is thinking about Simon Sanchez. What's he got to do with the draconite?'

Jock slammed his fist into his pillow. 'Thank you Sammy. You were doing so well hiding what you were thinking but your friends have told me your secret.'

Sammy groaned and gripped his duvet. Why wasn't he better at focussing on something else? Maybe he should have thought of sausage rolls instead.

'That's what Amos meant when he said Simon has told you,' said Jock. 'He said he would tell me so the four of us could stop the Shape. But he didn't know about what else is going on.'

'No way,' said Gavin, stepping up to the tower door with his staff in his hand. 'You can count me out of this. I've made a big mistake. I want dragons to live. I'll fight the Shape! I'll fight you!'

'Remember what I said about sticks and stones?' demanded Jock. 'I said I would make you pay for all the things you said about me! Let me out now!'

Jock snatched Gavin's staff out of his hands and smashed it down heavily across Gavin's knees.

'Owwwww!' shrieked Gavin, leaping high in the air and then he crumpled to the floor howling in pain.

Toby raised his fists but Jock had already drawn his ruby gemstone and created a red mist that made Sammy's eyes water.

Sammy wished he had some of Commander Altair's black powder to throw as Jock teleported out of the fourth year North boys' tower bedroom, leaving a devastating blue oilslick covering the floor, the walls and the ceiling of the tower room, rendering the four boys prisoners.

Sammy took out his staff and unfroze Gavin, Toby and Darius. He pushed them on to his bed so their feet were off the blue oilslick floor. He'd only seen vertical oilslicks before and there was no knowing what would happen if they put their entire weight onto a horizontal oilslick on the floor for any length of time.

'Sammy, I'm so sorry,' said Darius quietly. 'I should have known. I could have stopped him.'

'Gavin's hurt,' said Toby, tears in his eyes.

'My knees,' groaned Gavin. 'My knees are broken. Take me to Mrs Grock's,' he mumbled, his eyes closing.

'How's he going to get to Mrs Grock's?' asked Darius.

'Obviously not through the door,' snapped Toby.

'I'm ok,' started Gavin. 'Ug, no I'm not. The Dwarf breath has bust both my knees. I can't walk.'

'We can't stand on the floor at the moment either,' said Sammy. 'We'll have to think of something else.'

Sammy reached into the top drawer of his bedside chest of drawers and took out a small bottle of healing potion.

'No, try this,' said Darius, reaching over to his bedside chest of drawers and taking out a much larger bottle. 'I'm going to be a Healer. My healing potion will be better than yours Sammy.'

'I've got broken knees!' shouted Gavin. 'Your stupid potion won't work!'

'Try it anyway,' suggested Sammy. 'Or we could always freeze you with the ruby again so you wouldn't feel anything and we wouldn't have to listen to you complaining all the time.'

'Don't you dare do that!' threatened Gavin. 'Can't you get a dragon up here? Can't someone go for help out of the window? Teleport or whatever?'

'You can't teleport,' said Darius. 'It's not safe with the sapphire oilslick there. What if we end up in the blue oil and can't get out?'

'Who cares,' grumbled Gavin.

'I'll try it,' said Sammy.

'No!' shouted Darius. 'I've read about it and you can't. You'll disappear and we won't know where you've gone.'

'Well, maybe we could jump?' suggested Sammy.

'Too high,' said Toby at once. 'Gavin is right. We'll have to summon a dragon and fly down.'

'We could try shouting,' said Sammy, shifting sideways along his bed to get to the window. 'Someone might hear us.'

'Watch my knees,' growled Gavin.

'You should have knocked Jock flying,' said Toby. 'It's your fault Jock created the oilslick. We're only trying to think of ways to get us out of here so we can get help for you. Don't be so ungrateful.'

'Thanks,' muttered Gavin. 'Just watch my knees. They really hurt.'

Sammy pushed open the tower window and leaned out.

'Help!' Sammy shouted out of the window. 'Professor Burlay! Dr Shivers! Dixie! Help!'

'Professssssooooor Burrrrlaaaaay!' yelled Toby, three times as loudly. 'We're up here!'

There was silence. No one answered. No one had heard them. No one was coming to help.

'It's no use,' said Darius. 'They're all at breakfast in the Main Hall and that's too far away.'

'We could try projection,' suggested Sammy.

'It's no good with "that" there,' said Darius, pointing at the oilslick. 'Doesn't anyone listen to me?'

'You said we can't teleport,' said Sammy. 'You didn't say anything about projection.'

'What are we supposed to do then?' asked Darius. 'No one will look for us until at least lunchtime.'

'Professor Burlay will notice,' said Toby. 'Astronomics is after lunch.'

'My knees can't wait that long,' moaned Gavin.

'I'll try calling Kyrillan,' said Sammy, leaning out of the window as far as he dared. 'Ky-rill-an!'

'Try it inside your head,' snapped Gavin. 'You've been here for four years and you still don't know anything.'

'Use your Angel whistle!' said Darius suddenly. 'You have got an Angel whistle, haven't you?'

'So what? It won't call Kyrillan. It will only call our dragons,' said Gavin. 'Oh. I get it. We'll call our dragons here instead of Kyrillan.'

'Here it is,' said Toby, holding up their orange plastic, half-moon shaped Angel whistle. He blew into the device and then handed it to his twin brother.

Gavin put the plastic Angel whistle up to his mouth and puffed out his cheeks, blowing hard into the device.

No sound came out but Sammy knew the small orange Angel whistle would be calling Syren and Puttee to the tower room as fast as they could fly.

# CHAPTER 33

# EVIDENCE

In what felt like less than thirty seconds, Captain Duke Stronghammer appeared at the fourth year tower windows. He was riding on Gavin's pink dragon, Syren, and Toby's grey-green dragon, Puttee, was right behind him.

'Holy smoke!' shouted Captain Stronghammer. 'What in the dragon's name is going on here? I've just come from a scuffle in the East tower. Can't you cause trouble on different days and give me a break!'

'What happened in the East tower?' asked Sammy.

'Some fourth years trashed their bedroom,' growled Captain Stronghammer. 'Tom Sweep isn't happy. He's had a stinking cold for weeks and he wanted to take some time off. With that mess to clear up, Sir Ragnarok will never let him go now. What's worse is my Jock's been involved.'

'Can I go and look?' asked Sammy. 'Can I ride on Puttee?'

'Only if I come with you,' said Toby. 'Darius, can you go with Gavin to Mrs Grock's house?'

'I want to come with you to the East tower,' said Darius. 'It's all my fault Jock found out where the draconite was hidden.'

'Two is the most I'll allow on a dragon,' said Captain Stronghammer. 'An' jus' you be careful jumpin' out of windows. Whatever next?'

'My knees hurt,' groaned Gavin. 'Can't you hurry up?'

'Fine,' said Darius. 'What did you have to provoke Jock for anyway?' he scolded Gavin. 'If you hadn't had a go at him then none of this would have happened.'

'Whatever,' said Gavin, lying flat out on the bed.

Darius shook his head and passed Toby his pocket sized television.

'You can take some airborne videos,' said Darius. 'I've been meaning to do some for ages.'

Toby put the pocket television into his pocket and stood on Sammy's chest of drawers, holding onto the window frame for support. He steadied himself and then leapt onto Puttee's back. The dragon wriggled as Toby bounced along his back and into the rider position.

'Ow!' squawked Toby. 'I sat on a spike!'

Sammy stood on his chest of drawers and waited for Puttee to hover as still as possible, the dragon's wings beating rhythmically to maintain the position, then he too leaped out of the fourth year bedroom window and landed on Puttee.

To lessen the impact, Sammy rested his palms on Puttee's scales and brought his knees forward behind the dragon's wings as he landed smoothly on the dragon's scaly back, carefully avoiding all the spikes.

'See you later!' Sammy shouted to Darius and Gavin. He watched as Gavin hobbled to the window and dropped himself neatly onto Syren's back so he was sitting slightly awkwardly behind Captain Stronghammer.

Toby guided Puttee around the castle walls to the East tower. Sammy found the experience similar but not as smooth as when he was riding on Kyrillan. Puttee seemed to enjoy the challenge of having two riders on his back and he flapped his grey-green wings in perfect synchronisation, gliding around the castle walls.

'Higher Puttee!' shouted Toby. 'We need to go to the East Tower.'

Puttee obligingly swooped up to the second floor of the East Tower, where the fourth year East boys had their bedroom and where Sammy had spent the Christmas holiday.

Sammy leaned past Toby, craning his neck to see inside the tower windows. He could see some hooded shapes beside one of the beds.

'No!' shouted Toby as soon as he saw the figures. 'Get out!'

One of the hooded figures looked around. It let out an angry cry and pointed a staff in their direction. Then there was a scuffle and Sammy saw Simon Sanchez get up off the floor and stare at them.

'What are you doing here?' asked Simon. He looked rather surprised to see a dragon flying outside his bedroom window.

'What are you doing here?' asked Toby. 'We heard there was some trouble in the East tower and we have come to have a look.'

'I was giving the draconite to my mother,' Simon shouted through the open window. 'She came here and then the Shape came here!'

Toby swung Puttee close to the window. They could see Professor Sanchez kneeling on the floor.

'We'll help you!' shouted Toby, switching places with Sammy in mid-air.

From the back of his dragon, Toby took out the pocket sized television and turned it on. He pointed it towards the East Tower.

Then Jock came to the window. He was holding lumps of draconite in his hands. When he saw Sammy and Toby flying outside the window he dropped the draconite and took out his staff.

Jock fired green sparks all around the tower room. Some of the sparks flew through the window, narrowly missing Sammy and Toby. One of the sparks caught Simon off guard and it exploded on his chest. Simon collapsed onto the floor.

One of the hooded figures lowered their hood. Sammy gasped. It was Mrs Hubar, her face covered with charcoal black camouflage paint.

'Got her!' said Toby, holding up Darius's pocket television triumphantly.

'You'll never stop the Shape,' Mrs Hubar laughed manically out of the window. She took the pieces of draconite and held them up in front of the television recording. 'Now we have all of the draconite!'

'Uncle Alfie's getting them,' said Jock. 'Now get off that dragon!'

As if invisible strings were pulling them, Sammy and Toby flew into the fourth year boys' tower room, leaving Puttee squawking and breathing thick plumes of smoke.

Jock leaped onto the grey-green dragon's back and flew off with Puttee still breathing violent smoke rings that filled the air.

Mrs Hubar dropped the draconite stones into a black velvet bag and suddenly she too was gone, teleporting out of the tower in a thick grey mist.

Between the plumes of dragon smoke and the thick teleporting mist, the occupants remaining in the tower room coughed and spluttered in a heap on the floor.

'Whatever next,' puffed Professor Sanchez, wiping the dust off her dress with her hands. 'Get up Simon. Whatever will Sir Ragnarok say about you storing draconite in your bedroom?'

Sammy leaped to his feet. 'We have to stop Mrs Hubar!' he shouted. 'Where's she gone?'

Professor Sanchez looked kindly at him. 'That will be all Sammy. Leave it to me to speak with Sir Ragnarok. You have an Alchemistry lesson this morning, yes?'

'Yes, but,' started Sammy.

'Good,' said Professor Sanchez briskly. 'Then we will learn about the formula for immortality. Draconite is very instrumental in this.'

Professor Sanchez nodded briefly, as if agreeing with herself. Then she wrapped her black cloak around her shoulders and vanished in a grey mist.

'What were you thinking coming here on a dragon,' groaned Simon. 'Me and my mother, we could have stopped the Shape.'

'But you didn't,' said Toby, looking out of the window. 'Now Jock has my dragon and all the draconite.'

'What did Mrs Hubar mean when she said "all of the draconite"?' asked Sammy.

'She meant all the draconite that is harvestable. They are killing the newborn dragons and they will kill our dragons too.' Simon sat on his bed and cried into his hands. 'We have failed.'

'We have not,' said Sammy firmly. 'We've got proof Mrs Hubar is in the Shape.'

Toby held up Darius's television recorder and replayed the digital recording of Mrs Hubar, Jock and the draconite. They were tiny images on the small screen.

'You have a television recorder, like Sir Ragnarok,' said Simon, his black eyes shining with tears. 'That is amazing.'

'Darius!' said Toby suddenly. 'We have to rescue Darius from our tower room!'

'And check on Gavin,' added Sammy. 'Hopefully Mrs Grock has been able to help him.'

Simon reached for the television recorder. 'I will take this to Sir Ragnarok.'

'No way!' exclaimed Toby. 'Darius gave it to me. Let's all go to Sir Ragnarok's office.'

'We must use another way,' said Simon. 'The whole school will be at breakfast. We must be discrete.'

'Then we must wait,' said Toby. 'But the longer we leave it, the more time Mrs Hubar has to escape.'

'No,' said Sammy. 'I know another way. When Sir Ragnarok gets back from breakfast we will already be in his tower.'

Simon smiled. 'I like this idea,' he said and turned to Toby. 'Do you have a better plan?'

Toby shook his head. 'No.'

'Then it is settled,' said Simon. 'Sammy, tell us, which is the way that we must go?'

CHAPTER 34

# SIR RAGNAROK'S OFFICE

Sammy led the way down through the thick yellow carpeted East tower, down to the stone floored corridors and then up to the seventh floor, where Professor Sanchez had her Alchemistry classroom.

'Is this your great idea?' demanded Simon Sanchez. 'You want us to be on time for our lessons? I would have brought my books if I had known that.'

Sammy laughed and pushed open the Alchemistry door. The classroom was empty.

'Please give me your Dragon Minder pin,' said Sammy. 'I need it to open the secret passage.'

Simon did as he was asked, unpinning his silver dragon with the yellow eyes from his shirt collar and handing it to Sammy.

Sammy crossed the classroom and went over to the oak panelled wall. He carefully checked each panel, looking for the one oak panel that was slightly older and dirtier than the others. Halfway along the wall, he found the right panel with the slot to insert the Dragon Minder pin.

Sammy pressed Simon's silver Dragon Minder pin into the dragon shaped groove and turned it ninety degrees. With a soft "click" the secret door hidden in the oak panels opened.

'The secret passage,' said Simon, nodding approvingly. 'That must be how my mother gets around the castle so quickly.'

Sammy lit a small fire at the end of his staff and held it in front of the dark hole that was their entrance into the secret passage.

'I'm going back,' said Toby. 'You take Darius's television recorder and find Sir Ragnarok. I want to go and find Darius and Mrs Grock and make sure Gavin is ok.'

'That is good,' said Simon. 'The passage looks much too crowded for three people.'

'Ok,' said Sammy. 'Tell Darius I'll bring his TV back safely.'

Toby nodded and sprinted out of the Alchemistry classroom, banging the door behind him.

With the fire at the end of his staff, Sammy led the way down the narrow steps and along the passage. He didn't stop at the round room where the dragon massacre had occurred. He felt queasy as they walked past. There was the fading stench of dragon bones in the air.

'This place is death,' said Simon.

'Come on,' whispered Sammy, unsure why he was whispering as there was no one else around.

They walked on down the passage, the faint shadows cast from the fire looked eerie and spooky on the walls. At the end of the passage, Sammy found the steps and they began the near vertical climb of stairs to the wooden door at the top of Sir Ragnarok's tower.

Sammy pushed the door but it wouldn't budge an inch. He pulled the door towards him but nothing happened.

Sammy had a moment of panic and pulled and pushed against the door, willing it to open, then his fingers found an empty keyhole.

'It's locked!' said Sammy, horrified their journey had been wasted.

'Let me look,' said Simon, perhaps there is another way. 'Ah, yes, look at this. We must knock. It is written in these runes.'

Sammy looked closer at the door. There were five lines underneath the keyhole.

KNOCK
AND
YE
SHALL
ENTER

'Knock and ye shall enter,' said Sammy. He tapped nervously on the door.

'Louder!' hissed Simon. 'Try once more. Then if it doesn't work then we will go back.'

Sammy tapped the door with the base of his staff. Then he swung his arm back and gave an earth shattering blow to the door. His hand vibrated as the staff kicked back towards him. The door let out a faint hiss and crumbled away into oblivion, the dust sprinkling down the steps in a fine brown powder.

'Oh no,' muttered Sammy, coughing as the door dust circled in the air around them.

'You're in trouble!' grinned Simon. 'Let us go in.'

Sammy tiptoed through the broken doorway, catching his breath as he took in the magnificence of Sir Ragnarok's innermost quarters.

Rainbow sparkles from a diamond chandelier refracted from sunlight filtering through skylight windows in the coned roof and landed on the Headmaster's possessions.

They didn't have time to look around as Lariston was standing at the top of the spiral staircase that led down into the office. If cats could show emotion, Sammy was sure that Sir Ragnarok's smoky grey feline companion would be extremely disapproving of their ungainly entrance into his quarters.

'We're here to see Sir Ragnarok,' said Sammy, breaking the silence. He was tempted to add "Your Majesty" as he now knew Lariston was one of the Kings of the Dark Ages, but with Simon Sanchez standing next to him, it seemed rather inappropriate.

With his tail in the air, Lariston circled around Sammy and Simon and sniffed around their legs. Eventually he purred and nudged them towards the spiral staircase.

In amongst Lariston's purring, Sammy thought he could almost translate what the cat was saying. It sounded as though Lariston was saying "wait here" as he sat, preening himself, on the bottom step.

In the distance, Sammy heard the bell chime to signify the end of breakfast. He knew they had ten minutes to see Sir Ragnarok and get back to the seventh floor for their Alchemistry lesson.

After eight minutes, Sir Ragnarok appeared in a gold teleporting mist and he seemed genuinely surprised to see Sammy and Simon in his office.

'I have just been dealing with the problem in your tower room, Sammy,' Sir Ragnarok smiled. 'It was quite advanced magic indeed.'

'What about the problem in my tower room?' demanded Simon.

'Problem?' enquired Sir Ragnarok. 'What problem?'

'The Shape have been here,' said Sammy. 'Mrs Hubar is the "H" in the Shape,' he thrust forward Darius's television recorder and pressed "play". 'Look!'

Sir Ragnarok pursed his lips. 'What nonsense are you bringing me?' he demanded.

Simon took Darius's pocket television and showed Sir Ragnarok. 'This is not nonsense,' said Simon. 'It is perfect sense.'

Sir Ragnarok took the device. 'Please let me look for myself.'

Sir Ragnarok held the recorder in one hand and pointed his staff towards the floor-to-ceiling television screens he used to show the comings and goings at the school. He watched in silence as the pocket television recorder replayed the morning's events.

As the recording finished and the large screens went blank, Sir Ragnarok was very quiet. He went very pale. His face looked tired and drawn, as though he had aged fifty years in five seconds.

Sir Ragnarok sighed deeply, the lines on his face deep and prominent. 'I owe you a sincere apology Sammy,' he said, his voice choked and distant. 'It was my reluctance to believe you that has killed many more dragons than needed to be killed. I am sorry. I am truly sorry.'

Sammy felt a rock form in his throat. 'It's ok,' he said, rubbing his throat with his hand. 'I just wish...'

'We should have shown you the draconite sooner,' said Simon, looking down at his feet. 'If only I had not wanted to keep them safe myself. Or, maybe if I had told you or my mother...I am sorry too.'

Sir Ragnarok cleared his throat. 'Apologies will get us nowhere,' he said matter of factly. 'We have much to do and very little time. Simon, try to find your mother and see if she and Commander Altair can reach Mrs Hubar before she gives Alfie Agrock the draconite.'

'Yes Sir Ragnarok,' said Simon and he walked out of the office, using the stairs to go down to the Main Hall.

Sir Ragnarok turned to Sammy. 'I would like you to return to your next lesson and bring Jock to me when he turns up please.'

'Will he turn up?' asked Sammy.

Sir Ragnarok nodded. 'I believe he will be back shortly.'

'What will happen to him?' asked Sammy.

Sir Ragnarok paused. 'Jock has betrayed my trust and is no longer welcome at Dragamas. He will be sent to the Snorgcadell with his mother,' said Sir Ragnarok, his hands steepled together, his pale blue eyes looking sad. 'We met in the first ever Draconian Convention in Inverness. Helana Hubar was on Moon-Silk, her silvery grey dragon and I was on Fortune, a navy blue dragon, much like Darius Murphy's dragon. We were representing Great Britain to discuss the future of dragons. Now I understand only she attended the convention to receive one of these.'

Sammy looked at the device Sir Ragnarok was showing him. It was a globe suspended by metal prongs, roughly the size of a Dragonball.

'This will be her undoing,' said Sir Ragnarok, more to himself, as Sammy backed towards the door. 'She thinks she can come here to observe the dragons. Sammy, do you know we are the talk of the Dragon World?'

Sammy shook his head. He had no idea about things outside of the school.

'You in particular are quite famous,' continued Sir Ragnarok. 'You are famous for being there when the Angel of 'El Horidore was blown. That was an event that will rewrite our future.'

'I see,' said Sammy. 'I'll try and find Jock for you.'

'Do not underestimate him,' warned Sir Ragnarok. 'We both know he is capable beyond his years. Perhaps I should send Professor Burlay.'

'I'll find Jock,' said Sammy. 'After what he's done. I'll find him.'

'Take care Sammy,' said Sir Ragnarok, putting down the globe and shuffling papers on his desk.

As Sammy turned to go, he saw Sir Ragnarok meant his words. On top of the pile of papers, Sammy saw the coloured drawing of the Stone Cross. It was now mostly blue-green with very little white space left.

Out on the stone stairs, to save time, Sammy teleported, without thinking, and he arrived in the boys' toilets, in the end cubicle, which was luckily empty.

'Teleport somewhere else,' grumbled a voice from the next cubicle. 'Blooming third years. Always messing about.'

'I'm in the fourth year actually,' said Sammy, grinning. He checked his watch. The Alchemistry lesson would be well underway, with or without Professor Sanchez.

'Outside the Alchemistry classroom,' said Sammy, putting a bit of thought into his destination, hoping he would end up in the right place this time.

# CHAPTER 35

# WEDDING PLANS

Sammy looked through the Alchemistry classroom window. Everyone was sitting in neat rows facing Professor Burlay, who was standing at the front of the classroom.

Toby had his hand up as if he was going to answer a question. Everything looked normal, except that Professor Sanchez was nowhere in sight.

'Come in Sammy,' said Professor Burlay. 'We've only just started.'

Sammy pushed the classroom door open. He glanced at the blackboard. Instead of the usual Alchemistry words and diagrams, it looked as though Professor Burlay was using the lesson time as an opportunity for an extra Astronomics class.

'We are just discussing my wedding plans,' explained Professor Burlay.

Sammy looked again at the blackboard. The coloured dots he had mistaken for stars and constellations were supposed to represent people and seating arrangements. It looked as though Commander Altair was going to be Professor Burlay's best man.

'Have you seen Jock?' asked Sammy. 'Sir Ragnarok has asked me to find him.'

Professor Burlay surveyed the class and frowned. 'No, he's not here. I must have missed him when I took the register. Perhaps he is in the Dragon Chambers? Sit down Sammy and we'll move on to some Alchemistry in a few moments.'

'But,' started Sammy.

Professor Burlay pointed at one of the empty seats. 'No buts Sammy, sit down please.'

Sammy sat next to Dixie in the front row. Due to coming straight to Alchemistry from Sir Ragnarok's office, he didn't have his rucksack with any books, pens or paper, so he quickly borrowed some from Dixie.

'Professor Burlay is getting married,' said Dixie, her eyes shining. 'Isn't it exciting!'

'I know,' whispered Sammy.

'Humph,' muttered Dixie. 'Well, you've been here since the beginning of term, haven't you?'

Sammy nodded and projected to Dixie his meeting with Simon Sanchez and Sir Ragnarok.

'Oooh,' said Dixie out loud.

'Yes,' said Professor Burlay, mistaking Dixie's "oooh" for excitement about the gold rings he was showing the class. 'The design is so pretty. It's dragon tails, intertwined. Professor Sanchez has made them for us. A perfect fit,' he added proudly. 'I took the measurements from her old ring.'

'The balloons were our invitations to the wedding,' added Dixie. 'Oh and thanks for my Valentine's card.'

'What?' asked Sammy, trying not to laugh as Professor Burlay demonstrated a "you may kiss the bride" pose, bending forward and pouting his lips.

'My Valentine's card,' repeated Dixie. 'The one with the teddy bear on the front.'

Sammy looked puzzled and shook his head. 'I didn't get you a card, I uh, I guess I forgot. Besides, I didn't think you were into all that?'

'I'm not,' said Dixie quickly. 'I just thought, well, it was a nice thought. I didn't send any cards.'

'You're not into what?' asked Holly, eavesdropping into the conversation.

'It was probably Jock,' said Toby, who had also overheard them. 'He's got a thing for you.'

'Yuck!' exclaimed Dixie.

'What's he doing sending you Valentine's cards?' demanded Sammy. 'He's working for the Shape.'

'I got seven cards,' boasted Milly.

'Is anyone else listening in?' grumbled Dixie.

'It's the last card Jock will send you,' muttered Sammy. 'Sir Ragnarok's going to send him to the Snorgcadell. He asked me to find him.'

'Well he's not here,' said Toby. 'He's probably killing my dragon right now. Tearing the draconite out of my dragon's brain and killing my Puttee.'

'It would be a long walk for him,' said Sammy, feeling desperately sorry for Toby. 'Perhaps Jock will keep Puttee alive.'

'Shut up Sammy,' said Dixie. 'Puttee isn't old enough for the Shape to want his draconite. It wouldn't be any good to them. I've seen Alfie Agrock reject draconite that wasn't strong enough.'

'You don't have to say that,' sniffed Toby. 'Gavin's injured. My dragon's dead. I'm going to kill Jock if I see him again.'

'Professor Burlay should let us go and find Jock,' said Dixie. 'I'll shove his teddy bear card...'

'Dixie? Are you listening?' interrupted Professor Burlay. 'Please copy out these star charts and label the six major constellations.'

'It's supposed to be an Alchemistry lesson,' said Dixie, turning a string of paperclips from silver to bronze to gold and back again.

'Very well,' conceded Professor Burlay. 'Why don't you stand at the front of the class and show us all how it's done?'

'It's ok,' said Dixie.

Professor Burlay took a sip from the coffee cup on Professor Sanchez's desk. He instantly screwed up his face.

'Eugh! Rat's blood,' he said, spitting the liquid back into the cup.

'Red berry juice?' asked Sammy, instantly alert.

'What?' asked Professor Burlay, rubbing his hand across his beard to get rid of the liquid.

'Nothing,' said Sammy, thinking of sausage rolls to hide his thoughts.

Professor Burlay shook his head in despair. 'Sammy, please concentrate, there's barely half a class as it is. Are Darius and Naomi still in the Dragon Chambers?'

'Yeah,' said Toby. 'Hopefully Darius is waiting for Puttee to come back.'

Amos sniggered. 'I bet I know what they're really doing. Where's Simon?'

Professor Burlay looked around the class and checked his register. 'Yes, where is Simon? Sammy, do you know where he is?'

Sammy looked at Professor Burlay. 'Simon went after Professor Sanchez. I don't know where.'

'Well really,' said Professor Burlay. 'Is it any wonder why half the class is missing. She's not setting a very good example.'

'Can we draw some star charts?' asked Milly, who, Sammy noticed, was clutching her handful of Valentine's cards as well as scoffing chocolates with Holly.

'How about we actually use some star charts,' said Professor Burlay, flicking through a well read "You're the Groom" magazine. 'Instead of Astronomics this afternoon, why don't we have a late lesson at ten o'clock tonight. Meet me at Mrs Grock's house and I'll show you how to plot a course around the castle. Please tell the others,' said Professor Burlay as the end-of-lesson bell rang.

'Ancient and Modern Languages is next,' grinned Dixie. 'Shall we skip it?'

'I can't,' said Sammy, putting his arm around Dixie's shoulder. 'I have to be there just in case Jock turns up.'

'He's long gone,' said Toby.

'Come on Sammy,' begged Dixie. 'We could go to the den.'

'Maybe later,' said Sammy. 'I have to find Jock.'

'I'll skip Ancient and Modern Languages with you,' said Toby enthusiastically.

'Never mind,' grumbled Dixie. 'Sammy's probably right. Jock might be there.' She marched out of the Alchemistry classroom, muttering something about needing to see Commander Altair.

Sammy shook his head as Dixie marched down the corridor, her green ponytail swishing behind her.

'Come on Toby,' said Sammy. 'Let's go to Ancient and Modern Languages. Jock has to be there.'

## CHAPTER 36

# BACK TO MRS GROCK'S HOUSE

To Sammy's dismay, neither Dixie nor Jock showed up for Miss Amoratti's Ancient and Modern Languages lesson.

Miss Amoratti asked the students who had turned up to write a three-page essay on the essential language structure differences between Troll and Dwarven.

When everyone groaned, she wasted no time informing them that they should be grateful she hadn't asked for the differences between Elvish and Goblin.

In Sammy's opinion, it had been a wasted hour in which he could have been searching for Jock, or getting close to Dixie again. Not that there had been much time together since the kiss.

At least Darius and Naomi had turned up. Darius's neck was covered in a sticky looking pink lip gloss that was rubbing off on his shirt collar.

Sammy's arm was aching when he finally finished the essay on what he thought were the essential language structure differences between Troll and Dwarven.

'Everyone gets an "A",' said Miss Amoratti jovially as the end-of-lesson bell chimed. 'Put your papers in the waste paper bin on your way out.'

Sammy choked back his disapproval as he crumpled the seven double sided pages he had handwritten into a ball and slammed it into the bin beside Miss Amoratti's desk.

'Thank you Sammy,' said Miss Amoratti, as if she thought there was absolutely nothing wrong with this at all.

'Unbelievable,' Sammy grumbled to Darius and Toby as the three of them walked to Mrs Grock's house.

'She always does something like that,' agreed Darius. 'I didn't bother writing very much.'

'Well I did,' said Sammy. 'I want to learn everything I can about Trolls.'

Darius and Toby laughed hysterically. Darius kicked open Mrs Grock's garden gate and inside Mrs Grock's house, Sammy, Toby and Darius found Dixie, Commander Altair and Professor Burlay enjoying mugs of steaming hot chocolate with Mrs Grock and Gavin.

Both of Gavin's knees were in plastic wrappings and Sammy guessed Mrs Grock had run out of eggs again. A folding stretcher was resting up against the wall next to the fireplace. Above the flames, a string of chestnuts was roasting and giving off an enticing aroma.

'Hello boys,' said Professor Burlay. 'Have you found Jock?'

Sammy shook his head. 'He didn't show up in Miss Amoratti's class.

'He's off the Directometer too,' said Commander Altair, pointing to the silver dial on his watch, the same watch Sammy wore, which had been given to him by his uncle, Peter Pickering.

'I never thought of that,' said Sammy, suddenly ashamed of himself. Out of him, Toby and Darius, he had the best tools. He had been given emerald crystals and he had a Directometer built into his wristwatch.

'That was why I wanted you to skip Ancient and Modern Languages,' said Dixie. 'I just didn't want to say it in front of everyone.'

Sammy stared at the floor. 'Please can I see my parents' dragons?'

'Sure,' said Commander Altair. 'But it won't enhance the signal. Did you know that your parents' dragons are the only adult dragons left? Apart from the Dragamas teachers' dragons, there aren't any adult dragons. We took in another ten bodies over the weekend.'

'Oh,' said Sammy, feeling stupid as he realised the teachers would already have tried that long before he had even thought of it. 'I'll see them later then.'

'Ooch, the dragons are coming here all right,' said Mrs Grock. 'Now, Dixie, if you can keep a secret, I will let you help me with my wedding plans.'

'Cool, said Dixie, putting her hot chocolate mug on the coffee table and standing up. 'Please can I get Milly and Holly in on it too and Naomi, her cousin got married at Christmas so she knows all about weddings.'

'Ooch yes,' said Mrs Grock, nodding. 'I want everything to be perfect.'

'Everything "will" be perfect,' said Professor Burlay. 'Professor Sanchez finished our wedding rings and gave them to me yesterday evening.'

'Two gold rings with beautiful intertwined dragon tails,' said Commander Altair, patting his jeans pocket. 'They're now both safe with me.'

'When will your family be coming John?' asked Mrs Grock. 'They canna stay here if they wish.'

Professor Burlay looked at Dixie and then looked a little embarrassed. 'Molly will be here next week. But Dad's home so he and Mum won't come to Dragamas until the day before our wedding.'

'I expect they'll have a lot of catching up to do,' said Commander Altair, squeezing Dixie's shoulders.

Sammy heard the Dragon Commander whisper "I'm here for you" to Dixie and he found himself thinking "me too".

'Did you find Mrs Hubar?' asked Sammy out loud.

'Should I have found Mrs Hubar?' asked Commander Altair. 'Why?'

'She's in the Shape,' said Sammy. 'Toby and I caught her stealing draconite from the East tower. We've seen Sir Ragnarok and everything.'

Commander Altair flinched. 'I knew it,' he spat. 'Vermin often live underground.'

'Scum from the mines,' added Dixie, helping herself to some of Mrs Grock's roasting chestnuts.

'Simon was going to find Professor Sanchez to go after Mrs Hubar,' said Sammy. 'She was supposed to be going with you as well.'

Commander Altair reached for his coat, which was folded over one of the chairs by the dining table. 'I'll find her,' he promised.

'Ooch, be careful,' said Mrs Grock, helping Commander Altair into his coat.

'Aren't I always careful?' Commander Altair flashed Mrs Grock a smile. 'I'll leave this here,' he indicated towards a pouch of black Zyon powder. 'It might be useful,' he nodded to Sammy.

'Ooch, go on with you,' said Mrs Grock, holding open her cottage door.

Professor Burlay slapped Commander Altair's shoulder. 'Be safe.'

'Good luck Sir,' said Gavin. He stood up and wobbled. His knees were on the mend even if they weren't completely healed.

Commander Altair nodded. 'See you soon.'

The door slammed shut behind him and Sammy shivered. Who knew what Commander Altair would face or what battle he might have against Helana Hubar and Alfie Agrock.

'Who's for a nice cup of hot chocolate?' asked Mrs Grock, trying to lighten the mood.

No one answered. Mrs Grock's offer fell flat and she bustled around her lounge straightening cushions trying to keep herself busy.

'We should find Jock,' said Sammy. 'We should go back to the castle. We're not going to find him sitting around here drinking hot chocolate.'

'Let me at him,' scowled Gavin. 'I'll break his neck.'

Toby nodded. 'Me too.'

'Now, there's no need for talk like that,' reproved Mrs Grock. 'Sir Ragnarok will be the one to assign whatever punishment is due.'

'Jock may not have had a choice,' added Professor Burlay. 'But I think Sammy is right. The castle is the most logical place to look for him.'

'I'd like to stay here,' said Dixie, sitting back down on one of the beanbags by the fire. 'I want to make sure Orion comes back safely.'

'I'm afraid that's not possible,' said Professor Burlay looking kindly at her. 'I know he's important to you, but you must return for your afternoon lessons. As I am preparing you for a trek using night navigation this evening, you may use the Astronomics lesson this afternoon for general study, if you wish,' he added brightly.

'Great, that'll be fun,' said Dixie, not looking like she meant it in the slightest.

'I've seen him up against worse adversaries than Mrs Hubar,' reassured Professor Burlay. 'He'll eat her for breakfast. She's no match for a Snorgcadell Commander. Orion has been a Dragon Knight since he was fifteen and he was the youngest person in the Snorgcadell to become a Dragon Commander.'

'Really? Cool!' said Sammy. He picked up the Zyon powder Commander Altair had left for him as discretely as he could and stuffed it into his pocket.

'You may get the chance to become a Dragon Knight someday Sammy,' said Professor Burlay. 'Dragons have been around long before you or I were born and they'll be around long after we're gone.'

'Come on,' said Dixie, casting a long look at the chair Commander Altair had sat in. 'If we can't stay here, let's get going.'

'Use the Astronomics lesson for revision for your exams,' said Professor Burlay firmly. 'Leave the finding of Jock and Mrs Hubar in our hands.'

Darius held open Mrs Grock's green front door and they filed out in silence. Dixie entwined her arm with Sammy's and he squeezed her hand gently. It wasn't until they reached the North Tower common room that Professor Burlay turned to Sammy, Dixie, Darius, Gavin and Toby.

'Sometimes it's hard to wait for things to play out,' said Professor Burlay. 'I know it can be very hard at times.'

'Will Commander Altair really be all right?' asked Dixie. 'I'm not a kid any more. You don't have to pretend it's all ok when it's not.'

'No, you're not a kid.' Professor Burlay ran a hand through his hair and stroked his beard. 'We will just have to wait and see what happens. Hey! Come down off those chairs!'

Two first years playing "jump" scuttled away from the rows of chairs they had arranged into an assault course. They disappeared up the boys' tower looking terrified of Professor Burlay.

'It will be all right,' said Professor Burlay reassuringly. 'Fetch your books and meet me in room fifty-three. I will see Sir Ragnarok and be there in fifteen minutes to supervise your studies. I hope I can trust you to start work quietly without me.'

CHAPTER 37

# DEATH OF A TEACHER

Up in the Astronomics classroom, Sammy didn't think Professor Burlay would have approved of the paper aeroplane contest organised by Gavin and Toby. The air was filled with streamlined paper jets flying from one end of the classroom to the other.

However, no stars were lost when Professor Burlay eventually marched into the classroom, a grim smile on his usually cheerful face.

'Thank you for entertaining yourselves so studiously,' said Professor Burlay, catching one of the aeroplanes in mid-flight and crumpling it into a ball. 'All lessons are now postponed for the day. Sir Ragnarok has asked to see the whole school in the Main Hall immediately.'

'Why?' demanded Gavin. 'What's happened?'

'Did Commander Altair find Professor Sanchez?' asked Peter Grayling from West.

'News travels fast,' muttered Professor Burlay. 'Hurry please and Sir Ragnarok will explain everything. Simon, would you wait behind please.'

Sammy exchanged a look with Simon. He projected "what's going on?" but Simon just shrugged.

The fourth years scraped their chairs back and packed books and papers into their rucksacks, their feet clattering on the floor as they filed out of the classroom.

Sammy caught snippets of a conversation between two East girls. It sounded as though they were speculating that Mrs Hubar had been caught red-handed.

In the Main Hall, most of the other students were already seated at the house tables. The second years were in their sportswear. Mr Cross and Mr Ockay were standing beside the second year tables. Neither of them looked happy that their lesson had been interrupted.

Tom Sweep was standing at the back of the Main Hall, resting his chin on his long wooden broom handle. Captain Duke Stronghammer and Captain Avensis Firebreath were standing next to him. They were flanked by thirty or so Dwarves, all wearing white shirts specked with dirt, denim dungarees and black boots. The Dwarves' faces were sooty from coming straight from the mine.

The fifth years filtered into the Main Hall accompanied by the first years, who looked very small in comparison. There was a murmur of noise, the creaking of chairs and general unease as the students of Dragamas waited for Sir Ragnarok to appear.

After a couple of minutes, Sir Ragnarok ducked out from behind the Knight tapestry along the side wall of the Main Hall. He was dressed in a long black velvet robe that covered him from his collar to his toes. He swept up to his chair at the teachers' table and asked everyone to sit.

'Thank you for coming here at short notice,' said Sir Ragnarok slowly, pronouncing his words carefully. He was reading from a small white cue card in his left hand.

The Main Hall fell silent. Every student turned to face their headmaster. Sammy thought it was so quiet you could have heard a dragon scale drop.

'I have disturbing news about the Shape,' continued Sir Ragnarok. 'They are among us and they have been among us for some considerable time. Gemology teacher, Captain Stronghammer's wife, mother of two children at this school, my personal friend,' Sir Ragnarok paused. 'It has come to my attention that from the outset, she has been working against me. She is a key figure in the Shape, the corrupt individuals who are intent on gaining personal power at the expense of our way of life. Mrs Hubar has been caught passing draconite to the Shape to re-build the Stone Cross.'

At the back of the hall there was a deathly howl. Sammy spun round. Captain Stronghammer had collapsed to his knees. Captain Firebreath took a bottle of cider out of his dungaree pocket and passed it to Captain Stronghammer, who drank it all in one noisy gulp.

Captain Stronghammer passed the bottle back to Captain Firebreath and shoved his way out of the Main Hall. Captain Firebreath and several Dwarves scurried after him.

'I realise this must be a shock,' said Sir Ragnarok. 'Two Gemology teachers found to be in the Shape and perhaps the worse news should be saved until tomorrow…however there may be worse news again and I like to keep Dragamas students involved and informed. I must treat you with the respect that you deserve.'

'I wish he'd get to the point,' muttered Dixie.

'Professor Sanchez is dead,' said Sir Ragnarok abruptly, his voice choking. 'She and Commander Altair sought out our traitors, but…but, I'm sorry…' Sir Ragnarok backed away from the teachers' table, his face in his hands.

Sammy turned to the East table to see Simon's reaction, but he had gone and Professor Burlay stood rigidly alone beside Simon's empty chair, his mouth slightly open.

'Woah,' said Gavin. 'No more Alchemistry with Professor Sanchez.'

'Poor Simon,' said Milly.

'Professor Sanchez is dead,' said Sammy numbly, as though speaking the words out loud would make it untrue, someone would laugh at him, or tell him he was stupid for believing it.

Professor Burlay took Sir Ragnarok's place at the teachers' table and addressed the school.

'Lessons will be suspended until tomorrow morning,' said Professor Burlay sombrely. 'Please use the time to study quietly in your common rooms or in the library. This is a very difficult time for all of us.'

## CHAPTER 38

# JOCK RETURNS

Sammy led the way out of the Main Hall. There were whispered rumours ringing in his ears as students behind him discussed grisly stories about how Professor Sanchez and Mrs Hubar had fought each other to the death.

Back in the North common room, Sammy sat with Dixie, Darius, Gavin and Toby on beanbags by one of the windows. They saw two long black cars arrive and park in the castle courtyard. Men and women in long black robes spoke briefly to Sir Ragnarok and went inside the castle.

'There's going to be no Alchemistry until Sir Ragnarok finds a replacement,' said Gavin, flicking through the latest copy of In-Flight magazine.

Dixie fidgeted. 'I want to make sure Commander Altair is ok.'

'Is he your boyfriend?' asked Gavin. 'Isn't he a bit old for you?'

'Dixie's Dad was in the Snorgcadell with Commander Altair,' said Sammy. 'I'm her boyfriend.'

'Oh,' said Gavin. 'Ooooh!'

Dixie grinned and nudged Sammy's shoulder. 'Since when?'

'Since now, I guess, if it's ok…' grinned Sammy.

'Sure.' Dixie looked shyly at him through her green lashed eyes. 'So, are we going to find Commander Altair?'

Toby put down his homework. 'No one's going anywhere with Dr Shivers and Professor Burlay guarding the door. Anyone would think the Shape were after us and wanted something out of human brains instead of draconite out of dragon's brains.'

'Dragonball!' said Darius suddenly. 'We'll start a game, then Dixie and Sammy can go out after a ball that went out of the window.'

'Accidentally of course,' grinned Dixie.

'I'll get my Draconis Plus with Invisiballs set,' said Sammy. 'We used yours last time Toby and yours doesn't have the Invisiballs.'

'Hurry,' said Dixie, standing up to open one of the ground floor windows.

'It's cold enough in here, thank you,' Dr Shivers called across the common room.

To Sammy's dismay, Dr Shivers came over to them, armed with a large Dragon Studies folder, and he sat on a beanbag next to Dixie and Darius. Dr Shivers opened the folder and started handing out Dragon Studies notes.

Sammy stomped up the boys' staircase, cursing Dr Shivers under his breath. He wished Professor Sanchez had stopped to ask for Commander Altair's help finding Mrs Hubar. He shoved open the fourth years' dormitory door and knelt on the floor to retrieve his Dragonball set from under his bed.

Toby, Gavin and Jock's curtains were drawn, but Sammy had a nasty feeling he wasn't alone in the room.

'Hello?' called Sammy.

There was a slight rustle from behind Toby's velvet curtain.

Sammy picked up his shiny silver Dragonball case and crept past the closed curtain. He paused, feeling silly for being scared and pulled open the green veil.

He immediately took a step back. Jock was there, packing his suitcase full to the brim with books and clothes.

'Hey!' exclaimed Sammy.

Jock looked up. 'What are you doing here?' he glared.

Sammy braced himself. 'I was looking for you.'

'How did you know I'd be here?' demanded Jock.

Sammy shrugged. Jock didn't need to know the real reason he had come upstairs. Let him think what he liked.

'It doesn't matter,' said Jock. 'I'm done here anyway. Everything's packed. I'm gonna get out of here. Castle Court...'

Sammy reached into his pocket and scooped out the black Zyon powder. He showered it over Jock in a huge cloud of tiny black shards that bit and stung his face, melting through his clothes as the black dust rained down.

'You're going nowhere!' shouted Sammy. 'Nowhere!'

Jock rubbed his bleeding arms. 'You'll pay for this Sammy! You don't know what you're dealing with!'

'Oh yeah?' said Sammy, raising his fists. 'What am I dealing with?'

'Me!' shouted Jock, lunging forward, his eyes bulging and bloodshot. 'You're nothing to do with dragons! You shouldn't be here!'

Sammy cracked his fist at Jock's jaw. 'I am supposed to be here!' he shouted and punched Jock in the stomach. 'It's you who doesn't belong here! Ow!'

Jock pulled tufts of Sammy's hair out and kicked his shins.

'Let me go!' squealed Jock.

'No!' roared Sammy. 'You killed dragons! You're going to Sir Ragnarok's office!'

Jock kicked out again and Sammy threw him onto the floor, landing on top of him. He grabbed Jock's wrists and brushed Jock's head away as he turned to bite Sammy's arm.

'Castle Courtyard!' shouted Jock. 'School gates! Darned Zyon powder. Where did you get it?'

'From Commander Altair,' puffed Sammy, closing his fingers tighter around Jock's bony wrist. 'He said I might need it.'

'What about your Cross for Bravery? I showed you how to turn it into a dragon scale and back again. We're friends. You were good to me when I got here and didn't know anyone,' whined Jock, twisting and turning as he tried to escape.

'Shut up,' said Sammy, squeezing harder.

Jock wriggled. 'Mum said she'd let me run things with her. If you let me go, I'll share it with you.'

'No,' said Sammy firmly. 'Your Mum's been caught. They've got your Mum now. You're wrong to be involved with the Shape. They'll never win.'

'Liar!' screeched Jock. 'Join the Shape and you'll have everything you've ever wanted!'

'No,' said Sammy.

'Your parents could see dragons again,' said Jock. 'That's what you want most of all, isn't it? I could give that to you...just let me go.'

'No,' said Sammy. He felt something stirring inside him. He felt torn at the possibility of his parents seeing dragons again.

'It's what you want, isn't it,' said Jock. 'I can give that to you.'

'Shut up,' said Sammy, grabbing Jock's shirt collar. 'My parents will never see dragons again and there's nothing I can do about it.'

'What if there was something you could do about it,' said Jock.

'Shut up and get up,' said Sammy. 'We're going downstairs.'

'Make me,' retorted Jock.

Sammy dragged Jock out of the tower room by his legs. He had to pull really hard as Jock grabbed hold of the end of his bed to stay in the room.

'Fine,' puffed Sammy. 'Are you going to walk, or do I have to push you down the stairs?'

'What in the dragon's name is going on here?'

Sammy spun round. 'Dr Shivers?'

'I came looking for you Sammy. Sir Ragnarok insisted Professor Burlay and I look after all of the North students. We are under strict instructions to supervise you all and keep you all safe and you all out of trouble. You will lose three stars for disobedience,' said Dr Shivers, flicking his wrist and creating three black stars out of thin air.

'But I found Jock!' exclaimed Sammy.

'So I see,' said Dr Shivers. 'Sammy, please go back downstairs to the common room and stay with the other North students. Jock, you come with me.'

Jock leaped to his feet as soon as Sammy released him.

'But Sir, it's nothing to do with me,' whined Jock. 'You know it's not. It's me Mum who's in the Shape. You know it is.'

'I know that Sir Ragnarok would like a word with you,' said Dr Shivers frostily.

'Sammy's in the Shape!' shouted Jock suddenly. 'It's him you want. I was trying to stop him with the Zyon powder.'

Dr Shivers paused and turned to Sammy.

'He's lying,' said Sammy. 'Commander Altair gave the Zyon powder to me.'

Dr Shivers's gaunt face narrowed but he remained calm. 'This is an advanced tool Sammy. It is a powerful weapon. I don't think Commander Altair would have given you this. It's more than his job is worth.'

'He left it on the table at Mrs Grock's house,' admitted Sammy.

'Sammy stole it,' said Jock. 'Thief! Thief! Thief!'

'Silence!' hissed Dr Shivers. 'You have given yourself away Jock. Come with me and you will answer to Sir Ragnarok.'

Sammy stood back as Dr Shivers forced a green pellet into Jock's mouth. Instantly, Jock stopped kicking and shouting and slumped to the floor. He could hear the sound "step-bump, step-bump" as Jock was dragged down the spiral staircase.

Sammy picked up the forgotten Dragonball suitcase and followed at a distance. Dixie and Darius were at the bottom of the stairs.

'What took you so long?' demanded Dixie. 'Dr Shivers has found Jock.'

'I found Jock,' said Sammy.

'You're cut,' said Darius, handing Sammy the familiar bottle of healing lotion that he called "Heal All" and told anyone who would listen that he was going to sell it when he left Dragamas.

Sammy rubbed the foul smelling ointment into his face, hands and neck, everywhere that had taken the brunt of the black Zyon powder. He rolled up his right trouser leg and smeared the ointment over a bruise which was forming on his shin where Jock had kicked him.

'I found Jock,' repeated Sammy, thinking no one was listening. 'We had a fight.'

'Cool,' said Darius, looking at Sammy with respect. 'Dr Shivers brought Jock downstairs and he was unconscious.'

'Dr Shivers gave Jock a green pellet,' admitted Sammy. 'That wasn't me.'

'Are you ok?' asked Dixie. 'If you are, then I'm going to Mrs Grock's house to see if Commander Altair is back yet.'

'We'll come too,' said Sammy. 'Professor Burlay has gone with Dr Shivers and Jock so there are no teachers telling us to stay here any more.'

# CHAPTER 39

# A BAD DAY FOR DRAGAMAS

Sammy checked the corridor in both directions to make sure nobody was around. He slinked out of the common room with Dixie and Darius following closely behind him.

'I'm sure Commander Altair will be ok,' Sammy tried to reassure Dixie.

'Yeah,' added Darius. 'If he wasn't ok then Sir Ragnarok would have told us.'

'Maybe he's injured,' said Dixie, looking worried as she pushed open the castle door. 'Maybe Sir Ragnarok hasn't found him yet.'

'He'll be fine,' said Sammy, taking Dixie's hand as they walked across the castle courtyard and out into the school grounds. 'You know he'll be ok. Commander Altair is the best at Armoury in the whole of the Snorgcadell!'

'Get a room!' giggled Darius. 'You're so soppy Sammy.'

'Shut it,' instructed Dixie, and Sammy was disappointed when she let go of his hand.

Sammy pushed open Mrs Grock's garden gate. Mrs Grock was outside in her garden, plucking turnips from her vegetable patch. Two rabbits were jumping in circles around her and seemed to be fighting over a long orange carrot. A rooster crowed among her brood of hens, which were clucking in the open pen.

'Ooch, go on with you, silly rabbits!' said Mrs Grock. 'Leave me turnips alone. I expect I'll be needing many more of these to patch everyone up again.'

'Hi Mrs Grock!' shouted Dixie, skipping up to the school secretary and nurse and making her jump.

Mrs Grock dropped one of the turnips she was carrying. 'Ooch Dixie dear, you scared the life out of me!' she said, picking up the turnip and putting it into a wicker basket by her feet.

'Is Commander Altair back?' demanded Dixie. 'I want to see him!'

Mrs Grock smiled. 'Ooch yes Dixie, he's back. But I must warn you, he's not a pretty sight.'

'I'll go first,' said Sammy. He pushed open the green front door and went inside.

Commander Altair was standing by the fireplace warming his hands and helping himself to some of the chestnuts Mrs Grock always had tied to a piece of string and roasting above the heat. His grey overcoat had great slashes across the back and he was hunched over, coughing into his coat sleeve.

'Orion!' squealed Dixie, running over to him.

Commander Altair smiled and put an arm around her shoulder. 'I got him,' rasped Commander Altair, trying not to cough. 'Alfie Agrock who killed your father. I got him.'

'You killed him?' asked Sammy, his eyes wide.

Commander Altair shook his head. 'I wouldn't stoop to his level. No, I handed Alfie Agrock over to my father. You knew his real name is Alfred Agrock, didn't you?'

Sammy nodded. 'He told us last summer, when he took Dixie.'

'Yeah,' said Darius. 'That's how Professor Burlay can marry Mrs Grock. It was all a sham.'

'Ooch, are my ears burning?' asked Mrs Grock, bustling in through the doorway with her wicker basket full of fresh vegetables.

Sammy spun around and grinned. Under her velvet bonnet, Mrs Grock's cheeks were pinker than the turnips and radishes she grew in her garden.

'Will the Snorgcadell punish Alfie Agrock?' asked Dixie. 'I hope they kill him.'

Commander Altair sat on the sofa nearest to the fire and rubbed his wrist. Sammy saw a streak of the brown healing potion dribble onto the floor and he wondered how many cuts and injuries Commander Altair had sustained.

'The Snorgcadell is our justice system,' said Commander Altair. 'For Alfie Agrock's crimes against Dwarves, humans and Trolls, he will be punished, maybe in prison or maybe by death. It will depend on the evidence brought against him.'

'I'll be there,' said Dixie, folding her arms defiantly. 'He'll pay for what he's done to my family.'

Dixie unhooked two of the hot chestnuts from the string above the fireplace and crushed them in her hands. She threw the remains into the fire and they fizzed and crackled.

'By the rule of three times three, he'll receive what's done to me,' Dixie muttered, eating the nuts and crunching them into pieces with her teeth.

Though he knew the words were just from a television programme, they chilled Sammy and he drew closer to the fire, rubbing his hands to keep warm.

'How about a nice cup of hot chocolate? Sammy, perhaps you would like to check on your parents' dragons as well?' asked Mrs Grock. 'I've got two girls upstairs with colds and Jeremy Beaston who broke his ankle playing Firesticks to attend to, but I could sort something after that if you like?' she added and bustled her way upstairs to check on her patients.

'Good idea,' said Commander Altair, rubbing some more of the brown healing potion into his wrist. He took out his staff from inside his grey overcoat.

Sammy gasped as the staff fell apart in Commander Altair's hands. It was broken in half and was missing most of its crystals.

Commander Altair noticed Sammy looking at his staff. 'It's a shame Sir Ragnarok hasn't been too good at choosing Gemology teachers recently,' he smiled. 'I'll have to see if Mrs Hubar has left any good gemstones behind.'

'I wouldn't trust her gemstones,' muttered Dixie.

'Come on Dixie,' said Commander Altair kindly. 'Mrs Hubar just got turned. No one in life is all good or all bad.'

'She killed Professor Sanchez,' said Dixie.

Commander Altair shrugged. 'Maybe, but Simone's as good as me at Side Splitting and Shape Shifting.'

'What's Shape Shifting?' asked Sammy, hovering by the store room door, wanting to find out before he checked on Cyngard, Jovah and Paprika.

'It's like turning stuff into stuff,' said Dixie. 'Show him.'

Commander Altair held out the two parts of his staff, one in each hand, and pointed them at Mrs Grock's dining table.

There was a burst of light. The dining table shuddered and suddenly turned into a bright orange sports car, then back to the table again.

'Darn it!' spat Commander Altair, throwing his staff into the fire. 'It was supposed to be a lion!'

'Ooch,' exclaimed Mrs Grock, coming back downstairs with a thermometer in her hand. 'It canna be a bad thing it

271

didn't work. A lion in here! Whatever next! Maybe you're not as fit as you think you are.'

'Maybe I need a new staff,' growled Commander Altair.

'Yeah you just burnt your old one,' said Dixie.

Commander Altair shrugged. 'I could get it back,' he said dismissively. 'It wasn't much good at the best of times. I should have used my dragon's power instead.'

'And perhaps it's best you didn't,' said Mrs Grock. 'Now, let me get you all your mugs of hot chocolate.'

'Are you supposed to be in the castle?' Commander Altair asked suddenly, checking the silver dial on his watch. 'Professor Burlay and Dr Shivers are coming this way.'

'We'd better go,' said Sammy, although he was unable to stop staring at the remains of Commander Altair's staff burning in the grate and unable to stop thinking of the Armoury teacher's promise that he could recreate his staff at any time.

Despite himself, Sammy was really impressed and had the utmost respect for his teacher.

'Please can we use the passages?' asked Dixie. 'We can see Sammy's parents' dragons on the way.'

'We don't want to lose any stars either,' said Darius.

'No one is allowed to use the passages until Sir Ragnarok says it is ok,' said Commander Altair. 'I'm sorry, it's just too dangerous at the moment.'

There was a loud knock at the door. Sammy looked out of the lounge window. It was Dr Shivers and he looked angry. Professor Burlay was a few paces behind him, staring into the wishing well.

Sammy saw Professor Burlay toss a coin into the well. Inside his head, he thought he heard Professor Burlay wishing for a fine day for the wedding.

'Sammy? Dixie? Darius? Are you in there?' shouted Dr Shivers, beating again on the door with his fist.

Sammy noticed Mrs Grock shrinking away into the corner of the room. She was twisting her hands, muttering "it's not Alfie" to herself.

Sammy answered the door. He ducked out of the way as Dr Shivers barged past him.

'Back to the castle! Now!' barked Dr Shivers. 'And you can thank your lucky gold stars the North house is bottom of the house stars, otherwise I'd be giving out black stars, ten black stars for each of you!'

'Yes Dr Shivers,' said Darius meekly.

'Ooch Zacharius, you'll not take any more stars from my helpers,' said Mrs Grock looking most put out. 'Why, the young Dragon Knight has come to check on his parents' dragons which I am looking after for him. Darius has learned my healing potion and Dixie has come to check on Commander Altair...'

'That I can believe,' interrupted Dr Shivers. 'Very well, Dixie, I understand Commander Altair is a close family friend, but I must insist that you all come back to the castle at once. Sir Ragnarok has news about Mrs Hubar.'

'I was there,' said Commander Altair, raising himself from the sofa. 'It has been a bad day for Dragamas.'

'Indeed,' Dr Shivers frowned, long grey lines deepening on his face. 'Come with me please.'

Back in the castle, the corridors were dark and cold. Valentine's Day banners and pink balloons hung in the hallways, but they seemed hollow and empty in the wake of Professor Sanchez's death. Black balloons would have been more appropriate, Sammy thought.

Dixie seemed unusually quiet and for the first time, she pecked Sammy on the cheek before going up the girls' tower staircase to bed.

Sammy went to the boys' bathroom and rubbed everywhere on his face except where Dixie had kissed him on his cheek as he washed for bed.

A stray pink balloon bobbed in one of the sinks and Sammy tossed it onto the floor. A third year Sammy only knew as "Chuckie", since his parents ran a chicken farm, came in and stamped on the balloon making Sammy jump.

Sammy finished in the bathroom and went up to the fourth years' tower bedroom. Darius's study light was on, but Sammy didn't want to disturb him. Gavin and Toby's curtains were drawn, albeit slightly askew from Sammy's fight with Jock earlier.

Sammy stared at Jock's empty bed. All of his things had gone, from his photos and textbooks to his bedding, which Sammy half-hoped would be thrown away or burnt to get rid of the memories.

CHAPTER 40

# AN UNEXPECTED FIND

Several weeks later, the summer sun woke Sammy from a fitful sleep. He had been dreaming about his fight with Jock, with the Dwarf kicking and punching, spitting and swearing at him.

Sammy racked his brains but he couldn't piece together why Jock had turned and joined the Shape. He had said he wanted "to have the power" and Sammy could hear the words "join the Shape and we'll make your parents see dragons again" spinning in his head.

'No,' Sammy said out loud and he got out of bed, shaking his head to get rid of the bad dream.

Darius was already awake and studying quietly at his desk. Gavin and Toby were asleep with their green velvet curtains drawn tightly around their beds.

Sammy picked up his Gemology books and put them inside his suitcase under his bed.

Sir Ragnarok had cancelled all Gemology lessons in the wake of Mrs Hubar's capture. Instead of Gemology lessons, he had handed out Gemology course material to the fifth year students so that they could help teach the subject and what to revise for the exams to the younger students in the evenings.

Despite a few initial complaints, Sammy knew that some of the fifth years were secretly enjoying the assignment. It meant they had the opportunity to go back to the basics they had learned five years ago.

Sir Ragnarok had also ordered the destruction of all of the crystals and gemstones Mrs Hubar had in her classroom, in case they contained any negative energy or curses.

On the first Friday following Mrs Hubar's capture, the fourth years had been given brand new sapphires, dug out of the mine under the school by Captain Firebreath himself.

At the time, Sammy had thought this was pointless, since they hadn't had the rubies they had been given in the second year, or the amber gemstones they had been given last year replaced.

Nor had Sir Ragnarok replaced the onyx gemstones they had been given by Dr Lithoman in their first year at Dragamas. Considering the onyx was given to them for protection, Sammy couldn't understand the logic.

Darius had been quick to point this out and he had spent hours cleaning his crystals in soapy water to try and purify them and remove all influences apart from his own.

The results hadn't been altogether successful. Sammy looked over at Darius's study desk where Darius had lined up his gemstones. Darius's onyx was now black with white spots.

Sammy had his doubts that it was even onyx, or that it actually had any healing properties. He much preferred to touch his Cross for Bravery necklace any time he needed extra confidence or courage.

Inside its magic illusionary properties, Sammy felt he drew deeper strengths when he held his cross. It gave him the self-belief that he could save the dragons from the Shape and staved off his feelings of sadness that his parents couldn't see dragons any more.

Sammy picked out his polo shirt and leather lined sports trousers and his double ended Firesticks staff.

'Do you want a game of Firesticks?' asked Sammy.

Darius looked up from his textbook. 'Sure!' he said enthusiastically. He slammed the book shut and the noise woke Gavin and Toby.

'We're playing Firesticks!' said Darius. 'Are you playing?'

'Absolutely!' said Toby, leaping out of bed.

'Where's my Firestick?' demanded Gavin, rummaging through everything on top of his chest of drawers. 'Got it!' he yelled triumphantly as it emerged from under a pile of clothes.

Five minutes later, Sammy, Darius, Gavin and Toby were downstairs and outside on the sports pitch wearing their full Firesticks kit with black tracksuit bottoms with brown dragonhide patches sewn down the inner thigh to the ankle and white polo shirts.

With Darius's help, Sammy raised the golden dragon statue in the centre of the pitch. It spun round and around, grinding the cogs inside until it had its own momentum and spun around rapidly on its own.

Sammy fed the pink balls, purple balls and Invisiballs into the slot under the golden dragon's front paws. He ducked as an Invisiball flicked out of the dragon's mouth and vanished. It reappeared about ten feet away and then it was gone again.

'Are you ready!' shouted Sammy.

'Me and Gavin against you and Darius!' yelled Toby, holding his double ended Firestick close to the ground.

Toby scooped his Firestick along the grass and whacked one of the purple balls so hard that it flew up in the air, aiming towards the dragon's mouth to score the goal.

The ball cracked against the side of the golden dragon's jaw with a metallic clang.

'Darn it!' shouted Toby, racing towards another ball. 'Here Gavin, have this one!'

Darius intercepted Gavin's wild pass and flung the ball to Sammy.

Sammy picked up the ball with his stick and looked at it, a puzzled expression on his face. The ball was covered in a pattern of chequered green and blue.

It wasn't one of the Firesticks balls. It looked more like a juggler's ball and when Sammy picked it up, it felt like it was filled with rice or dried peas.

Toby ran over to Sammy. 'You're not supposed to pick them up,' puffed Toby. 'Hey! That's not one of our balls.'

'I know,' said Sammy. 'It must be one someone dropped.'

'It looks like a juggler's ball,' said Toby, taking the ball and squashing it in his hands.

Gavin and Darius ran over to Sammy and Toby. They stared at the ball.

'What's that?' asked Gavin.

'Beanball,' said Toby.

'Where's it from?' asked Gavin, looking upwards. 'Do you reckon it fell out of the sky?'

Darius let out an explosive giggle. 'Someone probably dropped it.'

'Finders keepers,' said Gavin, taking the ball from Toby. 'I remember these beanballs. That juggler had them at the Floating Circus. I wanted some for Christmas but I didn't get any.'

'There's another one over there,' said Darius, pointing to the edge of the pitch.

Sammy looked and he could see two more blue and green chequered beanballs and another one sticking out of the bushes.

'Do you really think someone dropped them?' asked Gavin. 'We had Sports yesterday and they weren't there then.'

'No,' said Sammy, looking up at the sky and then down at the beanball. He spotted tiny silver and blue sequins in the shape of the letters "S.H." sewn into each of the chequered squares.

'It says "S.H.", look,' said Sammy. 'Could they belong to Susan Horsham?'

'Or Stevie Hendon,' suggested Darius. 'He's a first year in West, but he hates sport. There's no way he's been out here.'

Sammy looked around. They had found four identical beanballs.

Toby pointed to the bushes. 'There's another one!'

They ran across to the bush that Toby had pointed to. But when they got there, it wasn't a beanball, it was a small green ballet shoe.

'That's weird,' muttered Gavin, poking the bushes with his Firestick.

'Holy dragon,' whispered Darius. 'Look at that!'

Sammy looked and gasped. Beyond the green ballet shoe was a pale white foot, half covered in torn and bloodstained purple lycra. Further into the bushes was the rest of the body. It belonged to a girl of about their age with blonde hair. Her eyes were tightly shut but she was breathing gently.

# CHAPTER 41

# SARAH HAVERCASTLE

'It looks like she's asleep,' whispered Toby.

'Apart from the blood,' muttered Gavin. 'Let's get Professor Burlay. He'll know what to do about her.'

'We should take her to Mrs Grock's,' said Sammy, kneeling on the grass beside the girl's head. 'Maybe she can do something for her.'

'Like bring her back to life?' asked Gavin.

Darius knelt down beside Sammy. 'She's not dead. The bushes have cushioned her.'

Gavin peered at the girl and flicked some of her hair out of her eyes. 'She's dead,' he said dismissively. 'Pity. She's hot.'

'Shut up Gavin,' snapped Darius, taking off his jumper. 'She's not dead. Keep her still and warm and I'll go and get Mrs Grock myself.'

'There's no point,' said Gavin. 'If we're not playing Firesticks any more, I'm off.'

'Yeah Sammy, I don't think anything can be done for her,' said Toby. 'It's really weird seeing a dead body,' he added, then he turned around and was violently sick in the bushes. 'I can't do this, I'm sorry.'

'It's fine. I'll be ok here' said Sammy. 'You go with Darius to get Mrs Grock,' he added, looking again at the girl in the purple lycra suit.

Although her hair was scraped tightly back and she had flamboyant makeup on her face, he thought he recognised her. He looked again at the beanball with the "S.H." initials.

'Sarah Havercastle,' said Sammy. 'The Ringmaster's daughter at the Floating Circus.'

He tucked Darius's jumper over her legs and took off his own jumper which he lay over the rest of her body, tucking it gently under her and pressing the edges to keep her as warm as possible.

Sammy looked up to the sky. Surely she hadn't fallen? There were high walls at the Land of the Pharaohs at the edge of the land. Presumably there were the same high walls at the Floating Circus. It simply wasn't possible to walk off the edge of the land. But the lands were so high up. How could she have fallen? More importantly, how could she have survived?

Sammy checked the jumpers he had lain over her like blankets. She was very cold. He tucked the edges in tighter and she stirred ever so slightly

'It's ok,' said Sammy.

'Mm,' said the girl, opening her eyes. 'Rolaan?' She tried to sit up but her leg caught on a twig.

Sammy moved the twig and helped her get comfortable, leaning against a silver birch tree.

'Just relax, they've gone to get help,' said Sammy, handing her the four beanballs they had found.

'Rolaan,' said the girl. She took the four beanballs and stroked them. 'The circus. It was tipping. Everyone fell.'

Sammy frowned. She wasn't making any sense. Things had been easier when they thought she was dead.

'You're Sarah, aren't you?' asked Sammy.

The girl nodded. 'I'm Sarah Havercastle. My father Andradore runs the circus. He'll give you free tickets for helping me.'

'Don't worry about that,' said Sammy. 'I'm just really glad you're ok.'

'We've got all sorts of things at the circus,' said Sarah, tossing the four beanballs into the air and juggling them expertly. 'I'm a juggler and an acrobat, but we've got lions, tigers and there's even an elephant called Grandma.'

'Grandma!' Sammy laughed.

Sarah laughed too. 'My Dad called her that. He said she reminded him of his mother. Oh, is that your help arriving? They were quick.'

Sammy turned around. Darius and Toby were running over to them. Mrs Grock and Sir Ragnarok were trotting more dignifiedly behind them. Mrs Grock was holding her skirt up to her knees so she could move faster. Behind them were two dark haired men that Sammy instantly recognised.

'Hullo Sammy,' said one of the dark haired men.

'Hi Antonio!' said Sammy, shaking his friend's hand.

'Ringmaster Sammy Rambles!' said the second dark haired man that Sammy knew was Sarah's father, Andradore Havercastle, the Ringmaster of the Floating Circus and Sir Ragnarok's close personal friend. 'I am twice in your debt young Dragon Knight,' he said and took Sammy's hand, shaking it vigorously. 'Twice in one lifetime!'

'Sammy Rambles. I remember you now,' said Sarah, twisting around to look at Sammy. 'I'm sorry. I should have recognised you earlier. Thank you for helping me.'

Sammy blushed. 'It's ok,' he mumbled.

'Nasty cuts you have there,' said Mrs Grock. 'I'll see what I canna do for you here and then you canna come to stay at my house until you're better.'

Sammy helped Sarah to her feet and he watched as she left with Sir Ragnarok, Mrs Grock and the brothers, Antonio and Andradore Havercastle, heading back to Mrs Grock's cottage.

Sammy made his way back to the castle with Toby and Darius, chatting nineteen to the dozen about what had happened.

'I shouldn't have left,' apologised Toby. 'I honestly thought she was dead.'

Sammy shrugged. 'It's ok. She should be dead really. It's a long way down from the Floating Circus.'

'Andradore said the whole land just tipped up,' said Darius. 'He said it was like it was being pushed.'

'Yeah, he said it was only luck that there was another land passing underneath and they all fell into that, buildings, people, everything,' said Toby.

'Except Sarah,' said Sammy.

'Andradore said she fell,' said Darius. 'He came straight here to find her.'

'Horrible,' said Sammy, imagining the feeling of falling helplessly through the sky and landing unconscious in a strange place. 'Hopefully Mrs Grock will be able to help her.'

'She'll be fine,' said Darius. 'I guess we won't be allowed up to the Floating Circus again.'

'I wonder why it moved,' said Sammy thoughtfully. 'Dixie told me the lands operate at different heights so when they move around there aren't any accidents.'

'Something obviously pushed it up from underneath,' said Toby. 'Logically, that's the only reason it would tip, if something pushed it up at one end.'

'Then they were very lucky the other land was passing underneath,' said Sammy. 'Maybe there are other people who fell from the Floating Circus?'

Darius shook his head. 'Andradore said everyone's been accounted for. Shall we get some lunch? I'm starving!'

In the Main Hall, Sammy made a point of seeing Simon Sanchez to offer some awkward condolences. It was very hard and neither of them knew what to say. It was even more awkward as Simon was sitting with Amos at the East table, waiting for dinner to be served.

'It was her time,' said Simon sombrely. 'Maybe now my father will be interested in looking after me. He walked out on her when she took this job as Alchemistry teacher at Dragamas. Dragons will kill you Simone, he said, and he was right.'

'Mrs Hubar killed her,' said Amos. 'Now her, Jock and that Alfie Agrock will pay for it.'

'Yes!' said Simon, thumping the table with his fist. 'When I am in the Snorgcadell, they will all pay, even your uncle, Sammy. They will all pay and the dragons will live.'

'Yeah,' agreed Sammy, privately thinking Simon was being a little bit ambitious.

There was still one member of the Shape they knew absolutely nothing about and there was also the problem that Mrs Hubar had vanished.

'You will see,' said Simon. 'You Sammy, of all people, you know what must be done.'

CHAPTER 42

# MRS HUBAR IS FOUND

Over the next few days, Sammy went with Dixie and Darius to see Sarah Havercastle at Mrs Grock's house. Each time they went, Sammy checked on his parents' dragons, pleased to see that Cyngard, Jovah and Paprika were as healthy as ever.

Sarah went from strength to strength. At first, she was just able to sit up in bed. Then she was able to sit up in bed and juggle with the four beanballs. According to Mrs Grock, Sarah would juggle from dawn to nightfall, stopping only to eat or when visitors came.

At the end of the first week she was able to get up and out of bed, taking her first steps after her fall. Mrs Grock wouldn't let her overdo it and Sarah's recovery was slow but steady.

Then one Friday, when Sammy came in alone, hot and sweaty from a furious Firesticks match, which had seen his double ended Firestick broken in half, Sarah was trying on one of the bridesmaid's dresses that she had helped Mrs Grock to sew.

'Wow!' said Sammy, stunned at the sight of Sarah with her hair curled in beautiful golden tresses down to her shoulder and the silver and peach meringue off the shoulder dress with a delicate dragonscale necklace and dainty peach ballet shoes.

'Ooch!' squawked Mrs Grock. 'I thought you were John for a moment and he canna see my dress at any price, and stop gawping young Dragon Knight. You've seen women in dresses before, haven't you?'

Dumbly, Sammy nodded. 'Are those the bridesmaids' dresses?'

Sarah laughed. 'Yes! Mrs Grock said as a thank you for me helping with her dress that I can be a bridesmaid at her wedding too!'

'Cool,' said Sammy, trying to think of something to say but struggling to find the words. 'It suits you,' he mumbled.

'I prefer my circus clothes,' admitted Sarah, loosening the lace on the corset. 'At least in the lycra suits there's room to breathe!'

Sammy nodded. 'Is it ok if I check on my parents' dragons, please?'

'Ooch, of course,' said Mrs Grock, ushering Sarah back upstairs.

When she had gone, Mrs Grock leaned close. 'A word of advice young Dragon Knight. Finish with one before you start with another.'

'What? I wasn't...' said Sammy, not entirely truthfully. In her own way, Sarah was as different as Dixie. Besides, Mrs Grock wasn't the best of examples to follow.

'Don't go causing any trouble,' warned Mrs Grock.

'No Mrs Grock. I don't...' started Sammy.

Mrs Grock laughed at him. 'I never said you were!'

Sammy checked Cyngard, Jovah and Paprika quicker than usual. They hurrumphed as he spilt their grain, rushing to load it into the bathtub sized food bowl and then they hurrumphed louder when he didn't bother to refill their water basin. He lit a fire and made his way through the underground passage to the castle to avoid seeing Sarah or Mrs Grock.

At the fork in the passage, something nagged him to take the path to the Dragon's Lair instead of back to the castle. Without thinking, he followed the rocky path, half feeling, half judging, his way along the narrow passageway.

Just before he reached the point where the tunnel should have come out by the lift that they used to visit the lands above the school, Sammy stopped. His pathway was blocked by a rockfall of earth and stone.

With a little concentration, Sammy enlarged the fire at the end of his staff. Now there was enough light to see from the rocky floor to the passage ceiling.

Sammy scraped at some of the loose earth. He was frustrated that some of the solid rock slabs lay jagged and haphazardly beneath the surface. He stepped back, scaring himself as the heavy slabs slipped towards him.

It looked as though the rockfall hadn't happened very long ago and the rocks and earth were still settling. Sammy kicked a loose stone. He was surprised when it fell between the cracks that there was a small cavity and that he could see through to the other side. Beyond the rockfall, he could hear a voice that sounded like Mrs Hubar talking to someone.

'Not so clever now, are we?' said Mrs Hubar, her voice quiet and echoing. 'To think, I've waited all these years. Not even with you as a dragon could you be banished from Serberon's thoughts.'

Sammy leaned forward and a stone rolled from under his feet making a small noise.

'Who's there?' demanded the voice from behind the rubble.

Sammy ducked as an enormous bright green flame shot through the earth and stone, sending the rockfall scattering into tiny shards.

Bloodied and stained, Mrs Hubar stepped through the gap created by the green flame.

Sammy stood firm, although his heart was racing and his hands were shaking. 'I know who you are,' he said bravely.

'Do you?' hissed Mrs Hubar. 'How could you possibly know that I am the great, great granddaughter of Helana Horidore. I have come here to put the right blood on the throne. Dragons should never have been born this way. Power must be given back to the earth where it was stolen from.'

'You're in the Shape,' said Sammy. 'You don't care about keeping dragons alive. You only want their power for yourself.'

Mrs Hubar stepped forward, swaying menacingly from side to side.

'Power!' she laughed, a throttled, blood clotted, murderous laugh that echoed up and down the passageway.

Sammy suddenly had flashbacks of the dragons that had been murdered in cold blood. The dragon called Kelsepe that had belonged to Mary-Beth, the massacre of the fifth years' dragons in the East wing, Anita Reed's black dragon lying dead in the field, the blaze of black dragons belonging to the Nitromen, Jock's dragon, Giselle, and Toby's dragon, Puttee.

'Look!' Mrs Hubar held out her hand. Sammy saw a blue-green lump of draconite with the dragon's flesh still attached and oozing with marmalade coloured blood and brains. 'This one is too small to bother with.' She tossed the draconite into the cavity behind her.

Momentarily distracted, Sammy noticed the "Max 10 Persons" sign on the floor. It looked as though the pearlescent lift that connected Dragamas to the lands above the school had collapsed. He felt sick, hoping no-one had been inside the lift when it fell.

'I am in the Shape,' said Mrs Hubar, edging closer to Sammy and speaking in the same silky, slippery, slimy voice that Sammy remembered hearing in the Great Pyramid. 'I have waited so many years for this opportunity. It will not slip through my fingers again. I deserve this power. I have worked hard. I have played the game. I have delivered all my promises. I will not be stopped by a fourteen-year-old boy, no matter who you are.'

'How can you do this?' asked Sammy. 'How could you kill Giselle?'

Mrs Hubar stopped in her tracks. 'Jock understood it needed to be done.'

'No he didn't,' said Sammy.

'For me, it was just one more dragon,' said Mrs Hubar. 'Killing Giselle was one more piece of draconite. One step closer to my goal. All of the dragons must die and then we will have the power to complete the Stone Cross which will give us our invincibility, our immortality and our control of the elements of earth, air, fire and water.'

'You'll never succeed,' said Sammy resolutely. 'Sir Ragnarok will never let you succeed.'

'We will see,' said Mrs Hubar, laughing cruelly. 'For all his words, he is a poor judge of character. Look at me, I am his closest friend and then look at you, he thinks you will be a Dragon Knight!'

Sammy drew his staff, the black onyx crystal burning furiously at its tip. The staff vibrated in his hands.

'I will be a Dragon Knight!' shouted Sammy.

Mrs Hubar eyed Sammy closely, surveying him with her eagle eyed stare. 'I think you might be right,' she conceded. 'But just not in this lifetime!'

She drew out a pocketful of large draconite stones in one hand and a large emerald in the other. A cool green mist emanated from the emerald and started to fill the passage.

'I can command the stones in your staff,' whispered Mrs Hubar menacingly.

Sammy looked down at his staff. The sapphire, the amber and the ruby gemstones were melting and dripping onto the stone floor. He grabbed the onyx and tore it off the end of his staff. He felt a burning sensation in his hand.

Removing the onyx was draining his strength but when the stone was released and his staff was empty of crystals, the staff stopped vibrating and Sammy felt his head clear.

'Old magic,' hissed Mrs Hubar. 'But that staff doesn't belong to you. It is too powerful. Who did you steal it from?'

'It is my staff,' said Sammy. 'I chose it on my first day at Dragamas.'

'You did not choose that staff. It chose you,' said Mrs Hubar, dropping the stones she was holding. 'Old magic will be beaten.'

Sammy stepped forward. He could feel Mrs Hubar's fear as an invisible source of energy surged forward, pushing her and her green mist back towards the lift.

Mrs Hubar tripped on a stone slab and fell over backwards, squirming on the floor. She picked herself up and shrunk back as thick black smoke poured into the passageway.

'Let me go,' Mrs Hubar wept. 'It will destroy us. We must escape.'

'What's in there?' asked Sammy, thinking nothing could be worse right now than Mrs Hubar. Yet she seemed so afraid.

'Something which should remain in there,' said Mrs Hubar. 'You must believe me. You must put aside our differences and we can escape together.'

The dense smoke poured into the passage, flowing effortlessly through the cracks in the rockfall. Keeping his staff outstretched, Sammy wrapped his jumper sleeve over his mouth and nose, crouching so that the smoke drifted over his head.

'Save us both, Sammy,' wept Mrs Hubar. 'We must leave now.'

In his crouched position, Sammy stood still, his feet gripped to the rock floor as if an invisible thread held him there. He could hear Mrs Hubar's thoughts "kill the wretch" he heard, "kill him, then escape the smoke", her thoughts were nagging at him, urging him to move aside to save his own life.

'No,' said Sammy. 'Not unless you promise to give yourself up to Sir Ragnarok.'

'Anything!' said Mrs Hubar, unaware Sammy could hear her thoughts screaming "never".

'We must leave,' said Mrs Hubar, her smooth, silky, sugar sweet voice full of urgency.

Sammy agreed. The smoke was closing in and he was having trouble breathing. He turned around and stepped backwards out towards the passage fork. This time, he took the path to the castle, hurrying as the smoke threatened to envelop him entirely.

Sammy saw Mrs Hubar reach the fork. Suddenly there was an almighty explosion overhead. The passage roof fell in completely and Mrs Hubar disappeared into the thick black smoke.

# CHAPTER 43

# DEATH IS NOT OURS TO GIVE

Daylight shone in and Sammy looked up. He was flat on his back, his feet had given way and he was lying sprawled out in the rubble. The sun was shining brightly in his eyes. Sammy saw shapes jump down towards him.

'He's here.'

Sammy recognised Commander Altair's voice and the Armoury teacher knelt beside his head.

'A word of advice,' whispered Commander Altair. 'Act like you're injured or you'll get expelled for this.'

Sammy looked up. Commander Altair was smiling grimly.

'Do you make a point to go out looking for the Shape?' asked Commander Altair, roughly dragging some loose stones over Sammy's left leg.

Sammy shook his head. 'My leg really hurts,' he said as realistically as possible.

'Good,' said Commander Altair. 'Did Mrs Hubar tell you who's above her? Who's pulling the strings? Who is the "S" in the Shape?' Commander Altair spelt out his questions in no uncertain terms.

'No,' said Sammy, looking over Commander Altair's shoulder. 'No, she didn't.'

Quite a crowd had gathered in the opening. Dixie and Sarah were at the front, peering through the smoke at him. Sammy waved at them, thinking perhaps if his "bad leg" could hurt a little after all then he might get some sympathy and attention from the girls.

'Is she still there? Is Mrs Hubar still down there?' asked Commander Altair.

Sammy nodded.

'Then I'll finish the job.' Commander Altair stood up and leaned out of the open passage roof. 'Can I get a stretcher down here for Sammy please?'

Sammy closed his eyes as people jumped down beside him, kicking up dirt and debris. Commander Altair disappeared over the rockfall and into the belching smoke.

Professor Burlay and Mr Synclair-Smythe picked Sammy up, his left leg sounded like it was crunching as the stones fell away. He was lifted up and out into the school grounds. The hole in the passage was just beyond Mrs Grock's wishing well, halfway between the castle and Dragon's Lair.

As he was carried out of the fallen passage and onto the grass, Sammy recounted his story for everyone who wanted to listen.

After a few moments, Sammy saw Commander Altair drag Mrs Hubar out of the hole. Commander Altair was black with soot and sweat and Sammy realised he must look the same. Mrs Hubar was limp and lifeless, her body caked in soot and scars.

'Is she dead?' Sammy whispered, gripping Dixie's hand.

Dixie looked at Mrs Hubar and shook her head. 'No, look, he's giving her a kiss.'

Sammy cricked his neck as he jerked around.

'It's the first rule of being a Dragon Knight,' said Dixie. 'Death is not ours to give. Life and death are not our choices. Death is not our purpose. Alfie Agrock told me when I asked him if he was going to kill me and he said it. Death is not ours to give.'

'He killed your Dad,' whispered Sammy.

'He said it was an accident,' said Dixie.

'He would have killed you,' said Sammy, stroking Dixie's hand. 'You only stayed alive so you could bring up those dragons.'

Dixie snatched her hand away. 'He said it was an accident.'

Sammy sat up straight. 'You don't slit someone's throat by accident. Alfie Agrock killed your Dad so no one would know he was in the Shape.'

'You're lying.' Dixie's face cracked. She stood up, turned around and ran off across the Dragonball pitch.

Sarah took her place. 'Stay there and rest your leg,' she hushed him as he was about to call after Dixie. 'Look, Commander Altair has brought Mrs Hubar back to life.'

'My leg is fine,' snapped Sammy, standing up.

Dixie was nowhere to be seen. Mrs Hubar, freshly resuscitated, shook her fist angrily at Sammy. Captain Stronghammer and Captain Firebreath watched her from the back of the dispersing crowd.

Commander Altair bound Mrs Hubar's hands with his belt with the silver stars and led her away towards a silver car parked at the school gates.

Sir Ragnarok approached Sammy and waved for the other students to step back. He reached around Sammy's neck and pulled out the stone cross necklace. Sir Ragnarok ran his hands across the metal and turned the cross into a glowing dragon scale.

'Did you know your cross could do this?' Sir Ragnarok asked so quietly that only Sammy could hear him.

Sammy nodded. 'Jock showed me.'

'Did he say where they came from?' asked Sir Ragnarok.

'No,' whispered Sammy, aware Sir Ragnarok was about to let him in on a secret.

'The dragon scales we use to make the Crosses for Bravery were found outside the Dragon's Lair at the beginning of the century. It is believed they were forged by Karmandor herself, that they were her scales. Legend says that she prised some of the scales off her skin because she was desperate to regain her Troll form.'

Sammy stood dumbly next to his headmaster. He knew of the strength contained within his Cross for Bravery. He knew the confidence he had drawn from wearing it. His Cross for Bravery against untold dangers, awarded for his efforts fighting the Shape.

'Alas, although we find one or two scales every so often, no one believes she will be successful. You know she is down there, don't you?' Sir Ragnarok pointed to the hole. 'Karmandor was buried alive, enslaved by Helana Horidore. I feel you are owed some answers Sammy. Please accompany me to my office. I will tell you the whole story.'

Sammy felt his jaw drop. The slight pain Commander Altair had induced on his leg was quickly forgotten. All his questions would be answered. All the answers laid bare.

'Could you please tell everyone in the Main Hall at tea?' asked Sammy, knowing Dixie and Darius would want to hear everything. He wasn't sure he would remember it all to recount in their tower room later.

'I would prefer to tell you alone first,' said Sir Ragnarok. 'Then, as it usually does, the truth will be revealed, travelling by watered down gossip. I think I will ask Dr

Shivers to update the Dragon Studies syllabus. These events will be talked about for many years to come.'

Sammy looked up. He and Sir Ragnarok were alone in the grounds. Professor Burlay was finishing escorting the straggling students away for tea. Sammy knew the news had spread. As he walked with Sir Ragnarok, he could feel their eyes on his back, staring at him.

Captain Duke Stronghammer ran, clomping in his black boots, up to Sir Ragnarok and tugged at his robes.

He held out his red and white neckerchief. 'I'll resign, Sir Ragnarok,' puffed Captain Stronghammer. 'I knew me wife was in on it all. She made me keep quiet. She said I'd lose her and me job and me son as well as me daughter. You have ter understand I couldn't say anything…' Captain Stronghammer tailed off.

Sir Ragnarok laid his hands on Captain Stronghammer's shoulders.

'I understand,' said Sir Ragnarok slowly and calmly. 'Captain Firebreath's cider has made you less than discrete on several occasions. But in times of peril, we must remain focussed on our common goal.'

Sir Ragnarok pressed the red and white neckerchief into Captain Stronghammer's trembling hands.

'You are a good man Fignus Hubar. Let not a stain on your family dissolve your character. In the future, you would be wise to stand up for yourself. Speak your mind and hold your own thoughts above outside pressure. You can do this. I believe in you.'

Captain Stronghammer nodded, his eyes glazed. 'You're a gentleman Sir Ragnarok. You're too good to me. I deserve to go to the Snorgcadell. I deserve to lose me job and me family. I shoulda come forward. I'm a coward when it comes down to it. I've bin drowning me sorrows when I shoulda bin helping the cause. I'm too weak. I'm…'

'Be strong from now on,' said Sir Ragnarok, taking Captain Stronghammer's hand and shaking it firmly.

Sammy looked back. Captain Stronghammer was staring at them open-mouthed. His hand was still outstretched from the handshake.

'Thank you,' said Captain Stronghammer. 'Thank you Sir Ragnarok. Thank you Sir.'

'What will happen to Captain Stronghammer?' asked Sammy, plucking up the courage to ask Sir Ragnarok as they stepped through the tapestry in the Main Hall and began climbing the steep stone spiral staircase.

Halfway up the stairs, Sir Ragnarok paused. 'He will continue to work here, for me and for Dragamas. I will protect him from those in the Snorgcadell who believe a man is responsible for his family and their actions.'

Sammy nodded. He wished he hadn't told Dixie the truth about her father.

Sir Ragnarok started climbing again and soon he and Sammy reached the oak door at the top of the stairs. Sir Ragnarok pushed open his office door and let Sammy climb up the seven steps into his circular office.

CHAPTER 44

# SNORGCADELL TRAINING

Looking out of the window in Sir Ragnarok's office, Sammy could see that most of the Dragamas students were outside. Some were curled up with their dragons, reading and revising while others were playing Firesticks.

Sammy could see belches of black smoke pouring from the large hole in the castle lawns. In the distance, he could also make out the Church of a Thousand Graves on the horizon. It looked tiny. Sunlight splashed on its slate roof, making it shine silver, almost as if it was a mirror, signalling for Karmandor to come home.

'Take a seat please Sammy,' said Sir Ragnarok. He pulled his draconite chart down from the wall and laid it out on his desk.

Sir Ragnarok turned on the television monitors that showed him everything that was going on in the school.

Sammy saw the silver car enlarged on the screen. Mrs Hubar's face was pressed against the window. Captain Stronghammer was holding onto the car bumper. He was on his knees. It looked as though he was begging the car not to drive off with his wife inside.

Sir Ragnarok took a file from his bookshelf. He laid it on his desk next to the draconite chart and opened the file. It contained several photographs.

'Firstly, I would like to show you a man named General Alaze Ramadere. He is the Troll Commander of the Snorgcadell and he is equal in rank to General Aldebaran Altair, who you already know is the Human Commander of the Snorgcadell.'

Sammy stared at the picture of the green skinned, hook nosed giant. He looked like Jacob Deane, only bigger.

'For your services helping Dixie…' started Sir Ragnarok.

Sammy gulped. He wished he could take his words back. He wished he could undo how upset he had made Dixie earlier when he had told her exactly how her father was killed by Alfie Agrock.

'…and to the Troll community as a whole. For deeds that I believe are yet to be done, General Ramadere would like to train you.'

'Train me?' spluttered Sammy. 'What for?'

Sir Ragnarok chuckled. 'To fulfil your wildest dreams Sammy. You can train to be a Dragon Knight.'

Sammy's eyes widened. 'A Dragon Knight?'

Sir Ragnarok nodded. 'But, you have a tough choice to make because General Aldebaran Altair also wishes for you to train under him.'

'What if I don't…' started Sammy.

'It would be walking away from a great honour,' said Sir Ragnarok, his blue eyes twinkling. 'To think that in my time at Dragamas, I should send not one, not two, not even three, but four students to be trained at the Snorgcadell.'

Sir Ragnarok turned to face Sammy. The Dragamas headmaster looked suddenly serious. 'You will go, won't you?'

Sammy stared blankly. 'To the Snorgcadell?'

'Of course I will need to seek your parents' approval. With their permission, you would be able to train over the summer and then take your apprenticeship at the end of your fifth year at Dragamas,' said Sir Ragnarok.

'Who else was chosen?' whispered Sammy.

'You were chosen,' said Sir Ragnarok, counting on his fingers, 'Simon Sanchez, Amos Leech and Dixie Deane. All students from your year which is most unusual.'

'What about Darius?' asked Sammy.

'Ah yes, Darius Murphy,' said Sir Ragnarok, shifting some papers on his desk. 'He has won a Dragamas award and he will teach Gemology in the Healing Division. I understand that both of his parents are qualified Healers and Darius certainly shows plenty of promise to follow in their footsteps.'

'Oh,' said Sammy.

'You would like him for company in the Snorgcadell?' asked Sir Ragnarok. 'I am afraid he lost his chance for that when he aided Jock to recover more draconite. The Snorgcadell see that as a major character misjudgement to show leniency against the Shape.'

'What about me?' asked Sammy. 'I gave Alfie Agrock the Angel of 'El Horidore. He used the whistle to call all the dragons here.'

Sir Ragnarok nodded. 'And King Segragore and King Serberon are very grateful. You have no idea how long they too have been searching for it.'

'But it was wrong!' exclaimed Sammy. 'It's killed so many dragons. Dixie was captured.'

'But how many dragons has it saved?' said Sir Ragnarok quietly. 'We should soon see Princess Karmandor again and she will hopefully offer us some answers. She may be able to fill in the gaps in our history. It may even flush out the source of the Shape. We may find out who is the "S" in the

Shape. We may also find out how the Shape knew about the unimaginable powers which would be released if the Stone Cross is rebuilt,' finished Sir Ragnarok.

'They'll have to kill all the dragons to complete the Stone Cross,' said Sammy. 'I thought you wanted to save all the dragons.'

Sir Ragnarok pointed to his television monitors. They changed from the silver car to Dixie, huddled alone in her tower room bed.

'You owe her an apology,' said Sir Ragnarok, swiftly changing the subject.

Sammy nodded and stood up. 'I'll fix it.'

'Very good,' said Sir Ragnarok. He gestured to Lariston, who uncurled himself and led Sammy to the office door.

'Thank you,' said Sammy, smiling to himself. He was still tempted to bow in front of Lariston, but he decided against it.

Once outside of Sir Ragnarok's office, Sammy teleported to the North house common room and ran up the spiral stairs leading to the girls' dormitories, two steps at a time.

Sammy knocked on the fourth year girls' room door. The wooden door was ornately decorated with flowers and multi-coloured dragon scales.

No one answered and Sammy pushed the door open slowly with his foot.

Through a gap in one of the curtains, Sammy could see Dixie sitting on her bed. She was hunched up with her staff lying across her knees. A pile of torn up paper was at the end of the bed.

'Hi Sammy,' said Dixie. She looked as though she'd been expecting him.

'Hi.' Sammy wrung his hands together awkwardly.

'I'm getting rid of my Nitromen stuff.' Dixie pointed at the paper which, Sammy was surprised to see, was automatically shredding itself into tiny pieces. 'I've also written to Mum to tell her to clear everything out of my room as well.'

'Why?' asked Sammy.

'You know why,' said Dixie. 'Nitron Dark hates Trolls. I've been hanging on to this stuff, hoping he'd change, maybe even ask me out, uh, no offence.'

Sammy grinned. 'He'd never ask you out.'

Dixie laughed, her pretty tinkling laugh Sammy had come to notice especially recently.

'Besides,' added Sammy, sitting himself on the bed next to the automatically shredding paper, 'you've got me.'

Dixie grinned. 'What else do I need?'

'I'm sorry about earlier,' said Sammy.

Dixie shrugged. 'I'm sure you probably had the best of intentions.'

Sammy nodded, leaning close. 'Like this one?'

He saw Dixie close her eyes as they kissed, a long, lingering, smouldering kiss with all of the passion of the last six months rolled into twenty seconds of passionate silence.

'Caught ya!' shrieked a voice from the doorway. 'I'm not speaking to him. He won't know what he's missing. Ha!'

Sammy flicked his eyes open. Naomi was standing in the doorway, holding Darius's television recorder.

'Caught you Dixie Deane!' squealed Naomi.

Dixie blushed. 'So what?'

'Humph! Well don't come crying on my shoulder,' Naomi held up the toilet roll and bars of chocolate she'd brought with her from the bathroom and the canteen.

'I'll still need the chocolate,' said Dixie, grinning mischievously.

Naomi laughed and threw Dixie the chocolate.

'I'm meeting Darius in the Gemology room,' said Naomi. 'Holly and Helana are doing extra Ancient and Modern Languages and Milly's been invited to a party with Tom Hill from the fifth year. You'll be on your own,' Naomi winked.

Sammy felt his cheeks burn. 'We're not…'

'Shh,' Dixie laughed. 'They all think we've done it.'

Naomi cackled. 'She's joking Sammy!'

'Oh.' Sammy knew his cheeks were crimson.

Dixie leaped out of bed and wrestled with Naomi to take the television recorder.

'It's mine!' shouted Dixie.

'No, mine!' replied Naomi.

Dixie and Naomi were in hysterics as the recorder was finally handed to Dixie, who danced triumphantly around the tower room with it. She stopped by Sammy and showed it to him.

'Cool,' said Sammy, touching his cheeks. They felt hot.

'Sammy's embarrassed,' teased Naomi. 'See you later!'

Dixie brushed her green hair in front of a mirror on her chest of drawers.

Sammy noticed there were some un-Dixie-like items on top of the chest of drawers. There was a lipstick, a blusher and a tube of what looked like the same mascara he'd seen his mum use at home.

'Are you going all girly?' asked Sammy, picking up the mascara and examining it.

'What?' Dixie scooped the items into a pale green bag and put them out of sight. 'These are just some things I'm experimenting with. I want to look good at Professor Burlay's wedding.'

'Oh,' said Sammy, wondering if Dixie had been practicing with make-up for a while as her appearance kept changing in lessons from day to day.

'Mum said I could get my hair done as well,' added Dixie enthusiastically. 'After, you know, what happened to me, I think she's just glad I'm still here.'

Sammy nodded. 'Are we going to go back to the Dragon's Lair? That's where Sir Ragnarok said Karmandor was buried.'

'Yeah, Sarah was saying she saw some smoke,' said Dixie. 'I reckon she's still alive.'

'No, the smoke would have been from the explosion in the passage when I found Mrs Hubar,' said Sammy. 'They can't be connected.'

Dixie shrugged and bent down to put on a pair of slightly high heeled boots.

'We'll soon find out,' said Dixie. She grabbed Sammy's hand and shouted, 'clearing in front of the Dragon's Lair.'

Sammy jolted as they landed inches between two trees.

Dixie clutched him in a fit of giggles. 'That was close!'

'Mm,' agreed Sammy, extracting a bramble from his ankle.

The clearing was the same as ever. The floor was covered in loose leaves left over from the Autumn with bits of moss peeking through. It was almost like a tropical rainforest with leaves casting an eerie green light overhead. The sky was almost invisible. Faint traces of smoke wisped out of the giant cave opening and the milk white "Dragon's Teeth" on the ledge suddenly looked real.

'Sammy, meet Karmandor,' said Dixie solemnly.

CHAPTER 45

# WEEDON SIEN YARDON

For a second, in his mind's eye, Sammy pictured the purple heather covered rocks above them flickering and loose gravel rolling down the cliff.

Dixie nudged him. 'Look.'

Sammy felt his jaw drop. The rocks "were" falling and the clumps of purple heather he had always thought could be eyes, were actually two giant purple dustbin lid sized eyes staring down at him and Dixie.

As they watched, the cave mouth closed. The milk white stone teeth clashed together. Loud hissing and spluttering smoke poured out of what Sammy saw, the split second before his legs turned to jelly, were nostrils. The smoke scattered amongst the leaves.

Dixie stepped forward. 'Arug eventa Karmandor.'

With a roar that shook Sammy's bones, the cave mouth opened and a pink forked tongue crept out towards him. He gulped but, copying Dixie, Sammy took a step forward.

'Ve sank amisha,' Sammy called and held up his silver Cross for Bravery, running his hand across the metal to reveal the blue-green dragon scale.

The forked tongue stopped inches from his chest.

'Amisha,' repeated Sammy. 'We are friends. We won't hurt you.'

'Ve navna vatar,' added Dixie, translating Sammy's reassuring words into Troll for Karmandor's benefit.

'Hurrumph!' Karmandor exhaled a plume of jet black smoke straight into their faces.

'Sien!' cried Dixie.

'Dragons can't speak!' shouted Sammy, taking several steps backwards. 'You have to stop her moving or she'll bring the land down on top of us.'

'Holy smoke,' muttered Dixie. 'We don't want that.'

Dixie pointed up to Karmandor's pearlescent tail.

'Frijida!' shouted Dixie.

Sammy struggled to remember whether that meant "cold" or "stop". But it did the trick and Karmandor stayed still.

'Ka,' said Dixie.

Sammy felt Dixie shaking beside him. He held her close to him. 'That was close,' he whispered.

Dixie nodded. 'What should I say to her?'

'Tell her we've seen her Dad and King Serberon,' whispered Sammy.

At Serberon's name, Dixie's eyes glazed over. Up in the cliff, a large splash of water fell, just missing them.

'She's lost far more than I have,' said Dixie slamming her jumper sleeve across her eyes.

'I know,' whispered Sammy.

'King Serberon,' started Dixie. 'We've uh, ve sank, ve sank, what's "met him"?'

'Irikola,' said Sammy.

'Ve sank irikolum,' corrected Dixie, ducking as another teardrop fell from the scaly cliff, 'King Serberon na King Segragore.'

Sammy pulled Dixie aside as a deluge of silver crystal tears threatened to drown them.

'Vantom se avendor,' said Dixie, pointing to herself and then to Sammy. 'Frijida! Please stop! You'll crush us if the land falls!'

'Actse-veri-su,' Sammy thought he heard the words inside his head. The voice was so quiet. It was the hoarsest of whispers.

'I trust you,' whispered Dixie. 'She will hold the land for us.'

'Vlandar vorton,' said Sammy, hoping his Troll slang "we'll be back" was right.

'Tromi,' said Karmandor, in another hoarse whisper.

Sammy nodded. 'We'll hurry.'

'Weedon sien yardon...' Karmandor's voice petered out.

'Weeks not years,' translated Dixie, laughing nervously. 'That gives us some time.'

'She's still moving,' whispered Sammy as they left the clearing. 'I don't know if she'll last until the end of term.'

'She's being called by the Angel of 'El Horidore,' whispered Dixie. 'It's calling her to our den and then we will have to take her to King Serberon at the Church of a Thousand Graves.'

Sammy stared. He almost couldn't bring himself to speak. 'The Shape will try to kill her now they know she's alive,' he whispered, his voice choking.

'Maybe she has to die,' said Dixie, reaching for Sammy's hand. 'She doesn't belong in our time.'

Sammy didn't answer. He couldn't. In all the pictures he'd ever seen of Karmandor, he remembered her as a beautiful golden dragon with scales the colour of the sun reflected on the sea.

She was the first dragon, the great, great, so many greats, grandmother of his dragon Kyrillan. Karmandor was locked in time and locked in stone. Her tail had been used as a common transport between the school and the lands above, whilst her rightful kingdom was squandered by those who didn't even know or care who it belonged to.

'Are you ok?' asked Dixie.

Sammy nodded, his eyes prickling uncomfortably.

Dixie squeezed his hand. 'I know,' she whispered.

Sammy let go. 'I want to be alone for a while.'

He saw the hurt in Dixie's green eyes, but she shrugged it off.

'Will I see you later?' asked Dixie.

Sammy nodded. 'Treestump in our old den,' he said silently and teleported himself out of the Dragon's Lair.

The landscape blurred into focus and Sammy barely recognised the clearing where he had first encountered the Shape. The remains of their den were scattered far into the woods. Had it been darker, Sammy knew he would have been afraid of the leaves rustling in the wind and the occasional pattering of hidden animals.

Sammy looked up at the horse chestnut tree. It was easily the largest tree in this part of the forest. He felt his staff vibrate against his chest and he took it out and examined it closely.

The wood was gnarled, knotted and very old. Sammy closed his eyes, imagining when he'd found his staff four years ago. He remembered his first encounter with the Shape and how good it had felt to pick up his staff. It was as if it belonged in his hand. The staff had called him. It was his, Sammy's. The power had been transferred through time to be in his hands.

'Yeah right,' Sammy broke his thoughts. 'It's just an old branch that I channel magic through.' He stroked the staff, enjoying the small quiver as he touched it.

Sammy looked up at the sound of a twig cracking near him. Sir Ragnarok was there, watching him intently.

Sir Ragnarok frowned. 'I suppose I should have begun my search for you here,' said Sir Ragnarok. He held up his Directometer and Sammy could see the green dot flashing. 'I have a message for you, from Lariston in fact. He feels he should warn you.'

'Warn me?' asked Sammy, looking around nervously. He half expected the Shape to pounce on him. 'Warn me about what?'

'Yes Sammy,' said Sir Ragnarok softly. 'I am afraid of what is beginning. Of everyone who could have found Karmandor, it is strange, yet perhaps foreseen and not unexpected, that she should talk to you.'

Sir Ragnarok lowered his head and wrung his hands. 'I knew it would either be you or Simon Sanchez who would speak with her. Tell me, did she say anything to you?'

Sammy nodded. 'She said "weedon sien yardon". She will be free in weeks not years.'

Sir Ragnarok took out a small black book from within his black robes. He turned to one of the pages and nodded. 'Weedon sien yardon, weeks not years, your translation is very good Sammy.'

Sammy blushed. 'It was Dixie's translation.'

Sir Ragnarok chuckled. 'I might have known.'

'Will everything be ok?' asked Sammy.

'That is an interesting choice of words Sammy,' said Sir Ragnarok kindly. 'Do you think "everything" can, or should, be well? By doing one thing, we may be undoing something equally as worthy.'

Sammy understood. By freeing Karmandor, they would lose their access to the lands above the school. Sarah Havercastle and her family wouldn't be able to get home.

'I think Karmandor should have the choice,' said Sammy.

'We can only see what eventually comes to pass,' said Sir Ragnarok. 'What will be, will be.'

Sammy nodded, holding his staff tightly.

Sir Ragnarok came and stood next to him. 'I've always thought your staff had an interesting past. I came across it in a reference book just the other day.'

Sammy could feel Sir Ragnarok's breath brush past his cheeks. He could see every pore and wrinkle in the old man's face.

'Your staff Sammy, I believe it belonged to Karmandor,' said Sir Ragnarok.

Sammy felt his jaw drop. 'They had staffs back then?' he stuttered. 'Why me? Why did I find it?'

Sir Ragnarok laughed. 'They say a lost staff chooses its new owner. Nearly all Dragamas students select new branches as their staffs. They choose their staffs from younger trees. It is also a popular tradition for grandparents to hand down their staffs when they retire from magic or if they pass on.'

'I can feel it sometimes,' said Sammy. 'I always knew my staff was different, not just because its old. It just feels different.'

'You mustn't feel let down that you are different Sammy. Do you remember that you bonded with your dragon the day before you chose your staff?'

Sammy nodded. 'But even my dragon is different.'

'Ah,' Sir Ragnarok smiled. 'You have been brought up to believe you should choose your path in life and not that your path has already been chosen. There are many forces at work Sammy and not all of them can be moulded to our bidding.'

'I think I've chosen,' said Sammy. 'I would like to train at the Snorgcadell with General Aldebaran Altair.'

'I see,' said Sir Ragnarok solemnly. 'Even if Dixie is to choose to learn her skills with General Alaze Ramadere?'

Sammy nodded. 'I'm not a Troll.'

'Both paths are a great honour,' said Sir Ragnarok. 'I will let the Generals know of your choice.'

'Is it the right choice?' asked Sammy nervously.

'The right choice?' Sir Ragnarok raised his eyebrows. 'Sometimes we can only do what feels right at a particular moment in time.'

Sir Ragnarok pulled the Directometer out of his pocket. 'Would you excuse me? I have some trouble in the East wing. No one realised quite how much Professor Sanchez did to maintain order amongst her students.'

Sammy watched as Sir Ragnarok disappeared in a golden mist. When the mist evaporated, the headmaster was gone. Sammy held tightly to his staff and it quivered again, jolting in his hands.

'So, you're Karmandor's staff, are you?' Sammy asked his staff. The wooden branch stopped moving. 'I can take you to her,' said Sammy quietly. The staff stayed still, as if it was expecting something. It felt warm under his fingers, the remains of his gemstones dripping onto the ground.

Out of his jeans pocket, Sammy took the four emerald crystals Dr Shivers had given to him and seated them on the scooped end of the staff. The emeralds glowed brightly and the staff was suddenly hot. Sammy let go of the staff as it burned beneath his fingers.

'Hey!' exclaimed Sammy. 'My hands aren't Troll. I can't hold something that hot!'

As if in reply, the emeralds stopped glowing and the staff cooled enough for Sammy to pick it up. He noticed straightaway that the four emeralds were now one big stone and there were trails of green liquid flowing down the staff.

Sammy saw that the green liquid was spelling words and he saw that the words were spelling out quotations.

One string of green letters spelled the words "Be Bold When Darkness Engulfs You" and another said "Courage Comes From Within". The third string of words said "Mighty is the Golden Dragon".

'Mighty is the Golden Dragon,' said Sammy out loud. 'Yes, I will take you to Princess Karmandor. Right now.'

The staff seemed to quiver its agreement and, briefly pausing to check he wasn't going mad talking to a piece of wood, Sammy stood up.

The air was cool around him. The sky was starting to darken and it would soon be pitch black. Sammy stepped over a log which had once been part of the wall of their den. He made his way through the overgrown paths to the clearing in front of the Dragon's Lair.

'Arug eventa,' said Sammy. He was half hoping Karmandor would be asleep and half wishing Dixie was there in case Karmandor was awake and things got complicated.

'Arug...ow!' Sammy jumped as his staff quivered and the emeralds glowed brightly.

'Do you want me to go?' Sammy asked the staff. 'I've only just got here.'

With a great effort, Sammy heard a faint whisper.

'Thank you for bringing what is mine. It gives me strength. I will hold on as long as I can.'

Sammy smiled. The whisper was inside his head, a silent thought, projected from Karmandor, spoken just for him.

'Alshara,' said Sammy, saying, "I understand", in the best Troll he knew. In the half light, Sammy saw one of the purple rock eyelids flicker.

CHAPTER 46

# DRAGON KNIGHTS, BREEDERS AND HEALERS

'So, we'll go up to see Karmandor, like, every day,' said Darius at dinner, tucking into the evening meal, which tonight was grilled chicken and an assortment of garden vegetables.

'Mm,' agreed Dixie, her mouth full of mashed potato and swede. She gulped it down. 'Guess what?' she asked, her green eyes sparkling brightly.

'What?' asked Sammy.

Dixie held up a piece of crisp white paper with a gold twin-tailed "D" logo.

'I'm going to the Snorgcadell to learn how to be a Dragon Breeder!' announced Dixie, waving the paper from side to side.

'Hah!' snorted Gavin. 'Dragon Breeder! That's a great job for you!'

Toby nudged his brother. 'She said she's going to the Snorgcadell!'

Gavin's eyes widened. 'The Snorgcadell?' he repeated.

'I'm going too,' said Sammy. 'Sir Ragnarok told me.'

Dixie grinned at him. 'Cool! We can train together.'

Sammy shook his head. 'I'm training under General Aldebaran Altair. I want to be a Dragon Knight.'

'Oh,' Dixie looked sternly at him. 'How come you...'

'Sir Ragnarok said it was mainly Trolls who train under General Alaze Ramadere,' interrupted Sammy.

'Third generation,' said Dixie. 'They're as human as me!'

Sammy shrugged. 'I've already told Sir Ragnarok.'

'So change it,' said Gavin. 'I bet you don't. The Dragon Knights get much better stuff to do.'

'Better than raising dragons for the Dragon Knights to ride into battle?' retorted Dixie. 'Without Dragon Breeders they would just be Knights, not Dragon Knights. Anyway, Darius is going to be a Healer and he'll need dragons to heal.'

'I'm going to be a teacher first,' said Darius. 'It's really funny. I haven't finished learning things myself, let alone thinking about teaching anyone else.'

Gavin pulled a face. 'Boring! Anyone want to play Dragonball?'

'Yeah,' said Toby, standing up and pushing his chair under the table. 'I'll get my Dragonball set, then I've got to read up on the Art of Descaling. Has anyone else realised our exams are only four weeks away?'

'Four weeks,' muttered Sammy, hoping Karmandor would stay still for that long.

Toby returned with his Dragonball set and they played a furious game of indoor Dragonball in the North common room until Professor Burlay arrived to send all the North students off to bed.

Instead of going straight to sleep, Sammy sat at his study desk to look through some of the Dragon Studies notes and text book to see if he could find any more information about Karmandor.

'So, why aren't you telling Sir Ragnarok everything about Karmandor?' asked Darius, sticking his head around the green velvet dividing curtain.

Sammy closed his Dragon Studies book and looked at Darius. 'What if Sir Ragnarok said Dragamas has to close? I would have to go back to my parents in Switzerland. I'd have to go to a new school and then I'd never get to be a Dragon Knight.'

Darius looked keenly at Sammy. 'Are you sure that's what you want? I'd love it if my parents wanted me to be with them. My Mum said she'll only let me near her dragon once I've passed all my Healer exams.'

Sammy nodded. 'It's different for me. I feel I've got something to live up to. I've got something to fight for. I want to be a Dragon Knight. It might be my chance to help my parents see dragons again.'

'Yeah, I can see that,' said Darius. 'It's just not what I want to do. You know I really love learning about all the gemstones. It's what I've always wanted to do.'

'Cool,' said Sammy absentmindedly. 'I just want to make sure there are dragons in the future, for our children and their children.'

Darius laughed. 'Are you going to have children?'

Sammy shrugged. 'Who knows! Are you?'

'No idea,' giggled Darius. 'Let me have a look at your staff. Dixie said it's changed.'

Sammy took his staff from behind his chest of drawers, where it was leaning against the tower wall. Though it was ancient, the wood was strong and the crystal gemstones were glowing brightly.

'Wow!' said Darius, staring at the large green emerald and the snaking lines of letters. 'It's got writing on it.'

Sammy nodded. 'I think I've translated it properly. It looks as though Karmandor has been out there in the school grounds under our noses all this time.'

'She's been there for centuries,' said Darius. 'I want to come and see her with you tomorrow.'

'That makes it four adult dragons plus Kyrillan I've got to check on,' laughed Sammy.

'You need the practice,' said Darius, collapsing in a fit of the giggles. 'Pillow fight?'

'Staff fight?' asked Sammy, raising his staff.

'Nah, I'll never beat your emeralds,' said Darius, juggling with the onyx, ruby, amber and sapphire crystals he had detached from his own staff. 'Maybe next time!'

# CHAPTER 47

# THREE WEEKS LATER

'Wake up sleepy!' yelled Darius.

Sammy opened his eyes at the exact moment Darius poured a glass of ice cold water over his feet. They'd stayed up revising until three in the morning and Sammy had kicked his duvet off in the night.

'Darius! That's freezing cold!' yelled Sammy, sitting bolt upright. Through his sleepy, half-closed eyes, Sammy saw Darius had his hands on his hips.

'Serves you right,' retorted Darius. 'I've called you twice already. You need to get up!'

'Sorry,' muttered Sammy. He checked his bedside clock, rubbed his eyes and checked it again. 'Hey! You should have woken me up earlier!'

Darius raised his hands above his head. 'I tried! Gavin and Toby have already gone.'

'I wanted to check on Cyngard, Jovah, Paprika, Kyrillan and Karmandor and now there's only just time to get dressed, have breakfast, and get to the Armoury exam!'

Darius was unsympathetic. 'Why don't you eat dragon food at Mrs Grock's house while you see your parents' dragons. You'll need Kyrillan for the Armoury exam anyway, so you'll see him then.'

'And then I can see Karmandor later. Good idea!' said Sammy, jumping into his jeans with the leather dragon hide patches on the thighs. 'What do you reckon Haycorn tastes like anyway?'

'I was joking!' giggled Darius. 'Dragon food tastes horrible. I should know. I once ate the remains of a sack of Haycorn while my parents were out one day!'

Sammy laughed and dragged on his new black leather dragon riding boots. He snapped the buckles shut and tightened the laces.

'Staff, jeans, boots,' counted Sammy. 'What am I forgetting?'

Darius held up a piece of card. 'Here's your number for the test. You're first!'

Sammy nodded, taking the card embossed with the words "Number One" in gold letters.

'That's why I couldn't sleep last night,' said Sammy. 'I have to fight against someone from the Snorgcadell to pass my Armoury exam.'

'Yeah,' said Darius. 'That's extra pressure because if you lose then you won't be allowed to train at the Snorgcadell next year.'

'I know,' said Sammy. 'Come on, let's go.'

Sammy and Darius ran out of the tower room, down the spiral stairs, through the North common room. They stormed past caretaker Tom Sweep, who was mopping the corridor floor, and burst out of the castle door.

Nearly out of breath, they ran across the courtyard and out into the castle grounds, approaching Mrs Grock's garden gate at top speed.

When they arrived, Mrs Grock was in her front garden, pulling weeds out of her colourful flower beds.

'Ooch, good morning boys,' said Mrs Grock.

'Morning,' puffed Sammy, leaning on the gate to catch his breath. 'Is it ok to see my parents' dragons please?'

'Ooch, of course it is Sammy, but just you, not Darius today,' said Mrs Grock. 'I heard Sir Ragnarok wants all the fourth year Dragon Minders at a special breakfast this morning.'

'I completely forgot!' shrieked Darius. He turned and ran out of the gate. 'I've got to be there! I'll get Kyrillan out of the Dragon Chambers for you for the Armoury exam. That'll give you ten minutes here!'

Sammy checked his Casino watch, given to him by his uncle. It was nearly nine o'clock. He flicked the button to turn the watch to the Directometer setting and saw himself and Mrs Grock represented by the tiny dots.

Looking beyond Mrs Grock's garden, Sammy could see a car arriving at the school gates. He clicked his watch back to tell the time and went into Mrs Grock's house through her unlocked front door.

Professor Burlay was sitting at the dining table, wearing his dressing gown and slippers. He was eating toast and marking books.

'Morning Sammy,' said Professor Burlay.

'Morning.' Sammy walked awkwardly past Professor Burlay and into the store room. He lifted the trapdoor and was pleased to see Cyngard and Jovah's heads craning up to see him.

'Hey Cyngard! Hi Jovah!' said Sammy, climbing down the steps, holding onto the rail for support. 'Where's Paprika this morning? Paprika? Where are you?'

Sammy stared into the darkness. He felt a cold chill seeping into his skin. The three dragons were always nudging each other to be first to see him. Paprika was always at the front. As he dropped into the circular room, Sammy saw that Cyngard and Jovan were shaking.

Sammy quickly assembled his staff and lit the four lanterns Commander Altair had installed for him with a quick burst of fire.

Instantly, the room was filled with a warm glow of amber light that reminded Sammy of Bonfire Night with the warm embers glowing in amongst the sticks.

Sammy checked Cyngard first as his father's dragon was closest to him. The jet black dragon was shaking, his scales clacking together and his amber eyes were enormously wide with fear. His mother's dragon, Jovah, was shaking as well and there was absolutely no sign of his uncle's dragon, Paprika.

Sammy reached for one of the bales of hay stacked up around the walls. He wanted to make sure the dragons had a clean and comfy bed to lie on, but Cyngard nudged his arm towards the underground exit that led to the Dragon's Lair.

'What is it Cyngard?' asked Sammy. 'Is Paprika down there?'

Sammy created a new fire and held it above his head, guiding the flames towards the dark entrance.

'No!' shouted Sammy as he saw the words written in scrawling blood red letters. With a clatter, he dropped his staff and the fire went out.

Sammy hastily picked up his staff and relighted the fire. He pushed the flames up towards the ceiling and peered closely at the words. They said, "The Shape requires what you have taken care of".

'No!' Sammy shouted again and Professor Burlay appeared at the trapdoor at the top of the steps.

'Is everything ok Sammy?' asked Professor Burlay.

'No!' shouted Sammy, then he paused, levelled his voice and checked his words. 'It's not ok, look at this.'

Professor Burlay scuttled down the steps. 'I was just on my way to get dressed…big day today…oh my…'

'Paprika's gone,' said Sammy, tears prickling in his eyes. 'The Shape…they've taken her.'

Professor Burlay squeezed Sammy's shoulder. 'I'm, er, I'm sure she'll turn up.'

'Turn up dead,' said Sammy, dragging the back of his hand over his eyes. 'I've got to go anyway. I'm first for the Armoury exam.'

'I'll tell Commander Altair,' said Professor Burlay. 'I'm sure he'll let you have a moment or two.'

Sammy shook his head. 'I don't want any special treatment. Paprika was my Uncle's dragon. He was in the Shape. It's not like they took my parents' dragons.'

Professor Burlay paused for a moment. 'That's odd,' concluded Professor Burlay. 'Well, if you're sure you don't want me to mention it then I won't. But perhaps you should mention it to your Snorgcadell Challenger. They may be lenient.'

'No,' said Sammy firmly. 'This just makes me more determined. Nothing's going to stop me knocking him out to get my place as a Dragon Knight.'

'I'm not sure the Armoury exam is quite what you're expecting,' said Professor Burlay.

'I've got my staff and Darius is getting Kyrillan,' said Sammy, wiping his other eye. 'What else do they want?'

'Three things,' said Professor Burlay without hesitation. 'The three things that the Snorgcadell requires are that you are strong, compassionate and just.'

'Just what?' asked Sammy.

'Just,' said Professor Burlay frowning slightly. 'Just, just.'

'Never mind,' said Sammy. Through the thick cellar walls, he heard some kind of foghorn, which he guessed was part of the exam. 'I'll give it a hundred percent.'

'Can't say fairer than that,' said Professor Burlay, slapping Sammy on the back. 'Good luck!'

Sammy arrived in the castle courtyard out of breath from running at top speed from Mrs Grock's house. The whole class and Commander Altair were waiting for him.

Darius was on the edge of the group of students. He seemed to be having trouble restraining Kyrillan. As soon as the blue-green dragon saw Sammy he wrenched himself away from Darius. With his metal harness trailing on the ground, Kyrillan stomped up to Sammy hurrumphing as if he was complaining that Sammy was late to the class.

Sammy reached for Kyrillan, stroking his scaly neck. He jumped as an enormous Troll man appeared out of a shimmering green mist the other side of Kyrillan.

'Lateness is a filthy habit,' said the Troll, his wide green eyes bulging. 'I am Alaze Ramadere, General of Trolls at the Snorgcadell.'

'I'm Sammy, er, Samuel Rambles, fourth year, North,' said Sammy, stumbling over his words, in awe of the Troll General.

General Alaze Ramadere shook Sammy's hand. The Troll's hand was leathery and his handshake was firm.

'Very well, Sammy Samuel Rambles, fourth year North. You will duel me. I have heard many things about you and I am extremely keen to see if you match up to my expectations.'

Sammy felt his mouth dry up. 'You Sir?'

'I'll be gentle,' said Alaze Ramadere. He seemed grim, but Sammy spotted a twinkle flashing in his green eyes. The Troll General wanted a challenge.

Sammy knew he had to prove himself and he wished he'd got out of bed later so there wouldn't have been time to find out that the Shape had taken Paprika. He would have to concentrate very hard so that it didn't put him off.

# CHAPTER 48

# THE ARMOURY EXAM

'Mount your dragon, boy,' commanded General Alaze Ramadere.

Sammy was painfully aware that all of the fourth year students were watching him intently and scrutinising his every move in anticipation of their own Armoury exams.

Out of the corner of his eye, Sammy saw Professor Burlay speaking quietly to Commander Altair.

Commander Altair started walking quickly towards General Ramadere. Professor Burlay reached out and held Commander Altair's arm. He said something that Sammy couldn't hear and Commander Altair stopped and nodded.

They both looked at Sammy, making him rather nervous. To avoid looking back at the teachers, Sammy looked up and he was surprised to see a white mist in the early morning air above Commander Altair and Professor Burlay's heads. In the mist he could see some strange grey shapes.

With a jolt, Sammy recognised the grey shapes. They were the ghosts from the Church of a Thousand Graves. King Serberon and King Segragore.

'There is no pressure,' said General Alaze Ramadere, interrupting Sammy looking at the ghosts. 'When you are ready, mount your dragon and take him or her up to the height of the castle turrets. I want you to hover and listen and I shall relay what you are to do next. Samuel Rambles is to go first and then each student will follow, one by one.'

'Ok,' said Sammy. He swung his right leg over Kyrillan's back and sat astride his dragon. He nudged Kyrillan's flanks and they started moving forwards. 'It can't be that hard,' Sammy thought to himself.

Kyrillan broke into a run and within seconds he spread his blue-green shimmering wings and launched Sammy into the sky.

As soon as they were in the air Sammy relaxed. He guided Kyrillan upwards. They were higher than his classmates. Higher than the trees.

Sammy looked down. General Alaze Ramadere's jaw had dropped and Sammy knew it was because of Kyrillan's colouring. He could feel the General's amazement and he looked down proudly.

Sammy was proud that he had a dragon, despite the Shape trying to kill all the dragons and even more proud that his dragon was a direct descendant of King Serberon and Princess Karmandor.

'Up Kyrillan,' said Sammy, nudging his knees against Kyrillan's flanks.

Kyrillan soared higher. They were level with the Alchemistry classroom windows on the seventh floor. Sammy nudged again and they flew higher and higher, up to the very top of the castle, where, as instructed, they hovered.

Sammy strained his ears against the wind, trying to listen for commands from General Alaze Ramadere. He pulled on Kyrillan's harness to make his dragon circle around the turret. Waiting. Listening.

Sammy circled the turrets twice more, then in the very faintest of whispers, he heard a rasping, dead-sounding voice.

'I have waited for you to come,' whispered the voice.

Sammy spun round on Kyrillan, even though he knew no one would be there.

'You can help me,' said the rasping voice. 'Follow me. Yes, come this way.'

Sammy guided Kyrillan north, towards Mrs Grock's house and the woodland behind. He felt as if he was in a trance, carried by Kyrillan on the ever so slight breeze in the air. He felt his eyes close and tried desperately to open them.

Inside his eyelids, he saw a flash of light, so bright it felt like it was burning his eyelids. Then after the flash of light, Sammy saw a glimpse of the Valley of the Stone Cross. Then his vision zoomed in on the Stone Cross. It was covered in tiny blue-green stones. Draconite.

'Wait Kyrillan!' shouted Sammy, dropping the harness to wrench open his eyes. 'It's a trick! Go down! Down! Down! Down!'

Sammy leaped from Kyrillan's back almost before his dragon's paws touched the ground. He rubbed his eyes until they hurt.

'What was that?' demanded Sammy, storming up to the group of students and teachers.

General Alaze Ramadere's green eyes were blazing like tiny emeralds. 'That was a disgrace!' shouted the Troll.

Sammy looked directly into General Alaze Ramadere's eyes. There was no humour there. The huge Troll was far from joking.

'Sir,' started Sammy, noticing that Commander Altair's father, General Aldebaran Altair had joined the group, 'I heard your voice up there. You told me to follow you.'

General Aldebaran Altair looked firstly from Sammy to General Alaze Ramadere and back again. He seemed to be judging the situation from each angle.

'Perhaps it was the pressure?' suggested General Aldebaran Altair. 'The instruction was to circle around the turrets twice and then come back down.'

'Thought he'd show off in front of his friends, more likely,' said General Alaze Ramadere, tearing up Sammy's notes into tiny pieces. 'I won't need these and we won't bother with the other tests. Who's next?'

'Gavin Reed,' said Commander Altair, handing the General another set of papers to mark.

Gavin stepped forward and called for his dragon, Syren, to come to him.

'Unlucky,' said Gavin, looking like he meant it. The dark haired twin slapped Sammy on the shoulder and mounted his pink dragon.

Sammy stepped aside, his cheeks flushed, and he led Kyrillan to the edge of the Dragonball pitch. Commander Altair teleported beside him.

'You did well Sammy,' said Commander Altair. 'Just ignore General Ramadere. You'll have other chances to get into his good books.'

'I thought I was following his instructions,' said Sammy, digging his hands into his pockets.

'It's a trick he uses. You wouldn't have heard anything. The idea is that you obey him like a puppet on a string,' said Commander Altair. He lowered his head kindly. 'If you'd been here on time, you would have heard me tell you that.'

'Oh,' said Sammy. 'So the voice I heard was someone else?'

Commander Altair frowned. 'What voice?'

'Follow me...come this way...' Sammy imitated the croaky, dead-sounding, rasping voice.

'Maybe it was an echo?' said Commander Altair, scratching his head. 'I've never heard of any student able to hear Silent Calling before.'

'What's Silent Calling?' asked Sammy.

Commander Altair nodded. 'Good question Sammy. It is the unwritten words. It is the sound of silence. It is the very essence of being. General Ramadere has the gift of being able to tap into your subconscious. He can make you do anything or go anywhere. Don't look so worried, the first lesson he teaches is how to prevent it. That's what upset him just now. You disappeared off on someone else's instructions.'

'How does he know it wasn't my choice?' asked Sammy.

Commander Altair leaned close and whispered. 'You had your eyes shut. I think he's worried who spoke to you.'

'Who was it?' asked Sammy, feeling a chill run down the back of his neck.

'General Ramadere would probably suspect it was my father. There is friendly competition between the Generals in the Snorgcadell. Perhaps he thought my father was showing him up,' Commander Altair gave a nervous laugh.

'But...' whispered Sammy.

'But I listened to my father as he stood next to me,' said Commander Altair, 'and he said nothing at all.'

Sammy felt another cold twinge sending more shivers down his neck. 'So, who was it?'

Commander Altair shrugged. 'Who says you heard anything? You occasionally seem to hear things and see things that no one else does.'

'I saw the Valley of the Stone Cross,' said Sammy. 'It looked like the Stone Cross was nearly complete, like it was only missing a few stones.'

'I'll mention it to Sir Ragnarok,' said Commander Altair. 'This could be what he was looking for.'

'What?' demanded Sammy.

'Leave it with me Sammy,' said Commander Altair, 'and please, try not to think any more about it.'

CHAPTER 49

# THE DRAGON STUDIES EXAM

'Try not to think about it!' exploded Dixie when they were back in the common room after everyone in the North fourth year had taken their Armoury exams. 'How does he expect us to think of anything else?'

Sammy stayed silent. He hadn't felt more miserable in his entire life. Not only had Paprika been stolen from under his nose at Mrs Grock's house, but he'd messed up his important Armoury exam and even worse, he had upset General Alaze Ramadere, one of the most senior people in the Snorgcadell, who now probably thought he, Sammy, was in the Shape.

'It can't be that bad.' Dixie tried to reassure him.

But, when they stopped for lunch in the Main Hall, it was "that bad" as Sammy found they had a lousy meal of some kind of unidentified smelly fish that had been curdled beyond recognition in a mashed parsnip and potato bake, followed by cheese and biscuits when usually there would be some sort of cake. Chocolate cake was Sammy's favourite and he wasn't in the mood for cheese and biscuits at all.

'Captain Firebreath has been fishing in the sewers,' said Gavin, holding his nose.

Sammy just pushed the sludge around his plate and didn't eat anything. He had brought some Dragon Studies revision cards to lunch but he found the cards were blurred because he couldn't focus on anything.

It was impossible not to think about the Armoury exam or about where Paprika might be. Sammy was glad when the afternoon bell rang and he could follow the fourth years into the Dragon Studies classroom. They all sat down at separated desks and got out pens and paper ready to take the next exam.

Dr Shivers and Miss Amoratti were adjudicating the exam. Miss Amoratti was wearing her usual blue and black tunic and was perched like a blackbird on her desk. She was observing the bowed heads of the fourth year students whilst simultaneously filing her fingernails.

Dr Shivers paced in a circuit around the desks, making sure everyone was ready. When he got back to the teacher's desk, he flipped a three-hour wooden egg timer filled with purple sand.

'You may start,' said Dr Shivers and he sat next to Miss Amoratti on the edge of the teacher's desk.

Sammy turned his exam paper over and spent a minute watching the purple sand falling through the narrow middle of the egg timer. Out of the corner of his eye, Sammy saw Dr Shivers frown at him and he picked up his pen and started writing.

After two and a half hours, Sammy thought he had got most of the answers to the exam questions as right as he was going to get them, no matter how much time he was allowed. Most of the purple sand had fallen into the bottom half of the egg timer and some of his classmates had put down their pens.

Sammy closed his eyes. He found himself remembering the voice he'd heard when riding on Kyrillan up at the top of the castle by the coned turrets. "Follow me…this way" the voice had said. It wanted him to go towards Mrs Grock's house, beyond Mrs Grock's house, into the Forgotten Forest.

'To Karmandor,' Sammy muttered.

'No talking please Sammy,' said Miss Amoratti, looking up from her fingernails, 'otherwise you'll lose five percent.'

Behind him, someone snorted. It sounded like Darius trying to supress one of his explosive giggles. Sammy bowed his head, trying not to laugh. It was common knowledge that Miss Amoratti couldn't count and that she awarded grades based on how much in her favour you were at the time.

'Silence please,' barked Dr Shivers. 'You only have fifteen minutes left.'

Sammy checked his answers for the third time and he was extremely glad when Dr Shivers eventually called for the exam papers to be handed to the front of the class.

'You will have your results at the beginning of next week,' said Dr Shivers. 'Until then, please refrain from concerning yourselves about your marks. If you have done your very best, then you have nothing to worry about. You may leave,' he finished, waving his hand towards the classroom door with a flourish.

Sammy hurried with Dixie and Darius back to the North common room. They took a brief detour to the school kitchen and persuaded Captain Firebreath to let them take plates of sandwiches and sausage rolls he was preparing for the finger buffet tea back with them to the common room. Other students were taking their plates of food outside.

With his usual gruffness and a little grumbling, Captain Firebreath produced a feast for Sammy, Dixie and Darius to take with them, on the promise that there wouldn't be any crumbs and they would return the plates later.

Sammy, Dixie and Darius took a large plate of food in each hand and scurried back to the common room, where they sat on beanbags next to the fireplace.

Feeling a little bit cold, Sammy took out his staff and lit the common room fire. Outside it was still light and they could see streams of students carrying plates and finding places to sit and eat in the school grounds.

'Weird, isn't it,' said Dixie, her mouth full of sausage roll. 'In a couple of weeks, we won't have any lessons, ever again.'

Sammy looked up from his plate. 'There'll be lessons at the Snorgcadell, won't there?' he asked.

'If you get in,' teased Darius. 'Yeah, there'll probably be sword fights, advanced flying, that sort of thing. You'll be expected to know ten times what you know now.'

'Are you seriously staying here for the fifth year?' asked Dixie.

Darius nodded. 'Yes, I'm doing next year at Dragamas, then I want to go to a Gemology college, maybe St. Agates, then I want to take a gap year and then do some sort of degree in Advanced Gemology and Medicines. After that, I'll probably do two years' work experience with Mr and Mrs Gravenstone and then I can choose whether I want to become a full time Healer like my parents or go somewhere like Dragamas and be a Teacher.'

'You should become a full time Healer,' said Dixie promptly. 'Then you can help me if anything goes wrong with my dragon breeding.'

'Hah!' snorted Darius, spitting out pieces of sausage roll. 'Like you'll need any help! You're a natural with dragons!'

'Well I have been around them all my life,' said Dixie thoughtfully.

'Exactly,' said Darius. 'I should be really good with dragons as well but it's hard to concentrate when we have to keep our own dragons as well. Dr Shivers was really sarcastic to me the other day when I asked if dragons can eat watermelons.'

'What did he say?' asked Sammy, picking up a magazine and not really caring about the answer.

'He said orange dragons like it best. He told me to tell you that for Paprika…uh, sorry,' said Darius sheepishly.

'It's ok,' said Sammy.

'No it's not,' said Darius. 'Me and Dixie are supposed to be your best friends. We should be looking out for Paprika, trying to find where she's gone.'

'There's no point,' said Sammy, snapping the magazine shut. 'You know that as well as I do.'

'Maybe we could listen for her, you know, like we tried to do when we were looking for Dixie,' suggested Darius.

Dixie scowled. 'Do you have to mention that? I want to forget I was ever down there.'

'Sorry,' apologised Darius. 'I didn't think.'

'I loved those dragon pups,' said Dixie, a far off look in her green eyes. 'Commander Altair said he'd let me keep them but then he tells me Sir Ragnarok wants them for breeding and they got sent away somewhere.'

'When can dragons breed?' asked Sammy. He'd never given it any thought, other than all the first years getting dragon eggs on their first day at Dragamas.

'That was question forty-two in the Dragon Studies exam,' said Dixie, 'and the answer is typically after fifteen to twenty years.'

'Just in time for our kids,' said Sammy, laughing.

Dixie looked worried. 'Steady on there!'

Sammy and Darius laughed hysterically, rolling around on the beanbags.

'I didn't mean us!' said Sammy. 'That's really weird!'

'Totally,' agreed Dixie. 'So, now that's sorted, I'll ask Commander Altair where he thinks Paprika is. I said I'd see him after tea.'

'Are you in trouble again?' asked Darius, rolling off the beanbag onto the floor.

'No,' laughed Dixie. 'He thinks he's responsible for me while I'm at Dragamas and my Mum will just give me an earful if I don't speak to him. I've tried telling her he's not my housemaster, but she won't listen.'

'It's nice of him,' said Sammy. 'While you do that, I want to check on Cyngard and Jovah anyway.'

'I'll come with you,' said Darius. 'It's weird they weren't taken as well.'

'That's what I'm worried about,' said Sammy.

'In case the Shape comes back for them?' asked Darius.

Sammy shook his head. 'It's strange because they weren't taken and they weren't killed. It's kind of like my parents' dragons are still needed somehow.'

'Very strange,' agreed Dixie. 'I'll see you later,' she added and teleported in a grey-green mist without revealing her destination.

Darius looked at the mist enviously. 'I wish I could do that.'

Sammy laughed. 'It's ok, we'll take the stairs.'

CHAPTER 50

# DWARVES ON GUARD

Outside it was still hot and Sammy unbuttoned the top buttons on his shirt after he and Darius had run to Mrs Grock's house. Her garden was deserted and the front door, as usual, was unlocked.

Sammy and Darius pushed open the green front door and stepped quietly inside Mrs Grock's house. There were murmuring voices and groans coming from upstairs.

Sammy remembered there had been an outbreak of mumps that was being contained and someone in the second year had broken a leg in an unfortunate Firesticks accident.

Ignoring the voices, Sammy followed Darius into the store room next to the kitchen. He pushed aside a sack of Haycorn and opened the trapdoor, surprised to find a flame hovering above the opening.

'Who's there?' demanded Darius stepping forward and looking down the hole in the floor.

Sammy had enough past dealings with the Shape to know not to jump in feet first. He held the trapdoor open, ready to shut it and call for help at a moment's notice.

'Commander Altair,' a voice called up the steps. 'Is that you, Sammy?'

'It's me, Darius, and Sammy's here as well,' said Darius, pushing Sammy towards the flames.

Using just his mind, Sammy extinguished the fire and started walking down the steps.

'Hey!' said another voice that was unmistakably Dixie's voice.

'Sorry,' said Sammy. He lit a new fire and stepped down into the circular cellar room.

To his relief, Cyngard and Jovah were still there. Sammy checked them and they looked in perfect health. He felt a pang of jealousy when they stomped over to Dixie instead of him. But his jealousy evaporated when he saw it was just because she had some sweets in her pocket.

'Do you want some of these?' Dixie asked the dragons as she shared the sweets equally between them. 'I'll tell Kiridor you ate them and he won't be happy!'

'I'm going to ask Sir Ragnarok to put someone on guard at this entrance,' said Commander Altair. 'I don't think it will be a problem now that Paprika has gone, but it won't hurt to be on our guard. I'll see if we can use Captain Stronghammer.'

'Are you sure about him?' asked Sammy, thinking this was an odd choice.

Commander Altair nodded. 'Captain Stronghammer has been on our side for as long as I've been alive. He would have come forward sooner if he'd stayed away from that cider.'

Sammy grinned, remembering the taste he'd had of Captain Firebreath's home brewed cider. 'It's not bad.'

'It's not good either,' said Commander Altair. 'We use it at the Snorgcadell to get people talking. They get the chance to do things the easy way and if they refuse then we give them a hangover to remember! That's a joke Sammy, you'll find out soon enough who we are and what we do.'

'We still live at Dragamas, don't we?' asked Dixie. 'I heard the Snorgcadell is really close.'

Commander Altair straightened himself. 'I needn't ask where you got that information from. As for the exact location of the Snorgcadell, like I said, you'll find out soon enough.'

Sammy gave Cyngard and Jovah some of the sausage rolls he'd saved for them and he noticed a pile of meaty bones that made his contribution seem tiny in comparison.

'Commander Altair brought them,' explained Dixie. 'He does it all the time.'

'Oh,' said Sammy, 'Thank you.'

'You're welcome.' Commander Altair smiled at Sammy. 'I know it's hard for you looking after the adult dragons as well as Kyrillan.'

A patter of footsteps caught Sammy's attention. He spun around. Captain Stronghammer was there with a cider bottle in his hand. Captain Firebreath was running after him.

'Will yer wait fer me?' growled Captain Firebreath.

'Glad I found yer,' grunted Captain Stronghammer. 'I got summit important news to tell yer about that dragon.'

Commander Altair leaned close, an arm resting on Sammy's and Dixie's shoulders. 'What do know about Paprika,' he asked kindly.

Captain Stronghammer took a swig from the cider bottle and coughed. Captain Firebreath took the bottle away from him and, staring wistfully, he poured the entire contents away.'

'I saw who it was. Him who took the dragon,' said Captain Stronghammer, swaying slightly on his feet. 'I was here. I checks on these three dragons as well. Sir Ragnarok's orders,' he added importantly.

'Get yer story out,' growled Captain Firebreath. 'They haven't got all day.'

'Well, it were dark,' said Captain Stronghammer, tucking his thumbs into his dungaree straps. 'An' I've had a lot of trouble lately. Things I need ter think about.'

Commander Altair cleared his throat, moving to the side as Captain Stronghammer staggered forward and stood in front of him, an eerie shadow cast across his face from the light of the fire at the end of Sammy's staff.

'He were as tall as yer, Commander. He were dark, shapeless, a cold figure, wore a long black coat, nasty smell behind him,' Captain Stronghammer paused and peered down the corridor as if he half-expected the man to be there, watching them.

'We know that already,' said Dixie impatiently. 'Alfie Agrock wore that when he, you know, when he kept me prisoner in the Church of a Thousand Graves.'

Commander Altair drew close to Dixie. His hand gripped his staff and Sammy knew the Armoury teacher would protect her from anything in the future.

'Alfie Agrock,' repeated Darius thoughtfully. 'We know it can't have been him because he's been captured and he's at the Snorgcadell along with Dr Lithoman, Sammy's Uncle and Mrs Hubar.'

Commander Altair nodded. 'If what I'm thinking is right, then we're looking for someone with the initials "S.S." who will be the last person in the Shape.'

'Simone Sanchez!' shouted Darius.

Sammy shook his head. 'She's dead. Paprika was taken this morning.'

'A ghost,' joked Dixie.

'You'll frighten yourself with stories like that,' said Commander Altair. 'Come on, I need to find Professor Burlay. He's asked me to check his suit,' Commander Altair laughed. 'What he means is that he wants to make sure I haven't lost these,' Commander Altair took a black velvet box out of his pocket and opened it to show them two gold rings in the shape of dragon's tails inside.

Sammy liked the look of the intricately intertwined tails and remembered how Professor Sanchez had made them. He braced himself as he heard more footsteps approaching the cellar, but it turned out to be two Dwarves who had come to be the new guards, replacing Captain Firebreath and Captain Stronghammer.

'...he ain't no punk,' sang one of the Dwarves as he entered the chamber.

The other Dwarf laughed. 'He's bin saying that all the way here, "drunk as a skunk, he..."'

'There's nowt wrong with my cider,' growled Captain Firebreath. 'Have yer found any more draconite stones?'

Sammy, Dixie, Darius and Commander Altair left the four mining Dwarves arguing about draconite and cider and they went back out into the sunshine in Mrs Grock's garden.

'Which exams have you got left?' asked Commander Altair.

'Most of them,' grumbled Darius. 'I need more time. If I don't get a good Gemology mark I can forget about asking my parents to let me go to St. Agates or train with Mr and Mrs Gravenstone. They won't want me wasting their time.'

'I doubt it,' said Dixie. 'You're easily the best in our class at Gemology.'

Darius blushed faintly. 'Maybe I'm worrying too much,' he conceded. 'Let's get something to eat.'

# CHAPTER 51

# GEMSTONES AND DREAMS

A few days later, after the exams were over, Sammy lay in the sun with Dixie and Darius wondering what the fuss had all been about. They had spent hours and hours revising and stressing over possible answers. Then suddenly almost as soon as the exam period started it was over.

Professor Burlay and Mrs Grock's wedding was going to be held on the Saturday after the summer term had finished, but everyone was invited to stay the extra night and be collected by their family or friends, who were also welcome to come and celebrate the wedding.

'Have you packed?' asked Darius.

'Nearly,' said Sammy. 'I've got most things packed and I've handed in all my books.'

'Me too,' said Dixie. 'Milly was terrible at packing. She packed, unpacked and then packed again, at least three or four times. She still doesn't know Naomi has taken her hair brush. She'll be looking for that for about a week!'

They laughed and Sammy thought back to the beginning of term. How could he ever have felt close to

Milly while Dixie had been held prisoner. He squeezed her hand.

'You're hopeless Sammy,' laughed Darius.

'Hey! I am here,' said Dixie indignantly. 'And Sammy, I'm not going anywhere. You can stop beating yourself up. You did rescue me. You found me. You came down into that chamber.'

'Eugh!' said Darius, shoving his fingers into his mouth and pretending to be sick.

'You're just jealous,' said Dixie.

'I am not!' retorted Darius. 'Me, Nelson and my brand new gemstone, we're going to cure the world!' Darius held out a large green stone. 'I asked Dr Shivers for this.'

'Cool,' said Sammy, assembling his staff. 'What extra things do emeralds do?'

'Onyx is protection,' said Dixie. 'Protection to look after ourselves and others.'

'Ruby to freeze and unfreeze objects and people,' said Darius.

'Amber to see things and listen for things,' said Sammy.

'Sapphire for moving matter, creating event horizons and oilslicks,' said Darius, as if he was quoting from a text book.

'And emerald to control yourself,' said Sammy. 'I bet that's what it is. I bet that's why I was given it. To stop the Shape calling me.'

'Emerald?' asked Darius, holding his green stone. 'Mine is jade. It has healing powers.'

'Cool,' said Dixie.

'Not really,' said Darius, looking a little envious. He touched the single emerald, the only gemstone left on Sammy's staff. 'It's weird how that's the only one left after all your other gemstones dissolved.'

'Dr Shivers gave it to me,' said Sammy.

'Zacharius Shivers,' said Dixie. 'Funny name.'

'Zach...' started Darius, his eyes round. 'Z Z Z, S S S.'

Sammy thought Darius had gone mad. Then he had a sudden thought about Paprika.

'Ooh,' said Dixie, picking up on Sammy's thoughts. 'There's no way he'd do that.'

'He knew my Uncle,' said Sammy. 'Maybe he's spoken to my Uncle while he's in prison at the Snorgcadell. Maybe I should ask Dr Shivers about it. Did my Uncle know where Paprika would be?'

'Half the school knew where Paprika would be,' said Dixie with a grin. 'You're famous for having three adult dragons, Sammy!'

'Yeah,' added Darius. 'I heard two first years saying that adult dragons eat humans! They asked me if it was true and I said it was,' Darius grinned wickedly.

Sammy laughed. 'Let's go up to the tower. I want to see if I can find my Firesticks ball.'

'The Invisiball?' asked Dixie. 'Unless it changes back to black, or you trip over it, you'll never find it again. While you look for that, I want to try my dress on again.'

'Yeah,' said Darius. 'You've only tried it on a million times. You never know, it might not fit!'

Dixie put her hands on her hips. 'Darius Murphy, are you saying I'm fat?'

'Turn around,' said Darius, winking at Sammy.

'No!' said Dixie. 'And don't you come looking in Mrs Grock's windows while I try it on either!'

'We'll see you tomorrow then,' said Darius.

'Remember to bring Kiridor for me,' said Dixie.

'Sure.' Sammy gave Dixie a quick hug as he and Darius said goodbye to her.

Up in the fourth year North tower room, Sammy and Darius searched high and low for the missing Invisiball, which refused to be found. They abandoned the search when Gavin and Toby arrived and suggested a game of Dragonball to finish up the evening.

When he finally got back to the tower room, Sammy checked his shirt was ironed and his trousers were clean and ready for the morning. He folded the items into a pile and placed them on the top of his chest of drawers next to his glass of water and sank into his bed, exhausted.

During the night, Sammy woke in a cold sweat. He threw his duvet off and reached for the glass of water.

'Last day today,' Sammy muttered, wondering why he had woken so early. It was still quite dark.

As he reached for the water in the darkness, Sammy looked out of the window and noticed the Church of a Thousand Graves, where the wedding would be held in the morning.

Sammy sat up straight. It looked as though grey smoke was rising out of the church spires. He stared into the darkness, wondering whether the grey smoke was in fact the ghostly King Serberon and King Segragore. He took a small sip of water and lay down.

Within minutes, Sammy was asleep, dreaming about Dixie wearing her bridesmaid dress, Mrs Grock, Professor Burlay and his family and of his own parents who would be coming later in the day.

In the dream, Charles and Julia Rambles could see dragons and they rode around the Dragonball pitch, his mother on Jovah and his father on Cyngard. He was riding on Kyrillan and they flew higher and higher until they disappeared into a bright white light.

Sammy flicked his eyes open. The bright white light was Darius, shining his torch on him.

'Are you ok?' whispered Darius. 'It's just you've been talking about your parents and their dragons in your sleep.'

'Sorry,' whispered Sammy, blushing. 'Sorry everyone.'

From behind Gavin's curtain there was a snigger.

'It's ok Sammy, we know you're weird,' said Gavin.

'Shut up Gavin,' said Darius. 'You'd be the same if it was you and your parents.'

'I would not!' shouted Gavin, ripping open his curtain.

Sammy grinned as Gavin held his pillow over Darius and brought it down with a thump on Darius's head.

'Oi!' shouted Darius, snatching Sammy's duvet and wrapping Gavin up like a mummy.

Sammy leaped out of bed. It was cold on the stone floor. He snatched up both of his pillows, one in each hand, and flung them at Gavin.

'Oi! Toby!' yelled Gavin. 'Help me out!'

Toby stuck his head around the curtain. He grinned at the debris and grabbed his pillows.

After a ten-minute furious fight, Sammy collapsed on his unmade bed, exhausted. His pillows were in pieces and his duvet was spread on the floor between his bed and Darius's bed.

'I win!' said Gavin, shaking the last feathers out of one of the pillows.

'Look at the time!' shrieked Darius. 'We're supposed to be at Mrs Grock's house with our dragons!'

Sammy checked his watch. Darius was right. Without thinking, he threw on jeans and a t-shirt.

'You can't wear that!' squawked Darius.

Sammy looked across. Darius was getting dressed in a sparkling white shirt, school jumper and freshly ironed black trousers. He remembered the pile of clothes on his chest of drawers he'd put out last night.

'Oh yeah,' said Sammy and he changed his clothes in record time.

CHAPTER 52

# THE WEDDING

Down in the Dragon Chambers, there were only a few dragons left to be collected. Most of the South, East and West students had already left for the summer holiday.

However, almost all of the North students had stayed to celebrate Professor Burlay and Mrs Grock's wedding. Sammy knew this was because Professor Burlay was a North teacher and everyone liked him. All of the North students were happy for him and Mrs Grock.

Sammy followed Darius into the North section of the Dragon Chambers. He sought out Kyrillan, who was drinking from one of the large water basins. He couldn't quite place a strange feeling he was having, but it felt like he was being watched. He remembered he'd promised to bring Kiridor for Dixie and he took the two blue-green shimmering dragons outside.

Darius fetched Nelson and Mrs Grock's enormous purple dragon, Xenon, who had spent the night in the Dragon Chambers instead of under Mrs Grock's house so that Darius could prepare her dragon for the ceremony.

Sammy and Darius marched up the ramp leading out of the Dragon Chambers and went outside into the early morning sunshine with the four dragons in tow.

Kyrillan kept nudging Sammy. It was almost as if the young dragon knew it would be their last day together for a while. There was no way Sammy could take Kyrillan to Switzerland for the summer holiday with his parents.

Sammy squeezed Kyrillan's scaly neck affectionately. He wished they didn't have to split up over the holiday. Kyrillan seemed to feel the same and Sammy loved the bond they shared.

As they reached Mrs Grock's house, there were two dragons already in the garden. The front door opened and Mrs Grock came out with Dixie, Milly, Naomi and Sarah Havercastle closely behind her.

Mrs Grock was wearing a beautiful pale peachy-pink dress with a matching bonnet. But Sammy felt his eyes lock on Dixie. She was wearing a mint and avocado two-piece dress that complimented her striking green hair to perfection.

Sammy noticed Dixie's hair was tied back in a plaited crown with wisping strands falling down the side of her face. She was wearing sparkling diamante earrings and a matching necklace. He thought she looked radiantly beautiful and he wanted to tell her but she was laughing at something Sarah had just said.

Next to Dixie, Sammy thought Sarah Havercastle seemed extraordinarily plain. Even though she was wearing the same coloured dress, Sarah was scowling. Sammy guessed she was feeling uncomfortable wearing the dress instead of her usual gymnastic circuswear.

Dixie waved frantically and Sammy saw she was wearing a sparkling bracelet on her right wrist.

'You're late!' said Dixie. 'Commander Altair and Professor Burlay are already on their way!'

'We had to get Mrs Grock's dragon,' explained Sammy, pointing to the shining purple dragon.

'I cleaned her until I could see myself reflected in her scales,' said Darius proudly.

'Ooch, bless you Darius!' said Mrs Grock and with a vibrant bounce, she mounted her purple dragon, her dress flowing behind her. 'Up! Up! Up and away!' sang Mrs Grock and Sammy thought he'd never seen her look so happy.

Sammy took a step back as Mrs Grock flew over his head. It was odd seeing the Dragamas school secretary and nurse flying thirty feet above them.

Sammy felt his heart skip a beat as Dixie took Kiridor's reins out of his hands. He helped her up onto Kiridor's back and she sat on her blue-green dragon with her dress falling neatly between her dragon's wings.

Sarah vaulted onto Kiridor's back and sat in behind Dixie. She took bunches of brightly coloured flowers and tubs of confetti from Naomi and tapped Dixie's shoulder to say she was ready.

Dixie tapped her heels against Kiridor's flanks and her dragon took steps forward, going faster and faster until he spread his shimmering wings, pushed off the ground and the girls were flying.

Milly and Naomi mounted their dragons and followed Dixie, Sarah and Mrs Grock into the sky.

'Let's go to the Church of a Thousand Graves,' said Darius, slinging his leg over Nelson's back. There was a loud "rip" as the back of his trousers split open.

Sammy roared with laughter at Darius's surprised face.

Darius shrugged. 'I'll just take my jumper off and put it round my waist. No one will see!'

Still laughing, Sammy mounted Kyrillan and with a gentle nudge, Kyrillan sprouted his wings and took off. They were away. The ground was fading fast beneath them.

Darius waved vigorously as he and Sammy soon overtook Dixie and Sarah, Mrs Grock and Milly and Naomi. Sarah sprinkled confetti over them and Kyrillan blew smoke rings as the coloured paper flew around his head.

Soon, the church spires loomed close and Sammy saw that each spire was laced with purple and gold banners. As they got even closer, he could see hundreds of pink balloons tied to the trunks of all of the blossoming cherry trees in the graveyard.

Sammy guided Kyrillan towards an empty space on the path leading up to the church entrance and they landed smoothly without kicking up any of the white pebbles.

Darius, Milly, Naomi, Dixie, Sarah and Mrs Grock landed their dragons in a neat line behind Kyrillan. The dragons folded in their wings and allowed the riders to dismount safely.

Commander Altair and Professor Burlay scurried to meet them. They were both very smartly dressed in black suits with white shirts and green ties.

Professor Burlay helped Mrs Grock down from her purple dragon.

'You look beautiful,' whispered Professor Burlay, loudly enough for everyone to hear. He turned towards the church doors. 'Mum! Molly! Elsie's here!'

There was a pattering of high heels on the stone floor and Molly Burlay appeared at the church entrance, followed by Merry Megan, who looked older and frailer than Sammy remembered. Both women were wearing dresses made of pastel pink and white silk.

Molly looked gushingly at Commander Altair and she and Merry Megan tinkered with the mens' suits and their green ties.

'It's fine, Mum,' said Professor Burlay, as Merry Megan re-adjusted the tails of his tie, trying to keep them level.

'Sammy, you and Darius can go in,' said Commander Altair. 'Sir Ragnarok will be inside and he will show you to your seats.'

'Ooch yes,' interrupted Mrs Grock. 'I'll need all of my pretty bridesmaids out here for a moment and then we will go in together when we are called.'

Sammy and Darius took Commander Altair's advice and went in through the church doors. It was dark, but they found Sir Ragnarok in the entrance and the Dragamas headmaster ushered them inside, pointing to two empty chairs at the back.

Commander Altair and Professor Burlay followed Sammy and Darius inside. They made their way to the altar and sat in the front row of seats, waiting in nervous silence.

Most of the other seats were filled. At the front, next to the altar, a man in an extremely tight tuxedo was playing the organ. Next to him were twelve choir boys and girls wearing long white ruffle collared garments. Each boy and girl was holding a black leather songbook. They were singing at the tops of their voices.

Sammy recognised Tristan Markham from the South house and he waved.

Holding his songbook like a trophy and his face tightly concentrating on the high notes, Tristan simply nodded at Sammy and Darius and he carried on singing.

Sammy sat in the chair nearest to the arched window and stared up at the scene of battle and bloodshed. He drifted his eyes out of focus, hoping to see signs of the Kings of the Dark Ages.

Nothing happened, so Sammy picked up his copy of the songbook from under his chair and sang, slightly out of tune, along to "Summer Beautiful" and then "Homefires Burning Bright".

As the music died away, Sammy looked back towards the church entrance. Mrs Grock, Dixie and Milly were there, followed closely by Naomi and Sarah.

The organ struck up a rhythmic wedding march and Mrs Grock stepped forward, shuffled, stepped forward, shuffled and stepped forward in time with the music, her long peachy-pink train fanning behind her.

Dixie and Milly picked up the corners of the train, so it wouldn't drag on the stone floor. Mrs Grock was beaming, her face half-hidden beneath the peach bonnet.

Everyone turned to look at Mrs Grock. There was an audible happy sigh from the audience as she made her way down the aisle. Sammy found himself staring into space, mesmerised by the procession.

Dixie awoke him with a sharp projected thought into his mind asking him what he was looking at. Sammy grinned at her, projecting back that she should try not to trip.

Sir Ragnarok joined Mrs Grock, slipping his arm into the crook of her arm and they walked together to the front of the church. Sammy guessed he was standing in for Mrs Grock's father, who was perhaps no longer alive.

Professor Burlay and Commander Altair were at the front, both looking back down the aisle expectantly. They stood up as Mrs Grock approached.

Commander Altair touched his chest pocket and Sammy guessed it was to make sure the rings were still there.

The music faded and the choir finished their song. Mrs Grock stepped up to the altar with Professor Burlay. Tristan Markham's father, the vicar, Howard Markham opened a large book and addressed the congregation.

'Ladies and gentlemen,' said Howard Markham, his voice as clear as a bell in the quiet church.

There was a murmur as everyone swivelled round to look at the vicar. Some people coughed briefly and others cleared their throats. Then there was silence.

'We are gathered here today,' continued Howard Markham, 'in the presence of the ghosts of the Kings of the Dark Ages.'

Sammy jerked in surprise. He could now see the Kings of the Dark Ages. One in each of the two end windows. By the sudden increase of murmuring, it seemed that everyone else could see them, apart from Professor Burlay and Mrs Grock, who had their backs to the stained glass windows.

'To join together Jonathan Franklin Burlay and Miss, er, Ms Elizabeth Louise Fernes, whom you know as Mrs Grock,' continued Howard Markham. 'I would like to reinforce to those present that her violent, abusive marriage to the member of the Shape, Alfred Agrock, was built on a lie and by a technical error of my predecessor, I am delighted to proffer her as a legally single, vibrant, adorable, kind, generous, beautiful...'

'Ahem,' interrupted Professor Burlay.

'...soul of a woman, who has accepted the proposition of an equally generous gentleman, whom I wish every success and happiness,' Howard Markham paused for breath.

Sammy was sure if he dropped a coin it would make everyone jump.

'Now,' said Howard Markham, his voice hushed to a stage whisper, 'do you Elizabeth Louise Fernes accept...'

'Yes!' squealed Mrs Grock. 'Yes! Yes! Yes!'

'Very well,' Howard Markham took out a gold fountain pen and scribed in his book. 'Now, do you, Professor Jonathan Franklin Burlay...'

'Yes!' said Professor Burlay. 'All of it! Yes! Marry us and make my life complete!'

'Very well,' said Howard Markham, looking rather disappointed. 'I now pronounce you man and...hey, you're supposed to wait for that...wife.'

Professor Burlay and Mrs Grock, who was now Mrs Burlay, were locked in a deep embrace.

Howard Markham wrestled them apart momentarily so that Commander Altair could give them both their rings, then Professor Burlay and his wife snapped back together as if they were on elastic.

Above them, Sammy saw King Segragore put his arm around the shoulders of King Serberon. They both seemed to be weeping slightly, their tears falling like rain down the windows.

## CHAPTER 53

# A PROMISE TO COMPLETE

Everyone clapped and cheered. Professor Burlay waved at the congregation, showing off his gold ring, which glistened on the third finger of his left hand.

Merry Megan, wrapped in her shawl, patted his arm. She hadn't stopped beaming ever since Howard Markham had pronounced her son a married man.

Molly Burlay was still looking at Commander Altair when she thought no one was looking.

'Right,' said Professor Burlay, loudly enough for everyone in the Church of a Thousand Graves to hear. 'I believe we are going back to Dragamas for lunch, then I and my beautiful wife will be whisked away to the Land of Paradise,' he pointed to the sky, 'where we can spend the entire summer in the finest hotel in the world, surrounded by tropical blue sea and golden sand.'

The congregation groaned loudly. It sounded a lovely place to go for the summer and Sammy hoped he could go there one day.

'With not a single star in sight,' said Mrs Burlay, laughing and linking hands with her husband.

'I promise, my love!' sang Professor Burlay. 'Now, to Dragamas!' He clutched her hand and disappeared in a vibrant golden mist that absorbed Molly, Merry Megan, Commander Altair and Sir Ragnarok.

'I suppose we're walking,' grumbled a lady in a pink taffeta skirt and jacket with a hat that looked like it was made of edible strawberries and cream.

Sammy nudged Darius. 'Come on, let's get our dragons.'

'Ok.' Darius got up, rubbing his legs and complaining he'd got pins and needles.

Dr Shivers was already on his feet. He was deep in conversation with an elderly couple, talking about the history of the church.

Trying to leave discretely, Sammy followed Darius to the church doors. Darius went first, but as Sammy stepped across the cattlegrid, something jerked him back. It was a cold hand pressing firmly on the back of his neck.

'Hey!' exclaimed Sammy, turning around quickly.

Behind him were the two grey ghosts of King Serberon and King Segragore.

'Before you run off for the summer...' said King Serberon.

'...You have a promise to complete,' finished King Segragore.

'Yes, I know,' said Sammy, glad they had let go. His neck was damp and clammy from their touch. 'Karmandor is in the Forgotten Forest at Dragamas. It's like she's been turned to stone. We use her tail as a lift to get up to the lands that visit above the school.'

King Segragore slammed his ghostly fist through the stone wall beside him. 'My Karmandor,' he moaned.

King Serberon hung his head. 'My Karmandor. How could she do that to her?'

'Karmandor's tail is the only thing holding the land above Dragamas,' said Sammy. 'If she moves, she'll pull the land down and crush the castle. We have to wait until the Floating Circus moves on.'

'I regret she cannot be free sooner, but I understand,' said King Segragore. 'I have waited several hundred years to see my daughter. A few days won't hurt me any more than I have already been hurt.'

'You have done well, Sammy,' said King Serberon. 'You have settled your end of our bargain very well.'

'Why don't you come to Professor Burlay and Mrs Burlay's reception at Dragamas?' asked Sammy. 'Then you could see Karmandor.'

'Yes,' said King Serberon at once. 'To think she has been so close for all these years. I have so much to say to the woman who will be my Queen.'

'Starting with an apology,' interrupted King Segragore. 'You owe my daughter and myself that much.'

King Serberon lowered his head, the grey jewels in his crown glimmering in the shadow of his former glory. 'And haven't I told you, every single day how much I regret things and how I would do things differently if I could?'

King Segragore nodded. 'Yes, but you must now say these things to my daughter.'

Sammy backed over the cattlegrid in the church entrance. Darius reached for him, pulling Sammy outside.

'What on earth took you so long?' asked Darius. 'Where have you been?'

Sammy looked around, dazzled slightly by the sunlight. Dixie, Naomi and Sarah were staring at him.

'You just disappeared,' said Dixie. 'We went in and out a dozen times.'

'I was with King Segragore and King Serberon,' said Sammy. 'I was between them,' he added thoughtfully.

Darius shrugged. 'Well, you're here now. Everyone else has gone.'

Sammy looked back as they walked down the cherry tree lined path to the patiently waiting dragons. He could see King Segragore and King Serberon following them at a distance.

Sammy mounted Kyrillan and used his mind to ask his dragon to fly back to Dragamas. Kyrillan instantly spread his large blue-green wings and took off, his iridescent scales casting shimmering rainbows down onto the gravestones.

Dixie and Sarah climbed onto Kiridor's back. Naomi mounted her dragon, Quentina and Darius climbed slowly onto Nelson's back, taking care not to rip his trousers any further. Together, the five humans and four dragons flew the short distance back to the castle.

The coned turrets of Dragamas Castle with the black flags and the golden "D" motifs flying high from the rooftops soon appeared underneath them. Several cars were parked in the layby opposite the school gates.

Dozens of tables with pink and white chequered tablecloths and hundreds of chairs with pink cushions were laid out in neat rows on the Dragonball pitch.

Sammy knew that Merry Megan and Molly Burlay had arranged with the Dwarves to prepare a banquet for everyone who wanted to come back from the Church of a Thousand Graves for food and drink. The invitation was open to all of the parents and guardians picking up their children from Dragamas as well.

'Look!' yelled Darius, pointing to a multi-coloured blob on the ground. 'My parents are here!'

Sammy guided Kyrillan down to the ground, flying downwards in the gentle spirals that Mr Cross had taught them for when they needed to land in confined areas.

Dixie landed Kiridor neatly next to Kyrillan and she and Sarah jumped off Kiridor's back just in time as Darius came careering down with Nelson breathing smoke rings and puffing and panting and scattering the dragons.

'That was amazing!' said Sarah, straightening out her dress and smoothing her hair back into place.

Dixie grinned and nudged Sammy's elbow. 'We do it all the time.'

'You're so lucky. I wish I had a dragon,' said Sarah.

'We've had them for nearly four years,' said Darius, patting Nelson's back to calm his dragon down. 'We hatched them out ourselves.'

'Amazing,' said Sarah. 'Although I suppose I do have a lion.'

'Is that your parents Darius?' asked Sammy, pointing to a smartly dressed couple at the front of the stream of adults who were coming up the drive to meet their sons and daughters.

'Yes,' said Darius. He quickly straightened his tie. 'Do I look alright?'

'You always look alright,' said Naomi, planting a kiss on Darius's cheek.

'How are you Darius?' asked his mother, moving Naomi aside and giving her son a hug. 'Did you have a good term?'

Darius's father gave Darius a stiff handshake and said nothing. Sammy remembered Darius's parents were quite formal but was surprised his father didn't greet him.

'Yes,' said Darius, trying to free himself and failing. 'We've just been to a wedding.'

'One of your teachers, I hope?' said Darius's father, checking his watch. 'We have time for a short drink and something to eat and then we are meeting Mr and Mrs Gravenstone to discuss their findings at Stonehenge.'

'Can't we stay longer?' asked Darius, finally extracting himself and putting on his best beseeching face, hoping to persuade his parents to enjoy the banquet at Dragamas. 'This is Sammy, Dixie and Sarah,' Darius added, pointing to his friends.

'And you must be Naomi Fairweather,' said Darius's mother, eyeing Naomi with caution.

Darius's father checked his watch again and tutted. 'Where's all this food then?'

'It's this way,' said Sammy. 'The banquet is being held on the Dragonball pitch.'

'Barbaric sport,' said Darius's mother. 'As if we don't have enough to do without curing injuries that could have been prevented.'

'There's Professor Burlay and Mrs Grock,' shouted Dixie, pointing across the Dragonball pitch at the bride and groom.

'Mrs Burlay,' corrected Sammy. 'She looks really happy.'

Both Professor Burlay and his wife had changed out of their wedding clothes. Professor Burlay was wearing a pair of blue denim jeans with a green and white chequered shirt.

Elsie Burlay had changed out of her wedding dress into a pair of purple corduroy trousers with a white blouse. It looked as though she had dyed her hair under her bonnet and she looked much younger.

In fact, she looked younger than Professor Burlay and Sammy wondered if she had been younger all along. Perhaps her grandmotherly appearance had been brought on by her unhappy marriage to Alfie Agrock and by not taking care of herself. She was carrying a tray of freshly baked pastry slices in the shape of dragon tails.

'Ooch, hello there young Dragon Knight and friends. 'I've got ham and mushroom, tomato and cheese and beef and onion slices,' said Mrs Burlay, pointing to each of the slices in turn.

Darius's father took one of each variety of pastry and Darius did the same.

'Pig,' muttered Dixie under her breath.

'Let's sit at this table,' said Sammy, seeing that Darius had overheard Dixie and was about to retaliate.

'We're off to the Land of Paradise in a few minutes,' said Mrs Burlay.

'We need to leave soon as well,' said Darius's father, helping himself to another three pastries.

'Ooch, well, it's a pleasure to have met you,' said Mrs Burlay, eyeing the disappearing pastries with approval.

'Darius is very talented,' added Professor Burlay. 'He's a natural with the gemstones.'

'That remains to be seen,' replied Darius's father curtly. 'He has a lot to learn.'

'Definitely a natural,' repeated Mrs Burlay. 'Now, you all have a wonderful summer and we'll see you in September!'

Mrs Burlay smiled and turned on her heels. She linked hands with her husband and they half walked, half skipped over to Merry Megan's ice cream van, where Commander Altair, Molly and Merry Megan were serving ice creams, hotdogs, candyfloss and popcorn to Dragamas students and their parents and guardians.

Sammy, Dixie, Sarah, Naomi, Darius and Darius's parents followed them. Darius's father ordered hotdogs for everyone and two for himself.

'Don't they make a lovely couple,' said Molly Burlay as she handed Darius's father the last hotdog and his change.

Sammy noticed Molly was trying to catch Commander Altair's eye and the Armoury teacher grinned at her.

Sammy took a bite out of his hotdog, wondering when his parents would arrive and whether he would need to meet them at the gates.

Professor Burlay finished his hotdog. He wiped the ketchup from the corner of his mouth, then he and Mrs Burlay collected their two honeymoon suitcases from Mrs Burlay's cottage that they were now going to share.

'Goodbye!' called Professor Burlay, shaking hands with Sir Ragnarok and then with Dr Shivers. He gave Commander Altair, Molly and his mother a hug. 'We'll see you soon!'

Everyone waved as Professor Burlay and Mrs Burlay wheeled their suitcases across the Dragonball pitch to where their dragons were patiently waiting on the grass that was covered with pink and white confetti.

Sammy waved but he felt sad and empty, even though he was so full of food he could barely move. It had been a long and busy day and he was sorry it was nearly over.

As Professor Burlay and Mrs Burlay disappeared into the trees, Darius's father checked his watch again.

'Well, it looks like it's all finished now,' said Darius's father. 'Fetch your things son and we'll make a move too. I'll get the van and you can have a minute to say goodbye.'

Darius pulled a long face. 'We'll meet up over the summer, won't we?' he asked Sammy and Dixie.

'Yeah,' said Dixie. 'You're still coming over to mine at the end of the summer holiday, aren't you Sammy. You're not spending the whole summer in Switzerland, are you?'

Sammy pretended to think about it and Dixie threw a play punch at him.

'Of course I'm coming round,' said Sammy. 'I'll ask my Mum if you can come to Switzerland for a week, you too Darius.'

'Yeah, call me,' said Darius, holding his hand up to his ear like a telephone with his finger and thumb outstretched.

They stepped back as Darius's father returned in the Murphy family purple, orange and lime green minibus.

Captain Firebreath appeared with Darius's suitcase. Grumbling under his breath, the Dwarf climbed up onto the roof and balanced the suitcase precariously on top of the minibus. Nelson took off and circled overhead.

Darius gave Dixie and Naomi a quick hug, Sammy a quick handshake and then he jumped up onto the back bumper and climbed into the minibus through the open window.

Naomi was the next to leave. Her father arrived to pick her up in his company car. He stopped only to say hello and goodbye in the same breath.

Sammy, Dixie and Sarah waved to Naomi and sat at one of the pink and white table clothed tables finishing their hotdogs and discussing whether there might be time for an ice cream or not.

They were just deciding it would be a good idea to have an ice cream when a large black limousine pulled up into the castle courtyard.

# CHAPTER 54

# THE SKY IS FALLING

Sammy craned his neck to see what was going on. Two men and a woman got out of the black limousine. The first man reached back into the car and pulled out a small child, clasping its hand.

'It's my parents!' shouted Sammy, leaping out of his chair. 'And General Aldebaran Altair!'

Sammy ran up to Charles and Julia Rambles and gave his mother and father a huge hug.

'Hello Sammy!' said Julia. 'You've grown up so much since we last saw you! Hello Dixie, how are you?'

'I'm fine, thank you,' said Dixie, blushing a little as Julia Rambles surveyed her and her green hair.

'Don't you have any boys as friends Sam?' asked Charles Rambles. 'What about Darren? Where's he?'

'Darius,' corrected Julia. 'I expect he's already gone home for the summer with his parents. We've just flown in from Switzerland and Al brought us here from the airport. Our plane was briefly delayed as well, so that's what's made us a little later than we intended.'

Sammy looked at General Aldebaran Altair and it dawned on him. 'Al, Aldebaran, I get it,' Sammy murmured to no one in particular.

General Aldebaran Altair nodded. 'I've been following your parents for twenty-four years, helping them where I can. Have you seen Sir Ragnarok? Where can I find him?'

Sammy pointed to the Gymnasium. 'I think he went over there.'

At a gurgle by his ankles, Sammy looked down at his baby sister Eliza. She'd grown more than he had expected.

'She's grown,' he said to his mother.

Julia laughed. 'They don't stay small forever.'

'Good,' said Sammy, wiping some of Eliza's dribble off his shoe. 'Is she always this dribbly?'

'Respect your sister Samuel,' warned Charles. 'She isn't old enough to know any better yet.'

Sammy shrugged. Nothing really mattered at the moment. It had been a perfect day. Professor Burlay's wedding had been a huge success. They'd had plenty to eat and drink and there were six weeks of the summer holiday to enjoy. Darius had invited him to come camping with him and his parents. He'd promised they could stay in tents and even go to a Dragon Healing Convention.

Sammy closed his eyes, picturing the green field by the river that Darius had described and told him they'd have to boil their own drinking water and that the campsite was at least twenty miles away from any shops.

He jerked back to reality as overhead there was an almighty rumble as loud as thunder. As if it was an orchestra made entirely of drums. Or someone banging with sticks on dustbin lids but magnified a thousand times louder. A gold mist descended through the air.

Sammy instinctively pulled his staff together, the emerald glinting in the strange light.

Julia Rambles stared at the staff, a question poised on her lips.

'What on earth is that?' started Julia.

'It's my staff,' said Sammy, painfully aware of his acceptance of things in the Dragon World and of his mother's ignorance.

Sammy pointed his staff at the sky, aware the students and teachers around him were doing exactly the same.

The ghosts of King Serberon and King Segragore appeared beside Sammy. They were both looking in the direction of the Forgotten Forest, where the sleeping hillside of Karmandor's golden head lay exposed. The ground was tumbling around her. Her sharp milk white teeth were bared and she was howling in an unearthly cry of pain and despair.

'Run!' yelled Sammy, clutching baby Eliza and his staff in one hand and Dixie's hand in his other hand.

At full pace, Sammy, Eliza, Dixie, Charles, Julia, Sarah, General Aldebaran Altair and Sir Ragnarok fled towards the castle gates. Kyrillan and Kiridor took off and flew after them, their wings beating in perfect synchronisation.

Above them, there was an even louder earth shattering noise and a gold mountain started erupting from the ground. Karmandor was rising from her tomb. The air was filled with falling rocks, sparkling gemstones and boulders.

Sammy cast a look back. General Aldebaran Altair had fallen behind. The human leader of the Snorgcadell was using his ruby gemstone and firing a red mist into the sky. Sammy understood. General Aldebaran Altair was trying to slow Karmandor down so they could escape.

Instinctively, Sammy handed Eliza to his father and pointed his staff towards the sky. Even though he no longer had the ruby gemstone on his staff, he had the skills within him.

Sammy fired red sparks up as high as he could. His sparks joined with General Aldebaran Altair's red sparks and it looked as though it was working.

Behind him, Sammy felt Dixie stop and with her own staff, she fired a sapphire protective mist over himself, her, and his parents. She created a thin blue tunnel down to the school gates to keep them safe from the debris.

Sarah and Sir Ragnarok ran in single file down the tunnel, the rocks and gemstones banging against the protective layer but not penetrating through Dixie's shield.

'The land is falling!' shrieked Dixie. 'Go to the Shute!'

'Down here!' Sammy yelled to his parents, who were watching with their mouths open, as if they had been frozen.

Sammy clutched his parents' hands and pulled them down the stone steps not a moment too soon. Dixie leaped down beside him. Pieces of rock smashed through her protective sapphire tunnel. Within seconds, rocks and sparkling debris had sealed the entrance.

Julia Rambles let out a whimper and she rummaged for her family. 'Charles? Are you there? Charles? Sammy? Eliza?'

'Dad?' asked Sammy, panicking suddenly. 'Where are you?'

A gurgling somewhere near his feet made Sammy look down. It was almost pitch black. The lanterns that usually lit the passage were out. The gemstones in the wall and floor gave out an eerie green glow.

'Light a fire Sammy,' whispered Dixie. 'Who's down here?'

Sammy touched the end of his staff and immediately bright orange flames appeared by his feet. He was standing half-in, half-out of the shallow underground stream, which explained why his right foot was soaking wet.

'Dad?' called Sammy.

'Gerrof me!' spluttered Charles Rambles, emerging from under Sammy's foot. 'Sam, take your sister from me. I nearly drowned!'

'Oh Charles, really,' said Julia Rambles. 'Look at the state of you and you're wearing your best suit too!'

Sammy felt a nudge on his elbow. Dixie was looking at him and she was even paler than usual.

'We can't get out,' said Dixie in an unusually quiet voice. 'We're trapped.'

'No we're not,' said Julia Rambles matter of factly. 'We will just have to go north.'

'What do you mean, go north?' asked Sammy.

'That way,' said Charles Rambles, pointing his finger. 'There's no other choice.'

'Oh,' said Sammy, barely hiding his disappointment as he remembered that his parents couldn't see dragons or Dragamas, or anything in the dragon world.

He was surprised neither of his parents had commented on the sudden creation of fire but perhaps they thought he'd just used matches. He dragged his feet as they made their way underground through the Shute back to the castle. Sammy wished harder than ever that his parents could see dragons.

At the steps which usually led up to the castle courtyard, the way was blocked with heavy boulders. Several sweets, toys and trinkets lay among them. Sammy felt sick, these things weren't from Dragamas. They had come from the Floating Circus.

'Karmandor couldn't hold on,' whispered Dixie.

'The land fell,' said Sammy.

'Land?' laughed Charles Rambles. 'I'll say it has! More like the sky has fallen!' His laugh fell on worried ears.

'Then we must go to the house. This passage, Charles, you know where it leads,' said Julia Rambles.

Sammy held his breath. It was as if his parents were remembering things from their past, from a long time ago.

'Yes,' said Sammy enthusiastically. 'It goes to...'

'Mrs Burlay's house,' finished Dixie.

'Aha!' said Charles Rambles. 'That woman who got married to one of your teachers today.'

'Whatever we're doing, we should get on with it,' said Julia, picking Eliza up off the floor. 'There's a good girl, hush now.'

Along the tunnel, bits of debris blocked their path. Sammy, his father and Dixie heaved the pieces of tunnel roof out of the way.

Even the gaping hole where Sammy had fought Mrs Hubar was blocked, this time the debris was shards of glass, desks and chairs he guessed had fallen from the atrium entrance at the Floating Circus.

Dixie bent down and picked up a pen and a broken mug that was missing its handle.

'Property of Immigration. Floating Circus,' she read out loud.

'Floating...Circus,' said Charles Rambles. 'Julia, do you remember, didn't we...?'

Julia stopped in her tracks. She clasped a hand over her mouth. 'Andradore,' she mumbled.

'Yes!' said Sammy, eagerly.

Dixie nudged him and he knew she was as pleased as he was.

'Andradore,' echoed Charles. 'That sounds familiar. Do they have lions at this circus?'

'Yes,' said Dixie. 'Andradore has a lion called Rolaan. Sammy saved him...ooooh,' Dixie trailed off.

Sammy looked ahead. There was a large golden lion in the middle of the passage only about twenty feet away from them.

'Rolaan,' said Sammy, stepping forward and holding his hand out.

Charles Rambles clutched the scruff of Sammy's shirt collar. 'No you don't boy. Your mother will see to this.'

'Mum?' asked Sammy.

Julia Rambles nodded. 'It was a long time ago, but I think I remember.'

'What?' asked Sammy incredulously. This was only his mother who couldn't see dragons, yet she was apparently a full-on lion tamer.

'I'm a lifetime guardian for Andradore's daughter,' said Julia. 'She'd probably be about your age. It was a long time ago but Andradore and I were close friends.'

'He's your guardian Sam,' said Charles. 'He's never met you mind, but he's out there. Maybe you'll meet him one day.'

'I have!' said Sammy, at exactly the same time as Dixie said, 'he has!'

'Oho!' said Charles. 'Well, you do it Sam. Let's see if you can.'

Sammy nodded, not stopping to think about why his father was suddenly happy for him to approach a fully grown lion. He stepped up to the lion, staring into its deep black eyes.

'Hi Rolaan,' said Sammy, a little nervous and very aware that everyone was watching him.

'Grrrrrrrrr.'

Sammy saw a flicker of recognition in Rolaan's eyes and he held out his open palms like Dr Shivers had shown him when approaching adult dragons.

'Grrrr.'

Rolaan growled again, but this time it was a little less ferociously.

'I won't hurt you,' said Sammy. 'We just want to get past.'

'Hurry Sammy,' said Julia. 'The tunnel is collapsing.'

Sammy looked back. Beyond Dixie, Eliza and his parents, more of the tunnel roof was slipping and sliding and starting to cave in on itself.

'Come on Rolaan, let us past,' said Julia. 'There's a good lion.'

At his mother's voice, Rolaan lifted his heavy paws and stepped aside. From behind him, a silvery, torch-lit, face appeared.

'Who's there?' came a cold, stern voice. 'We've got you covered.'

'Who are you?' demanded Charles Rambles. 'Identify yourself!'

'Identify myself?' said the voice, followed by a sarcastic laugh. 'I don't think so!'

Sammy pushed past. 'General Ramadere?'

'Who's that?' demanded the voice.

'It's me, Sammy Rambles. I'm with Dixie and my family.'

There was a muttered murmur and Rolaan backed away completely.

'Come through,' said the voice.

Sammy led the way. He was slightly nervous at who to expect to see behind the lion. Perhaps of the two options, the lion was preferable.

Dixie gripped one of his arms and Sammy held his staff in the other. The tunnel opened up into a small craterous room that Sammy instantly recognised was the cellar underneath Mrs Burlay's house where Cyngard, Jovah and Paprika had been living.

Sir Ragnarok was lying against Paprika, a great gash in his leg which was being tended to by Sarah and two of the acrobats from the Floating Circus.

Andradore, General Aldebaran Altair and General Alaze Ramadere were standing at the entrance. King Segragore and King Serberon were wafting behind them.

'Paprika!' said Sammy, rushing towards the large dragon and stroking her head. He turned to General Alaze Ramadere. 'It's just us and my Mum and Dad,' said Sammy, 'and Eliza.'

'Aha!' said General Alaze Ramadere. 'You've caught one of them!'

'I what?' started Sammy.

'Eliza Elungwen! Surely you remember her? You found out she was the "E" in the Shape and showed us the evil Dwarf she really is!' said General Alaze Ramadere.

Sammy choked back a laugh. 'Eliza is my sister. She's two years old.'

Relief poured over the Troll General's face. He turned to General Aldebaran Altair.

'That's one less to worry about,' said General Alaze Ramadere. He took Sammy's hand. 'I was wrong about you Sammy Rambles. You are welcome to join my ranks or the ranks of General Aldebaran Altair next year.'

Over General Alaze Ramadere's shoulder, Sammy saw King Segragore give him a thumbs up.

'Thank you,' said Sammy.

'So, the real Eliza is not here,' said Sir Ragnarok.

'She has vanished,' said General Alaze Ramadere.

'Has she teleported?' asked Dixie. 'I didn't think you could do that at the Snorgcadell?'

General Aldebaran Altair frowned. 'I suppose Orion told you?'

'I guessed,' said Dixie, pointing at the floor.

Sammy looked down. Beneath his feet was an engraving of a dragon's tail coiled around a set of broken bars.

'They've escaped,' muttered Sir Ragnarok.

'Yes,' said General Alaze Ramadere.

'But...' stuttered Sammy.

'It was all of us,' said General Aldebaran Altair. 'We used sapphire and Karmandor to seal it. Now she's gone, the magic binding that once protected the Snorgcadell has weakened and dissolved altogether.'

'Your dragons are down there,' said Sir Ragnarok.

Sammy knelt on the stone floor and looked. There was Cyngard, Jovah, Kyrillan and Kiridor and many other dragons he didn't recognise.

'This links through to the castle,' explained General Aldebaran Altair. 'These dragons are the ones we have saved.'

Behind him, there was a thud and Sammy saw his mother had crumpled to the floor. His father simply stood there with his mouth goofily open, as if he was about to speak but had been frozen by a ruby in mid-breath.

'Sammy,' whispered Charles Rambles. 'Are those...are they...'

'Dragons,' finished Sammy. 'Yes, lots of them. That's yours,' he pointed at Cyngard, 'and that's Mum's. Uncle Peter looked after them for you.'

'Dragons?' echoed Julia. 'But they're...'

'Here,' said General Aldebaran Altair kindly. He helped Julia to her feet. 'I understand this is difficult for you, but we have to find the Shape before they go too far.'

'Is it safe to go out?' asked Sammy.

'Yes Sammy,' said General Aldebaran Altair. 'We have been monitoring everything for the last hour. It's as safe as it's going to get.'

# CHAPTER 55

# KARMANDOR

Sammy looked around the room. Sir Ragnarok was standing up, holding Sarah's arm for support. Andradore was stroking Rolaan's mane and the two acrobats were standing together, waiting to be told what to do.

'We will start by implementing the Five O's,' said General Aldebaran Altair. 'I just hope Orion managed to get his people to safety.'

'Overview,' said General Alaze Ramadere. 'Deep darn dragon dung by the look of it. I don't have the time for all this, let's get straight to "Operation" and find the Shape. They can't be far away with all this chaos going on.'

From General Alaze Ramadere's firm tone, Sammy knew the Snorgcadell leader wasn't messing about so he made his way with Dixie quickly towards the steps leading into Mrs Burlay's house.

'Sorry lad,' General Alaze Ramadere gripped Sammy's shoulder. 'You can go first when you're the General of the Snorgcadell.'

Sammy stepped aside and followed at a short distance behind General Alaze Ramadere and General Aldebaran Altair. He gasped as he reached the top step.

Although they were in a bubble of red steamy smoke left over from slowing the fall of the Floating Circus, Sammy could see the vast extent of the destruction all around him. He could see everything and it didn't look good at all.

Debris from the Floating Circus was falling in slow motion. The red sparks Sammy had helped to send up into the sky were protecting Dragamas from the Floating Circus falling directly on top of it.

'Mrs Burlay's house has been destroyed,' whispered Dixie and Sammy realised that she was right.

The contents of Mrs Burlay's store room were pulverised. There were torn strips of the yellow and red canvas from the Big Top at the Floating Circus melted onto her powdered books and crushed furniture.

Sammy was glad everyone in the hospital rooms had already gone home for the summer. The beds were now in the space where Mrs Burlay's lounge and kitchen had been.

'Well you're here, so you might as well help,' said General Aldebaran Altair, conjuring a spade with his staff. He threw it to Sammy. 'Search for survivors.'

'Allow us,' said King Segragore, floating seamlessly through the floor. 'We can do these things so much easier in our disposition.'

Sammy grinned and stepped back for the Kings of the Dark Ages to slide in and out of the rubble. He climbed up onto a large rock with grass growing on it and felt like he'd been stabbed in the heart.

The once magnificent Dragamas Castle was in ruins. The North and East towers had collapsed into a small mountain of rubble.

'Look at that!' breathed Dixie, climbing onto the rock beside him. 'Dragamas is gone.'

'Half gone,' corrected Sammy, shuddering slightly. 'We were in those towers this morning.'

'And we're here now,' said Dixie, taking his hand.

Sammy nodded, privately thinking, "only just".

'Very lucky you made it to the Shute,' said Sir Ragnarok, wheezing as he climbed the steps. 'Oh my! Look at my castle!'

'My castle,' said King Serberon, popping up haughtily between a crevice of two concrete slabs. 'Actually, it is really Karmandor's castle.'

'Old Samagard Farm, Dragamas, Karmandor Castle, take your pick,' grumbled King Segragore. 'I take it that my daughter is responsible for this carnage?'

'At least she is alive,' said King Serberon. 'We can marry, just like we should have all those years ago. Then Princess Karmandor will become Queen Karmandor.'

'There's just two problems with that,' said Sammy, pointing at King Serberon. 'You're dead and she's a dragon!'

'Technicalities boy,' said King Serberon, a scowl spreading across his grey face. 'We will find her and see what can be done.'

'Very little, I'd imagine,' said Sir Ragnarok, slipping on the stone steps.

Sammy caught his headmaster and realised how old and frail he looked.

'Let's go over to those trees so you can sit and rest for a bit,' suggested Sammy. 'Maybe there are some chairs left from the wedding banquet.'

'At least it's a nice day,' said Sir Ragnarok. 'A nice day for finding dragons.'

'Let's take Kyrillan and Kiridor up in the air and see if we can see anything,' said Dixie.

Sammy nodded. 'Good idea.'

As if they had read Sammy's mind, Kyrillan and Kiridor swept up beside them.

With a kick to the floor, Sammy leaped onto Kyrillan's scaly back. He perched like a hawk, scouring the rubble for flecks of gold.

At nearly forty feet in the air, Dixie yelled and jerked Kiridor's reins to the right.

Sammy pulled Kyrillan's reins to follow her, but his blue-green dragon needed no prompting. In a split moment, Sammy wished his parents could see him riding bareback on Kyrillan, the wind in his face, a cool breeze contrasting against the afternoon sun.

'Down Kiridor!' shouted Dixie. 'There she is!'

Sammy lurched forward into a dive. The gold flecks below turned into a golden dragon shaped mountain. A golden dragon shaped mountain surrounded by four figures wearing black capes.

'Dixie! Wait!' shouted Sammy.

Dixie screamed. She pulled Kiridor up as he swept through the vanishing figures.

Instinctively, Sammy sent a light red mist over them, bringing Dixie safely down to earth.

'I'll get everyone!' Dixie shouted and set off at a run, covering the path with her staff outstretched in case the Shape returned.

Sammy landed and dismounted. Kyrillan swished his scaly tail. Karmandor's eyes opened and she growled, a deep, throaty howl of pain, opening her mouth like a ginormous tunnel. Kyrillan shivered and Sammy rested his hand reassuringly on his dragon's back.

'Hi Karmandor,' said Sammy.

Karmandor howled again, her mouth stretching wider. She was bleeding, dark red liquid covering her teeth.

Sammy saw something inside her mouth that made his own blood run cold. He ran forward, his staff outstretched, the green emerald on the end glowing. He leaped up the roughly hewn steps to the Dragon's Teeth stones that now belonged to the real dragon.

A bolt of freezing cold air rushed past him and the light dimmed to darkness in the forest. Sammy tripped, landing on his back, yelling in pain as Karmandor closed her mouth, cutting a hole through his right leg.

Out of the empty, cold darkness came a solitary hooded figure.

'Welcome Sammy Rambles,' said a rasping voice from the hooded figure. 'Welcome to my world. I have waited and waited for this day. You will feel pain like you never dreamed possible. My power transcends time. No one can defeat me and those who I command.'

## CHAPTER 56

# WHAT'S DONE CAN BE UNDONE

Sammy froze, his leg dripping with blood. Karmandor's sharp tooth was still deeply embedded in his calf.

The ground moved slightly and dozens of unhatched dragon eggs rolled out of a crevice from somewhere underneath him.

'Yes,' said the shadowy figure, circling him. 'You are Samuel Richard Rambles, Keeper of Dragons, at last, under my control. Together we shall complete what was said in the stars aeons before either you or I were born.'

'What was said before I was born?' asked Sammy, forgetting to be frightened. 'How do you know?'

'There are things even I do not know about what is written in the stars,' said the hooded man. 'But I warn you this…You will be sorry if you cross me. This is something I cannot do alone and something a boy like you cannot prevent.'

A growling rumble emanated from behind the hooded man. Sammy felt Karmandor's tooth shudder and it was suddenly wrenched out of his leg. Sammy screamed. The pain was unbearable.

'Fifteen years I have waited,' said the hooded man. 'A little longer will make no difference.'

The hooded man knelt beside Sammy's face. 'Fear not, for I shall return,' he said menacingly. 'I will be stronger and I will be ready to complete my powers that cannot be surpassed. I will have powers beyond your wildest dreams. There will be no childish magic like you learn at school.'

The hooded man created a wall of fire, encircling himself and Sammy, trapping them in a bright orange halo.

'We shall experience the power of earth, air, fire and water embodied in our veins. We will be immortal and invincible. No man shall control us and we shall control all men.'

'Why do you need me?' asked Sammy. He tried to stand. He was sure he had seen a brief flash of blue and gold behind him.

The pain in Sammy's leg from where Karmandor's tooth had torn his skin had spread from his knee to his ankle and it was unbearably painful.

'I need you because you were there,' said the hooded man. 'You have seen me and you will die once you have seen my face.'

The hooded man raised his right hand and started to take off his hood.

'Behold!' he shouted. 'Stand up and you will see the face of universal power!'

Sammy closed his eyes. There was a burning white light searing directly in behind his eyelids. He reached for his staff. He felt himself being seized up from the ground. The pain in his leg magnified tenfold. It was an exploding pain like he had never felt before.

'Behold my face!'

Sammy was wrenched to his feet and pushed down the rough steps. With a nasty crack, he felt his left elbow crush under his weight. His eyes jerked open.

Ahead, the man had removed his hood and was covered in shimmering rainbows and sparkling diamonds. He was standing in Karmandor's cave mouth.

'Behold for I am here!' shouted the man. 'I am here! This is now! Behold!'

Sammy closed his eyes again. He was on the verge of passing out. Beneath the rainbows, he had seen the ghostly face of the man, withered skin, so many wrinkles and a cruel thin mouth with yellow teeth. His eyes, where the eyeballs should have been, were just empty sockets, bleeding as though they had been torn out. The skin on his face was drooping and loose membranes were splashing down his hollow cheeks.

After what seemed like ages, Sammy opened his eyes again, unable to erase the horror he had seen. He looked up at Karmandor's cave mouth. The man was gone but there was a rumbling as loud as thunder.

The orange circle of fire was dwindling. Sammy saw the fire was fading because it was raining. Soft summer rain was pouring down like someone had opened a giant tap in the sky.

Karmandor's mouth was higher up than he remembered and it seemed to be moving and climbing higher. Her two ginormous eyes were focussed on him and on Kyrillan who had walked through the ashes.

Sammy tried to stand on his good leg. He rested his hand on Kyrillan's back for support.

Karmandor opened her mouth and a pale pink tongue came out from between her rows of sharp milk white teeth and reached towards him.

Sammy didn't know if she was trying to speak or preparing to eat him. He shuffled backwards and was stopped by Kyrillan's tail coiling around his legs.

'Let me go Kyrillan!' shouted Sammy.

Kyrillan didn't budge. If anything, Sammy felt himself being nudged forward. The pink tongue was close to him, inches away and he could feel her hot breath.

In a split second, Karmandor's tongue split into two forked prongs. One prong touched Sammy's leg, rubbing his wound like used sandpaper. The other jabbed twice at his elbow, clicking it back into place.

Sammy gasped. It was so quick and the pain was gone instantly and completely. He touched his trouser leg. The material was still ripped beyond repair but his skin had healed without a scar.

'Seeta mai,' said Sammy, thanking Karmandor in the shared Troll language they both understood.

'Mai arug,' replied Karmandor, shaking herself and stamping her giant feet.

Sammy ducked as trees that had been growing on her back were uprooted and scattered. They missed him by mere inches.

Karmandor opened her huge mouth and growled. She stamped her feet again and more dirt and rubble fell into the clearing.

Sammy looked up, shielding his eyes. Her golden wings seemed to be badly torn but then as they spread, dirt fell off and they were as perfectly formed as Kyrillan's wings.

Karmandor clenched her milk white teeth together and pulled the grass, twigs and brambles out of the ground as she arched up her back and pulled herself free.

Darkness descended briefly as Karmandor's wide, pure gold wings spanned the horizon. She flapped her wings up and down, scattering boulders and more debris.

Sammy clung to Kyrillan, shielding himself from being hit in the face with earth and twigs. He leaned back as Karmandor took off from the ground completely. She showered him in glitter, gold and diamonds.

Karmandor circled the cavity she had been buried in. Her golden wings cast rainbow shadows on the ground. She swept past the gaping hole where she had been buried and with one long flap of her wings, she disappeared behind where Mrs Burlay's cottage had been.

It seemed suddenly dark when she had gone and Sammy stepped nervously to the edge of the great hole. He peered over the precipice, crouching down as he felt dizzy looking into the abyss.

The hole went down by more than the height of the castle. It was a huge pit that was riddled with lots of tiny passageways, stretching down into a deep black void.

Sammy crawled backwards. The depth of the chasm was making him lightheaded and faint. He reached Kyrillan and stopped. He rested his hand on his dragon's head.

'It's all over Kyrillan,' whispered Sammy. 'I have no idea what just happened there.'

Kyrillan nudged him and Sammy climbed onto his dragon's scaly back. Sammy held Kyrillan's neck and they trotted over to the remains of Mrs Burlay's house.

When Sammy reached the flattened garden gate, he saw that Sir Ragnarok was with General Alaze Ramadere, General Aldebaran Altair and Andradore Havercastle. They were digging a path through the rubble using metal spades and their bare hands.

'Ahoy there Sammy!' shouted Sir Ragnarok. 'Tell me, was she everything you expected?'

The two Generals stopped digging and looked keenly at Sammy.

'Karmandor,' said Sir Ragnarok. 'You saw her.'

'What is the meaning of this?' demanded General Alaze Ramadere. 'You assured us of protection. We were told that our sealing magic would transcend time.'

'And it did,' said Sir Ragnarok. He sounded mildly exasperated. 'But it did not transcend the calling power of the Angel of 'El Horidore. How many times must I tell you? Dragamas is not at fault.'

'We will discuss this later,' said General Alaze Ramadere, his black eyes burning like liquid onyx. 'I have business to attend to elsewhere.'

'Is your business really more important than what is happening at Dragamas or the future of the Snorgcadell?' enquired Sir Ragnarok.

'We will have to see,' spat General Alaze Ramadere. He buttoned his long green cloak and vanished in an emerald teleporting mist that made Sammy's eyes water.

General Aldebaran Altair and Andradore Havercastle stood up and shook hands with Sir Ragnarok and with Sammy. Then they too departed. General Aldebaran Altair disappeared in a cool green mist and Andradore set off on foot towards the castle gates.

'All that is done can be undone,' Andradore called over his shoulder. He whistled loudly and Rolaan stepped out from behind where Mrs Burlay had kept her chickens. The lion had a few feathers in his mouth but no one except Sammy noticed.

'I don't know what they'll make of that lion in the village,' chuckled Sir Ragnarok.

Sammy grinned, imagining the screams and shock. He knew that Rolaan was harmless but everyone else didn't.

Sir Ragnarok beckoned for Sammy to come closer to him. Sammy felt suddenly cold in the afternoon sun now that the rain had stopped. His clothes were damp and he leaned close to his headmaster.

'You must believe Andradore,' said Sir Ragnarok. 'It can be undone.'

'What can be undone?' whispered Sammy. He was aware of how close Sir Ragnarok was standing to him and he could feel the Dragamas headmaster's power radiating from his body.

'Karmandor,' said Sir Ragnarok in a hoarse whisper. 'There is a way she can return to us in her Troll form and then she can be with King Serberon as it should have been all those years ago. She will become Queen Karmandor.'

Sammy nodded solemnly. 'King Serberon would like that.'

'And so would Karmandor's father. King Segragore would like his daughter back. It would be a difficult undertaking, but I believe it could be done,' Sir Ragnarok paused and grimaced. 'I have just promised it to King Segragore. He trusts my plan and we will achieve it. There are many things to do and a lot to plan. Go and enjoy the holiday. Things will be very different in six weeks time.'

Sammy looked around him. He could see the cavernous pit where Karmandor had been held prisoner, the destroyed Dragamas Castle towers and the exposed Snorgcadell headquarters. He privately hoped things would be different in six weeks time.

'Yes Sammy, there are many tasks,' said Sir Ragnarok, 'but remember our school motto, our full motto, which is, "In the darkest of dark, in the deepest of deep, keep us hoping for a new beginning, for mighty is the golden dragon".'

'Validus aureus draco,' said Sammy.

Sir Ragnarok shook Sammy's hand. 'We will recover from this.'

Sammy let go. 'I hope so, Sir.'

At a call from the castle courtyard, Sammy looked around. His mother and father were there with his sister Eliza, Dixie, Kyrillan and Kiridor. They even had a couple of bags with them, the remains of their possessions, salvaged from the castle.

'Come on Sammy!' shouted Dixie. 'Your parents are dropping me home! We're going in the limousine!'

Sammy ran across to them. He could feel his mother staring at his torn trousers.

'I can explain,' said Sammy. 'I think.'

'There's no need,' said Julia Rambles, hugging him. 'You have good friends, good marks and now we're going to have a good holiday.'

'We're also moving back here Sam,' said Charles Rambles. 'Your friend says she knows someone who can help us find a good house.'

'Cool.' Sammy linked arms with Dixie and half walked, half danced to the car.

Apart from a light layer of chalky dust, the black limousine was unscathed.

Sammy put the bags into the boot and sat on the plush leather seats in the back of the car next to Dixie and his sister, Eliza. Julia started the car, put the radio on and they set off on the short journey back to the village.

Above the limousine, Kyrillan, Kiridor, Cyngard, Jovah and Paprika flew in a "V" shape formation, their wings beating in perfect synchronisation.

As they rumbled over the cattlegrid, Sammy looked back at the ruins of Dragamas. It was now only half hidden by the damaged pearlescent bubble that used to cover the school and protect it from being seen by outsiders.

'Goodbye Dragamas, see you in six weeks,' whispered Sammy, squeezing Dixie's hand.

Then in a split second, they had turned the corner and the castle was gone.

The End.

# Dragon Talks

The journey writing the Sammy Rambles series has been full of ups and downs. It has been an adventure starting with a pen and a piece of paper, through to publishing and promoting the books around the world.

I've created a series of Dragon Talks and Writing Workshops to share my experiences and help inspire children in their writing. In the sessions everyone is encouraged to create their own story with memorable characters, layers of detail and inventive plots.

Dragon Talks and Writing Workshops are available for schools, libraries and clubs with tailored content suitable for children from Year 1 to Year 6 (KS1, KS2, KS3) either as a full school assembly or class sessions.

Find out more about:

- The inspiration behind Sammy Rambles, the reason for writing.
- Philosophical influences, mythology, love of words, hidden meanings within the stories.
- Writing the stories using pen and paper in every spare minute and very unusual places.
- Editing, proofreading, aiming for 95%.
- Agents, Publishers, Rejection and the route of self-publishing.
- The reason for publishing the books in quick succession.

- Promoting the stories, creating the website and Facebook page.
- Visiting fairs, events, schools, meeting the readers.
- Writing more stories in the future.

In the Dragon Talks, children are encouraged to create their own dragons and their own fabulous stories to share.

These are some of the comments following Dragon Talks in schools, libraries and clubs.

"The Canadian and British Sections were delighted to welcome JT Scott, author of the Sammy Rambles series of novels, to SHAPE International School. Over the course of two days, the children were privileged to experience a series of writing workshops designed and delivered by this celebrated British author. The two sections learned all about the grit and resilience required to get a book published; how to structure and develop a story arc; and how to utilise a rich and powerful vocabulary to engage and enchant the reader. The children were also enthused to learn a plethora of facts about everybody's favourite mythical monster: dragons! The two days were an unqualified success and packed full of exciting writing experiences. It also allowed the British and Canadian Sections the time to start developing the close relationship that will be an incredible boon of their new shared school. This was an amazing learning opportunity, and both Sections would like to extend their gratitude to JT Scott and to Common Services for making this unforgettable two days a possibility." – SHAPE International School.

"The children enjoyed creating their dragons. Some really good ideas." St. Nicholas Church of England School.

"Thanks a lot for coming in yesterday. It was lovely to meet you and thank you so much for coming to talk to the children. I know the children found it really exciting and got loads of great ideas from it." - Pelynt Academy.

"In Jenny's Sammy Rambles Dragon session boys who usually refuse to write anything spent the hour engrossed and they did not stop writing. Thanks for all the work and time you've given us. I will recommend you to our other schools! All my class were motivated and it was great to see their creative ideas." - Looe Primary School.

"Jenny came to visit our vibrant Year 4 class of 37 pupils and had them truly engaged with her stories. It was thoroughly enjoyable to have Jenny share her writing tips and enthrall our students with extracts from the books. The children relished the chance to write their own dragon stories, based on the adventures portrayed in Sammy Rambles and now they can't stop talking about dragons! Thanks Jenny, please come again." - Elmhurst Junior School.

"Thank you so much for coming over, sharing your work and inspiring our children. I know the visit was a huge success from our point of view and both children and staff, from both the British and Canadian Schools, loved the experience." – Acting Head, SHAPE International School.

www.sammyrambles.com

# Dragonball

Dragonball is the sport played by Sammy Rambles and his friends in the Sammy Rambles books.

It's a hybrid of football, netball and rugby where players use their hands or feet to kick, throw and pass the seven Dragonballs to score goals and the team with the most Dragonballs in the opposition goal wins.

Although in the books Dragonball is played whilst riding on a dragon the ethos of Dragonball translates into real life and Dragonball is a tactical game for social and competitive teamwork, fitness and entertainment.

Dragonball is a sport anyone can play. It's for all ages and all abilities. There's no "you're not good enough", "you can't play", "we don't want you on our team".

It's all inclusive and a great way for children and adults to keep active, fit and healthy, to make friends and work together to score goals and win games.

For more information or to book a Dragonball game or tournament, please visit www.dragonball.uk.com.

These are some of the comments from recent Dragonball taster sessions, sports lessons and tournaments.

"We are thrilled to be endorsing, promoting and delivering Dragonball as one of our inclusive sport options in The South West." - Sports Way Management.

"I think it's a really good game. Everyone is running about. It doesn't matter if it's crowded, there's loads of space and everyone's around the balls." – Oliver, Dragonball Player

"Your visit was brilliant, thank you so much for inspiring our pupils. Just to let you know that our KS2 children have all been playing Dragonball this morning courtesy of our Sports Coach! It has been great fun!" - Headteacher, All Saints CE VC Primary School, Dorset.

www.dragonball.uk.com

# Dragon Shop

You'll find lots of exciting things in the Sammy Rambles Dragon Shop and also in the Dragonball Shop.

Sammy Rambles Books / Audiobook
Sammy Rambles and the Floating Circus
Sammy Rambles and the Land of the Pharaohs
Sammy Rambles and the Angel of 'El Horidore
Sammy Rambles and the Fires of Karmandor
Sammy Rambles and the Knights of the Stone Cross

Sammy Rambles Kyrillan Soft Toy
Sammy Rambles Fridge Magnet
Sammy Rambles Keyring
Sammy Rambles Standard Mug
Sammy Rambles Colour Changing Mug
Sammy Rambles T-shirt
Sammy Rambles Hoodie

Dragonball Fridge Magnet
Dragonball Keyring
Dragonball Standard Mug
Dragonball Colour Changing Mug
Dragonball Kit
Dragonball T-shirt
Dragonball Polo
Dragonball Hoodie

Dragonball Equipment and Coaching Workpack

www.sammyrambles.com | www.dragonball.uk.com

# Sammy Rambles and the Floating Circus

## J T SCOTT

Sammy Rambles is given a dragon egg on his first day at his new school. The egg hatches into a dragon called Kyrillan and Sammy learns to look after his new pet.

He makes new friends, a girl with bright green hair called Dixie Deane and Darius Murphy, a boy with unusual parents. Things are going well for Sammy Rambles, until he learns of a dark fate hanging over the school.

An enemy, known only as the Shape, wants to destroy all of the dragons and close the school. It is up to Sammy Rambles and his friends to try and stop this from happening.

www.sammyrambles.com

# Sammy Rambles and the Land of the Pharaohs

## J T SCOTT

Sammy Rambles is keen to return to the Dragamas School for Dragon Charming for his second year with his friends Dixie Deane and Darius Murphy. There are new lessons, new teachers and new skills to be learnt.

On the school trip to the Land of the Pharaohs, Sammy learns his parents once knew about dragons but cannot see them any more. He finds out about the Stone Cross and discovers the enemy, known only as the Shape is trying to rebuild it.

When the fifth years' dragons are poisoned, Sammy has no choice but to find out more about the Shape and uncover why the Stone Cross is so important.

www.sammyrambles.com

# Sammy Rambles and the Angel of 'El Horidore

## J T SCOTT

A wedding gift from King Serberon to his future Queen, the Angel of 'El Horidore is an ancient whistle used for calling dragons. With one single blast, the whistle will call all of the dragons in the world together.

The Shape want to find the whistle and use it to kill the dragons, steal their draconite, rebuild the Stone Cross and obtain the powers of immortality and invincibility.

Sir Ragnarok cannot let this happen. He is sure the Angel of 'El Horidore is hidden near Dragamas and sets a task for his students to find it so he can protect it from the Shape. Sammy Rambles and his friends Dixie Deane and Darius Murphy embark on their most serious quest so far.

www.sammyrambles.com

# Sammy Rambles and the Fires of Karmandor

## J T SCOTT

Tying the past and the present together, Sammy Rambles needs to find his best friend and uncover the link to the ancient Queen Karmandor.

He must use all his skills and attempt a daring rescue, whilst staying on top of his schoolwork. As the legend of Karmandor comes true, it begins the systematic destruction of everything Sammy Rambles cares about in the Dragon World.

He finds himself yet again in the hands of the Shape and almost powerless to do anything about it.

www.sammyrambles.com

# Sammy Rambles and the Knights of the Stone Cross

## J T SCOTT

Bringing everyone together one last time, Sammy's final year at the Dragamas School for Dragon Charming sees him fight his fiercest battle yet.

Can he find the last member of the Shape?

Can he free Karmandor?

Will he escape with his life?

www.sammyrambles.com

Printed in Poland
by Amazon Fulfillment
Poland Sp. z o.o., Wrocław